KARL —

PRIVACY WARS:
A CYBERTECH THRILLER

WARM REGARDS!

JOHN D. TRUDEL

Privacy Wars is a work of fiction. Names, characters, places, and incidents either are products of the author's imagination or are used fictitiously. Any resemblance to actual events or locales or persons, living or dead, is entirely coincidental.

Author: John D. Trudel
Cover Design and Art: Bruce DeRoos

Privacy Wars is available on Amazon.com, through major book distributors (e.g. Ingram, Amazon, etc.), and in all major eBook formats. Please ask your local bookstore and library to stock it.

ISBN: 0983588635
ISBN-13: 9780983588634

DEDICATION

This novel is dedicated to my wife Pat. Without her bright spirit, patience, and untiring support, **Privacy Wars** would not exist. She made this all possible.

ACKNOWLEDGEMENTS

My agent, Tony Outhwaite, believed in me. Thank you, Tony. We're getting traction at last.

Ernest Hemingway once said, "There is no such thing as writing, only rewriting." Novels are indeed that way. I would never have made it without my small band of critical readers and editors who assiduously scanned years of drafts with eagle eyes and brutally honest criticism. Each time they touched my words, my novels got better. Kay Jewett deserves special credit.

Two departed friends deserve thanks: Captain Langford C. Metzger, a Vietnam hero who gave me early encouragement, and Gerry Drew who gave me a book about ancient civilizations and mysterious pre-history that inspired this novel.

I've been blessed to live in a culture that values exceptionalism, and to have a life that has touched interesting events and people. It was freedom, innovation, and a career in technology at the peak of "the American Century" that helps give context for my writings, and it is freedom, innovation, and technology that let me break through and get my books published.

A work assignment in Egypt let me visit pyramids and tour closed sections of the Royal Museum in Cairo. Another adventure let me pilot myself into dirt strips at inaccessible ruins in the Yucatan, allowing a unique view of these relics in the context of the local geography.

Over my years in High-Tech, I worked with ELINT (ELectronic INTelligence) systems. Later, as a consultant, I had assignments for commercial technology firms dealing with computer and network architecture, including trusted/managed networks and the Internet. Michael Crichton's novels were an inspiration. I regret that I never got to meet him in person.

Several inventors and legal experts helped with patent and Intellectual Property issues. Alex Johnson deserves special credit for keeping me true when writing against a complex landscape of high stakes innovation, constrained by technology, law, and global economic policy. Dr. Roger Smith applied his critical eyes to scrutinizing my final drafts for obscure errors.

Many have contributed to the publication and success of this book. Thank you all for your inspiration, friendship, and support. Finally, you, my readers, are most important of all. Meeting you at events, signings and book clubs is a special treat, albeit sometimes an adventure.

Thank you for choosing **Privacy Wars**. If you like it, please post reviews and tell your friends.

TESTIMONIALS FOR *PRIVACY WARS*

"You're in the first row of a slowly climbing rollercoaster. Behind you, closing fast, are the American President and his enforcers, assisted by UN Peace Forces and a powerful foreign government—all bent on your annihilation and that of your technology. Then prepare for a dizzying plunge into a breathtaking, unexpected conclusion. It's a ride worth taking with author John D. Trudel whose writing skills will captivate you."

WR. Park, Author of twelve acclaimed suspense-thrillers

"*Privacy Wars: A Cybertech Thriller* hit me as such a realistic storyline that it could easily be a non-fiction in the not so near future. The loss of privacy and the government intervention into the private and corporate worlds were way too real. I have a hard time focusing on reading, but this read was way too good to put down for very long. The characters were very lifelike and the descriptions were awesome. This is a definite "5-star" read. It is riveting and the action lends it to someday be a movie and definitely one I would love to go see. John Trudel has a winner here."

G. R. Holton, award winning Author of DEEP SCREAMS

"Trudel has a remarkable talent for maintaining an atmosphere of brittle tension. This, combined with an uncanny instinct for what perplexes most of us in this new tech age and its inherent threats to our privacy and our basic freedoms, makes for a gripping thriller."

Roger Croft, Author of Spy Thrillers in the le Carré tradition.

"In *Privacy Wars*, John Trudel knows his audience and like a guided missile seeking the target, accurately and explosively delivers in his new book on Cybertech."

John Zodrow, Author of THE SINS OF WAR

"In *Privacy Wars*, John Trudel pens a Thriller that is a sure bet to grab you, carrying you along on a trip into the darker side of technological intrigue. Trudel's characters are gritty, genuine, and vulnerable; his plots masterfully crafted. *Privacy Wars* will propel you into another fascinating read in the wake of last year's *God's House*."

David F. DeHart, Author, SHADOW PLOTS

"Remember when you read your first book by an authentically professional author? This is another one of those times. John Trudel's *Privacy Wars* is a unique work of sheer audacity, and is a certain winner among those who love a mystery that creates a futuristic-but-palpable synergy of international gangsters, brilliant technological acumen, the dynamics of irrational political power, and the essence of free-market societies. Don't miss this one!"

Ron Ruthfield, Author, THE CAPITAL UNDERGROUND

"John Trudel's *Privacy Wars* does more than just provide plenty of entertaining reading. It issues a warning to all lovers of freedom that freedom is what we lose when we grant power to others. This thriller has elements of *1984* and *Atlas Shrugged*, but is replete with modern technology and high-tech-based adventure. Highly recommended!"

Joseph Badal, Author of SHELL GAME

"You have zero privacy anyway. Get over it."
Scott McNealy
CEO, Sun Microsystems, January 1999

PROLOGUE

T he overall effect was deliciously subtle.

Keigo Ouchi and his men were dressed in Western business style with dark suits, white shirts, and subdued ties. Their clothes were expensive, the suits of Savile Row "bespoke" quality, and the fit was impeccable. Still, the image projected was subtly wrong, just a notch off.

They all dressed the same and little showed through the facade of genteel civility except slight bulges in their suits and the snake tattoos on their right hands, only partially concealed by Italian Super Fine Herringbone shirts with heavy gold cufflinks. The visitors showed just a little cuff, not too much, and each the exact same amount.

John put their shirts down as custom-tailored, and costing something north of $300. A person could buy a good dress shirt off the rack for thirty bucks and cover the tattoos if he wanted to. Obviously the lapse was intended. It sent a signal to those paying close attention.

They pretend to be businessmen and we pretend to believe it, John thought. *They look like textbook versions of 1960's IBM executives, except smaller, Asian, better dressed, with stylized crew cuts, and with an understated, thuggish overtone.*

John Giles might have dropped in from a different planet than his visitors. He was still adapting to civilian life, learning his job. Last year he'd gotten in trouble for being candid in public statements about the investment community and dysfunctional Washington policy. *The Wall Street Journal* called his remarks, "Refreshingly honest," but *The New York Times* dubbed him, "Brutish," and on its front-page, no less.

His casual remarks set off a media circus. He was called "Iron John," and the name stuck. His supporters spoke it with respect, lauding his integrity, but his critics were numerous, organized, and vitriolic with their demagoguery.

John's investors and directors weren't amused. The fact that Cybertech was closely held and doing well deflected some of their anger, but he got the message. *Stay under the radar.*

His son Will had been furious. "Jesus, Dad. Get some couth training. We don't have time for this shit."

Cybertech didn't need money, but did require goodwill. Global commerce was perilous. Free markets got the blame for societal problems, and garnered hatred from powerful enemies. So did success and prosperity. A small firm like Cybertech needed all the friends it could get.

Everyone in business did. A weakened America was struggling back from astronomical deficits and a dark period of crony capitalism, corruption, socialism, and frequent national embarrassments. It was a long hard road. Businessmen were no longer demonized, but neither had they regained respect.

This was a time for CEOs to tread softly and deliver results. *Best to keep a low profile, practice humility, create jobs, and regain trust.*

America was relearning how it had once become the shining city on the hill, but it was a slow process. The capitalists who'd created the greatest prosperity in the history of the world were gone, and, with a few exceptions like Bill Gates and Steve Jobs, forgotten.

John now accepted education and negotiation as part of his job, and diplomacy and patience as needed skills. He'd done his homework, but the *Yakuza* didn't pass out Org Charts or wear rank on their collars. He was watching his visitors politely, trying to assess their roles.

Ouchi was upper management. He was at least a sub-family chief, a brother or *Kyodai*, perhaps even a *Shatei-gashira* who reported directly to the country boss.

John glanced down at the cards arranged carefully in front of him on his dad's old desk. Engraved, not printed. He touched Ouchi's, feeling the raised letters and the quality of the fine card stock with his fingertips. It said "Economic Development."

Yeah, right.

Couth training or not, this meeting with the *Yakuza* was odd. The meeting had been strongly encouraged, but he had no idea why. *Max Banks said to meet with these people, and he's an undersecretary. Does that mean what they're doing is officially sanctioned?*

John wondered if even Wall Street stalwarts like Merrill Lynch or Goldman Sachs merited such special consideration from the State Department these days. It seemed unlikely. Someone in Japan's diplomatic corps must have been owed a favor.

Ouchi had been doing the talking while John kept a polite smile on his face and jotted notes. His mind raced as he tried to assess the man, to discern the true purpose of his visit.

The man on Ouchi's right was named Iwamoto. His card said "Technology Ventures." *Why is he here?* He'd not spoken, but his eyes were coldly alert, watching and analyzing.

John tentatively classified Iwamoto as non-operational. Probably one of the staff specialists, an advisor or *komon*.

The two on Ouchi's left – Kuroda and Kume – were enforcers. They were here ostensibly as bodyguards. That was obvious fiction. It was like keeping savage tigers to give kiddy rides at the zoo. *Intimidation*, John thought, *or is it more?*

Those two probably had their bodies covered from neck to calf with elaborate clan tattoos. Street thugs who'd worked their way up.

Kume was short but massive. John studied his hands, callused from years of martial arts. *His job is to hurt people. He's the muscle.*

Kuroda was gaunt, almost emaciated, with long slender fingers and dead eyes. *That one's a stone killer. When you stare into the abyss the abyss stares back at you....*

There was no soul behind those eyes. Kuroda didn't even blink. Whatever was inside that skull, it was dark and scary.

Ouchi finished talking and looked at him expectantly. John smiled, but said nothing. He'd spent duty time in Japan and knew the protocols. The person who spoke first was at a disadvantage.

The silence lengthened into minutes. Finally Ouchi spoke. "We offer you a substantial sum of money, Colonel Giles. And other considerations of even greater value. With our assistance and backing, you'll become wealthy beyond your wildest dreams."

No point antagonizing them, John thought. "Your offer is generous. Would you like more tea?"

Ouchi pinned him with a sharp look. "We'll help you with export licenses, permits, and distribution. We can triple your sales into Japan by the end of the year."

I'll just bet you can. John glanced over to the right at Cybertech's security chief, Harry Conners. Old Harry wasn't much to look at. He was bald as a bowling ball and had a face only a mother could love. His nose had been broken numerous times and part of his left ear was somewhere back in Tibet.

Harry was leaning casually against the wall with a short-barreled 12-gauge pump gun cradled like a baby in his massive arms. There was no one better to have covering your back when the fecal matter hit the fan. He shrugged and snuck John a wink.

Iwamoto noticed John's inattention and muttered something in soft, rapid Japanese.

Something ugly flickered in Ouchi's eyes. "He says you don't show us proper respect."

"I'm sorry he feels that way." John kept his tone neutral. "You're my guests. I just offered you tea."

"Don't patronize me. You test my patience, Colonel."

Unusually direct and unmannerly for a top Japanese executive. John frowned politely and said nothing, as if shocked at the outburst.

Embarrassment ghosted across Ouchi's face, and he dropped his eyes. *Interesting. I think he's been **directed** to threaten me. How far does he plan to take it?*

"We're here to do business," Ouchi said.

John put on his most attentive look. "I'm listening."

"You should listen with more care. I just made you an offer you can't refuse."

John moved his lips into a faint smile. "Do you watch old gangster movies?"

Ouchi gave a shake of his head.

"It's not important. Is there anything else you wanted to discuss?"

That prompted rapid words in Japanese from Iwamoto. Ouchi responded and a heated discussion ensued. John waited patiently until he saw the two goons starting to tense. Kuroda slipped a hand under his jacket.

Click. The group froze as Harry flicked his safety off. The sound was preternaturally loud in the quiet elegance of John's office. Harry eased to the side where he had a clear field of fire, his weapon leveled and his finger on the trigger.

"Excuse me." John cleared his throat. "Mr. Ouchi?"

Ouchi raised his hand and Iwamoto instantly fell silent. "Yes?"

"I've treated you with respect." John looked directly into Ouchi's dark eyes. "You're my guests. It would be unfortunate if our discussions turned unpleasant."

Kume spoke for the first time, a sharp question in Japanese.

"We don't want an accident," John said softly.

Ouchi looked at him appraisingly. "Do you threaten me?"

"I protect myself. If any of your men shows a weapon, my guard will kill him. His scattergun has seven magnum loads of double-ought buckshot. Each contains nine pellets a third of an inch in size."

A long moment passed. The room was very still.

"We're not your enemy," John said softly.

Ouchi snapped an order in Japanese. No one moved. He repeated his command more harshly, raising his voice and spitting out the words. His men slowly and carefully put their hands on John's desk in plain sight.

Ouchi took a deep breath. "We're here to do business, Colonel Giles, not to harm you. Why won't you take our money?"

"We do take your money. You're a good customer, and we appreciate your business."

"You know what I mean. We can offer more than simply being a customer, but you avoid discussion. Is it because we are *Yakuza*?"

John shook his head. *You almost lost control there, didn't you?* "We're not seeking investment capital at the present time. Not from anyone."

"I saw the article in the **Times** last year." Ouchi smiled, but the smile never touched his eyes.

"The reporter was arrogant."

"He has that reputation. An asshole, as you Americans say."

"I'm still learning patience."

Ouchi glanced left, at Harry's weapon. "Prudence might be a better lesson. You don't want me for an enemy."

"I agree. It would serve no purpose."

"We can offer you more than any investment banker, and the best time to raise money is when you don't need it. Surely you know that. You're a smart man."

"I'm sorry," John said. "I'm not in organized crime, nor do I wish to be."

"A limited viewpoint. We have much in common. At the core, you're no different than us. Our nations have both survived bad leadership."

"Barely."

Ouchi almost smiled. "You resist oppressive government. You earn your living by helping normal citizens live their lives without government intrusion and interference. So do we. It's our cause, our heritage."

John gave a hand signal. Harry lowered his shotgun, slowly relaxing and leaning against the wall. The tension in the room dropped slightly.

"Did he get that gun from a museum?"

"Possibly," John lied. "Some prefer vintage weapons." The *Yakuza* favored archaic armaments, especially exotic swords and knives.

The old pump-gun had been Harry's weapon of choice since the Tibetan campaign, and to hell with the Geneva Convention. It had no batteries or microchips to fail, a hot trigger, and a simple mechanism that resisted jamming. Only a fool would stand up to a 12-gauge at close range. He'd seen Harry fire it faster than most people could trigger an automatic.

Tibet was a forgotten war. Except at the Staff College, where it was taught to exemplify the ultimate foul up. They'd sent green troops commanded by an ambitious barracks officer. The mission was spawned by humanitarian concerns and a plan based on bad intelligence. It was implemented with unclear objectives, inadequate support, and no contingency plans.

The result was what you'd expect: disastrous. The chaos was unbelievable.

When the relief force finally made it through to the survivors on the Tibetan Plateau, the Roof of the World, they'd found John and Harry barricaded in a cave. The plain in front of them was marred by large craters and littered with bodies and the wreckage of fighting vehicles, helicopters, and strike aircraft. Sheltered behind them were seventy-four wounded men, all that was left of a battalion.

John had been a young Captain, and Harry was at his side when the President hung a Medal of Honor around his neck in a White House ceremony. That seemed a long time ago.

Ouchi looked left again, this time at Harry. "That's a most uncivilized weapon."

"But useful," John said. "You were talking about heritage."

"I was talking about common ground. Shared interests."

"I'm listening."

"We never had your Second Amendment. In ancient Japan, the servants of the shogun were the only people allowed weapons. Some were rogue *samurai* who terrorized citizens. They were called *kabuki-mono*, 'the crazy ones.' They'd kill for pleasure. Our forebears were called the *machi-yokki*, the 'servants of the town.' The *Yakuza* was founded by warriors who took up arms to defend the villages and towns from the crazy ones."

"What's that got to do with me and Cybertech?"

"Do you know how Interpol defines organized crime?"

John shook his head.

"The General Assembly of the Interpol member countries defines organized crime as 'Any enterprise or group of persons engaged in a continuing illegal activity which has as its primary purpose the generation of profits irrespective of national boundaries.' That definition fits your firm, Cybertech, perfectly, Colonel."

Ouchi held up one finger. "Cybertech is an enterprise." A second finger: "You generate profits worldwide." A third: "Some, including many in your own government, say your business, selling private encryption and security products, is, or should be, illegal." He spread his hands. "We are the same as you. You are the same as us."

"You play with words," John said. "Cybertech isn't in the same business as the *Yakuza*. We don't do loan sharking or money laundering. We do technology."

"You are naïve, Colonel. The reason the *Yakuza* can operate in the open is that we're not illegal. We're older than your country and we perform useful, even vital, services for our society. The financial practices you criticize are legal in Japan. We loan money when the banks refuse to do so. We help people.

"We keep neighborhoods free of violent crime. Because of *Yakuza,* Japan has one of the lowest crime rates in the world. People can walk around Tokyo with money sticking out of their pockets and not be fearful. The *Yakuza* provides needed professional services to our government. With our help, Japan has few terrorist problems."

"Except for sarin gas on your subways," John murmured.

"That was long ago and an isolated domestic incident." Ouchi waved a hand dismissingly. "*Aum Shinrikyo* lost its status as a religious organization, its top leaders were promptly hanged, and the few surviving members became social outcasts with unhappy lives and no future. We leave them alive as an example. It's a much better result than what America has achieved with Islamic fanatics, and the cost to Japan's government has been trivial."

John nodded. It was true. *Japan had avoided wars since Pearl Harbor, and had accumulated a hell of a lot of international respect over the years. If not for acts of God, like earthquakes and Tsunamis, Japan would be wealthy. Its technology was second to none.*

Ouchi held up his hand and turned it over, displaying the snake tattoo. "The *Yakuza* protects the downtrodden. The *Mamushi* is my clan's emblem. Are you familiar with it?"

"No."

"It's a pit viper, the most deadly creature in Japan. It thrives everywhere because it has adapted to our society. So have we."

"It's unfortunate the *Yakuza* is associated with so much violence."

"I blame it on television." Ouchi's expression was deadpan.

"Biased reporting?"

"Yes."

John suppressed a smile. "What's your point?"

"My point, Colonel, is that you need us, because Cybertech is small and weak. Powerful forces would like to take you over. You're an irritation to governments all over the world, and especially your own. All governments want to control their citizens. You know this."

John nodded.

"Your products get in the way of those in power. Someday a government agency or a crony competitor will take control of your firm. Perhaps the Chinese. It's just a matter of time."

"The problem concerns us. Why should it concern the *Yakuza*?"

"Any compromise of our personal privacy concerns us greatly," Ouchi said. "We have no suitable substitutes for your products. If your government took control of Cybertech, they'd put in trapdoors to monitor us."

"Just as they did with smart phones and the Internet? Just as China did with personal computers when they replaced IBM?"

"Exactly."

"They might."

"We can't allow that," Ouchi said. "We seek to invest in your company, to become your partner. Our offer is generous."

John was shaking his head. "It won't work. Think of Switzerland."

"What are you talking about?"

"May I speak openly?"

Ouchi shot his men a cautionary glance. "Yes. Please do."

"You don't want to invest. Or help. You want to take us over."

Ouchi was watching John carefully. "Go on…."

"As you say, Cybertech is small and weak. We're important only because we provide something needed by those who are powerful. History has seen analogous situations and gives clues for how to handle this one. During all the bloody centuries of European warfare, tiny Switzerland was left alone as an independent nation, even during times when the entire world was engulfed in conflict."

"I read history," Ouchi said. "How is this relevant?"

"Why do you think that was? Partially because Switzerland threatened no one. Mostly because everyone agreed it was best for all parties if Switzerland stayed neutral. It served as an honest banker for all. To a lesser extent Sweden did the same, acting as an arms merchant."

"What's your point?"

"Do you think you're the first group who wanted to control us, the first to pressure us or offer us wealth? Hardly. There have been many: telecommunications cartels, government agencies, foreign governments, entertainment firms, and others. In each case we've refused."

"Entertainment?"

"It was inevitable," John said. "Hard core pornography is a large market with many easily targeted segments. One half of one percent of men are pedophiles, a number which has included Hollywood Executives and Members of Congress. It's an available market of 1.5 million customers in the U.S. and 34 million worldwide. That's just one market segment. There are many others.

"Pornography for pedophiles carries severe penalties, but is hugely profitable. Adult performers do it for fun and the young stars aren't paid. I'm told the profit margins exceed seventy percent."

"You're not involved in anything like that," Ouchi said. "We've checked."

"We're not, but some in the entertainment industry are. The main thing is customers will risk everything to get the pornographic product. Police stings are common and it's easy for the authorities to search people's computers, but pedophiles persist.

"They are compelled. Compulsion overwhelms them. The consequences of being caught will totally destroy them, but they still risk it. I'm told if their needs can be fulfilled safely, their appetite becomes insatiable."

"I begin to understand," Ouchi said. "Some interests wanted to adapt your technology to allow hiding such photographic evidence from sight. But you refused?"

John nodded.

"Digital porn can have a better profit margin than drugs," Ouchi said musingly.

"Possibly true, but it's not a business we want any part of. We don't make moral judgments about what others do. That's their business. But part of **our** business is to avoid being compromised. We work hard to be completely neutral and incorruptible, partially because it's our personal preference, but also because we dare not act otherwise."

Ouchi was watching him intently. "You *dare* not act otherwise…?"

"My government considers our technology to be, ah, rather sensitive."

"Very sensitive indeed…."

"If the *Yakuza* gained control of Cybertech, there would be repercussions. Someone would discover the connection. No matter how many bribes you paid there would be consequences. America has strong child-pornography, racketeering, and technology export laws. Most likely, Cybertech would be nationalized or shut down. Where would that leave you?"

Ouchi blinked.

"It would leave you with nothing. Haven't your strategists considered that? If not, they're fools or traitors."

Ouchi frowned at Iwamoto, who cringed visibly.

So much for Asian inscrutability.

Ouchi turned his gaze back to John. "There is another problem. Regardless of what we do, Cybertech may not survive as an independent company much longer. A group of large Chinese and U.S. firms is lobbying your government to allow a hostile takeover."

John laughed and shook his head. "Including Hollywood, no doubt...."

"Yes, among others. You knew that?"

He believes me. Good. "We're used to it. The threat has been hanging over our heads ever since the day we started the company. We've beaten back several takeover attempts."

"The risk troubles my superiors."

"Then here's what they should keep in mind: The main thing is we're neutral, like Switzerland. In addition, we are patriotic Americans. You, Sir, are not. If you try to possess us, you'll damage yourselves in the process. And if you destroy us, you *will* lose access to our products."

"I'm instructed to make you accept our offer."

"Then those who sent you are confused or mistaken," John said. "You can save money and accomplish what you want by simply using the *Yakuza's* influence to discourage those who seek to take us over. Use your strength against them, not us. We're not your enemy."

"You'll continue to sell us your products?"

"Our government favors trade with Japan. We value you as a customer."

"You don't sell outright. You license your products with restrictions on use."

"Of course. So does Microsoft. So does Apple. So does Sony. Licensing is a common practice in the industry. It is how we keep ownership of our intellectual property."

"If your use restrictions are violated, you drop customers and terminate support."

"It's a policy for your protection as well as our own. We make our use restrictions clear before we take on new customers. And we review them with our customers each year when we renew our contracts."

"What if we don't want to be protected?"

"I'm sorry. Allowing customers to use our products improperly would create too many problems."

"You don't sell to the Islamists at all. We've checked."

"Your information is incomplete."

"Explain," Ouchi said.

"We keep our customer lists private unless the customer chooses to make them public. I am allowed to say Turkey is a customer, as is the Saudi Royal Family."

"It was in the press that you refused Iran as a customer."

"So they said. We didn't comment."

"It's legal to sell to Arab countries."

"Sometimes. Some countries. It's hard to know. The Mideast is still a big problem."

Ouchi said, "I worry that one day you may see us as a problem too."

"Not if you use our products responsibly. Do you know the parable of the golden goose? It's a cautionary tale about the consequences of excessive greed."

Iwamoto said something in soft Japanese. Ouchi didn't look at him or reply. His full attention was on John. "We need to trust you and your products. This is essential."

"That's the nature of our business."

"If we can't trust your products, you'll be dead. You need to understand this."

"We do, absolutely. If we betrayed our customers, you'd have to stand in line."

"There's another issue. We must deal with you as a normal company if you don't become our partners. Do you agree to pay protection money?"

"I'm sorry," John said. "I can't do that."

Ouchi scowled. "Can't or won't?"

"We don't pay anyone protection except for our legal taxes. Why should we pay for what you can't deliver? You may be able to destroy us, but I doubt even the *Yakuza* can protect us if we fail to stay neutral."

Besides, if we paid you, we'd have to pay everyone. There'd be no end to it.

Ouchi's men tensed. In Japan, the only ones who refused to pay were those who couldn't. The first warning was a brutal beating and only rarely was a second warning given. Most chose suicide rather than face the *Yakuza's* wrath.

Ouchi stared at John, taking his measure. The office was still, devoid of all movement and sound. The silence hung heavy. This was the key moment, and it could go either way. A word from either man and the room would explode in gunfire.

Kuroda and Kume kept their hands on the desk as ordered, pictures of frozen rage. Could Harry take out Ouchi and his killers before they reached their weapons? He couldn't get them all.

Or could he?

The tableau was frozen in time, a hairsbreadth from raw red violence.

John was calmly looking into Ouchi's eyes, waiting for a decision. He flicked his gaze to the right, then back, softly reminding him of Harry's weapon. "You know what buckshot does at close range. Think about it. Your men might get me, but you won't live to see it."

Harry was in a combat crouch, holding his scattergun in both hands, his finger on the trigger. It wasn't pointed at Ouchi and his men. Not quite.

Good. Let Ouchi think about it as long as he wants. No one needs to die. He has options.

The room was totally still, and a long moment passed. Finally, Ouchi nodded. "Under the circumstances, I think your independence is acceptable, Colonel."

Ouchi spoke in rapid Japanese and his men slowly relaxed. Iwamoto's hands were shaking and beads of sweat were running down his face.

John could smell the man's fear. Combat always sharpened his senses. Colors were sharper and sounds were more intense.

Ouchi took a deep breath. "I'm inclined to believe you. I think you're a man of honor."

"As are you, Sir. You lead your men well."

"One tries." Ouchi flashed his teeth, acknowledging the compliment. "I've taken courses at your Harvard University and from your military exchange program.

"Be careful not to assume too much, Colonel. You're fortunate, but this is not the end of it. I have considerable autonomy in this matter, for now. We're divided about how to deal with your company. I was chosen because you're in my territory, and I'm known to be more open-minded than some of my brothers. Your words make sense to me."

John nodded. Unseen, he quietly slipped his service .45 automatic from his lap into the soft briefcase on the floor.

"I'll argue your case. Still, I may be overruled, and I need not tell you that direct orders must be followed. The next time we meet, it might be as enemies."

There's such a deep abyss under this tightrope we walk, John thought. *Our friends are as dangerous as our enemies. Despite what I said, we're not a sovereign nation like Switzerland. Despite what you said, there is too much blood on your hands.* "I get the message. You'd kill me in a second if you had to."

"With regret, I would. I'd drink a toast to you afterwards."

John sighed, letting out his breath slowly. "We're not a threat to you. We treat everyone even-handedly in our business dealings. Now may I offer you tea?"

This time Ouchi's smile was genuine. "Perhaps another time. Our business is finished for the present. I'll do what I can to discourage your enemies."

"Thank you." *We could damn sure use the help.*

In the lobby, Ouchi paused, turned and extended his hand to John. "It was a good meeting, Colonel. It's a pleasure doing business with you."

John smiled and shook his hand. Ouchi's grasp was firm. "I'm glad we could reach an understanding."

John and Harry watched Ouchi and his men walk to a waiting limousine and enter. John waved, and they watched in silence until the limo was out of sight.

Harry heaved a sigh of relief and clicked the safety on his shotgun. "That could have gotten ugly. I'm not as quick as I used to be."

"You had them convinced," John said. "That's what counts. Besides, Ouchi is too smart to let things get out of control. He needs our products, and he knows it. We were as safe as being in church."

Harry rolled his eyes. "What happened to the peaceful retirement you told me about?"

"Nothing is more valuable than personal privacy in today's world. Even a saint has something she wants to keep secret."

"I don't know any saints. What are you saying?"

"How well do you know my son, Will? Cybertech is his company, at the core. He invented the things we sell. Do you know what motivates him?"

"I don't have a clue, Colonel. I've never really thought about it."

"Will's dream is freedom. He thinks people should be able to talk with friends in private without becoming targets. He's right, but he didn't realize how big all this was."

"What's that got to do with Ouchi?"

"Cybertech is a target. Will's encryption is covert and impenetrable. Our customers who use it can stay hidden, but we can't. We can't run, nor can we hide."

Harry thought for a time. "Shit."

"Ouchi wasn't here to invest. Not really. He came to check us out, to see us firsthand."

"To see if we could protect ourselves."

John nodded. "And if he could trust us."

"Our customers don't attract attention, but *we* do and it worries them."

"I'm afraid so," John said. "There's more. Think about it: Why'd he back down?"

"Because I would have blown his fucking head off and he knew it. I could have nailed him and his skinny-assed little gunman with the same pattern."

"I know." John suddenly felt very tired. "But we can't get them all, Harry. We're vulnerable. He who defends everything, defends nothing.

"Ouchi backed down, because he knows privacy is no better than the people who sell it to you. Cybertech is successful, because everyone knows we keep the faith. Our products do what they're supposed to, and we don't put trapdoors into them for anyone."

"Even crooks like the *Yakuza?*"

"Ouchi knows the rules. We follow the law, but we don't betray our customers. If one of them is indicted on criminal charges, we put their product orders and updates on hold. If they are convicted, we blacklist them and comply with whatever a U.S. court lawfully instructs us to do. Ouchi mentioned Iran, but we've also blacklisted the ATF and the UN. We don't talk about it, but the word gets out."

Harry blinked. "The UN?"

"They got nailed for raping the survivors in one of those squalid African conflicts. What we're selling is precious, like ice water in the desert. There are some we won't sell to, but none that we'll betray. It's a fine line, and the buck stops with me. If our customers think we can't be trusted, if they fear the water is tainted...."

Harry glanced down at the gun in his hands, frowning, then back at John. "We get hit from both sides?"

"All sides. Will's inventions tilt things a bit more toward freedom. That's going to stir things up. We're going to be a target. If people can't break Will's codes, someone, sooner or later, will try to break us."

"They should have made you a General."

John smiled. "Not much chance of that.

"I'm sixty-one years old," he continued in a soft voice. "I won't be around forever. My son is a genius at technology, but Cybertech is going to attract a lot of attention of the wrong kind. This was just the beginning. It's going to get worse.

"Will's never fired a shot in anger. Sharks like Ouchi would eat Will alive if he didn't have people like us to back him up. If anything happens to me, take care of Will. Find him some help."

"I'll do what I can, Colonel."

John punched his friend gently on the shoulder. "Thanks, Harry."

Side by side the two old warriors gazed out the glass doors across the parking lot. The clouds on the hills were dark, and the wind seemed to be picking up.

"I think it's going to rain," John said.

BOOK ONE:
THE STORM GATHERS

"A Nation of Sheep will beget a Government of Wolves."

Edward R. Murrow

CHAPTER ONE

CYBERTECH PLANT, 3 YEARS LATER....

William Patton Giles took a deep breath. He let it out slowly and pressed his back into the contoured Aeron chair. He closed his eyes and tilted his head back, letting the chair do its work and comfort him. Mentally he counted to ten, by thousands, willing his muscles to relax.

One thousand and one, one thousand and two... I wish Dad was still around, he thought.

He opened his eyes and looked down at the gouges and grain patterns in the beautiful rosewood desk. He remembered the dreams that led him and his father to start the firm. *We were going to do some good, make money, and have fun.* It hadn't been much fun recently, and it was getting worse.

The desk had been his father's, one of the first extravagances they'd bought when Cybertech started making serious money. Will touched it gently with his fingers, remembering the past. The old desk had gotten a little beat up over the years.

The desk didn't match the bird's-eye maple on the walls or the tan and gold industrial carpet on the floor, but what the hell. John had picked the décor, and said he wanted contrast. He liked Brazilian Rosewood, but declared it too dark for the walls. His office once made the cover of *Forbes*: the writer called it "eclectic." Will smiled. Those were good times.

He remembered one of his father's favorite ways to relax from the stress of running a business: field stripping and reassembling his M1911A1 Colt .45 with his eyes tightly shut. The scars and gouges on the desk held those memories.

After Will became CEO, he'd had the holes in the ceiling repaired. After all, they were really his fault. Will once mentioned to his dad that Bill Lear had sometimes fired into the ceiling of his office for psychological effect. John liked the story, and thereafter was known to bring rowdy meetings to order by capping off a round or two. It added to his mystique.

The desk was special. Will would never dream of having it refinished, and, fortunately, John had limited his fire to the vertical. The maple paneling was untouched, and beautiful.

Will glanced at the photograph on the wall in front of him. Iron John, not in scruffy fatigues or desert cammo, but wearing expensive microfiber slacks and a silk shirt that accented his ice blue eyes. His eyes held just a tinge of amusement. That was John's "genteel CEO" persona, one forced on him by the family.

Not a day went by without Will missing his father and blaming himself. The FBI would not declare that John was dead. They insisted on keeping the file open and investigations active. It was like a wound that never healed. Until all that was resolved, Will was responsible, and alone. *So very alone.*

He sighed and turned his gaze back to the small group seated in front of his desk. They were all but snarling at each other. He slapped his hand on the desk to get their attention and waited for silence. It took a few seconds, and then he spoke as softly and politely as he could under the circumstances.

"Would everyone *please* shut up long enough that I can get a clear thought in my head?" He scanned their faces. "Thank you."

He glanced at his Research and Development manager. "We spent over twenty-five million dollars to develop the Andromeda platform so we could move up into high-end privacy servers. It is the most expensive product launch we've ever had. Now we have a problem?"

Clive Stuart was short, introverted, and unkempt. He removed his wire-rimmed glasses and cleaned them carefully. Bill Gates used to rock in his chair, but Clive cleaned his glasses.

Mostly. When stressed, he rocked too.

Clive looked the *ubergeek*, right down to the ponytail and sandals. It fooled people who didn't know him well, which was to say, just about everyone. In reality, he was a superb project manager, a paradoxical cross between a slave driver and a mother bear with cubs.

"We're about to have our ass handed to us on a plate," Clive said. "Two large multinationals have copied our parallel processor system assemblies and cloned the product. They're selling them in Europe for half what we charge. *Half.* And I had to find out about it from my engineers instead of from sales."

Will glanced at his sales manager. Olivia was in her mid-30s and was beautiful in a thin, dark, fashion model sense. Her dress was soft silk, her shoes were Ferragamo, and she wore no jewelry. Someone who looked into her eyes saw intelligence and alertness.

If that person looked deeper, he saw festering anger. She'd apparently nurtured it from her childhood. He didn't know why. Her parents were dead, and she never discussed her family. In addition to her anger issues, she was obsessive-compulsive, a condition which, at times, created problems that spilled over into the business.

Will once had to get Olivia out of jail for starting a riot in a fashionable nightclub. She'd hit a man in the face with a glass. The settlement, and keeping it out of the papers, had cost the firm six figures. Will told her it was an investment, that he'd keep her secret if she'd avoid alcohol and get her shit together. That had been almost six months ago.

He suspected she was lesbian, but no one dared ask Olivia about her personal life. She'd made it clear such discussions were unwelcome. She seemed grateful to him, but told him to mind his own damn business when he suggested counseling.

Whatever her issues, Olivia did her job. She kept the engineers honest. They liked her focus. The ones he'd spoken with privately said it was better than working with the gregarious, shoot-from-the-hip, disorganized schmoozers that were typically selected for sales managers. The sales force liked her too.

To catch her unprepared was rare, though she did tend to take criticism personally. Her anger, rage actually, was something else. Since their talk, she'd not thrown anything. He supposed he should take comfort from that. Will looked at her, thinking it was best to get her to respond before Clive got more spooled up and set her off. Episodes like that had caused some of John's holes in the ceiling. "Olivia?"

Her green eyes flashed. "The products to which Clive refers are not yet on the market."

"Bullshit," Clive snapped.

Will silenced him with a look. "You're saying he's wrong?"

Olivia took her time answering. She frowned, carefully tucked a few errant strands of silky dark hair behind her left ear, and shook her head. "Not wrong – unproductive. He's overreacting. There's no need to get hysterical."

"Do we have a sales problem or not?"

"We don't have a sales problem, not yet, but there are issues on the horizon. We always knew we were moving into deep water as we expanded our markets. We may get to stress test our Intellectual Property Protection and design cleverness. This is not unexpected."

Will felt his eyes narrow. "What the hell does that mean, Olivia?"

"I'm inclined to believe Clive's speculations. I was going to brief you when we had verification."

"You fucking knew about this?"

Olivia gave Clive a disgusted look and glanced back at Will. "If I took up your staff time with every rumor that floated through, we'd never get anything done. You know how much misinformation and disinformation circulates around our industry."

"Just tell me what you are hearing."

"Iwata Industries and New Century Business Machines may have cloned our server designs. If the rumors are correct, they will be selling them for between forty and sixty percent of our prices, depending on the configuration."

Will didn't know whether to laugh or cry. *So why are they screaming at each other when it turns out they basically agree?* He put it down to nerves. They were both worried.

"Keep talking. Do you have anything actionable?"

"Nothing compelling. Hearsay. Unconfirmed rumors like those Clive's people picked up. I do have some smeary copies of a product brochure in German."

"No cancellations?"

"Not yet," Olivia said. "But we are starting to see delays in placing orders. One of my people has seen New Century's tech manuals and is express shipping me a copy. There's a trade show in Munich next week. They'll be showing there."

"Now you tell us." Clive was scowling at her. "What actions have you taken?"

"I had legal send the standard 'cease and desist' letter, warning them about infringing."

The lawyer cleared his throat, but Will waved him to silence. "Not just yet, Samuel." He looked back at Olivia.

She shrugged. "They told us to stuff it."

"Let me break in here, Will." Clive looked irritated. "I've got friends at our customers who've done technical evaluations. They told me in confidence these are *copies* of our products. Blatant copies. They infringe at least six of our patents. New Century and Iwata have a teaming arrangement. They're thieves. This is overt piracy."

Olivia started to say something, but Will silenced her with a headshake and an icy glare. When Clive grinned, he turned the glare on him until the grin faded. "New Century did hire a few of your people. We're suing them. How's it going?"

"Not worth a tinker's damn." Clive snorted. "Their lawyers are stalling. New Century is a forty billion dollar company. They can litigate forever if they want to. We haven't even gotten to taking depositions yet."

"What about the patents?"

"They admit to distributing copies of our patents and tech manuals to designers in the divisions that compete with us. There's no law against it; those are public documents."

"So what's the problem?"

"They say they can use our designs for free," Clive said. "I've heard it from several sources.

"That's crazy." Will glanced at Olivia.

"But true. I've heard it from six sources myself, two of them in the media." She shrugged. "It may be hopeful. It shows they are desperate, and they know our products are light years ahead of theirs. It could be bluster and bluff. Or a negotiating strategy."

Will closed his eyes again. He took a deep breath, looked at Clive, and spoke calmly. "Why would they say they could use our designs, pray tell?"

"Who knows?" Clive rolled his eyes. "They're thieves."

"Let me try to summarize." Will tried to keep a reasonable tone. "Two large multinationals, working in collusion, are introducing products that directly compete with ours. They hired away some of our key design talent. They say they can use our designs. Is that right?"

"Yes," Olivia and Clive chorused, nodding in unison. "Absolutely," Clive added.

"That's wrong," Sam interrupted.

They all looked at the lawyer. He was shaking his head.

"It's not that simple. Those statements are conjectures, and the allegations are speculative. We'll have to prove them in court."

Olivia and Clive started to protest, but Will waved them to silence. "Okay, Samuel, you have the floor. Why do you say that?"

"First off, these allegedly-copied, potentially-infringing products have yet to hit the open market. Nothing has been sold. Like Olivia said, we can't do much based on rumors. Even if Clive is right, the beta test units are being loaned under nondisclosure, so no one will talk on the record."

"So do your legal shit," Clive said. "Subpoena the bastards."

"I can't ask for a subpoena or restraining order based on rumors. We can't sue until they start shipping products, and then the burden of proof will be on us. There is quite a lot to prove."

Will frowned. "New Century did poach our people."

"Sure. That's legal, unless we can prove otherwise. They've hired five of our engineers over the past two years. One male, four females. They claim our non-compete agreements don't apply."

"Can that be true?"

"Not for the reasons they assert. New Century makes general-purpose industrial computers, while we make communications security gear. Different markets, they say."

Sam grinned. "There may be valid issues about when our non-compete agreements expire, but I'm not worried about that point. When they raise it, we'll assert our NDAs and ask for a preliminary injunction. Our Non-Disclosure Agreements don't have time limits. I can broaden the injunction to include non-technical issues and request expedited subpoenas. I can ask them things like if the first employees poached revealed proprietary information to help them target the rest, if they disclosed our marketing information, and so forth."

"But their machines are the same? Copies of ours?"

"Perhaps," Sam said. "We'll have to prove that too. That's messy. For one thing, we'd have to get the actual infringing equipment. That might not be easy."

Clive's fists were clenched in frustration. "The claimed functionality is identical."

"The products may *appear* similar to you or to your sources, but their lawyers will say you're biased," Sam said. "It's up to a court to decide the facts. You told me yourself that the ROM packs and software are different."

"So what?" Clive said. "They'll buy our ROMs and put them in their machines. There's already a thriving gray market in those chips. It's convenient our firmware just happens to run on their machines. We're looking into site license violations, but...."

Will glanced at his watch. "I've got another meeting in ten minutes, people. This is a rat hole. The bottom line is we'll still have to prove they copied our designs."

"Actually, we'll need to prove several things," Sam said. "First, we have to convince a judge that the designs are the same. Second, assuming they are, it would be helpful to establish our former employees worked on these designs. Conversely, opposing counsel is sure to claim the products were reverse engineered using a 'clean room team' who, of course, had no access to our confidential information, and that our former employees did not participate in these design efforts. Third, we'll...."

"Can we prove those two points?" Will interrupted.

"We might if we could get the case heard by a U.S. court. They'll want it tried in Geneva."

"On what basis?"

"Probably because all the indications so far are foreign." Sam shrugged. "We're arguing these now because of the employee non-compete issue. If we prevail, we can subpoena their design data, raise the NDA issues, and see if we can get ITC action to block imports."

"And sue them for copying our designs?" Will asked.

"Yes, we can do that. Eventually. They'll deny, stall, and raise the reverse engineering issue. That will take time. At least another year, and probably longer. I was about to ask you for more staffing. I now have three lawyers working on this, and we've not gotten to any product issues yet. If they get jurisdiction moved out of the country, it gets more difficult."

"They infringed our patents, Sam. Reverse engineering doesn't help them if they infringed." Clive was getting agitated. He'd started fidgeting. Will looked at his watch again.

"Samuel?"

"It's not that simple. There are many loopholes and ambiguities in the current body of patent law. They'll cite the 'prior user rights' clause as a delaying tactic."

Olivia frowned. "Would it be possible to talk about this in plain English?"

"If either organization, or any of their subsidiaries or affiliates, or any firm they've bought before we get to trial, can claim to have used our inventions before our patent disclosures were published to the world, they can use them royalty free. That's how it works, Olivia."

"I took courses on the U.S. Constitution and how it applies to technology business," Olivia said. "Article one, section eight, says inventors with patents will have sole rights to their inventions. It's quite clear. The Constitution specifically says *exclusive rights*."

"So now you're a lawyer?" Sam said.

She glared at him.

"It's not that simple. Times have changed."

"Can you tell me why without going off into lawyer mumbo jumbo?"

"Sure. Congress changed the law."

"He's right," Clive said. "When Congress started rewriting America's patent system back in the 90s, opponents labeled the bill the 'Steal American Technology Act.' It passed anyway."

"Is that true?" Olivia asked.

"Absolutely," Clive said. "The 1999 law passed on the midnight express: Totally underhanded. It was a cluster fuck."

"I was asking him," Olivia said, looking at Sam. "What happened?"

"WTO wanted legislation to aid 'Global Harmonization,' and the UN and big multinationals backed it. The bill that rewrote U.S. patent law passed without debate in 1999. They've been patching it ever since, again and again, endlessly."

"It's been a rolling disaster," Clive said. "It legalized theft, and dumbed-down our patent system."

"Congress called it the 'American Inventor's Protection Act,' actually," Sam said mildly. "That was the start. This was expanded in 2011 when the 'American Invents Act' passed. Both bills were modeled on European patent law."

Will sighed deeply and made a dismissing gesture, sweeping his arm. "We're drowning in details, Sam. What was the intent of this legislation? What does it mean, Sam?"

"The vote was technically legal. These days, Congress votes on unpopular bills its members haven't had an opportunity to read. Think about ObamaCare."

"Screw ObamaCare," Clive said. "Let's stick with patents. The first legislation crashed the Internet bubble and collapsed the stock market. Our property rights took a spear in the chest. That's what it means."

Sam shrugged. "You can't prove cause and effect. There were other factors: rampant executive fraud, terrorism, and a new administration. We also have major trading partners that pay no attention whatsoever to property rights, like China."

"And that makes it okay? I seem to detect a don't-give-a-shit attitude here. Look at your paycheck, lawyer man. It says Cybertech on it."

"Easy," Will said. "Sam, did this legislation harm or help America?"

"That's a political issue, not a legal issue. I can't answer your question."

"It troubles me," Olivia said, "but I think Clive is right on this one. You don't seem to give-a-shit, Sam."

"I didn't say the legislation was good, I said it was **legal**. In any case, it doesn't matter. It's old history, and it's irrelevant. We're wasting time."

Olivia's eyes narrowed. "How can you say that?"

"The Supreme Court upheld the legislation. It doesn't matter how they got passed, how bad the laws are, or what damage they do. It's now the law. My job is to work within the law to serve our corporate interests as best I can. God bless America."

"We have a lot invested here," Olivia said. "What should we do?"

"What we're doing. Litigation. It's the American way...."

Olivia glanced at Will. "Clive's right. Let me go on the record. I'm going to miss my sales targets badly if we don't fix this soon."

"This will take time," Sam said. "We'll argue the paragraphs that support our case. Their lawyers will argue those that say the opposite. Then a judge will decide."

"We're being robbed," Clive said. "*We* invented this technology. No one else used it first. Part of getting a patent is the search for prior art. If there was any prior art, we wouldn't have been granted a patent in the first place."

Will shrugged and gestured at the lawyer. "Samuel?"

"Irrelevant." Sam spread his hands. "We do a good job at that, and we keep good records. They won't break our patents. They might threaten, but I don't think they'll try seriously."

"What then?"

"Like I said: Prior user rights. They'll probably say they used our inventions internally without any public disclosure. Maybe at a plant in China or Brazil or someplace."

"And if they do?" Olivia asked. "So what?"

"If they can convince a judge they did, they get to use our inventions for free."

"How do we prevent that?"

"We send some lawyers down to wherever the hell they claim they were using it. We hire local lawyers who understand the legal system and are licensed to practice there. We get a local court to let us collect evidence and we file to get a ruling. Then we bring the ruling back here and sue in a U.S. court. It can be done. It just takes time and money."

"That could take years," Olivia said. "Our patents might expire first."

"It's the law," Sam said. "There are other issues. We'll get to argue the 'doctrine of equivalents'...."

Will was getting frustrated. "Okay, okay, enough already, Samuel. I want you to meet offline with Clive and Olivia to study these details and come up with an action plan."

"There's a downside," Sam said. "We'll get sued if we push this. Those firms have thousands of patents between them. They'll start rolling through them in batches of ten or so, claiming infringement and asking for massive damages. That's a standard tactic."

"It's legalized extortion," Clive said.

"I'm telling you how it works," Sam said. "Not justifying it."

Will sighed. He turned his attention to Olivia. "How much of our sales are at risk?"

Olivia looked down at her compute pad. She tapped some buttons. "Worldwide, this year's plan for these products is nine percent of our total sales. The target for the U.S. is 12%. Orders were ramping up nicely until last week, but at the current run rate we'll miss our plan by over 60%. Next year, sales targets triple, and the year after they triple again."

"That's a pretty deep hole to fill," Clive said.

"It sure as hell is," Olivia said.

"So we have to fight?" The question was rhetorical, but Will wanted a staff discussion.

Clive and Olivia nodded.

"Samuel?"

"It's going to be costly," the lawyer said.

"Can we win?" Will asked.

"We should prevail if we can get into a U.S. court. They'll settle before then, because if we win in court and prove bad acts, like willful infringement, we'll get triple damages. If these acts are deemed 'exceptional' by a court, that would be plus our legal fees."

"Fees which will be substantial...."

"Yes."

Will sighed deeply. "Thank you all for your time. At least we're pretty clear about the issues and threats. I want you to put together a task force to come up with a plan of what to do, along with timelines and budgets. I need options, people. Who's going to be the team leader?"

They looked at him blankly.

"Olivia?"

"Not me." She shook her head. "It's a legal issue."

"No," Sam said.

They all looked at him.

"This is a policy issue. It's about technology strategy."

Will took a deep breath and let it out slowly. "Okay, then, engineering's got the lead."

"I fucking knew it." Clive was rocking back and forth in his chair. "This sucks."

"Can't help it. That's a direct order."

Clive blinked. He stopped rocking.

"Do you understand me? I need to be able to depend on you."

"Yes," Clive said. "It still sucks."

"True," Will said. "Thank you. If you need help, ask."

"The rest of you will support Clive fully." Will looked around at his staff from left to right, meeting each pair of eyes. He held his stare until he saw a nod, and then moved on to the next until all had signaled agreement.

"All right, then. One more thing. In the future, let's try to be a little easier on each other. This is a crucial issue, and I want open discussion. Different viewpoints are fine, but let's remember we're all on the same side. Can we do that?"

They nodded again.

"On your way out, ask Kate to get me an aspirin and a glass of water and hold my next meeting for a few minutes. This day is going to have to improve a whole bunch just to make it to shitty."

The small group stood, collected their things, and left quietly.

Unknown Location

The woman turned from the strange mirror, shaking her head. Her mentor, the *Viracocha,* was watching her somberly. His oddly violet eyes reflected a deep inner sadness.

A person noticed the eyes first, followed immediately by the *Viracocha's* pale skin, thick white hair, and fine bone structure. He was tall and thin, over six and a half feet.

The *Viracocha* switched the device off and the images and sounds faded. After what seemed like a long time, the woman spoke.

"It's beginning, isn't it?"

"Yes. Do you wish to go to him now? Our ability to protect you is limited."

"I don't see an alternative. I'm the only one here who knows Dr. Giles personally. He might trust me."

"I could send some of our warriors to protect you."

She was silent for a long moment, clearly tempted, but finally shook her head. "Our warriors are few, and they're needed here. We both know that."

He looked at her fondly. "If we do nothing the man is surely lost."

"We can't allow that," the woman said. "I'll go alone."

"We need him, but we need you as well," the *Viracocha* said. "Please don't take unnecessary risks. Don't sacrifice yourself."

She looked into his eyes for a long moment. "I'll remember your teachings. All lives are precious. When I return with him, we'll all be safer."

"Go with God, Rebecca." He nodded somberly. "We'll pray for you. We'll watch over you and do our best to keep you safe."

"Thank you, *Viracocha*."

Cybertech Plant, Executive Conference Room

Here we go again, Will thought. He studied the faces of the people filing into the conference room. It was an odd assortment. Sarah from Human Relations, Jacob from regulatory compliance, Mary the PR lady, and several staffers. He recognized one of Samuel's attorneys.

Will glanced at Sarah questioningly. *What the hell?*

"Give me another minute or two. I've asked Clive to drop in as well." She looked around the room and raised her voice. "I want these discussions off the record and confidential."

Will looked around to see the others were paying attention. "You got that?"

Heads nodded.

"Phones and computers off. Remove the batteries." Sarah watched as they complied. "I've asked Harry's security people to go over the room."

"Fine by me," Will said.

At Sarah's signal, a team of technicians came in and swept the room with sensors. One had a metal-mesh basket. "Listen up everyone, here's the drill. What you will be discussing is restricted and attorney client privileged. Put all your smartphones and electronic devices in here. You can get them back after the meeting. No notes are to be taken. If anyone asks you what was discussed, you tell them nothing and report it to security or legal. Got it?"

The security man seemed nervous.

"Harry told me I need verbal responses." The firm's culture distrusted authority, but they cut a lot of slack for old Harry.

The group responded with a chorus of, "Yes, we understand." For Harry or Will, they'd go along. For anyone else, they'd be complaining about regulations and bullshit.

The earnest young man glanced at his security team. "Is it clean?" They nodded.

He looked at Will. "No bugs, Sir. Everything's clean. I'll cut the hardline and we'll get out of here. Everyone's electronic gadgets will be in our security safe. They can pick them up after the meeting."

"Fine," Will said. "No problem."

The man unplugged the Polycom speakerphone and hefted it off the table, wrapping the wires around it.

Will gave him a puzzled look.

"Harry says." He put it in the basket, and his security team filed out of the room. Clive was just entering. He shook his head, but handed them his smartphone as they passed.

"One more thing, Sir." The security man paused at the door, radiating discomfort. "Harry wants us to go to lock down. He wants no cell phones inside the facility whatsoever, and asks for your support."

"Why wasn't I informed about this?" Clive demanded.

"You are informed now," Will stated calmly. "Tell the group. I'll need your full support on this."

Clive blinked.

"You tell them **why**," Will said. "You're our technology guy. If you won't go hard core on this, we're all in deep shit."

Clive sighed. "Harry's right. Cellphones can't be allowed in a secure area. They can be used for tracking, eavesdropping, and video monitoring. Better make it the same for all wireless devices. Keep them offsite, and run full security scans on anything you hardwire to our internal networks **before** you connect. As for secure COM on hardlines, only go through our own gear. Do not trust DOD scramblers, they could have backdoors."

"Thank you," Will said. "This will now be our company policy until further notice. Violations will be a termination matter. I want this taken seriously."

"Clive, would you shut the door, please?" Sarah's voice was melodious. She weighed over two hundred and fifty pounds and was very competent. Her skin was jet-black, so dark it almost glowed. Sarah had a law degree, but had never taken the bar exam. Instead, she'd served two terms in the state legislature, elected from a predominately white district.

Something was bothering her. "I wanted someone here from accounting, but I don't want to wait. Can we start now?"

Clive sat down, looking questioningly at Will, who shrugged. Will looked at Sarah. "What's this about? I'm not used to meetings without agendas."

"There's weird shit going down," she said. "We need to talk about it."

He nodded, waiting.

"We're regulated by over fifty agencies and a number of them seem to be stirred up. I had a visit from the Equal Employment Opportunity Commission's regional director yesterday. She dropped by to complain in detail about the racist, chauvinist pig you have running R&D."

Will glanced at Clive. "You mean him?"

"Uh-huh," Sarah said. "I'm afraid she wasn't a happy camper."

Clive shrugged. "Remember our meeting about patents? This is related. The bureaucratic bitch claims we discriminate by not paying our female engineers enough. She says that because she has noticed competitors like New Century are paying the women they poached from us double what we did. The woman has rocks for brains. She ought to be horsewhipped."

Sarah gave a noncommittal grunt. "Tell him the rest."

"It's like Sarah says. EEOC is also alleging we discriminate by race. We're okay on blacks, but don't have enough Hispanics or Asians, and we don't have any Indians at all."

"We've never had problems before," Will said. "We've employed Indians for years."

"We have several programmers from India, but no American Indians," Sarah said. "None have ever applied for jobs. I can handle the Hispanic crisis and the Confederation of Tribes likes us because we outsource to them, but Clive pissed her off about the Asians."

Will was watching Clive. "What happened with the Asians?"

"She asked me why I didn't hire more Asians. I told her probably because they didn't go to the same engineering school I did. You know how we work: small teams that know and trust each other. I don't tell my people who to hire. I just tell them to get the job done."

"She says we're exploiting child labor too," Sarah said.

"One of my Senior programmers is a single mom with a really bright son," Clive said. "Kid's a whiz with computer games. Works for us after school. He did most of the work on the graphics user interface for Andromeda."

"So?"

"He's only seventeen. Underage. His mother would rather have him working here than hanging out. The kid would too. He likes the work."

"What's wrong with that?" Will asked.

"The state filed a grievance," Sarah said. "Child labor violation."

"We've appealed," Clive said. "It's bullshit."

Sarah scowled. "It gets worse. Jacob here does our environmental compliance and industrial safety. OHSA is on our ass and we've been warned EPA may join in too. OHSA says our model shop needs six different types of masks and four different types of shoes."

Will glanced at Jacob, a small man with thick glasses who looked like he wanted to be somewhere else, somewhere far away. "Are we having problems with National Safety and Health and World Environmental Pollution?"

"I'm sorry, Sir. OHSA is filing safety violations over the shoes and masks we use in our shop. They gave us a waiver years ago, but now they say it's invalid.

"We only have twelve people working in that shop. We've never had an accident, but there is a lot of wiring to trip over. Sometimes one of the machines leaks and we get an oil slick. We did have a small fire last year, but no one got hurt."

"So what's the problem?"

"They fined us $100,000 because of improperly labeled potential explosives," Jacob said. "They say we've failed to comply with asbestos documentation laws too. I don't think we've ever used any asbestos, but we don't have the records to prove it."

"It's not your fault," Clive said. "Why the hell would we have records for something we never had? We're a frigging software company, not a heating contractor."

"Do we have explosives in the model shop?" Will asked, puzzled.

Jacob shook his head. "No, of course not."

"Potential explosives," Sarah said. "We had a five gallon can of isopropyl alcohol to clean things. It wasn't labeled. Probably it had been, but the label fell off."

"Alcohol isn't an explosive."

"The government defines it as a potential explosive in quantities of a gallon or more," Jacob said. "Some rule they passed after 9-11."

"Oh," Will said. "What about gasoline?"

"It's in a different category," Jacob said. "Makes no sense, but those are the rules."

"EPA stuck HAZMAT stickers all over Jacob's can of alcohol and took it away to analyze it," Sarah said. "We're in trouble over drug testing too."

Will blinked.

"Not me," Jacob said. "Not my shop. They're after engineering."

"Yes," Sarah said.

"God freaking *damn* it," Clive said. "Let's not start that again. I've got a group of programmers who'll be happy to test drugs for you, Sarah, if they're not dangerous. You can bet most have smoked pot. So has most of the population. What's the big deal?"

"These people can shut us down," Sarah said. "That's the big deal."

"This is nuts." Clive's eyes were flashing and his face was flushed. "The damned woman acted like I was running an opium den."

Sarah started to reply, but Will waved her back. She was touchy about drugs, having lost a sister to crack. It wasn't a subject Will wanted to spend staff time discussing.

Clive looked at him. "There's no drug use at work. We don't allow that. One of my best software designers was busted recently because she failed a random drug test. Her crime was eating a hamburger with a poppy seed bun.

"Police came to her house in the middle of the night, arrested her, and threw her ass in jail. I had to go down at 2 AM and bail her out, and then we had to get her counseling for the trauma. Her computer code is still all screwed up. The woman's a basket case."

Will winced. He couldn't let this develop into a fight. "Sarah, I know how Clive feels. And I know how you feel. We keep trying to focus on business, customers, and technology, but we wind up spending time on things like this. Stick to business please."

"I am," Sarah said. "The reason I wanted this meeting is that everyone needs to know the heat is on. We're being targeted for some reason. If every agency that regulates us enforced all of the rules all of the time, we'd be shut down. Anyone would be. Remember Gibson guitars? Government goons with guns came in and seized their products because some bureaucrat suddenly didn't like the kind of imported wood they'd been using for 30 years."

Will nodded. Clive looked irritated. At least he wasn't fidgeting.

"I wanted to send an alert," Sarah said, "and to have Mary and her PR people in the loop. I think somebody – or maybe a group of some bodies – is out to get us."

"I see," Will said carefully, not really understanding where she was going. "What are you suggesting?"

"Not letting Clive's engineers piss off the regulators. General cover fire until we can figure out what's going on. Maybe a campaign about what good citizens we are and how much we contribute to society and the local economy. I've asked Mary to put something together."

"Let's hear it," Will said.

Mary and Sarah were physical opposites. One was petite and blonde, the other large and black. Mary dressed conservatively. Sarah favored flashy clothes and heavy jewelry, filling the room with vivid color.

"I'm still collecting ideas." Mary smiled brightly. "If Clive's engineers are smoking gourmet California weed, it probably helps interstate commerce. Maybe I should promote that?"

"Bad plan," Clive said. "Canadian's better nowadays."

Sarah glared at him. "Not funny, asshole."

Clive shrugged. "Just trying to help."

Sarah looked at Mary. "Don't encourage him, white girl. Some heavy shit gonna come down on you haid if we ain't real careful heah."

"I'll have a draft proposal by close of business tomorrow," Mary said.

"There's another reason I wanted PR here today," Sarah said.

"Let's hear it," Will said.

"You're on, girl," Sarah said. "You're not going to believe this one, people."

Mary looked uncomfortable as all eyes turned to her. "This isn't about any of the issues you've been discussing, I'm afraid." She hesitated. "I've had a most unusual call from investor relations. I'm not sure what to do about it."

Clive frowned impatiently and started to push his chair back, but stopped at a gesture from Will. "This meeting isn't over yet. Go ahead, Mary."

"We got a call from the WOW ladies. They're threatening a boycott of our products and to hold protests at our plant and any trade shows or events we attend."

"Who the fuck are the WOW ladies?" Clive demanded.

"I've never heard of them either," Will said quickly, looking at Sarah. "And, more to the point, why is this an issue we need to spend time on?"

"Because they could shut us down," Sarah said. "It's a splinter group: the Women of Waco. Their issue is child abuse."

"Jesus," Clive muttered. "That's all we need. A bunch of fucking Femi-Nazis."

Will kept his voice calm. "Let's back up, here. Other than Clive's programmer, we don't have any children working here, do we?"

"No," Sarah said. "We don't."

The lawyer cleared his throat, and spoke hesitantly. "Samuel asked me to sit in on this meeting. WOW is a fringe feminist group. It has only a few hundred members, but they're militant. It's loosely affiliated with the larger women's organizations, including NOW."

"They're a bunch of nuts, but their issue, child abuse, is taken very seriously," Sarah said.

"WOW NOW, brown cow," Clive said. "This is bullshit."

Sarah glared at him.

"If I fire the kid, can I go back to work?" Clive was fidgeting, and his face was scarlet. He'd started to rock back and forth. It wasn't a good sign.

"Wouldn't help." Sarah shook her head. "The complaint about your programmer is exploitation of a minor, not abuse. WOW's issue is child abuse."

Mary and the lawyer nodded agreement.

"I don't understand," Will said.

"There is no right to privacy if child abuse is involved." The lawyer spoke in a didactic tone, slowly, enunciating each word carefully.

"**What?**"

They all jumped, and the lawyer cringed. "I'm only quoting what WOW said to investor relations, Dr. Giles."

"Privacy," Sarah said. "That's WOW's issue with us. They say privacy is enabling child abuse. They say privacy is not a right where child abuse is involved. They cite case law to support their position."

"We're not abusing any children," Clive said. "This isn't an engineering issue. After that busted takeover attempt a few years back everyone knows we don't sell to pedophiles."

"Easy," Will said. "The issue appears to be privacy, not child abuse."

The lawyer said, "Actually, it's not been alleged we've abused anyone."

Will put his head in his hands and rubbed his eyes. *This gets worse and worse.*

Finally he looked up at the group and sighed. "Let me guess. WOW's grievance is our products allow privacy, and that someone, somewhere, somehow is, or might someday be, abusing children, talking about his nefarious deeds to his sleazy friends, and keeping his despicable communications private by using our products. Right?"

"I think so," Mary said.

Clive groaned.

"I know so," Sarah said. "That's exactly right."

"Tell me more about WOW," Will said. "Are they from Waco?"

"No," the attorney said. "They're a nonprofit based in Hollywood. Some of their members are well-known actresses."

"**Great….**" Clive stretched the word out: GRRRRR-EIGHT. They all looked at him. At least he'd stopped rocking.

"We get to see a movie about how we help perverts abuse children. We get to be a target for reality-show politics, like a deer in the headlights. Fucking fantastic."

Will frowned. "An Agit-Doc film like that Moore guy used to do?"

"Why not?" Clive said. "Isn't that what Hollywood does? They make movies."

"WOW has made such films," the lawyer said. "Propaganda framed as entertainment."

It gets worse and worse. Will kept his voice calm. "Could we prevent that?"

The lawyer shrugged. "Free speech…."

"I don't think so," Sarah said.

"Trying to prevent it would make it worse," Mary said.

"Okay," Will said. "What does Waco have to do with it?"

"There was an incident in Waco, Texas, in 1993," the lawyer said. "A religious cult had allegedly violated weapons laws. Arrests were attempted and a standoff resulted, with shooting and casualties on both sides. During the siege, it was alleged children were being abused."

"Were these cult people abusing children?" Will asked.

"Actually, no, but the Attorney General at the time thought so," the lawyer said. "She ordered federal agents to attack. An intense fire started, the buildings burned, and 82 people died.

"The abuse allegations and fire are what's remembered about Waco. The official report concluded the cult burned its own buildings. Others assert the government started the fire."

"Excuse me," Mary said in a subdued tone. She had a strange expression on her face.

"Yes?" Will said.

"Fire. That's what they said. WOW is advocating burning Cybertech to protect children from abuse. Those are the signs they'll be carrying."

Clive slammed his fist on the table. "I can't believe this shit."

"What do they want?" Will asked.

Sarah said, "They're demanding our products be licensed and registered. They want trap doors and clipper chips embedded so law enforcement agencies can monitor conversations."

Clive shook his head. "That's absurd."

"It would put us out of business," Will said.

"Yes," Sarah said. "It would."

Will thought for a time. "What can we do?"

They all looked at him silently.

"Sarah?"

"I don't know, but I'm declaring an emergency. Something's very wrong. I'm getting bad vibes. I like working here, and I'm afraid."

"She's got a point," Will said, looking at Clive.

"Okay, okay." He shrugged and spread his hands in surrender. "We *all* like working here. I'll be good, and I'll warn my troops to stay clean and not piss anyone off." He glanced at Will. "Can I go now? We're having a design review."

Will nodded. "Beat it. Just understand this is real trouble."

"I'll pass the word. We'll be good." Clive left looking somber.

The meeting wrapped up shortly afterwards. Will spent the rest of the week thinking about what to do.

CHAPTER TWO

CYBERTECH PLANT, ONE WEEK LATER

That fateful Thursday, Will had slept soundly for the first time in weeks. A soft rain had been falling all night. He'd always found the rain calming. He didn't wake up with one of his nightmares, not once. Not even the one where his dad was calling for help.

Will sighed deeply. There had never been demands or a ransom note. Will's intellect accepted John was dead, killed by professionals who'd left no trail and no clues. His subconscious apparently still had hope his father would come back some day. Counseling didn't help, and he dared not take drugs.

Not knowing was a wound that never healed. Will knew that. His problem was living with it. Today he rewarded himself with a long hot shower. Shaving, he looked at himself in the mirror, frowning at the stress lines around his eyes and the slight indication of softness in his belly. *I've got to get back on my exercise program.*

Instead, he took time for a decent breakfast. Granola cereal topped with fresh blueberries, one lightly buttered English muffin, and a single cup of strong black coffee. *Most of health is mental. Attitude, attitude, attitude… I'll work out tomorrow.*

Will arrived late at the plant. His assistant, Kate, glanced up when he walked in. Katherine Chambers, now almost 70, was Cybertech's employee number three, right after Will and his father. She was only five four, a lot of spunk in a small package. Kate's hair was gray, but her mind was sharp. Her green eyes still sparkled and she got things done.

Kate's husband had died a few years ago and she'd wanted to keep working. She didn't need the money, but said she wanted to work, to be active and to have purpose in her life. Her parents and brother were deceased, she had no children, and Cybertech was her family. Will was grateful to have her.

She looked worried.

"What's up?"

"I'm not sure." She was frowning and shaking her head. "Sarah's scheduled a meeting. It's on your calendar from ten to noon. Sam has one of the partners here from the law firm we use in Washington, and he apparently has something he wants to report."

"Who else will be there?"

"Finance and engineering," Kate said. "Clive, Herb, and Matt. Sarah says she's getting a special conference room ready."

Herb Walmsley was the Chief Financial Officer and Matt Cunningham, his assistant, was the firm's financial planner. Both were long-term, trusted employees.

"Please tell her I'll be there and clear my calendar for the rest of the day."

Kate nodded.

Will grinned at her look of concern. "It's okay. I once saw a tombstone that said 'I was expecting this, but not so soon.' "

Kate didn't smile. If anything, she looked more worried. "I'll hold your calls too."

"Good idea."

Sarah held the meeting out in Clive's test lab, in an odd chamber suspended from the floor on large springs and cables. Will remembered vaguely it had been purchased to fulfill contractual requirements from one of the government agencies. Harry's security team did their scans, collected personal electronic items and departed, leaving one man to guard the door.

The usual pre-meeting banter and chitchat was conspicuously absent. Will looked around the small table: Sarah, Samuel and his guest, Herb, Matt, and Clive. The Washington attorney was dressed formally in a dark three-piece suit and tie. The Cybertech people wore "business casual" – knit short-sleeved shirts and slacks, except for Sarah, of course.

Sarah always tended towards flamboyant dresses and jewelry. She'd grown up poor and dressing well was important to her. Today her dress was green and gold, and she was wearing heavy gold hoop earrings.

Will studied their faces. The lawyers seemed uncomfortable and Sarah looked grim. The others were simply waiting. The room was cramped, without ventilation, and the seating was on wooden folding chairs. The harsh lighting was one overhead bulb dangling on a cord, and the walls and ceiling were faced with deep acoustic foam wedges.

Actually, so was the floor. The table and chairs were sitting on a heavy metal mesh, which was suspended in place on springs. It flexed slightly as people shifted in their seats.

Better get started, Will thought. "Sarah, this is your show. Why are we meeting here?"

She didn't answer him directly. "This is a Class 1 vault. After we seal the door, we're cut off from the world. Before we start, is there anyone else you want here?"

Will thought for a moment. "Yes. Please ask Kate and Harry to join us. Get Mary and Olivia too."

As the big woman struggled to get out of her chair, Will realized she'd have to clamber over everyone to get out. "Clive, the guard's name is Tim. Please ask him to request those people attend."

The rest of the team must have been expecting something because they arrived immediately. After they were seated, Clive closed the door with a solid *thunk* and moved a large handle, forcing clamps into place.

"This room is triply shielded electronically," Sarah said. "The power is from our own generator, and we *know* those lines are clean. The acoustic dampers render any mikes in the lab useless, so we should be able to talk in private."

Will nodded. "Go ahead. It's your meeting."

"Be careful what you say outside this room." Sarah looked into each set of eyes, emphasizing her words. "Will's office is bugged. A friend sent me a transcript of the meeting about patents last week. It was complete, and accurate. I have that deer-in-the-headlights feeling."

Sam frowned. "I presume your friend works for the government and prefers to remain anonymous?"

"Yes...." Sarah left the word hanging in the air.

Will looked at her. "Everything we discuss here is confidential. It's also attorney-client privileged and not to be discussed outside this room. If they bugged us without a court order, they may have broken the law. It would help Sam if...."

"Don't ask. You know I don't reveal my sources."

Will shrugged. It had been worth a try.

Harry scowled. He started to say something, but caught himself, glancing at the Washington attorney. That brought a few smiles. Harry didn't trust outsiders.

Even Sam smiled, but grimly. "I've asked Mr. Boggs to join us. Jerry Boggs. He's a partner in the firm that handles legal matters for us in Washington.

"Jerry, feel free to take off your coat and be comfortable. We're pretty informal here."

"This won't take long. As your agents, we were served with three separate notices late yesterday."

Sarah groaned. "Why do bad things always come in threes?"

"Whoa," Clive said. "Think negative vibes, and you're gonna bring down bad karma."

"Let him talk," Olivia said coolly. "Karma's in trouble whenever you get lawyers involved. That's why he's here, Clive: To screw up your personal karmic condition."

"Easy," said Will. "Keep talking, Mr. Boggs."

"I caught the red eye flight out because I wanted to warn you personally. You're in big trouble."

"They need specific details, Jerry," Sam said. "We'll hold questions for later."

Boggs nodded. "To cut to the chase, the first set of papers is from the Patent and Trademark Office. They've opened twenty-seven of your patents to reexamination. If you fail to respond in thirty days, the PTO threatens to summarily declare these patents invalid."

"Jesus," Clive said. "It takes us an average of seven years to get patents granted, and they give us thirty days to defend?"

Sam said, "I agree it's outrageous, and unprecedented. One reexamination, maybe, two possibly, but I've never heard of twenty-seven in a batch. I can delay things for years, but the intent of this probably isn't about legal issues. It's simple intimidation."

Will frowned. "You just lost me."

"This won't ever get to court. It's a ploy to block us from enforcing our patents until it is resolved."

Boggs nodded. "I concur."

Clive muttered a string of profanity under his breath. His face was getting red.

Boggs looked at him. "May I continue?"

Clive shrugged.

"The second set is from the State Department. Another thirty-day notice. They're charging illegal export of encryption technology."

"What technology?" Will asked.

"2048 bit encryption keys," Boggs said.

Sam frowned. "Why is State Department involved? Commerce handles export licenses."

"I wondered about that myself. The Commerce Department's Bureau of Export Administration normally administers non-defense and dual-use products, those for military and commercial use."

"So you don't know?"

"I do not," Boggs said. "The third notice is from the Commerce Department. Actually, the patent office is part of Commerce, but this particular action is to investigate WTO claims that you're illegally using monopolistic practices against New Century and Iwata. I think FTC is a party to this as well, but we haven't researched that issue."

Will opened his mouth but before he could speak, Clive interrupted. "This is bullshit."

Sam frowned. "May we continue?"

Clive took a deep breath and let it out in a sigh of disgust.

Sam shrugged and looked at Will.

"I'm interested in the antitrust order," Will said. "Accusing us of picking on New Century and Iwata is absurd. It's like an ant raping an elephant. Why is Commerce…?"

"We have another problem." Sam held up his hands, palms forward and waved them emphatically, like a policeman directing traffic. *Stop.*

"What?"

"Before we discuss these matters in detail, Mr. Boggs has informed me his firm can no longer represent our interests."

Will blinked and shook his head. They'd used Boggs' firm since almost the beginning.

"Excuse me all to hell." Olivia's eyes were locked on the lawyer like laser beams. "We're in desperate trouble, and our attorneys are going to recuse themselves?"

"She has a point," Sarah said. "Breach of contract, legal ethics…."

"It seems the IRS has raised compliance issues about their tax returns." Sam's tone was caustic. "They're afraid."

"What the fuck are we paying these people for?" Clive snapped. His face was red.

"Easy," Will said.

The Washington lawyer shifted uncomfortably. "Samuel, my partners and I have discussed this. I'm your friend and you're a valued client, but I can't place the firm at risk…."

Sam didn't bother to argue. He waved his hand dismissingly.

"I understand, Jerry. We're suffering from the death of due process ourselves. Perhaps it's best you leave now. Time is short and we have a lot to discuss."

They all watched silently as Clive opened the door and Harry escorted the lawyer out.

Washington, DC.

The old man finished reading and closed the file. "This is in effect?"

"*Hai.* Cybertech's attorneys should be presenting the actions to their client today."

"It seems excessive."

"You told me to handle it, Sir."

"True." He was grooming this man for bigger things and didn't want to interfere. "What outcome do you expect?"

"Cooperation, eventually. Sometimes it's necessary to nudge, to give guidance."

"They may take offense."

The younger man didn't look concerned. "It doesn't matter."

"What if they resist?"

"Dr. Giles is not his father. He's weak."

The old man raised an eyebrow.

"He's not foolish enough to let his firm be ruined. He'll give us what we want."

"And if he doesn't?"

The younger man took a sip of his tea. "We'll take it anyway."

"Yes." The old man sighed and nodded slowly. He didn't like this unpleasantness, but the other options were more severe and best avoided. "Perhaps you're right."

CHAPTER THREE

CYBERTECH TEST LAB, SECURE ROOM, SAME DAY

Will had ordered a break to give everyone a chance to recover from the bad news. Boggs was already on his way back to Washington, but somehow the room seemed more crowded. They were almost sitting on each other's laps. Will shifted in his chair, causing mutters and a ripple down the table as everyone adjusted.

Clive gave a faint scream, high, falsetto.

They all looked at him.

"She grabbed me," he said, glancing at Olivia.

Sarah rolled her eyes.

Olivia shook her head slowly. "If that were true, he'd be missing some equipment." Her smile was frosty. "Guaranteed."

Clive shrugged. "Yeah...."

There were a few chuckles, but most looked solemn. Even Sarah was subdued.

Will said, "Let's get started. The agenda is how to deal with these legal notices."

"The timing is bad," Sam said. "My attorneys are already busy with the New Century and Iwata issues."

"Do you think that's a coincidence?"

"No."

"Nor do I." Will looked at Sam. "You read through the papers Boggs brought?"

"I'll need to study them in more detail, of course, but Jerry's report astonishes me. I've never heard of anything like this."

"Can you block these actions?"

"I don't know."

"What can we expect from Bogg's firm?"

"Jerry will do what he can. They'll not testify against us, and they'll not help the government. Attorney client privilege protects us." Sam shrugged. "We won't get any active support. They're afraid."

"This is a rat hole," Clive said.

The financial people looked puzzled.

"He's saying it's a waste of time to discuss this," Will explained. "Why?"

"I don't dare tell my people about this," Clive said. "It'd just frustrate and distract them. We need solutions, not to get entangled in a complicated, legalistic, cluster fuck."

"Solutions," Sarah said. "Can you suggest any?"

Clive shook his head. "I don't even know where to start."

"He has a good point." Will looked at Sam. "Where *do* we start?"

"I don't know yet. We need to understand the politics better. And to learn what's behind this. The legal issues are all serious, and any one of them could sink us."

"We need to do something while we're learning, Samuel. Where should we start?"

Sam shrugged. "The export law violation is a major felony. Why not start there?"

"If we stop shipping product, we won't be breaking any export laws."

They all looked at Will, startled. He kept his attention on the lawyer. "Well?"

Sam took a long time to answer. "Maybe."

"What's that mean?"

"It's an unusual defense, but I could argue we were in technical compliance with the first order, the export law violation, if we stopped shipping. It helps us deal with the third order too, the one about monopolistic practices."

"And you can stall on the patent issues?"

"Sure." Sam nodded. "The PTO moves slowly."

"This is not a solution," Sarah said. "Once these investigations get rolling, it's going to get ugly."

"It's already ugly," Will said.

"It's better than doing nothing," Clive said.

Will looked around the room. "Anyone have a better idea?"

"Not me," Sam said.

"Anyone?" Will rapped the table with his knuckles for emphasis. "I'm looking for suggestions, people."

He waited. There was silence.

"Okay then, let's run with it."

"My sales people won't have anything to do," Olivia said.

"Give them paid vacation with their families. Tell them we'll take care of them."

"I'll lose some of them if that goes on very long. I can't put them in a time capsule."

"Me neither," said Clive. "An out-of-date engineer is an unemployable engineer."

"I know." Will looked around the room at the tense faces. He smiled grimly. "Don't panic. I want everyone to take a few deep breaths and calm down. We need to keep clear heads."

"And to do what?" Clive asked.

"You've all had training in strategy."

They nodded.

"Time to use it, people. Sun Tzu: *Where the enemy is strong, avoid him.*"

Clive was starting to fidget in his chair. "We don't fight?"

"In a contest of strength, we'd be overwhelmed. We disperse. Each of you operates independently. Trust your training. Trust your instincts. Trust each other, but no one else.

"Sarah, you and Mary need to start a PR campaign so the right people know what's going on. This is 'open ground,' so don't block the enemy's path. Avoid direct confrontation. Snipe at them from secure positions and then fade away. Let them wear themselves out."

No one spoke. The room was totally silent. The acoustic baffles soaked up so much sound that Will could hear the blood moving through his ears. He searched the faces of his team, seeing what he hoped for. *Outrage.*

"We need a plan," Will said. "Suggestions?"

Sarah was ready. "On intersecting ground, you can join hands with allies."

"Exactly right. For example?"

"What happens if the public and the big firms like Intel and IBM knew we're being put out of business by our own bureaucracies and they can't purchase our products any longer?"

Will smiled. "They wouldn't like it."

"Correct," Sarah said. "What happens if we pull our ROM chips off the market?"

"They'd discover encryption products like ours won't function without our proprietary components, and that they have no second sources."

Clive looked startled. "Iwata and New Century would have to stop shipping product. You're going to force that?"

Will nodded.

Herb and Matt were frowning. Herb spoke first. "I don't think shutting down the chips is a good idea. Twenty percent of our profits comes from outside component sales. We're sure to get sued on anti-competitive grounds."

"We're **already** being sued," Will said. "We've just developed technical problems. I'm shutting the component lines down."

"That's not advisable," Matt said. "We have a fiduciary responsibility to our investors. We have outstanding contracts with our suppliers and customers."

"It's not about the damned numbers," Will said. "It's about survival, and I control the majority of the stock. All our contracts have cancellation clauses, don't they?"

"They do," Sam said.

"Then cancel them."

Sam nodded.

"Clive, I want you and your technologists to vanish. Scatter. Get lost. Get out of the country. I don't want anyone to know where you are until after those orders are due. Can you make that happen?"

"I think so. I'll talk to my engineers."

"Do it. I'll make sure you have enough money, and Harry can help you find remote vacation spots. If anyone gets found, they say nothing unless Samuel has an attorney present."

"And if they sell us out?" Harry asked, speaking for the first time.

"We pick our people for integrity," Will said. "Now we find out if we were right."

Sarah was shaking her head, looking worried. "You're going too far."

"Why?"

"We're not an army. I'm not Chinese, you're not a warlord, and the most powerful government in the world is coming down on us like a hammer. Shutting the company down would be the end of Cybertech. Once we do that, it's all over."

"The lessons live," Will said.

"What do you mean?" Sarah asked.

"Sun Tzu," Will said. "He said, 'Supreme excellence consists of breaking the enemy's resistance without direct conflict.' His writings on conflict are three millennia old and have never been surpassed in comprehensiveness and depth of understanding."

"We're not in school, professor. Sometimes being witty, clever, or right isn't enough. My granddaddy had his skull caved in by a Birmingham cop and was never the same again. Pardon me, but the government scares the shit out of me."

"My father wasn't a professor. He was a respected military leader, and he thought all officers should be required to take yearly tests on Sun Tzu's writings."

Sarah nodded reluctantly. "John said one of your ancestors did the first translation of those into English."

"The first translation was done by a P. F. Calthrop. But you're right. Lionel Giles published the second in Shanghai and London in 1910, and it's still used."

Sarah was watching him intently.

"I wish Dad was still around, but we'll have to do our best without him." Will met Sarah's gaze without flinching. "If you have specific concerns, let's hear them."

"How specific do you want? I don't want to get my head bashed in, and I don't want to see this company destroyed."

"If you know your enemy and know yourself, you need not fear the results of a hundred battles."

"Do we fight in court?" Sarah asked.

"Certainly. It's a good start. We're not criminals. I expect everyone to obey the law. But remember you have rights. Don't give them anything but your name unless a lawyer is present."

"If the company shuts down, there's no one left to defend our patents," Sarah said.

"She's got a point." Clive had started rocking back and forth in his chair. "If our patents are declared invalid, then their teachings become public domain, and all our competitors are free to use our technology. There will be nothing left of Cybertech. We'll be dead."

Will shook his head. "I didn't say we were dissolving the company. Cybertech will remain as a shell, like one of those holding companies with no assets but a bunch of lawyers and a patent portfolio. We're going to be closed without being closed."

"If we're closed, how do we resist?" asked Sarah.

"Ferociously," Will said. "With every fiber of our being."

Sarah shot him a puzzled look.

"The lawyers stay and fight. We can trust Samuel to defend Cybertech's interests. If I shut down our operations and order our employees to take a prolonged vacation, who's to say I can't? If you and others choose to keep working, who's to say you can't?"

"I can keep this tangled up in litigation for years," Sam said.

"But can you hope to win?" Sarah objected. "The big multinationals are plundering our technology. If the PTO negates our patents on top of that, how can the firm possibly survive?"

"Maybe it can't," Sam said. "I don't know yet."

"Screw the Patent and Trademark Office," Will said. "Do you think they can beat you?"

Sam sighed. "What worries me is maybe I can't beat them. They have limitless resources."

"It's my call. What if I order you to resist?"

"I'm your man," Sam said. "Until they tote me off to the reeducation camp...."

"That's it then." Will looked around the room. "Let Samuel handle the PTO and work on the things you can affect."

Sarah frowned.

"What's the best form of strategy?" Will asked.

"One where all possible outcomes lead toward victory," Sarah said automatically.

"One where we can survive long enough to win," Olivia said.

"You are both correct," Will said. "We must pick our battles carefully. George Washington fought only nine battles against the British. He lost most of them, but we still won the war. It took eight years."

Sarah said, "We could try to negotiate a settlement. The nail that stands up gets hammered."

Will shook his head. The room was silent.

"You're betting the company on this one. Do you **really** want to do that?" Sarah said.

"I don't see an alternative. We're overmatched. We don't have the bandwidth or resources to run the company and fight the government at the same time, not on multiple fronts. We need to focus."

"Why escalate?" Sarah said. "What's the advantage in that?"

"Something's rotten here. I want to shine a light on it. The courts have the power to find out what's going on. So does Congress, and we have a few friends there."

They all looked at him. A long moment passed in total silence. Sarah finally took a deep breath and let it out slowly. "I'll do my best."

"Thank you." Will turned his attention to the others. "Herb, when Sarah and Mary come up with a PR message, I want you to pitch it to the investment community. We're big enough and our products are crucial enough to get their attention."

"I can certainly get their attention," Herb said. "That's not going to be a problem."

"Just make sure Wall Street understands this isn't about Cybertech, it's about their right to privacy. If we go down, so does their ability to communicate privately by electronic means. They have a dog in this fight."

"Yes," Herb said, nodding. "I'll get notices out to the banks and credit card firms."

"We should go wider," Mary said. "I'll do press releases to the networks, trade press, and major papers. The loss of electronic privacy will concern everyone. It's not about us or our products; it's about our customers' Constitutional rights. Most American citizens want personal privacy. That's the high ground."

Will said, "Good idea."

"I can get groups like the Electronic Frontier Foundation and The Cato Institute involved. ACLU too," Mary said. "They can hold conferences and do white papers, and we'll embed that in our PR campaign."

"Excellent," Will said. "Run with it. Herb, I want you and Matt to set up a trust to ensure funding is available to do what we need."

Herb nodded. "What about the employees?"

"I'd like to cover half their salaries for a year. Can we afford that?"

"Probably," Herb said. "There will be cancellation fees. Some customers may sue."

"Whatever," Will said. "Work with Samuel and Sarah to get reserves set aside. Liquidate whatever is needed. We'll be engaged in expensive litigation, so get enough assets clear to cover things, including the things I haven't thought of yet. I'll sign whatever papers you want, but you need to get them to Kate today. What am I missing?"

"The government could freeze our assets," Sam said.

"Just handle it. Surely, they can't freeze the funds we need to pay your lawyers to defend ourselves?"

"I'll do my best," Sam said. "The bar association and several other groups would raise hell if they tried that. Maybe we can find allies. As long as the money holds out, I can keep them tied up in court."

"I want your litigators to be self-funding. Be aggressive. Sue the bastards for everything you can."

"Including the government?"

"*Especially* the government." Will rapped his knuckles on the table for emphasis. "Pick cases where the evidence is compelling and damages can be established. Get subpoenas out and discover who's behind all this. One sympathetic federal judge or Congressional Committee hot on the trail of corruption and why we're being harassed could make a big difference."

Sam nodded.

"Work with Sarah. The cold neutrality of an impartial judge is a wonderful way to inject some justice, accountability, and common sense into the government."

"Wait a minute," Clive said. "You're not going to manage this?"

"No."

Clive had stopped rocking. He had a stunned look on his face.

"I can't," Will said. "I'm counting on you. It's **vital** you and your engineers vanish. Make sure our design data and lab notebooks don't fall into the wrong hands."

Clive shook his head in denial. He suddenly looked very young.

"Can you handle it?"

"I don't like this."

"People will be coming after me with arrest warrants if I hang around."

"He's right," Sam said.

Clive took off his glasses and started cleaning them. "I'll do my best."

"Thank you." Will smiled. "Look on the bright side. Iwata and New Century will discover copying our products and technology does them no good. The demo systems they've been showing have *our* chips in them. We're going to cut off their oxygen. With luck, it will give them a new world view. They need us."

There was a pause as that sank in and they thought about it.

"Confusion to our enemies," Sarah said.

"Damn straight," rasped Harry in his gravelly voice. It was more like a growl. "Can't trust politicians. The bastards hang you out and leave you twisting in the wind."

Will looked around the group, pleased to see heads were nodding. "Since Clive's guys are targets, like me, we're all getting out of sight. With luck, the bad guys will waste a lot of time and resources looking for us.

"Our enemies made a major blunder. They thought we'd cave in and submit to extortion. But it's not just about money. It's about freedom and the American Dream. Think of the stories you'll have to tell your grandkids. Besides, what have we got to lose?"

"For starters, they could arrest me and put me in jail," Sarah said quietly.

Will nodded. "*Great idea!* All that free publicity would help. Look at Gandhi and King."

"If they bust you, make 'em use handcuffs." Sam grinned and pointed his finger at Sarah like it was a gun. "Wear your purple dress and big gold jewelry. Get photographs. Give interviews. It'll do your granddaddy proud."

"Way cool. We'll put it up on the Net." Clive was grinning.

"Don't bail her out until I can get the media there," Mary said. "We don't want to leave the interviews to those tacky courtroom reporters."

She studied Sarah carefully, pursing her lips, seeming to ponder. "Maybe a simple black dress would be better for the trial. What do you think?"

"I'll check with my litigators," Sam said, making a big show out of taking notes.

"Do it to 'em, big Mama," grated Harry, deadpan. He sounded like a friendly rhino.

Kate clamped a hand over her mouth. The rest were biting their lips and trying to hold back laughter. The expression on Sarah's face was worthy of a Kodak moment.

Her eyes narrowed with suspicion. She looked at Will. "Were you expecting this?"

"Not really, but Dad said to always expect the unexpected. If we make it through this, you'll be a celebrity and everyone on the planet will want our products."

Sarah groaned, but she was smiling. They were all smiling.

"Whatever happens, I love you people," Will said. "I can't tell you how much I appreciate your loyalty and support. Now get out of here. Good luck to you all."

Olivia was crying. She angrily brushed the tears away, kissed him on the cheek and walked out without speaking. Sarah and Kate gave him hugs. The rest shook his hand as they were leaving.

Even then, Will knew his life was about to be turned upside down. *What would Dad do if he were here?*

There was, of course, no answer. Only silence.

CHAPTER FOUR

CASCADE WILDERNESS AREA, TWO WEEKS LATER....

Bright sunlight filtered through the tall firs, tossing sharply variegated, shifting patterns of light and dark across the forest floor. A few high branches rustled, but the dominant sound was the soft rippling of a small brook as it rushed over its rocky bed.

The sun was lowering and the man shifted position, edging a bit farther into the glade, following the sunlight, moving towards warmth. Soon dusk would fall. The air would chill quickly at this altitude.

The man seemed mismatched to the rustic setting. Only experienced hikers ventured this deep into the high mountain wilderness, seldom alone. It was lonely country.

The nearest residents ran small tree farms or grubbed out crops, some legal and some not, farther down the slopes. They were a day or more away down the narrow, rocky trails. The nearest town, really a village, was an hour's drive down the mountain on poorly maintained farm roads, where patches of gravel interspersed stretches of crumbling asphalt.

This man didn't work a farm or ranch. His skin was pale and his hands were soft. He didn't fit.

Since restocking and reforestation initiatives had replaced the clear cuts of the last century, there were again large predators in the forest: coyotes, bears, and even wolves and cougars. Because of the large predators, solitary hikers usually hung noise makers or non-lethal weapons on their belts, but this man didn't seem to have any defensive devices whatsoever.

That was odd. Every year a few people were mauled. There were stiff fines for not taking suitable precautions, and "suitable" was changing to "serious."

Predators were increasing. America's original native Gray Wolves had been small. They looked like over-muscled coyotes, but the ones that were reintroduced were hybrids, aggressive, and much larger. Some termed them "Canadian Dire Wolves," others "Giant Idaho Wolves." The program goal had been to have 100 wolves, but the number was now estimated to be over two thousand, spreading across state lines, running in packs.

The government avoided the subject, simply calling them Gray Wolves, as if they were the original species. One more government program gone awry and in the process of being covered up by silence and disinformation. It was like an early Dean Koontz horror novel.

The giant wolves were fearsome predators. For every animal they killed to eat, these genetically modified wolves killed about three more just for the fun of it. The biologists called it "sport-reflex killing" or "lustful killing." Hunting dogs were found eviscerated, with their intestines ripped out, left to die slowly.

You didn't see it reported on the news, but mountain people woke up when an Idaho grandma, out bow hunting elk, got the scare of her life in 2011. She nailed a charging 180-pound wolf with a headshot from her .44. It fell dead at her feet, and she became an Internet sensation when she posted the photo.

Her wolf had been alone, but they hunted in packs of up to 20. After checking out the images, backwoods hunters prepared, trying to avoid becoming snack food for killing machines that were often larger than they were. They started carrying 12-guage shotguns loaded with a mix of slugs and 00-buck for camp defense.

Informed hunters and hikers were nervous, but this man was either ignorant or unconcerned. He wasn't armed. The man's clothing was a hodgepodge of shabby and new, city and outdoors, expensive and castoff. He wore Vasque hiking boots with Gore-Tex uppers and vibram soles.

There was a high-tech weatherproof jacket draped over a branch. These clashed with his ragged sweatshirt and faded jeans.

Nothing fit. There was nothing slung on his belt. He had no belt knife, and no walking pole. The required bright yellow emergency locator beacon was nowhere to be seen. Most hikers draped it around their neck. Even if he had a hiking permit, he was breaking the law.

He had none of the gear of a camper except for a battered blue backpack. Nor did he seem to have the gadgetry that most city dwellers carried, especially a cellphone with a camera and GPS as suggested for novices in the backcountry.

Mostly, though, the man's demeanor didn't fit the wilderness. People generally came to the high mountains to hunt, to hike and explore nature, or to commune and find serenity. He evidenced no experience or preparation for hiking, other than the fact that he'd gotten there somehow.

Clearly, he was not a hunter or woodsman. Just as clearly there was no stillness or serenity in him. He seemed edgy in an odd way, one that was incongruous for the actual hazards.

There was a constant tension in his motions. He'd not slept, though it looked as if that might have been his intention. Instead of basking in the warm sun, he fidgeted and shifted position. When he removed his dark glasses, his eyes were haunted. When he stood, it was to stretch, pace, and sip water from the canteen beside him.

He was tall, about six feet, but not large. He looked generally fit, but not athletic. It would be hard to guess his age, perhaps late 30s. The tension in his face made him look older, and there were flecks of gray starting to appear in his brown hair above his ears.

He finally gave up trying to rest, sat up and reached for his pack. He opened it, rummaged inside, and spread some of the contents out next to him – a few energy bars, and a mostly empty bag of trail mix. Digging deeper, he came up with a lone can of beer.

He shrugged and poked at an energy bar dubiously. He paused over the beer, but finally put it away. He slowly munched the bar, chewing carefully, and taking small sips from his canteen.

Decision time, he thought. *I probably should start back. Only seven days left before letters come due and they start issuing warrants.*

He frowned, knowing it would be dark long before he could make it to a road. He knew better than to hike the rugged trails at night. It was asking for a broken leg or worse.

He considered the meager remains of his rations, wondering how long he could make them last. *Not much longer.* He should have run for the border with the others.

Sun Tzu said, "On hemmed-in ground, resort to stratagem." *Good advice, but what?*

The man shook his head. He wasn't thinking clearly and knew it. That bothered him. He'd always had a plan for what to do next, but not now, not when it counted.

It wasn't good planning that landed him out here in the mountains, far from civilization without adequate supplies or even a proper sleeping bag. His careful plans and hopes had fallen apart. His whole damn life had fallen apart. In the end, he'd just cut and run, leaving others to do what he should be doing himself.

He'd run to the mountains to think, but that hadn't helped. He'd stayed close to home, in-state, trying to develop options, hoping he'd think of something. But the more he thought, the more hopeless it all seemed.

"Why does there always have to be conflict?" he'd once asked his father.

Dad just smiled. "It's the way of things. That's how this country started. Jefferson said a revolution was needed every few years so humanity could progress. A Republic run by and for the people makes those in power fearful. It takes courage and sacrifice to preserve liberty."

Dad believed in taking risks, in taking responsibility, in living up to American exceptionalism. He'd often told Will the story about how his many-times-great grandfather, unarmed and dressed as a farmer, had met General Washington's boats and guided his troops into Trenton for the Christmas Eve battle that changed the course of the war and won independence for a new nation.

Will imagined a long line of ancestors watching him down across the centuries. They were waiting confidently and lovingly for him to do the right thing, and his dad was standing proudly at the front of the line.

Do the right thing. Use your intellect and training. Resort to stratagem. Problem was, he didn't have a clue and he was letting people down. People who trusted him.

Unknown Location

The watchers studied the man through the strange mirror. Finally the priest spoke. "Do you still think he's the one we need?"

"He left his worldly possessions behind. He runs not from fear, but from love, to help his friends. That shows wisdom and maturity. If he'd stayed, he'd be a captive by now."

"He has ample reason to fear," the priest said. "The hunters will come soon. They're strong. We can't prevent that."

"We must do what we can, my brother. Keep watching over him. Time is short."

The priest bowed his head and put his hands together. "I fear there is nothing we can do."

The *Viracocha* sighed, his eyes sad. "The one we sent is resourceful. Do we know where she is?"

"She'll be into the mountains by now. We've scanned repeatedly, but without success. The spy satellites are active and there are drones up, so she and her team are keeping under cover."

"Then there is hope. Perhaps she will contact us. Perhaps she will find the man in time. In any case, we can pray. We can do that."

Cascade Wilderness Area

The dammed bureaucrats are going to destroy me, Will thought. It was like being nibbled to death slowly by ostensibly friendly, small animals. *Maybe killer ducks? Harmless looking animals, with tiny, sharp teeth.* At first, you could shoo them away. For a while, you could beat them back with brooms. But they kept coming....

People still had a right to privacy, didn't they? Of course they did. Citizens had rights, the First, Second, and Fourth Amendments, among others.

The terror wars were over. Osama bin Laden and the fanatical Muslim *jihadists* were gone, now just one more footnote in their thousand years of turmoil and bloodshed. The threats of brutal Sharia law, Theocratic Socialism, and a Caliphate were quashed, but the intrusive bureaucracies they'd spawned remained and continued to grow.

Yesterday's solutions become today's problems. Question: What's the cure and what's the disease? Answer: It depends on viewpoint and definitions.

"Definitions," Will said musingly. *That's it. Definitions. It's about defining citizens' rights. That's what I've been missing.* **People** *have rights, but* **things** *don't.*

His mind was racing. *"Pursuit of Happiness" might be too vague for a dumbed-down population. They've been led to think happiness comes from a government handout. The old meaning, what the founders embedded into the Constitution, was "happenstance," the pursuit of chance, the hopeful chaos of free enterprise. That God-given right, embedded into the highest law of the land, had created prosperity. It inspired the American Dream, the desire to improve things, better your life, and reap the rewards if you made the right choices.*

Might we be better off if the Constitution had listed life, liberty, and **property** *as our inalienable rights? Uneducated people could better understand the right to own "stuff" than the more subtle concept of having the freedom to fail along with the freedom to benefit from success.*

Still, it was happenstance that led to prosperity and self-reliance that led to exceptionalism and security. Not stuff.

The problem was that all was lost when governments turned to plundering their citizens. Under tyranny, citizens inexorably suffered a loss of their property, happenstance, liberty, and life. The real issue might be which to defend first.

His mind churned. It was as if an old-style light bulb had gone off over his head. The distinction between property and what made up a free person was important.

Trusting the justice system to protect his property rights might be a huge mistake. He was defending stuff. The real issue was liberty. New Hampshire was right, "Live free or die."

Mistake or not, I'm running out of provisions. I sure as hell can't stay here.

"Where the hell is Ayn Rand when we fucking need her?" he shouted at the forest.

There was no answer, just the wind in the trees.

Will struggled to his feet. He was stiff from lying on the hard ground and felt a tinge of pain in his back. Will stretched and gazed at the beautiful wilderness, wishing life was easier. He shuffled to the edge of the forest, picked a tree, stepped behind it, sighed deeply, and unzipped his pants.

"Don't turn around. Just keep doing what you are doing."

The voice came from nowhere and he jerked, startled.

"Keep your voice down, and don't turn around, Dr. Giles." The voice was soft, and female. It was vaguely familiar.

"I think I'm losing it. You're not Ayn Rand, I hope?"

"No." There was a soft laugh. "Act normal, and calm down."

"I'm so far from 'normal' I couldn't find it on a map, lady. Am I under arrest?"

"No." She sounded amused. "I'm a friend, and it's *very* important you continue to act naturally. Do what I say if you want to live and stay out of jail."

She knows my name. Questions raced through his mind. "Do I know you?"

"Yes. You're being watched."

"I certainly am." He was concentrating. "If you wanted to see how far I can...."

"By others. There are groups that keep track of people like you. Your car is bugged. Your company and house too."

He thought about that. They'd bugged his office for sure. "What do you want?"

"Right now I want to help you get away, and you need to get going. You need to be back on that trail and moving in the next minute or so. Hurry up."

"Lady, I'm going as fast as I can. You're making me nervous."

"Just hurry." She definitely sounded amused. "Are you listening?"

He nodded.

"I want you to walk as fast as you can down the trail. In about a mile you pass through a deep gully. There are dense trees and brush on both sides."

He remembered that spot. The path was badly overgrown. It was rough there. "Yes."

"When you get there, look down. There will be a small green box on the right side of the trail, with a wire and an earplug. It's a secure radio. Put the hood on your jacket up and the earplug in. Put the box under your jacket and keep it out of sight."

"I have some questions."

"Not now. It's important that you do exactly what you are told. Your safety depends on it, and so does ours. We're taking risks for you, so don't screw up."

What was he getting into? He hesitated and took a deep breath, letting it out slowly, trying for calm. *I don't have many options*, he thought.

"Would you *please* hurry up? I used to have a large Appaloosa stallion that didn't take this long...."

Her undertone of amusement had turned to irritation. Well, he was getting annoyed himself. "Give me a break. It's hard to perform with you holding a stopwatch on me. There, I'm done." He tugged on his fly.

"This isn't a game. I don't know about you, but I don't want to go to prison."

There is that.

"Well?"

"I'll do what you say," he said.

"The radio is undetectable even by Japanese technology. It uses micropower, pseudo-random spread spectrum techniques and transmits below ambient noise. Do you understand?"

"More than you can imagine." The range would be limited, but anyone trying to listen in would hear only static. Better yet, no one could home on it. "Did you know a woman invented spread spectrum?"

"Hedy Lamarr, the actress. Co-invented, actually. She was gorgeous."

"Glamorous," Will said. "She said any girl could be glamorous."

"I know." A brief laugh. "She said, 'All you have to do is stand still and look stupid.' "

"Right." The woman knew her science and history, whoever she was.

"The box has a black button. Tap it once for 'yes' and twice for 'no.' If you hold it down for more than ten seconds, it self-destructs."

"How soon?"

"There will be a warning beep followed by a one minute delay. The explosion is small. Just drop it, move away, and you'll be fine.

"Do exactly what I say and we'll get you to a safe place. If something goes wrong, play dumb. Above all, don't let anyone get the radio intact."

"I understand. One for yes, two for no, hold and it blows." He paused. "Who are you?"

"There's no time. The main thing is to stay calm and do what I told you."

"Who's following me?"

"A team of hunters. Don't worry about it. They've no reason to get close, and I don't think they'll interfere as long as you're heading back. But don't talk on open ground, especially not anywhere there is long distance line-of-sight contact, just screened like we are now."

"Why not?"

"They may have directional mikes. There's no time. No more questions."

"Right. Stay calm. Don't worry. Follow instructions. Don't talk in the open." His heart was racing. He took a deep breath.

"The 'play dumb' is easy. It's the 'stay calm' part I worry about, lady."

"If I were a lady, I wouldn't be out here in the middle of nowhere watching you pee. If they wanted to pick you up, they'd have done it by now. You'll be fine."

"I hope so."

"Time's up. Go. Go now."

He started down the trail at a brisk pace.

BOOK TWO:
FLIGHT

"Never, never, in nothing great or small, large or petty, never give in except to convictions of honor and good sense. Never yield to force; never yield to the apparently overwhelming might of the enemy."

Winston Churchill

CHAPTER FIVE

CASCADE WILDERNESS AREA

It's harder going down than it was going up, Will thought. *That was a bitch, but this is worse.*

His legs were starting to hurt in different places and the old aches were still there. The trail was steep, narrow, and rocky. The roots and rocks that afforded him traction on the way up reached out to trip him on the way down. He'd fallen twice.

Gravity pulled him to go faster and he had to resist. The fronts of his legs were starting to cramp, but he was afraid to stop. "Walk as fast as you can," she'd said.

He was thankful for his expensive boots. Without their support, he'd have twisted an ankle by now.

What's the purpose of having me hurry? Surely, his best rate of progress was snail-like compared to a good hiker. The shadows were getting deeper and the trail would be impassable in the dark.

He found the radio exactly where the woman – *Who was she?* – said it would be. The little green light said it was on, but that was the only indication of functionality.

He looked around and saw that he was well screened, even overhead, by the dense foliage. He carefully put the radio in his inside jacket pouch and ran the wire down his sleeve, putting the talk button where he could reach it easily.

He pulled up the hood as instructed and looked around. The downhill stretch was over, but the going ahead looked even worse. *Damn.*

Will clambered slowly up the steep ridge. He paused to mop sweat from his face frequently. The hood of his jacket added to his problems. He kept it as loose as he could and it flapped around his head getting in the way and interfering with his peripheral vision. His arm was starting to throb where he'd bruised it, but he needed to keep pushing branches aside.

His legs ached. Every part of his body was sending pain signals warning him to stop. He struggled on as best he could.

Stay calm. It's important to stay calm.

He was making too much noise, breathing hard. Sweat was running down his neck. He kept shifting loose rocks and gravel, stumbling, sometimes causing miniature avalanches.

He stopped at the top of the ridge, catching his breath, looking around, listening intently. He peered back down the trail, but didn't see anything. He took deep breaths, mopped sweat from his eyes, and waited for his heart to stop racing.

The trail dipped down again, but there was another, higher ridge ahead. Will sighed, took a few sips of water, slung his canteen, and doggedly trudged on.

The wind was picking up strength as the sun dipped below the peaks. Clouds were rolling in. That wasn't good. Will knew what to expect from spending the past few nights on the ground with only his jacket and a poncho wrapped around him for warmth.

He hoped it wouldn't rain. After dark, the wind would be shrieking in the high trees, whipping the branches around. Apparently, that was common at these elevations. The trail was almost blocked in places by fallen trees and branches.

"Can you hear me?" He recognized the woman's voice. The sound quality was good, though there was a slight hiss in the background.

Tap once for yes. He gave the signal. *Tap.*

"You're slowing down. I need you to pick up the pace."

Tap. Will was exhausted. He walked the level places, skittered down the slopes, and clambered over the obstacles. Then it was uphill and steep. He cursed, pulled his hood down, opened the jacket, and kept going, breathing hard, trying not to stumble. One bad fall and it would all be over.

"You should be almost on top of the ridge by now. Is that correct?"

Tap. He was moving as fast as he could.

"It'll be full dark soon. I need you to listen carefully. Are you ready?"

Tap.

"When you go down the other side of the ridge, be careful. It's steep."

He didn't like steep.

"Did you hear me?"

Tap.

"Okay. One tap is yes, but it's also, 'I understand.' I need you to acknowledge. This is a critical part."

Tap.

"Can you keep moving till you get to the bottom? Maybe another half hour?"

A half-hour? He groaned. *Tap*.

"After the steep part, you'll come to dense forest at the bottom of the slope. Someone will meet you. Do exactly what he says."

Tap.

"Be ready to peel off your clothes and give them to the man you'll meet. You need to make the exchange quickly."

Tap.

"Also your backpack."

No way, lady. His notebook and computer disks were in the pack.

Tap. Tap.

"If you have essential items in the pack, take them out and let him scan them. Just be quick about it."

She'd thought of that. *Tap*.

"He'll show you where to hide. There will be food, water, and shelter. The bad guys are coming down the trail two ridges behind you. Before they were just observing, but something has changed. They're moving faster and no longer sticking to cover."

Tap.

"Our man is very good in the mountains. He'll get you to a safe place and lead them off. You must keep out of sight and make no noise after he leaves."

Tap.

"I'll come for you in the morning. Signing off for now."

Tap.

Will concentrated on placing his feet carefully. He took deep breaths, trying not to fall, ignoring the pain in his legs. He was nearing his limit and knew he couldn't make it up the next slope without stopping to rest.

The man appeared out of the bushes without any warning. "Follow me. Don't touch anything. Watch where I put my feet and place yours there too."

He moved quickly, holding branches back to clear a path. They slipped through the dense overgrowth effortlessly and without any noise.

How does he do that?

The man led him to a well-concealed camp. "Get your clothes off. Socks and boots too. These should fit you." He lifted a camouflage net and pointed at clothing piled on top of a mottled black and green sleeping bag.

"I'm careful about bugs." Will stripped and handed his clothes to the man, who checked them carefully with a small device. He felt foolish standing there.

The man was scanning Will's boots. A red light blinked, and the man attacked the left sole with a Leatherman tool. He removed a tiny unit, studied it carefully, nodded, and held it up. "Not careful enough."

"What's that?" It looked like a pin with a small barb and an oversized plastic head. It had been stuck into the front of his heel.

"A passive tracer. It's Japanese. If you shine the right microwave frequencies on it, it resonates like a beacon. They put a GPS tracker on your car as well. Give me your keys, please." The man grinned at Will's astonished look, handed him a full water bottle, and stuck the tracer on his own shoe. "Take small sips. We can talk, but keep your voice down."

The man stuck Will's keys in his pocket. He scanned the personal items, checked that his computer's batteries had been removed, and carefully put them down on the sleeping bag.

"There's a new backpack for you in the kit." He pointed at a bag on the ground. "Food, extra water, and other goodies too." The man slipped into Will's shirt and jacket. "Jesus, why don't you just wear a neon sign on your head?"

"I love that jacket."

"I'll try not to get bullet holes in it." He looked at Will's jeans skeptically, then made a face and stuffed them in Will's backpack along with his fancy boots. "I'll take everything but your computer, battery, and disks. Okay?"

"Excuse me all to hell. I don't have much experience as a hunted fugitive."

"You'll learn." The man dumped everything into Will's pack and strapped a pair of bulky goggles on his head. He shrugged into Will's backpack and put the jacket's hood up.

"Now I'm you." He jerked a thumb at the goggles and grinned. "Night vision. I'm going to tease them a little. I'll pick up the pace and lead the goons off you."

"What do you want me to do?"

"Keep the radio on and the plug in your ear. You'll be safe if you stay out of sight and keep quiet. Get into the sleeping bag and stay there. It's shielded from sensors, but keep your head down and don't move around. They might have air support or infrared imagers."

Will blinked and shook his head. "Air support?" He had wild thoughts of jets screaming down out of the sky, guns and missiles blazing, like in the movies.

"Probably helicopters. Possibly drones. I'm out of here. There's a flask of brandy in the kit. Enjoy." The man vanished into the brush.

Will cleaned up as best he could, slipped into the fresh clothes, and collapsed gratefully into the sleeping bag. He sipped more water. A small bag contained food and there was a sandwich inside.

He forced himself to take small bites, chewing thoughtfully. His breathing slowed and his heart stopped pounding. He followed the sandwich with dessert, a candy bar. It tasted wonderful.

Will was warm and comfortable for the first time in days. He closed his eyes and dozed.

Will snapped to wakefulness. He'd heard something. He cautiously raised his head and peered through the underbrush. It was full dark and there were lights coming down the trail. Dim. Red. He could see them flickering through the trees.

Red light, he thought. *Doesn't destroy your night vision.*

They were close. When he strained his ears, he could hear boots crunching on the gravel. There was the sound of loose rocks sliding, followed by a dull thud as someone went down hard.

A flurry of muttered curses was silenced by a brusque command. There was a soft moan.

"Get up." The voice was harsh.

"I think my ankle's broken. I can't move it."

"I should leave you here. Giles has night goggles, and we don't. You're stumbling around like a child, the satellites have failed again, and we have no drones."

The voice had a foreign accent. Asian? Will wasn't sure.

"He didn't even have camping gear. How could we know?"

"It's your job to know. You were supposed to search his house when you bugged it."

"I didn't see any night eyes." The man gasped. "Damn that hurts."

"It's broken, Captain."

That was a new voice. American.

"Splint it and strap it. We need to keep moving. If he can't walk, carry him. A *gaijin* won't be allowed to slow us down."

The leader's voice was definitely Asian, his tone one of barely suppressed rage. *Japanese*, Will thought. *Gaijin* translated as "foreign," but the speaker's tone implied "subhuman."

Dear God, it's a Peace Enforcer squad. UN troops.

The United States had signed treaties allowing U.N. enclaves in major cities and exempting Peace Enforcer troops from U.S. law. The Peace Enforcers were officially there to protect foreign property and company managers from "barbarian criminals," but most Americans called them occupation troops. Not publicly of course. Critics suffered reprisals.

Why are they following me?

The injured man groaned.

Will kept very still. He was terrified.

The men grunted as they hoisted their comrade to his feet and shuffled off down the trail. Slowly the sounds grew fainter and the lights faded into the distance.

"Are they past you?"

She was still there.

Tap.

"Good. Just wait. If you see or hear anything, give me one tap."

Tap.

He lay still, listening intently, hoping the searchers wouldn't return. He didn't hear anything except the pounding of his heart. He forced himself to take deep breaths, and slowly he relaxed.

The adrenaline rush subsided. He lay there waiting and listening, but heard only the normal night sounds of the high mountains.

He wondered if he'd ever feel safe again. He didn't think so. He kept perfectly still, listening to the forest noises, straining his ears. They seemed to be gone.

In the end, he had to move, to crawl out and relieve himself. He eased the bag's zipper open one careful click at a time. It was cold and dark. *Very dark.*

Will strained his eyes, peering through the gloom. He couldn't see a thing.

He finally knelt and felt in front of himself for branches. The slightest sound could give him away. He took care not to step on anything, feeling helpless, moving as carefully as he could, knowing the terror of a hunted animal, and expecting a challenge from out of the darkness. His hands were shaking.

Nothing happened. They were really gone.

Afterwards, he climbed back into the bag and helped himself to a sip of brandy. The warmth felt good. He took another sip. The wind seemed to be picking up.

More time passed and the wind moaned in the high branches. Suddenly there was a bright yellow-orange flash of light, vividly back-lighting the trees on top of the ridge.

Will started counting, as bright spots faded from his vision. One thousand one, one thousand two, one thousand three…. He'd gotten to nine when the sound of the explosion came. How far away? He couldn't remember. Several miles, he guessed. I'd better check in, he thought.

Tap.

"I saw it too." She was there. *Thank God.*

Tap.

"I love it when the goons have problems." She chuckled, softly. "I think they just lost a helicopter. Get some sleep. I'll see you in the morning."

Tap.

Will couldn't see any stars. The night seemed preternaturally black. He sipped the brandy until he was too tired to be afraid and sleep finally came.

Will woke to the smell of coffee. She was kneeling in front of him, holding a thermos under his nose. His mouth tasted like cotton and his legs were stiff and sore. God, the coffee smelled wonderful.

"Hmmurrph?" he mumbled.

"Not a morning person, huh? Well, this will get your eyes open." She handed him a cup. "The kit we gave you has hygiene items in it if you want to brush your teeth and clean up. Sorry there's no hot water, but a fire wouldn't be a good idea."

It took half a cup before his blood started flowing. He grinned up at her. "Thanks."

She helped him out of the bag and watched as he stretched to get the kinks out. His muscles were sore, but everything seemed to work.

He excused himself, stepped behind some trees, and proceeded to try to make himself presentable. They'd even provided a battery-powered razor and a mirror. He studied himself critically. *You look like hell warmed over.* He splashed cold water on his face, cleaned his sunglasses, and combed his hair into less of a tangle.

The woman was leaning against a tree sipping coffee when he returned. She examined him critically. "That's better."

"Who are you? What's going on?"

She laughed. "I took some of your classes."

He'd not taught for years. Will looked at her closely, slowly shaking his head.

"Rebecca. Rebecca Rider." She looked at him expectantly.

He wrinkled his brow in concentration. He used to put photos of his students in his grade book. He remembered an R. Rider, a PhD candidate. She hadn't finished her degree. That student was girlishly talkative, chubby, and suntanned. She'd had long dark hair. A rich kid, or maybe one with a rich husband.

The woman in front of him was pale, oddly so, he thought, and serious, even intense. Her azure eyes were quite striking against her white skin. She was thin and her hair was short, a lighter shade of brown than he remembered. He frowned. The images didn't match.

Her gaze was direct, demanding recognition. "You said I was a good student. Encouraged me to get my Ph.D. A few times we drank beer together."

The R. Rider in his class had been a good student. He remembered her. She just looked different.

"Mrs. Rider? You were in my computer science class down at Berkeley?"

She nodded. "Wrong title. I've never been married, though I came close once. I had a posselque in grad school, but it didn't work out. You were a damned good teacher, by the way."

"That was a long time ago. Did you ever get your doctorate?"

"Not in computer science, but yes. Technical anthropology. Penguins. It changed my life." She looked more serious. "I got older and eventually I grew up. So here I am."

"What's a posselque?"

There was a sense of unreality about the conversation. She seemed to be speaking a different language. Military squads in the night. Distant explosions and a serious looking woman with mysterious friends.

"Posselque." She chuckled. "It's a census bureau acronym. P-O-S-S-L-Q. Person, Opposite Sex, Same Living Quarters. I expect you called it shacking up."

"I'm not *that* old. Did you say 'penguins'?"

"I did my dissertation on Adelie penguins."

He shook his head.

"Penguins. Birds that don't fly. They swim like fish. They have scale-like feathers." She made flapping motions with her arms.

"Are you serious?"

"There are eighteen species and six genera of penguins. The Adelie are the most common; black and white, they look like tuxedos."

"How the hell do you get a doctorate in Penguins?"

"It wasn't easy. They live in Antarctica, mostly, so I did my fieldwork there. It's hostile. Very cold, very windy, very dark. Coldest place on earth: makes the Arctic look balmy. It hit minus 110° F once. That's not the record. The wind hit 180 MPH once. That wasn't a record either."

It sounded like a dreadful place. No wonder she was pale.

"Who was following me, Dr. Rider?"

Her smile faded. "My friends call me Becky. Who do you think? A Peace Enforcer squad. Goons. How much do you know about the PEs?"

"I know their reputation," Will said. "It scares me."

"It should. Despite the propaganda, their job is violence. They kill people, or worse."

"Why are they following me?"

"Your privacy technology upsets world harmony, Dr. Giles. They don't like that. Neither does your own government. You know that. You're not stupid."

"The Peace Enforcers break up demonstrations and riots. They don't pursue citizens and make arrests."

"You're a special case," she said.

"I may have upset a few bureaucrats, here and there, but I'm hardly worthy of PE attention. I'm a peaceful, law-abiding citizen. A businessman."

She gave him a "You-know-that's-bullshit" sort of smile.

He had to smile himself, grimly. She was right, of course. *Okay, the big question.* "Why are you helping me?"

She stopped smiling, serious again. "I need your help. Rather, my friends need your help. We need it badly."

Well, he didn't think she'd gone to all that trouble because of old college memories. "Did you cause the explosion last night?"

She shook her head. "We're nonviolent, except for self-defense. *My religion is truth. My practice is non-cooperation with evil.*" She said the last part as if she was quoting someone.

"What happened?"

"Good question," she said. "Let's go see. I think there was a crash, and I want to get some photos. Whatever happened, they'll probably blame you for it. We need to get going."

Blame him? She could be right. He was already in trouble. He hesitated. "If there are PEs following me, they'll probably be tracking us with satellites. We'll stand out. There can't be all that many people walking around out here in the forest."

"That's one thing you don't need to worry about. Their military satellites and drones are sometimes... ah ... unreliable."

How can she be sure? He didn't ask, and she continued after a moment.

"We're safe from the satellites, but we need to get going before anyone comes back. I don't think they will, but why take chances? Here, let me help." She started stuffing his personal items and new belongings into his pack, wrinkling her nose as she got a whiff of him.

"You smell like a dead moose."

"Sorry."

It was a great lesson in how to impress a woman. He was a fugitive, he'd let down the people who trusted him, and he smelled bad.

She smiled and gave him an encouraging look. "You're in luck. Our next stop has soap and warm water. I could use a bath too. Let's go."

"I'm ready to start being lucky."

"You already are."

"It doesn't feel that way."

"Trust me on this one. You're *very* lucky. Near the end, they were jogging to catch up with you."

"Shit."

"Deep," she agreed, as they started off down the trail together.

CHAPTER SIX

THE WHITE HOUSE

Paul Harney, 49th President of the United States, sipped his coffee slowly. He wasn't a morning person, and this part of the day was invariably the worst. His staff knew he wasn't to be bothered until he'd gotten through his morning briefing packages. They were always there on his desk waiting, and the news was seldom good.

The bright yellow folder was the most urgent. Yellow was for caution, generally reserved for political embarrassments. Without quick attention, scandals had a way of building and spinning out of control. Fortunately, the garish folder contained only one minor item, with press clippings and photos of a black woman from Oregon.

She was claiming government harassment of her employer and demanding an investigation. Harney scanned the executive summary. A surprising number of news channels and video feeds had covered the story.

Cybertech. Why is it all those companies have similar names?

He vaguely remembered the firm had a troublesome technology that needed to be suppressed. He couldn't recall the details. Letting the regulators deal with such matters was routine.

To hell with the woman. Let her complain. Best to just ignore it. She can claim anything she wants, but she can't prove anything. Conspiracy theories were boring unless they prompted a response. There had been so many in recent years that the public barely took notice.

If he did nothing, the media would soon lose interest and move on to something else. He jotted, "This is trivial. Stonewall it!" on the first page and shoved the folder into his outbox.

The red folder, always the thickest, was important but non-urgent. These days it usually contained news about job riots, food or energy shortages, and economic sanctions or fines being levied on the U.S. by its trading partners.

Before entering politics, Harney had been a school teacher. That was his platform: *save the children*. The U.S. spent more per student than any other nation, but its students became more ignorant and less educated every year. Test scores had been falling for decades, and his programs hadn't helped. His opponents claimed they made things worse. It was a tiresome, depressing discussion, and one that never went anywhere.

Well to hell with them. I didn't create these problems.

The populace was cynical, and only a third bothered to vote. Most of the working population was dumbed-down, especially in history, economics, and critical thinking. Drug lords and gangs ran the cities, and the government slid ever-deeper into insolvency.

It was the new normal.

Harney was out of ideas, at least any he could fund. The tax rate was deep into the backside of the Laffer Curve long before he took office. Raising taxes would decrease revenues, but dropping them would cost his party the unions and the public sector vote. Either way, he was screwed, so he chose to do nothing.

The red folder was depressing. He poked at it idly, and then pushed it away.

Even with a national police force and surveillance cameras everywhere, it was difficult to persuade the wealthy nations to build more assembly plants in the United States. "Too dangerous. Too much liability. Not profitable. You have too much crime. Your workers are cheap, but poorly educated and disloyal. You need to offer us something more," they said.

He'd done what he could. No matter how many prisons he built, they stayed full. The government had to keep releasing people due to lack of space. Prisoners and ex-cons were a significant voting bloc. They had rights and he had to tread carefully.

Harney made the theft or destruction of foreign-owned property a capital offense. When that didn't help, he declared a national emergency. It was crucial to protect foreign assets. If he didn't they'd pull out.

Last month he'd humbled himself by going to the Pacific Rim Nation's Council to request aid. He came back empty handed.

To be forced to beg for table scraps was damned embarrassing. *"Hai. It is sad what has happened to your country, Harney-san."* He'd played the game long enough to know *hai*, though it translated as yes, was a polite way of saying no.

Harney had a feeling of helplessness. The British dominated the 19th Century, due to Empire, while the 20th was called "The American Century," because of prosperity. He wondered if this one would be tallied to Asia, to anarchists and terrorists, or to World Government and the end of the sovereign nation-state. Right now, he'd bet on the last.

The Mid East had settled down to its customary state of internecine tribal conflicts. Muslims were still killing people and blowing things up, but mostly each other and those unfortunate enough to be in close proximity. China had its own problems, as did India. America was broke, and Europe was in even worse shape. Socialism had not been kind to the Western Democracies.

His intercom buzzed. Harney scowled, glanced at his watch, and punched the button. "Damn it, Marta. I told you no interruptions."

"I know, Sir, but it's Dr. Kobayashi. He says he must speak with you before your cabinet meeting."

"Oh." This was unusual. "Just a minute, Marta." Japan's deputy ambassador for trade had been attached to the President's staff as part of the world harmonization treaty.

Ito Kobayashi was a professional diplomat, always subtle, careful not to cause embarrassment, impeccably polite and rarely intrusive. Harney was grateful for his discretion and good manners.

The two men had surprisingly little personal contact. Usually Kobayashi sent a substitute to Harney's cabinet meetings from a cadre of identical looking young Asian men in dark suits. Harney could never keep their names straight.

Kobayashi's men rarely spoke in the meetings, but they took notes that resulted in guidance from their boss. His advice was generally sound.

Almost everything Kobayashi requested was in Harney's best interests, if not always in his nation's.

Harney sighed, got up, and strode into the adjacent bathroom. He looked at himself in the mirror, splashed water on his face, combed his hair and straightened his tie. *Need to look presentable and calm.* He took several deep breaths, then walked back to his desk and punched the intercom. "Send him in, Marta."

Ito Kobayashi had dual PhD's from Stanford and Cambridge. One of his doctorates was in engineering, the other in global economics. He'd come to power from the commercial side of government, not the military. He'd served Japan's trade ministry well and had run the World Trade Office for the UN.

He was short and wiry, only five foot eight, but a bundle of carefully controlled energy. He bounced into the oval office with a spring in his step. His black hair was cut close and turning to salt and pepper. His eyes were dark and intense, reflecting fierce intelligence.

Kobayashi was highly respected. He approached the President's desk formally and made a short bow. Not deep, just a touching of the hands together, a slight inclination of the body, and a nod of the head. Still, it was a signal of respect. *He wants something.*

"Please sit down, Kobayashi-san. Would you like some coffee?"

Kobayashi frowned and shook his head, but seated himself.

No coffee. Of course not. Harney knew better than that. *Tea. He should have said tea.* He buzzed Marta.

"Yes, Sir?"

"Some Japanese green tea for our guest. Very fresh. Very hot. Coffee for me."

"Yes, Sir."

Kobayashi smiled approvingly. They spent a few minutes exchanging formal pleasantries as the tea was brought in and served.

"We have important matters to discuss Mr. President. Decisions are needed and your country has asked for help." Kobayashi left the *again* unsaid.

Harney nodded, paying close attention. "It's the economy...."

"I know your cabinet meeting is scheduled to be starting, Mr. President."

Harney nodded again.

"Would you please delay it for ten minutes?"

Always polite and considerate. He'd phrased it as a request. Harney buzzed Marta and gave the necessary instructions.

"We're aware of your needs. It is sad when harmony is disrupted, Mr. President. I know your government has its problems and we like to help our friends."

The President nodded, carefully.

"Your credit has been stopped."

Tell me something I don't know.

"Soon you will be unable to pay your officials, guards, soldiers, and national police. That would be bad for trade."

"We have some problems. It's not as bad as you see reported in the media."

"You know better," Kobayashi said. "Your treasury's line of credit expires next month. When your social agencies, police, and guards are not paid, there will be riots. Again. We don't want that. At best, your party will lose face, and there will be more impeachment talk. You don't want that, do you?"

Harney shook his head, feeling real fear. *This wasn't in the yellow folder.* His analysts had given it three months, but this man worked for the people who held his country's credit chits. He didn't estimate, he *knew*.

Now that China has stumbled, Japan provides us with cheap products and lends us the money to buy them. That can't be so bad, can it? Everyone wins. It's worked for decades.

In a year, his term would be up and the country's problems would belong to someone else. If it all fell apart now, he'd be blamed. He could feel the blood draining from his face. He needed time, and it was running out.

Kobayashi's lips were smiling, but his eyes were cold and intense. "Fortunately, you have good friends, Harney-san."

No, "Mr. President." Me personally. He'd said "Harney-san." What's he saying? That he'll help me out of this mess?

"You don't want my government to fall." Harney's throat was dry, and he could hear the undertone of anxiety in his voice. The fear was like a knife twisting in his belly.

He took a cautious sip of coffee and forced himself not to say anything more. His hand was shaking slightly. Long moments passed before Kobayashi's reply, the silence interrupted only by the clink when Harney put his cup down.

Kobayashi shook his head. "Of course not, Mr. President. That would be sad. And so unnecessary. This is a small thing. I'm sure we can work it out together."

Harney took a deep breath. "What can I do for you?"

His guest smiled, and this time the smile was warm and friendly. "Do you know a Dr. William Giles? He runs a company called Cybertech in Oregon."

Cascade Wilderness Area

The glare of the sun was warm, and they'd stripped down to shorts and t-shirts. Becky scrambled up the slope like a gazelle with Will struggling along behind her.

God, that woman has legs. Small tits, but nice legs. A man could get lost in those deep blue eyes.

The legs and eyes were her best features. He'd remembered her as a chubby girl, smart, but not particularly attractive. Either she'd grown up and slimmed down, or he'd been in the mountains too long. Maybe both.

She stopped at the top and looked back. "Want to take a break?"

Will nodded, saving his breath. Glancing around, he chose a large tree, shrugged off his pack, and gratefully collapsed against it. He took deep breaths, letting them out slowly until he could feel his heart rate slowing.

He looked her over carefully. "You're in good shape."

"I've lived in some hostile places, Dr. Giles," she said. "So hostile they're uninhabited. When we'd get a break in the weather, we'd have to hustle to do our research. You had to move quickly and lug your own equipment. Wearing cold gear and toting fifty-pound packs gets you into condition. If you can't pull your own load, it gets dangerous."

"I thought we were on a first name basis. What happened to Will?"

She placed her pack on the ground and pulled out a canteen. "Maybe it was the way you looked at me. You didn't used to give me looks like that."

"Um," Will said. "I have a feeling no matter how I answered, I'd be in trouble."

She looked at him.

"Am I wrong?"

She looked somber for a moment. "No," she said with a shake of her head. "I'm sorry. I'm not being fair."

"No problem," he said. "It's not easy being a dirty old man."

She smiled and offered him the canteen.

"Thanks." He took a few swallows. "Will you share my tree if I promise to behave?"

She nodded, pulled a sweatshirt out of her pack, spread it on the ground, and sat next to him.

They were quiet for a few moments. Finally, he said, "What's wrong?"

"It's not your problem. It's me. Don't worry about it."

"You're an attractive woman." When she didn't reply, he asked specifically. "What's bothering you?"

"I don't want to talk about it." She glanced at him, then down, not meeting his eyes. "I have a job to do. It starts with getting you to safety."

Will thought back on the chubby, playful girl who'd taken his classes. She'd been smart, but not serious. This woman was a different person: earnest and focused. "Don't you get to be human?"

"Not now. You're in more trouble than you know."

"More trouble than I know?" He shook his head and laughed without humor. "That's not possible, Becky. The government has my company, Cybertech, squarely in their sights. They're going to destroy us if they can."

"You're right about that. They didn't expect you to close Cybertech. You wouldn't *believe* how many important people are upset because you screwed up their plans."

"Shit." He sighed deeply.

"Deep shit. Your problems go far beyond Washington. If it was just the US government, the Peace Enforcers wouldn't be after you."

"Why *are* they following me?"

"Because they can."

He frowned, not understanding what she meant.

"We gave up our national sovereignty when our government requested help from the UN back during the food riots." Becky fanned the air with her hands. "Japan volunteered, and the UN approved. They came at our request. Now they're here acting under their own local commanders.

There's no accountability to our government, and certainly not to our citizens."

"That's not what I mean. What are Japanese troops doing here, in the mountains, in Oregon?"

She gave him an odd look. "You don't watch the news much, do you?"

"I have a company to run." *Or I used to.*

"Japanese troops have been used for pacification in America for years. It started with riot control, but, over time, the mission has broadened. The precedent comes from the last Century." She shrugged. "We started it actually."

"How'd we do that?"

"Helping people."

He blinked and shook his head.

"We put troops in Korea, Vietnam, Kosovo, Somalia, Iraq, Tibet, and on and on. Plus we initiated huge social wars: drugs, poverty, climate, and so forth. These actions were intrusive, ineffective, and draining. Many people around the world are angry at us, and now it's payback time."

"Payback for problems we didn't create."

"Doesn't matter. There were too many unintended consequences, and too many blunders. We got bloated, corrupt, and inept. Our huge bureaucracies and budgets depend on those problems continuing."

"You tend to get more of what you invest in," Will said. "You're saying the problems self-perpetuate and get worse."

"Exactly," she said. "All bureaucracies maximize friction and minimize output. Throwing money at problems usually makes them worse."

"We're the good guys. Americans have compassion. We do try to help. Some are grateful."

"Very few," she said. "There's a fine line between altruistic and stupid. Much of our 'helping' has been done under the auspices of the UN or WTO. We fund and support them. Problem is both are corrupt, and neither is accountable. Global Governance is the new tyranny, and we are both a victim and a sponsor."

"What does this have to do with me and Cybertech?"

"There has to be a fall guy. We get blamed for the UN's faults, which are massive, on top of our own. Few Americans remember that Harry Truman started the UN, but it's true."

"I'm one of them. I don't spend much time thinking about politics I can't do a damned thing about. I want to know why Peace Enforcers are chasing *me*."

"You have something they want and Washington is going along with it."

"Something Japan wants?"

"Them and the UN. Why not? Would you prefer the Chinese or the Arabs?"

"I'd prefer to be left the hell alone."

"Not an option. President Harney *asked* for UN help. In effect, he was trading our sovereignty for public safety. We needed foreign troops to ensure internal security, just like Iraq did after Saddam."

"Japanese occupation troops," Will said.

"They don't call it that, but, yes, that's pretty much where we are. It used to be that Japan was weak and broke, while we were wealthy and strong. Things change. We became arrogant, clumsy, and depleted our wealth. Now it's their turn on top."

"And Japan has its own agenda."

"Of course. Everyone does."

How does she know so much? A list of questions flashed through his mind. He picked the simplest. "You're part of a group. Who's the 'we' that you speak of?"

"It's a long story. My friends are people who value freedom. We don't like what the world government is doing to prohibit your technology and want to help. The rest takes too long to explain. Can you trust me on faith for the time being?"

"I've agreed to do what you want." *I don't really have much choice.*

He studied her intently. She met his gaze squarely. "This trust thing has to go both ways, or it won't work," he said. "You know that."

She thought for a time and then nodded. "Fair enough."

"I've learned to be careful around men. I spent a lot of time in polar camps out in the middle of nowhere. For most of that time, there were two women and over fifty men. Under the circumstances, the nerdy Dr. Rider was vastly preferable to Boom Boom Becky, the horny but deprived sex machine."

He grinned. "Boom Boom sounds good to me."

"It's not."

"Depraved might be hopeful."

Her lips twitched. "I said, '*deprived*.' With an 'I.' " She said it like a pirate, loud, stretching the word out. *Aye!*

"Horny? You said horny." Will's grin broadened.

"Don't even think about it...."

"I'll have to refine my fantasies."

"Restrain. Work on 'restrain,' not refine." Her eyes sparkled, and she finally smiled.

"I'll try to behave." He offered his hand. "Truce?"

That brought a smile. She held out her hand and he took it.

Somewhat to his surprise, she didn't pull away. She put her other hand on his. Her fingers were soft, as was her voice. "Truce. It's good to see you again."

He kissed her on the forehead, gently. "You saved me. I know what the Peace Enforcers do to people. Thank you."

"I was worried for you." She touched him gently on the cheek, then pushed him away, frowned, and looked at her watch. "We need to keep moving. I want to examine the site of the explosion we saw last night. Do you have any idea how far it is?"

"It was a couple of miles from my camp, I think."

"Did you count the time between the flash and the sound?"

"Nine seconds." He grinned, sheepishly. "I tried to recall the conversion factor to calculate distance, but couldn't remember. I'd guess about two miles?"

"Close. Multiply by zero point two. That's one point eight miles. It should be just over the next ridge."

The crash site was a two-hour hike. They were coming down in altitude, and the forest was thicker. The path turned into an overgrown deer trail, and they had to keep ducking under branches.

Suddenly she stopped, giving him a hand signal, one as old as the army of ancient Rome. *Down!* She turned and put a finger to her lips.

He crouched and nodded understanding, not moving until she gestured him to approach.

"This is it," she whispered. "Be very quiet and follow me closely while I check it out. Don't break any branches. Follow my footsteps exactly."

They silently moved to the edge of the forest, keeping to cover and listening intently. Ahead he could see bright sunlight, a clearing. There were no sounds, except for birds.

The warm breeze brought a pungent smell, unpleasant, like a mixture of burned rubber and something else, sickly sweet. Becky pulled out an odd looking pair of binoculars and scanned the clearing. Several minutes passed.

She pushed a button on the side of the unit and noted that a small green light came on. She scanned again, this time in a full circle, slowly, and then again. More time passed, and then the green light started blinking.

"Do you recognize the smell?"

He shook his head.

"It's kerosene, jet fuel, mixed with burnt flesh. You never forget it. In the Antarctic our greatest fear was fire."

He was horrified. "Human flesh?"

"That's the smell," she said. "It should be safe. Except for a few deer, there are no large animals or other humans within several miles. I need to look this over. Follow me if you wish, or wait here. It'll only take a few minutes."

"I'll come."

The first thing he noticed was a ball of crumbled, partially melted, fire-blackened metal in the center of the clearing next to a large boulder. Except for the tail rotor and engine, it was unrecognizable. That seemed to be where the smell was coming from.

On the far side of the clearing was another smashed helicopter. It hadn't burned, but it looked like a broken child's toy, strangely crumpled and out of proportion. It was flat black and the front was pushed back. It lay upside-down on the ground, its windows cracked, some completely broken out.

There was wreckage strewn all over the clearing. A third machine seemed intact until he noticed that the main rotor was missing. No, not missing, he corrected himself. He could see broken blades, tangled in the trees.

"What happened?" he asked.

She was preoccupied, snapping pictures carefully with a small camera. "I think it started with an accident. Some of their weapons went off."

"Weapons?"

"See the pods and chain guns on the farthest two copters?" She focused on them, taking more pictures.

He looked. "Yes." There wasn't enough left of the burned helicopter to tell if it was armed.

"The pods are rockets. Modern Japanese weapons are beyond smart, they're brilliant. They pick the biggest targets around. A man, a truck, a helicopter." She grimaced. "The guns can be slaved to an AI system as well. I think they were in combat mode, hot, with their safeties off."

"How do you know so much?"

"I was briefed," she said absently. "It was windy last night. Maybe a tree moved or a pilot accidently bumped his trigger."

Will looked around at the carnage and shook his head. "Artificial intelligence is no match for natural stupidity."

She didn't respond to his black humor.

They approached the upside-down copter. Something had shredded its armor. There were no markings. "The ubiquitous black UN helicopters," she murmured to herself. There were bodies inside, in Peace Enforcer uniforms.

Will counted four bodies, maybe five. It was hard to tell without sticking his head inside, and he wasn't about to do that.

She took more photos, then looked up at the sky. The wind was picking up again, and dark clouds were forming in the West.

The third machine was sitting forlorn with its doors and hatches standing open. There was dried blood all over the seats and instrument panel. It looked dark, not red. They swatted at a cloud of small insects and peered into the cabin.

"These models normally carry ten, plus a crew of two." She took more photos, frowning. "I count five bodies, all in uniform, and two of them are Japanese.

"I made a mistake. Peace Enforcers don't leave their dead or wounded. They'll be coming back for the bodies. A big storm is coming in tonight, and we need to get out of here. Are you up to three or four hours of hiking?"

Dumb question, he thought. *The alternative is being arrested and blamed for this.*

"Sure," he said.

She was already moving. Her swaying hips filled his view as she led off. Will smiled. *Nice ass.* It broke his tension a little.

Peace Enforcer Barracks, Portland, Oregon

Captain Tanaka's face was bruised, and one eye was blackened. His close-cropped black hair had been shaved on one side, revealing a gash with stitches that extended down his forehead. His left arm was wrapped to the elbow in an elastic bandage.

His head hurt, but he was used to pain. Pain, controlled violence, was his art, one he'd practiced since he was a child. The problem was that there was no enemy on which to focus his pain, no one to strike, no one to hurt. He struggled to think clearly and looked at his senior officer, seeking the proper response. *"Wakaremasan?"*

"Speak English, Captain. It's good practice, and it makes our hosts more comfortable."

"Hai." Tanaka stood at rigid attention, his eyes fixed straight ahead. Before his chief could correct him, he said, "Yes, Sir. I serve your orders."

Kobayashi was new to his added duties as Chief of Special Operations for the United States. He'd only been in charge for a month, and Tanaka wasn't used to serving a civilian commander.

Tanaka kept his face stoic. He'd failed in his mission. *A warrior who fails must offer atonement.* That was the way, centuries old. He didn't mind the loss of a few *gaijin,* but his own men, his *samurai,* had died, including the promising young Lieutenant Sasaki. As their leader, he was responsible.

"It was an unfortunate training accident, Captain. Dr. Giles can't escape. We have tracers on him and his vehicle."

"Yes, Sir!"

"You've earned no dishonor. We knew the risk when we decided to enhance our forces with native police. They're clumsy and ill trained. Mistakes are to be expected."

A long moment passed, with no response. "Answer me, Captain!" This time Kobayashi put a snap in his voice.

"Sir! Yes, Sir."

"What are you planning?"

Captain Tanaka had lost an officer and most of three squads. He was ashamed.

"Sir! I have my duty, and my honor."

"I will decide your duty," Kobayashi said.

"Sir."

"America is a large country and we are few. You do not serve us by atonement. You serve by loyalty and obedience, and I say you have served with honor. Your skills are needed."

"Sir! I must atone." Tanaka would go back, retrieve the bodies, and have the ritual ceremony. A small atonement, perhaps a finger, would satisfy honor. Then he could continue.

"It was not your error, Captain. You were ordered to use native police."

Tanaka nodded. That was true, and he'd questioned the directive at the time.

"I give you a direct order: *You will not atone.* If you disobey, you bring dishonor to yourself, to your family, and me. Acknowledge my order, Captain."

Tanaka bowed respectfully. "Thank you, master."

Master was a term of highest respect. *Samurai* owed loyalty to their master. Without a master, they were *ronin*, lost warriors, men without purpose.

"Thank you, Captain. You must be deadly serious in training. You had a training accident and will now be better prepared for battle. There is no dishonor."

"I understand, Sir." *Such is the warrior way.*

"Are you fit for duty, Captain Tanaka?"

"Yes, Sir. The medics have released me."

"Then I suggest that you get a good night's sleep. Certain things are happening and I will have need of your skills. You can recover the bodies after replacements arrive. There's a major storm coming, and I do not choose to risk more men in the mountains at this time. You are dismissed, Captain."

Tanaka saluted crisply, wheeled, and departed.

CHAPTER SEVEN

MOUNTAIN CABIN, CASCADE WILDERNESS AREA, THE NEXT MORNING....

The snow was still falling when Will woke up. His left leg was cramping painfully. "Son of a bitch," he muttered.

He groaned, extended the leg out straight and curled his foot back. At first, that made it hurt more, but finally the spasms passed.

There was total stillness. The wind had died down. There was that eerie half-light just before dawn. He poked his head up out of the sleeping bag and looked around, peering through the gloom. Through the small window, he could see heavy snow on the big firs outside, their boughs bending under the weight. The heavy blanket of white absorbed all sound.

He was cold, very cold, much colder than his night on the ground. He could see his breath even in the dim twilight. *A blizzard in March. This weather is crazy.*

He didn't want to get up, but nature was calling. Hell, it was screaming at him. His bladder was full, but it was much too cold to get out of the sleeping bag. *Life's little choices.*

"Are you okay?" Becky's voice was crisp. She must have been lying there awake.

"Just a muscle spasm in my leg. I haven't hiked so hard in a long time. I'm sore all over." *Running for your life is a great motivator.*

"Stretch carefully," she said.

"Huh?"

"You got a good work out yesterday. Before you get up, take each major muscle and extend it as far as you can for a count of ten. Do it several times and stretch your back by pulling your knees up. Take your time and do that. It'll help. For breakfast, I'll get you a banana. The potassium will help with cramps."

If you say so. Will wasn't overly fond of bananas, but he wasn't going to argue with her about it. "Thanks."

He loosened the zipper on the side and thrashed around in the sleeping bag, stretching, testing each muscle, and feeling like a beached whale. It seemed to help.

"Better?"

"Some," he said. "I'm on to the next problem. I need to piss like a racehorse, and it's freezing in here."

That got a chuckle. "It does sound like a problem."

"Where's the bathroom?"

She laughed. "It's conveniently located. Right outside."

"Outside? You expect me to use a snowdrift…?"

"Heavens, no," she said innocently. "We have all the comforts of home. There's a modern outhouse just behind the two big trees to the left when you go out the door. About fifty feet. Just stay under the trees so you'll be out of sight."

"Um." He wondered what a modern outhouse was. It sounded like an oxymoron.

Will fumbled the bag's zipper open and grabbed his jacket. *Think warmth, think warmth.* He slipped it on and struggled to his feet, looking for his boots. There they were, by the wood stove they'd never lit.

"I can't believe this. The water on the stove is frozen solid."

"You don't get out much, do you?" She giggled, obviously enjoying herself. "It's balmy, maybe ten degrees. In Antarctica, we'd wear bathing suits. It's a great day for a tan."

"Yeah, right." He laced his boots, zipped his jacket, and stumbled toward the door. He hurt all over. He'd wanted to stop and rest yesterday, but she wouldn't let him. "In case you haven't noticed, there isn't any sun...."

"Wrong." He could see the flash of her smile in the dim light. "The clouds outside are a lighter color. 'Isn't any sun' is when it's pitch dark for six months. This is morning and we call what you see outside 'daylight.' There's a sun up there somewhere."

"If you say so. If I'm not back in a few hours, send help." He eased himself outside and closed the door carefully behind him.

The snow had been coming down hard when they reached the cabin, and there was now a good two feet on the ground with a thin crust of ice on top. It crunched as he slogged through the snow to the outhouse, only to discover he couldn't open the door. He stomped the snow down, banged the door several times, and pulled hard, repeating the process until it finally opened.

Inside seemed warmer than the cabin, if only slightly, probably because he worked up a sweat getting the damned door open. There was a Maglite flashlight in a clip by the door. It worked. When he shut the door, he discovered quantities of toilet paper and noticed panels of translucent plastic that let in the light.

Someone had taped a note under the panels, printed with a computer using a large block font. "Check for spiders and snakes."

"Yeah, right," he muttered to himself. "It's frigging freezing. They have better sense. You don't find them this high in the Cascades anyway."

What's all this doing out in the middle of nowhere? he wondered idly as he followed the instructions. There was a broom by the door. He used it to brush cobwebs aside and poke into the dark corners, just in case, before he attended to his business.

On the way back to the shack, he picked up some of the split wood stacked by the door. Becky was up and dressed. She'd found a small propane cook stove somewhere and a lantern.

"I feel much better. Do you want me to build a fire?"

She looked up and frowned. "Not unless you want some of the goons who were following you to drop in for breakfast. You can smell wood smoke for miles, and the satellites are back online now. If the clouds break, a plume from a wood stove would show up like a flare. There may be drones up too."

Will could still see his breath. "Is there any way to get warm?"

She glanced out at the deep snow. "I'll take pity on you, since we're not going anywhere for awhile. There's a stealth heating system."

She took out a small screwdriver, removed a panel from the wood stove, threw a hidden switch, and replaced the panel. "Just forget you saw this."

He looked at her questioningly.

"Technology to the rescue. There are heating coils under the floor. We'll have to reset the system every day or it shuts down."

Whoever she was working with, they were well organized. A lot of thought had gone into preparing this cabin. As an engineer, he wondered how the system worked and how she could be sure it wasn't detectable, but he took her cue and didn't inquire. The main thing was they had heat.

"Don't you ever get cold?"

"Sure," she said. "There have been times when I thought I'd never be warm again. You'll feel better when you get some hot coffee. I'll brew some fresh."

He nodded.

"It'll be ready soon. The water will be boiling in a few minutes. They left us a stash of food. We have eggs, orange juice, and bacon. It's just like the Hilton."

The heating system was starting to work and soon he even had warm water for bathing. He shaved and washed up while she prepared the breakfast. By the time he finished, the cabin was warm, and the coffee smelled wonderful.

She handed him a mug, and he sipped it gratefully. "What is this place?"

"It was a Forest Service shack, years ago. It was purchased by friends, insulated, and modernized. They moved it to a good location, under the trees where it's out of sight. We helped them with improvements, and they let us use it. How do you like your eggs?"

"Over easy. Can I help?"

"There's only one skillet, but I could use some juice. It's in the cooler."

I hope it's not frozen solid.

It wasn't. He poured her a glass, and one for himself. The breakfast was delicious, and they chatted quietly while they ate. Afterwards, he helped her clean up.

"Excuse me," she said. "I need to check in."

She pulled a hard-wired telephone from under a loose floorboard and dialed a number. There was a box attached to the phone that he recognized, one of Cybertech's privacy units.

Becky spoke what was obviously a code phrase, then some words and a sequence of numbers. Then she listened for a few minutes, replying with another sequence.

"Okay, that should work. Four PM, code blue. You be careful too. Talk to you then." She put the phone back and glanced up at him. "So far, so good...."

He was watching her intently. "We have food, heat, and scrambled telephones. Somehow your friends can control the government's satellites. You didn't set this up just to rescue me."

"No, of course not. I'm with a private group that wants to move our civilization to a higher level before we use up this planet or have a major war."

"Greenies?"

She shook her head.

"Not a government?"

"Governments usually support vested interests and the status quo, not progress. I'm part of a private group of independent scientists who'd like to improve things."

"And they sent you to get me. Why?"

"My primary mission is to get you out of the country."

"Why?"

She rolled her eyes in exasperation. "Dear God, Will. I know you have a brain. Start using it. Think about the mess you're in. How many government agencies are targeting you or your company?"

"Several, but...."

"Let's pick just one. The State Department is investigating the illegal export of weapons to a hostile nation, right? At best, they can tie you up in litigation for years. Or they can have you tried offshore, in secret, perhaps by a UN court."

"I haven't done anything wrong," he said. "The *alleged* weapons were just computer disks, chips, and hardware. That scrambler unit on your phone is typical. The *allegedly* hostile nations are some of America's best trading partners. Some people prefer my company's crypto products to those of my Japanese, Russian, or Israeli competitors."

"They should. Your products are revolutionary. Everyone tells me that. How *do* you do it, by the way?"

"I get asked often." He shook his head and laughed. "That's what the National Security Agency and patent office people wanted to know. It's none of their damned business."

She wasn't smiling. "Export law violations are serious, and they consider encryption to be in the same category as nuclear weapons. The 'keeping little secrets' part is called treason. It carries the same sentence. Death. They may hang you twice."

"I'm innocent. A trial will prove it."

"If you even get a trial, it won't be fair. The government is in the process of closing your company and seizing your assets. After they do that, you won't be able to afford to defend yourself. They can drop you into a prison and no one will even notice."

He shook his head, not meeting her eyes.

"We have some horrific laws and executive orders on the books. What is supposed to save people is the Constitution. In your case, I wouldn't count on it. Hasn't anyone warned you?"

"Yes," he said. "Our Washington attorneys quit because they were afraid."

"You should heed their warning. Do you think those Peace Enforcers were hiking around in the mountains for their health? Do you think it was a coincidence?"

She stopped talking, and their eyes met. There was a long silence. She got up, walked over slowly, bent down and hugged him. He took a deep breath, put his arms around her, and a long moment passed.

"Let me help. Let us help you. You're in great danger. We can get you out of the country. There's a place where you'll be safe. Let me take you there."

"What do you want, Becky?"

"What do I want?" She smiled a sad smile. "I want you to live. I want you to be free. I want you to help me save the world. Right now, I mostly want you to get away before they kill you or throw you into a cell until you give them your secrets."

"What do you want me to do?"

"Come with me."

He hesitated. "I'm not sure I can do that."

"We want to use your technology, but it's your choice. We won't steal it. The people that I work with are principled. You can decide later if you want to help us. But I do need to know something now. Is there anything you need to duplicate your products?"

"I have the disks I need in my backpack. My engineers are in hiding. We plan to go dormant and scatter before the court orders hit. We're hoping allies will come out of the woodwork when our products are no longer available."

"I know." She smiled. "That was a clever strategy."

He blinked, and then stared at her. *How could she know? The meeting where we discussed it was totally secure.*

She met his eyes. "I need to go back and make sure the records at your company are destroyed. We don't want them to fall into the wrong hands. That's my second objective, keeping your technology out of the wrong hands. If I send people to the plant, do you have any way to let us tell your guards we're the good guys?"

"Yes," he said slowly. "But sending someone to the plant shouldn't be necessary. My staff knows what to do. They'll have already destroyed the records."

"Are you sure?"

She's got a point. Why didn't I stick around and check that myself? I should have.

He took a deep breath. "We're careful about such things. My people are *not* likely to make a blunder like that. Even if they missed some things, our technology is intrinsically secure. Our records are encrypted on locked, coded, memory chips. Our products are tamper proof. Any attempt to break them destroys the unit."

"It's important we get this right," she said. "We need to be absolutely certain your technology is safe. 'Trust, but verify,' like Kennedy said."

"I think Reagan said that." *Whoever said it, they were right. I may have screwed up.*

"Whatever." She seemed to sense his indecision. "I need to check this myself."

"Absolutely not. It's not safe, and it's not your problem. I don't want you or your friends put at risk. You don't owe me that."

"You underestimate how important this is. I'm not doing this for you. It's not about you or me, and it's not about business or money, it's about whether civilization is free to evolve or be controlled by elites."

"My dad used to say things like that."

"You're a nexus. You're good with computers, and your crypto work moved you all the way up to genius. I'm proud of you, Will. I was in Antarctica when you won the science prize, or I'd have called. I would have kissed you if you were available."

He grinned. "Boom Boom Becky emerges?"

She blushed.

"I like that idea, Dr. Rider."

"Not now."

"No. Bad timing."

"We need you safe, and we need your technology to be safe."

"That's why I came up to the mountains to think." He paused and looked at her. "You knew *exactly* where to find me and where the Peace Enforcers were, didn't you?"

She nodded. "Yeah."

"How do you know so much? It's as if you can see things without being there, and without remote equipment."

"Sometimes."

"That's not possible."

"Any sufficiently advanced technology is indistinguishable from magic...."

"I think it's time we trusted each other," he said. "I'll go with you. You don't need to tell me how you do it, but I want to know what capabilities you have. Maybe we can work out a plan for a safe return to Cybertech."

She shook her head. "Don't even think about going back yourself. I'm getting you to safety. You're not expendable."

"We can discuss that later. Just tell me what your friends can see."

Becky gave him a smug look. "It's all done with mirrors."

She started talking.

Peace Enforcer Barracks, Portland, Oregon

Captain Tanaka rifled carefully through the pack of papers. There were six sets.

The top paper of each set bore the seal of the office of the President of the United States and the President's signature. Chief Kobayashi had signed the next sheet. Tanaka skimmed the cover pages, and spent time studying the building plans and security system diagrams.

When he'd finished, he looked up at his chief seated across the desk and nodded. "The signed authorizations are only to be used if the local police attempt to interfere?"

"Correct," Kobayashi said. "We don't want to attract attention needlessly."

"I understand. How large a force do you suggest, Sir?"

"It's up to you. This is a simple mission. The plant is closed. There is only one guard on duty, an old man. You should be able to handle him easily. It will be like swatting flies."

"*Hai.* How much force is authorized for this fly?"

"You are to get the computer files and paper records and destroy the building. It would be convenient if it looked like an accident. We'd prefer not to have witnesses."

"I understand, Sir." *I'll make the death look natural.*

Tanaka imagined the killing chop to the neck. He spent two hours each day practicing on the dojo mat, but actual combat was so much better.

"Do you have any questions?" Kobayashi said.

"No, Sir. For a small task, I think a small force is best." His head hurt, and he still had bad dreams about the disaster in the mountains. "I'll take Sergeant Kami, Sergeant Kumakura, Corporal Sato and two men."

Kobayashi nodded. All he named were martial arts instructors with high degree black belts, and expert with small arms. They'd have no trouble with an old watchman.

"That's approved, Captain. If there are no further questions, you are dismissed."

Captain Tanaka stood, saluted crisply, about faced, and marched out of the room. He was smiling faintly.

Mountain Cabin, Cascade Wilderness Area

Will was concentrating, fascinated by Becky's strange story. "That's incredible. You can see clear images over any distance. It's better than television, and you do it without a local camera or equipment."

"There's nothing incredible about it," she said. "Think how a scientist from the 1950s would react to a nanocomputer, a flat screen, or even a sonic toothbrush."

"They'd lack context. Nothing in their experience or training would relate."

"Exactly. Our devices are based on a different view of science. The ancients knew more about such things than we do today.

"The Toltec believed everything is made of light, and the space in-between isn't empty. That matter is only a mirror that reflects light. That our senses perceive reality poorly, like seeing through smoke. Today's quantum physicists say pretty much the same things."

"Photon tunneling," he said. "Your devices spatially transfer photons."

"Clumsy words. Our science prefers to discuss photons and particles and wave packets, but my friends say it's better to think about high-dimensional quantum vibrations. Einstein said that communicating electronically was like wiggling the tail of a very long cat. You pull its tail in California, and it yowls in New York."

"He said that about the telephone." Will grinned. "He also said, 'Radio is just like that, but without the cat.' I've always liked the second version better."

She grinned and nodded. "Vibrations. Our devices lack both the cat and the radio."

"You said 'Toltec.' Isn't that an ancient Mexican civilization?"

"It's a common point of confusion, but no. Anthropologists refer to the Toltec as a nation or race, but they were actually scientists and artists who formed a society to preserve the knowledge and practices of what they called the 'ancient ones.' Much of that science was lost, but some *naguels* – it translates best as 'skilled ones' – tried to secretly preserve the ancestral knowledge about the nature of the universe. They argue that what we can sense is only illusion."

Will nodded slowly. "Modern quantum physicists are starting to come to similar conclusions. Some say matter is only vibrating energy in a ten-dimensional hyperspace. They call it 'superstring theory.' Unfortunately,

Congress shut down the supercollider back in the 90s and we lack the experimental tools to verify those theories...."

"Forget the theories. Our devices work reliably."

Will stopped, blinked, and looked at her sharply. "If you can see across distance, then you can find out who in the government is behind the attacks on Cybertech...."

"I don't need to find out. I already know. President Harney."

Will felt his jaw sag. "Personally?"

"Yes."

"Are you certain?"

She nodded. "Absolutely. It's part of a political accommodation he's made."

"No wonder you're fearful. Is that why they sent you to get me?"

"I volunteered. I wanted to see you. But, yes, we would have sent someone."

"Can you use your viewing devices to discover some private Internet addresses and passwords? Can you send the digital photos you took yesterday of those burned copters to someone I trust? Can your friends look in on Cybertech and tell us if the plant is closed down and empty?" Will fired the questions at her.

"It can be done. When we have secure communications, I can call them and get started. What are you thinking?"

"I have a portable security unit in my backpack. We can have secure communications from anywhere we can get to a phone on a hard-line. Here's what I want you to do..."

TV Studio, New York City

Samuel Goldstein turned his gaze from Sonny Boxer, the celebrity talk show host, and frowned into the cameras. "Yes, that's *exactly* what I'm telling you. Cybertech is shut down as a business. We've stopped shipping product. We regret it, but we had no choice."

Sonny flashed his famous smile. "It's causing quite a bit of turmoil on Wall Street, and my viewers are interested. Can you explain what's going on?"

"How can anyone explain Wall Street?" Sam said. "If I could do that, I'd be wealthy, retired, and you'd be interviewing me on my yacht...."

That drew laughter and applause from the live studio audience. Sonny paused until it had died down. "Your firm's HR manager, Sarah King, has been giving interviews saying that Cybertech is being harassed by the government."

"Sarah's quite knowledgeable about the regulatory aspects. You should interview her."

"I plan to," Sonny said, "but I'd like you to comment."

Sam shrugged. "We've been advised that several agencies have an interest in scrutinizing us. It does get one's attention…."

"So you gave up?"

"We chose to prioritize defending our legal rights over trying to do business."

"Ms. King said there are seven government agencies going after Cybertech. She says your right to produce and export products is being attacked."

"That's basically correct," Sam said. "They've served notice that they may wish to challenge our right to sell privacy products, so we stopped shipping until we can sort this out. As you know, the issue has come up in our industry before. There's been tension for years between citizens' rights to privacy and the government's export laws and national security issues."

"You sued the government a few years ago."

"We did. The case was settled amicably."

"And now the same issues are back?"

"They never went away. Dr. Giles and his father founded Cybertech to allow people and businesses to buy products to protect their privacy. I was one of the first employees. We wanted to help preserve people's privacy. That's our purpose."

"And to make money?"

"Yes, of course. It's a business, not a hobby. Dr. Giles wanted the technology developed. His father and I wanted to have some fun and make money. Our corporate culture reflects all three desires. But it's not been fun recently, and if we become enmeshed in extensive bureaucratic entanglements and litigation, it won't be profitable."

"Do the government's charges have any merit?"

"You'll have to ask them. I'm skeptical, but I really can't say and it doesn't matter. We've shut Cybertech down. They wanted us to stop shipping product, so we did."

"Mr. Goldstein, you're an attorney. How can you not have a legal opinion about the charges that have been filed against Cybertech?"

"It's important to understand that *no* charges have been filed against Cybertech. We were served with some 30-day letters that said various agencies **might** intend to investigate us in certain areas. There are rumors of more such letters. It's quite troubling."

"No charges have been filed?" Sonny said.

"None whatsoever. And if they were, the legal aspects would be outside my expertise."

Sonny raised his eyebrows. "You're Cybertech's top lawyer."

"Chief legal counsel," Sam corrected. "I have people on my staff who are experts in litigation. I'm a patent attorney. I was fortunate to have done the work on Cybertech's original patents, but I'm not a litigator. Also, government law is very specialized."

"If you're innocent, why don't you defend yourselves?"

"We are defending, but it's too costly to continue doing business and risk penalties. If we're charged with even half the stuff they're talking about, defending would be extremely expensive. A protracted legal action would consume the company. Dr. Giles decided to shut Cybertech down instead. That's his right."

Sonny's co-host broke in at that. She was blond, gorgeous, and not to be trifled with. Where Sonny played the genial host, Ashley enforced political correctness.

"Wasn't Dr. Giles charged with illegal exports two years ago? That's a felony, isn't it? Didn't Boggs and Harper, the big Washington law firm, defend him from those charges?"

Sam studied her politely. *She's as pretty as a coral snake and just as deadly.*

He smiled, nodded and spread his hands open, palms up. This was the moment he'd been waiting for. He looked directly at the cameras and spoke in his most reasonable voice. "As I said, there has been tension for many years over the privacy issue, Ashley."

"What about those charges against Giles?"

"All the charges against Dr. Giles were dropped. Such incidents are not unusual in our industry. Back when Cybertech was founded to sell privacy products, there were threats of similar charges being brought, but nothing ever came of it."

"You seem to have recurring legal problems."

"Not really," Sam replied. "The right-to-privacy issue does persist, though. The core grievance in the instances you mention was, in essence, that Cybertech is selling excellent security products. And, yes, Boggs and Harper has served as our outside counsel."

"Those were very serious charges," Ashley persisted. "Don't you agree?"

"That's not clear. The government sometimes considers privacy products to be regulated under munitions export laws, so, yes, the penalties are quite severe, if that law indeed applies. Those are the same laws that apply to the export of nuclear weapons materials like plutonium."

"What do you mean, 'that's not clear'? Doesn't Cybertech sell products that prevent our police and law enforcement agencies from doing their jobs?"

Ashley paused, but not long enough to give him a chance to reply. "You should be ashamed of yourselves," she added, raising her voice.

"I don't see why. Don't you value your right to have a private conversation with your doctor without the government listening in? Having Big Brother privy to and in control of all medical decisions was a huge issue for ObamaCare, to where all but the radical left eventually rejected it. Medical privacy is now one of our largest markets."

"That's not the same thing." Her eyes flashed. "You know that."

"I disagree. Some people think it is."

"You're encouraging terrorists, perverts, and criminals, Mr. Goldstein. Isn't that so?"

"I don't see how. Our products allow law-abiding people to protect their privacy."

"But aren't you empowering people to break the law?"

"I don't see how." Sam kept his smile friendly, his tone mild.

Ashley was losing her patience. She pointed an accusing finger.

"Why don't you admit it?" Her voice was becoming shrill. "You sell people the equipment to defy the government. You provide people with the equipment to become terrorists and criminals. Providing that equipment makes you criminals yourselves. Isn't that so?"

"I don't see how, Ashley." Sam repeated, keeping his tone reasonable, looking into the camera, and speaking distinctly. "You have all the equipment to be a prostitute, but you're not, are you?"

"You're an asshole!" Ashley totally lost it. Her face was red and she was screaming obscenities when her mike went dead.

Ashley stormed off the set, leaving the two men sitting there looking at each other. The look on Sonny's face was priceless.

Sam spread his hands helplessly, in a "What do I do now?" gesture. He kept his gaze focused on Sonny. Time passed.

Sonny looked stunned. He didn't say a word.

After a strangled silence, the cameras cut to a commercial. The interview was over, but it would be replayed for weeks on talk shows and over the Internet.

CHAPTER EIGHT

THE WHITE HOUSE

President Harney's demeanor was subdued. "I called this press conference to discuss the reports you've seen in the media and financial press. Some say our nation has credit problems and our dollar will be devalued."

Harney's presence wasn't imposing, with owlish brown eyes, stooped shoulders, a receding hairline, and a slight paunch. But he was skilled at politics, good at oratory, and knew how to play an audience. He paused and sighed deeply, covertly glancing down at the monitor in his podium as the cameras cut away, watching concern ripple through the audience, gauging the moment.

Not enough fear yet, he decided. Timing was everything. *Let them fret a tiny bit more. Just to set the hook. Never waste a crisis.*

The President shook his head sadly, running a hand through his thinning hair, his face a mirror of concern. "You know the talk here inside the beltway. My opponents say the government is insolvent, that a few more shocks will drive our economy into a deep depression."

He didn't have to look at the monitor – he could feel the emotion and hear the muttering. He had their full attention. *Good. Now I'll give them hope.*

"Don't listen to my critics," He squared his shoulders and smiled confidently into the cameras. "They're lying to you. They're trying to scare you."

The last was delivered in his loudest and most resonant voice. He held the smile and continued more softly. "Pay no attention to this fear mongering and partisan politics. Our economy has a firm fiscal foundation and is poised for a strong recovery."

Harney watched as relief spread through the audience. He'd packed the room with people from groups that supported him. His plants and supporters stood up, cheering and clapping loudly. This was what Harney did best. His speechwriters were excellent, and many voters lacked the intellectual equipment to detect propaganda.

Most had been indoctrinated to accept the government world view. Some were as fearful about Global Warming as an earlier generation had been about Global Cooling. Many were dependent on government handouts and not inclined to question policy so long as their checks and services kept coming. Crony capitalists went along, provided they made money.

You give 'em a crisis and then show them you can save them. First the stick, then the carrot. "Firm fiscal foundation." What a terrific sound bite. In his mind he could see tomorrow's headlines: "Harney Handles Financial Crisis."

The President paused, looking with compassion and sincerity into the cameras, waiting for the applause to subside. At just the right moment, he raised his voice and spoke in his most presidential tone. "My fellow Americans, there is no financial crisis. You've been misled. Our currency is secure, our dollar is sound, and your future is safe."

There was another round of applause from the audience, tentative at first, then gaining strength. He scanned the room casually, then glanced down at the small monitor, noting that the leaders of the opposition party, seated behind him, looked skeptical and weren't applauding.

Poor manners. Well, good, it'll cost them. Now we show the voters proof.

Harney held up a document carefully, steadying his arms on the podium and giving the cameras time to zoom in on it. "This letter of understanding is signed by me, Japanese Ambassador Kumakura, and Director General Mozard of the United Nations. It guarantees us an interest-free trillion-dollar revolving line of credit from the Bank of Japan and the International Monetary Fund.

There was a hush as that sunk in. He'd found other people's money to spend.

"Free is a very good price." The President smiled into the cameras. "This free money will finance our trade imbalance for some time. And our friends are offering more than money: they've agreed to help with our domestic problems.

"As you know, crime control and public safety consumes much of our budget. Japan, our valued friend and trading partner, will help us. They'll provide personnel for Peace Enforcer duty and for guarding our plants at no cost to the American taxpayer. The United Nations will supply up to one quarter of our national police force on the same basis. The signatories will also help us with our overcrowded prisons and court dockets. We're optimistic China will participate too.

"This agreement secures our nation's credit, and I urge Congress to quickly pass the legislation needed to move this forward. Just as we helped our friends rebuild after the wars of the last century, they'll now help us in return. Thank you, and goodnight."

The secret service agents swarmed around the President and escorted him out of the room. There was a strange silence as the cameras panned the room. The members started to leave, only to discover the hall was jammed with reporters seeking interviews.

The Senate Majority leader, an outspoken opponent of the President, paused for a moment and was instantly surrounded by a phalanx of reporters waving microphones. "I have no comment at this time. The Speaker of the House and I have agreed there will be no comment until we have time to review the documents the President referred to. Thank you."

Japanese Embassy, Washington DC

Ito Kobayashi clicked off the video and looked at the Ambassador. "Kumakura-san, why are you troubled? This is a historic moment. President Harney kept his part of the bargain."

Ambassador Teruyuki Kumakura was respected for wisdom and considering all sides of an issue. He took a sip of *sake* before replying. "Ito, my friend, you've done well. I just wonder if perhaps we move too fast. Our progress has been good. In a few years, America's market and technologies will be unimportant. The giant is weak, and the world is passing them by."

Kobayashi frowned. "Political resistance is mounting in America. Over thirty percent of their population uses equipment to block police monitoring, and the number is growing rapidly. That has to be stopped for our plans to succeed."

"What you say may be so, but we have time...."

"A fiscal crisis would topple their government."

Kumakura nodded. "It could."

"Harney's government accepts our guidance. Having it fall would bring others to power, and they might not be so accommodating. We cannot allow the protest movements and trends to gain strength. We require a docile population."

"*Hai.*" Kumakura sighed and took another sip of *sake*. "Still, history teaches us that direct, aggressive acts are not always wise."

"Do we still have your approval, Sir?"

"The policy is approved." Kumakura looked up and smiled gently. "These are just the thoughts of an old man who yearns for a peaceful retirement next year. The plans are set, and we shall proceed."

"We must take control and develop this resource area."

"Yes."

"*Banzai!!!*" Kobayashi raised his cup.

"*Banzai!*"

The two men bowed to each other and drank the toast.

Cascade Wilderness Area

Will looked thoughtfully out the window. "It's starting to clear, Becky. I see a patch of blue sky."

She picked up the phone. "I've got a dial tone. Before I call my friends, I need to ask you something."

"Go ahead."

"How sure are you no one can tap our conversations? We use your equipment, but are still quite careful of what we say. We always use code words or ciphers, but I want to speak directly this time. I need to discuss some complex issues we've not anticipated or planned for."

"You do well to ask about privacy. When the CALEA laws passed back in the '90s, few noticed the specifications: One out of a hundred conversations was to be monitored."

She rolled her eyes. "They damned sure noticed during Iraq when it hit the news."

"It was inevitable. Such an intrusion was beyond the wildest dreams of Hitler's Gestapo or Stalin's KGB, but modern technology makes it possible. After 9-11 and the Patriot Act, surveillance increased. CALEA embeds it into our communications infrastructure."

Becky frowned. "What's a caliee whatever? I've never heard of it."

"C-A-L-E-A. It's an acronym, 'Computerized Assistance to Law Enforcement Agencies.' When communications went digital, conventional wiretaps stopped working. The government's solution was to *pay* the phone companies to ensure their networks allowed monitoring. Under CALEA, backdoors for monitoring are built into all telephone and Internet infrastructure. The taps are built in and widely used.

"The Foreign Intelligence Surveillance Act, FISA, was amended after 9-11. Wiretaps and surveillance are conducted without court orders. Today, most everything can be monitored. Therefore, it is. Everything on the Internet is captured, archived, searched for patterns, and scanned for keywords."

"I know the risks of photos, cell phones, credit cards, and Social Networks, but not even the most totalitarian state could possibly monitor everything said over electronic media."

Will shook his head. "They can come close. China does it bluntly and without apology. Iran puts cameras in all their Internet cafes. Here, it's usually softer, but everything is captured."

"You mean all the phone calls and emails. All the communications."

"Please don't think that staying away from a phone or computer will save you from Big Brother. Most of the camera feeds are monitored and archived as well."

"Security cameras. I know that."

"Any camera that is connected to the net can be monitored unless the feed is encrypted. Your TV set at home can watch you. That's been built in since 2012."

"That's hard to believe. Why would people tolerate that?"

Will gave a little snort. "Where have you been? They not only tolerated it, they **embraced** it and paid more for the feature. In 2012 Samsung started putting always-connected cameras and microphones into their top-of-the-line HDTV sets. The TVs had built-in face recognition, so they could personalize the viewing experience for each recognized family member. If you had friends over, it could log their faces as well, and even link to their Facebook pages."

"Tell me they got sued…."

"Not really. The Samsung TVs came with warnings that they accepted no responsibility, and shall not be liable in the event that a product or service is not appropriate. The government, delighted, raised no legal objections. Do you know how much time the average American spends in front of a TV?"

"No idea. Probably a lot."

"Nielsen Media Research claims the average American household watches 8 hours and 15 minutes of television in a 24-hour period. That's why networks can charge so much for ads."

Becky blinked. "So how do you avoid that?"

"I don't watch live TV. I watch streaming video, and only on a computer I trust, one that is sitting behind a good hardware firewall. I personally avoid the smart TVs. So far we've not been forced to buy them."

"I can't even imagine processing that much data. How can anyone keep up with it?"

"With great difficulty, and a lot of taxpayer money. Are you familiar with *Stellar Wind*?"

"Never heard of it," she said.

"How about the Utah Data Center?"

"No."

"*Stellar Wind* is a National Security Agency project. It came on-line operationally in 2014, and is housed in a massive data center in the Utah desert near Salt Lake City, in a town called Bluffdale. The public name is 'Utah Data Center,' which sounds harmless. The purpose, however, is to track **all** forms of communications."

"Like emails and phone calls?"

"Much more. **All** forms of communications, from cell phones to the complete content of emails, photos, rich media, and all. They call it the "deep web' and also track what is called 'digital pocket litter." That includes all sorts of personal data trails– parking and meal receipts, travel itineraries, political donations, memberships, pictures, Google searches, bookstore purchases, smartphone GPS locations in real time, and on and on...."

"That's legal?"

Will shrugged. "The legal construct is 'triaging anonymized data'...."

"What the hell does that mean?"

"No one knows for sure at a detail level. It's the old 'needle in the haystack' problem. The Watchers are looking for a few words of information buried in Petabytes of prattle. 'Triaging anonymized data' is what the lawyers say. The assertion is that personal privacy is somehow protected by a focus on content. It is, of course, the same bullshit logic TSA uses. Rather than profiling terrorists, they grope Grandma and take her nail clippers away."

"Triaging is a legal trick to avoid Constitutional Rights issues?"

"Absolutely. It's also for political correctness and to avoid embarrassments and having to discuss operational details in court. The IRS has used that dodge for decades. They **never** reveal why a citizen was targeted for an audit, and the courts have never challenged them. The spooks are even more hard core about their OP SEC."

"I don't understand."

"Spooks. The agencies. The blackest secrets in the intelligence community are sources and methods, but there's a general consensus that face recognition and keyword matches are widely used. The monitoring computers tag words like 'bomb,' 'money,' 'drugs,' and the like to save messages and flag them for human attention. You can defeat face recognition and keyword searches by encryption, but encrypted messages are obvious. They stand out like a sore thumb.

"Obvious encryption is asking for big trouble, be it an IRS audit, bureaucratic harassment, surveillance, or a police raid. Once you get flagged and put on one of the special interest lists, you're in trouble. It's not wise to attract the attention of the Cybercops."

"Do you think all calls to or from Cybertech are monitored and traced in real time?"

"That would be a reasonable operative assumption. Because of the business we're in, we're a target. People would love to crack our systems. We log probes from all over the planet."

Becky frowned. "Just how solid is your encryption?"

"Cybertech's design goal is 100 years, a human lifetime, for the best supercomputers to break it. We think that is, for all practical purposes, adequate security."

"Can people be safe if we avoid sensitive topics or targeted phone numbers?"

"Not safe, but it helps. There's more to it than technology. Even if the cybercops can't read your communications, they can use a wide variety of other means to watch you." He shrugged. "Or they can just save the files, arrest you, and put pressure on you to produce the keys.

"It's best to not be noticed. It's safest to hide in plain sight. That's what our products do."

"How?" she asked.

"The science is called steganography. We don't discuss our methods, but there's literature. Published techniques include chaffing, winnowing, and covert channels. A primitive method is using the LSBs of pixels in an image to hide a message."

"I didn't understand a word you said."

"Our scramblers make messages appear normal, to appear **not** to be encrypted. Anyone listening in or reading a message would observe a totally normal, if perhaps nonsensical, conversation. Our basic concept is camouflage, steganography, coupled with several layers of strong encryption, just in case."

"This is too complicated."

"The notion is quite simple. Like I said, we hide our clients' conversations, images, and data in plain sight."

"So I can talk to my friends privately if I use Cybertech's gear?"

"You can with a few provisions." Will chose his words carefully. "Because of Echelon, inherent cell phone tracking, and for a variety of other technical reasons, it's prudent to avoid wireless or international conversations. Provided you do that, no one is physically listening, and your friends are trustworthy, our equipment lets you communicate privately."

"Don't use cell phones?"

"Use them all you wish, but not for anything you need to keep private. The lowliest, dumbest gangbanger knows to use a pager, not a cellphone.

I personally don't trust anything wireless or any computer that hasn't been checked for bugs, spyware, and the like. Cell phones are an easy target."

"And no one has ever broken your encryption…?"

"There have been no known breaches for the past six years that were attributable to our equipment."

"I was hoping for a simple yes or no answer."

"There's no absolute safety this side of the grave. It's all relative, but we're the best there is. Why do you think I'm in so much trouble? We've consistently refused to allow backdoors in our equipment. That makes people nervous."

"Okay." She nodded and took a deep breath, letting it out slowly. "I'm getting us extracted from here on an urgent basis. I need to get you to safety."

"No."

She looked at him sharply. "What did you say?"

"I can't agree to leave."

"Why not?"

"I have to go back. I'm responsible."

"Damn it, Will, be reasonable. I'm here to take you to safety, not deeper into danger. Neither of us is armed, and those Peace Enforcers are killers. We can send someone else to the plant, someone with the right equipment and skills."

"Great idea." He felt a surge of relief. "Your friends can handle it for us."

She wouldn't meet his eyes. "We're a small group, not an army. We're not militant. Most of us are scientists and healers. We have a few people who are trained to protect us, but none of them are in Oregon."

"Can your friends handle it or not?"

"I've asked for help and someone appropriate will be sent."

"But you don't know when. Even if they've been dispatched, this storm will delay them…."

She nodded, reluctantly. "Yes."

"Let me guess. You were going to send me to safety and then go back and secure the plant yourself, weren't you?"

"I can't take a chance. I'll get everyone out and burn it to the ground."

Will closed his eyes. "That's what I was afraid of."

He was silent for a long time. "Becky, this is my fight. Dad's not around, so now it's up to me. If my people left confidential information lying around, it's my responsibility."

"I can take care of it."

"Not as well as I can." He glanced into her intense gaze. "I can be in and out of the plant in a few minutes. I know exactly where everything is."

She shook her head. Her eyes were like laser beams. "You are *not* expendable."

"We don't have time to argue."

"Don't be an asshole. I'm trying to keep you alive."

He looked at her solemnly. "It's my responsibility."

"And it's *my* responsibility to get you to safety."

"You will. I'll go with you. I just need to go back first and finish things."

"You're a target. I'm afraid for you."

I'm scared shitless. If we talk about it, we'll both lose our nerve. "It'll be perfectly safe. We'll use my portable crypto unit and your 'mirrors' to make sure no hostiles are around."

Becky stared at him. "Bad idea."

"Hear me out. All I need is five minutes inside. The trick will be getting us out of these mountains in this storm."

"That part's easy. Local help was planned for our extraction. Someone will come for us as soon as the weather breaks. The problem is at the other end, at Cybertech."

"I can be in and out before anyone notices. I know exactly where to go and what to do."

"What if something goes wrong? What if it's a trap?"

"Portland's a major city. We still have laws, and I have excellent lawyers. The Peace Enforcers wouldn't dare harm me there."

"Maybe not," she agreed reluctantly. "But what if you're arrested?"

"I'll give you my backpack. I'll tell you how to find my technology team and give you some additional code words so they'll know that I want them to help you. If I'm arrested, hide yourself and tell my people who took me. My lawyers will get me out."

Her eyes widened. "You trust me that much?"

"You've gone to a lot of effort to help me, and I have to trust someone. Without you, the Peace Enforcers would have taken me days ago."

"Are you sure you want to do this?"

"Dead sure. It'll be fine."

She paused for a moment, thinking, and then sighed. "I can't think of a better plan. You know your way around Cybertech, and we don't. I'll take you back to the plant if you *promise* to let me get you to safety after that."

"Let's do it."

"All right." She started dialing the phone.

Russell Senate Office Building, Washington DC

Senator George Margolin pushed his chair back and looked around the room. "All right, Ernie, let's get the decks cleared so we can talk."

Ernesto Salvador Morales had been George's senior Chief in the Navy and was now his Chief of Staff with a bachelor's degree from the University of Arizona in Political Science, courtesy of a Navy scholarship Margolin helped him acquire.

Ernie was born in Arizona, the son of a legal immigrant. He was stocky, swarthy, and, even after all these years he lapsed into Spanish when excited, which was frequently.

Ernesto was nothing if not passionate, and, like most legal immigrants, he was a fervent believer in the Constitution, liberty, and democracy. His dad was now set up in a retirement community in Arizona living out the American Dream. He still flew the flag every day, taking it down before dark, and folding it with respect.

Ernie nodded and got out his notes. A technician scanned the room one last time for bugs, while an aide carefully unplugged and removed the telephones. It was unlikely that anyone would dare to bug a Senior Senator's office, but Margolin, a retired Navy Captain, was careful. The workers nodded and left, closing the door behind them.

"Let's go through Harney's speech again, Ernie. What's this about?"

"I've watched that damned clip ten times now. There is minimal content. It's political fluff. His entire speech took two minutes and twelve seconds. The only documentation we got for backup is the letter of agreement he was waving, along with a few attachments and a codicil. Our analysis is in the folders I passed out."

Six men and one woman shuffled the papers before them, each opening the indicated folder. It contained a single sheet of paper.

"I have five issues to cover," Ernie said. "Point one: The loan is a trap for the next President. A trillion dollars. It sounds like a lot of money. Hell, it *is* a lot of money, post Obama. Problem is it taps out at about the time Harney leaves office. Interesting coincidence."

"Are you sure?" It was the Senator from Maine, Helen Branson, a former Wall Street analyst who'd gotten rich and retired to the woods. After her husband died, she'd become bored and run for the Senate. She was an intense woman, quick and meticulous with numbers.

"It's pretty close."

She shook her head. "Can't be." She was asking for more data.

"Check it yourself."

She nodded, waiting for him to continue.

"That's not the whole picture. Commerce Department numbers don't consider foreign-owned domestic assembly plants. Assemblies built offshore are passed through plants in the U.S., where they are screwed into cases and stuffed into boxes by minimum wage workers. The assemblies don't count as imports. The finished products are counted as domestic, maybe even as exports, if they are re-exported.

"It's a shell game, Helen. This hidden deficit increases the real trade imbalance by a factor of three or four."

She nodded. "Figures lie and liars figure. You are touching on a difficult topic for taxpayers to understand. The assembly jobs are dead-end, as you say, but some are dependent on having them."

"Harney has another 18 months in office. By then all that money will be gone." He looked around to make sure he was understood. "Incidentally, the 'interest free' part is a lie. It's interest free, but only for two years."

Margolin rapped the table. "Ernie, I'm going to pull rank. You are right, but so is Helen. We don't mention the assembly jobs. Just the fact that this is a financial trap that only adds to our nation's problems."

"Got it."

"Thank you," Helen said.

Heads nodded. Margolin signaled for Ernie to continue.

"Point two: We do need the money. Badly. Our credit was about to be pulled."

Heads nodded again. That was well known. Harney's administration had apparently dodged that bullet, but at what price?

"Point three: This is the classic deal with the Devil. The sucker gets gold in trade for his soul. In effect, we give up our national sovereignty and control of our justice system."

Margolin frowned. "God, what else? Do you have any good news?"

"None whatsoever. Harney's letter legitimizes Peace Enforcers on U.S. soil. We have that already on a limited scale, but this amounts to occupation troops. We give their courts purview of our economic and drug cases. We let them house our prisoners offshore. Who do you think will get to pick the people who get shipped out as slave labor? Not us.

"Most of our prison population consists of non-violent criminals, kids busted for pot or tax offenders. Prisons provide cheap industrial labor. Our enemies can skim the productive workers out of our prisons for their labor camps, leaving us the thugs and psychos. They'll use our citizens to build cheap products, which they'll sell at a profit."

Everyone nodded, but Margolin said, "Careful, Ernie. You'll be nailed for that. 'Opponents' or 'trading partners,' not 'enemies.' "

Ernie made a sour face. "Noted." He continued, "Point four: We've just legalized technology theft. I doubt the details of that codicil will ever see daylight, but…."

Just then, there was a knock on the door. They all looked at the Senator. He held up his hand. "Someone open the door and see what Grace wants. She wouldn't interrupt unless it was important." Ernie, already standing, jumped to obey.

Grace stuck her head in the room. "Excuse me, Senator, but I think you should see this. Flip on the SATNEWS channel. Something interesting is happening." Margolin hit the remote. The display lit with the image of an earnest commentator, seen as a talking head framed against an image of carnage and twisted wreckage.

"These videos were sent to all the major networks by an unknown source that apparently had access to the private Internet addresses for their news directors and CEOs. The coordinates and time stamps in the upper left indicate this was recorded in the Cascade Mountains of Oregon three days ago."

The camera flashed some coordinates, in red. The background shifted to a map, with the location highlighted. Then it zoomed back to show its relationship to major cities. "This location is some two hundred and fifty miles southeast of Portland, in an unpopulated, roadless area."

The view shifted back to the shattered helicopters. The weapons pods and shredded armor showed up clearly. "These are the latest models of Yamada Industries 'black swan' gunships. As you can see, they bear UN markings." The camera zoomed in and held to show the lettering on the copters.

"A Yamada spokesperson told our reporter that these models are built for the Japanese Defense Force and not available for export. Sources at the UN tell us that they can find no record of having purchased these advanced weapons." The screen split, to show a helicopter firing missiles at tanks.

"The text that came with these clips asserts that a foreign military force is operating against U.S. citizens. It claims the Harney administration authorized this. White House press secretary Susan Myers denies that, saying, 'This is obviously a political attempt to discredit the President and disrupt his economic recovery program.' She went on to say the White House declines further comment at this time.

"The UN has issued a statement saying that peace enforcer operations on U.S. soil are limited to WTO enforcement actions and closely coordinated with state and national officials. It denies knowledge of any such operations in Oregon.

"A severe storm is limiting movement in the Northwest, but we're sending reporters and will have more to report soon. News at six."

Senator Margolin punched a button and the display vanished. "We need to wrap this meeting up now. I'd better get to my committee meeting. If the phones were connected, they'd be ringing off the hook about this. I want you to finish, Ernie. What's your last point, number five?"

Ernesto shrugged eloquently, and the gesture spoke volumes. *¿Quién sabe?* "Harney's plan makes me want to puke, George, but there's no smoking gun. Except for averting our imminent economic collapse, everything that I'm alleging here is debatable. Nothing is provable until after it happens, and then it's too late."

"The old Rahm Emanuel strategy: Never Waste a Crisis? Panic people. Force emotion over rational debate?"

"Yes, Sir."

"What's your assessment?"

"There's pressure to do something fast, to not look Japan's gift horse in the mouth. The public is scared. Whatever Harney's hidden agenda is, he'll get away with it."

"Unless we can come up with tangible evidence of malfeasance or corruption. I want to get out ahead of this one. Let's find out more about the agreement and whatever happened in the mountains out west. I want to know who sent those video clips. This is now our top priority. I'll have Grace schedule a meeting to continue this tomorrow."

Ernie nodded. "Can do. Anything else?"

"Get me a briefing. Japan used to be in the toilet. Now they're a superpower. I want an explanation of how they recovered so fast economically despite their string of earthquakes, tsunamis, and nuclear disasters. I'll need it boiled down into a short presentation the public can understand, maybe seven talking points."

"Let me handle that one, George," Helen said. "I'm interested myself. It might be very useful for the next campaign cycle."

"Thank you, Senator," Margolin said. He waved over his shoulder on the way out.

Cascade Wilderness Area

"Becky, hold up. I need to catch my breath." Will shook the wet, clinging snow off his snowshoes for what seemed the thousandth time. "I hate these damned things."

She came back, breathing easily, and did the same. "It's getting warm. The snow's melting so it sticks to our shoes. But we wouldn't have gotten this far without them."

"How are we doing for time?" Time was the imperative, he knew. She'd kept them moving because time was running out.

"We're almost there. It's just over this ridge and we have ten minutes left."

"Thank God. Just let me catch my breath, then we'll get going."

She nodded.

A few minutes later, they cleared the ridge and stood looking down into a small clearing with a lake. There were no roads and no signs of habitation.

"Do you see anything?" he asked.

"No." She looked at her GPS. "The location they gave me is only 150 yards ahead. It must be down in the clearing by that lake.

She took out her strange binoculars and scanned the area. "Not a thing."

"No sign of intelligent life?" He smiled, recalling the old Star Trek videos.

"Right," she said. "No large life forms in the area."

Soon they were standing at the spot. Will looked around, turning in a slow circle, straining his senses. Nothing. "Are you sure this is the right place?"

"Positive." She was scanning again with the binoculars. The day was warming, but there was still solid cloud cover, just over the tops of the surrounding hills. "There's nothing here."

"So what do we do?"

"We wait." She was preoccupied, concentrating. "Do you hear anything?"

"Just the wind and my own breathing."

"No, something else. I can't tell…"

Suddenly they both heard it, an engine. An instant later, a small plane popped over the hill to the west. It was white, blending with the clouds and snow. As it approached, they could see that it had struts bracing the wings, and floats.

Its flaps came down and it slowed as it slid down the contour of the hillside. It seemed to barely be moving as it touched down just offshore with a splash that set small waves rippling across the lake.

The plane turned, and the pilot saw them. He gunned his engine and pulled up on the beach in front of them as the prop slowly spun down to a stop. A door on the right side popped open, and a small man with dark hair and a crooked grin stepped out.

"Name's Murphy. Heard you folks needed a ride. I can have you on the Willamette River near Cybertech in about an hour. Got ground transportation arranged, but the special help you wanted hasn't checked in yet."

Becky looked at the little plane skeptically. "Does it need to have all those wires and things hanging off it?"

Murphy's grin got wider. "That's what holds it together. We call it rigging, lady. All airplanes used to use rigging and struts. It's much stronger."

She looked dubious, but Will nodded his encouragement.

"Hop in," Murphy said.

They did, throwing their packs behind the seat.

Murphy hit the starter, but there was only a whir. "Damn. I need to fix that," he muttered. He poked the starter again, and this time the prop turned and the engine caught.

"Gonna be tight getting out," he yelled over his shoulder as they taxied out. "I'll take off downwind, back the way I came in. We gotta clear that hill. Just hang on, and keep clear of the stick and rudder pedals."

At the far side of the lake, he spun the plane around and jammed the throttle full open. The engine roared loudly and they pounded across the lake. The engine was screaming and the plane was shaking furiously, but it accelerated slowly. Finally, they struggled into the air.

Becky leaned close to Will's ear. "Was that normal?"

"Absolutely." In truth, he had no idea, but he did know he'd never seen trees so close from the air. They cleared the hill, barely, and headed northwest just under the clouds. The engine noise softened, but the air was bumpy. The plane kept lurching and dropping.

"I don't feel well," Becky said.

"Don't think about it. It's a short flight. Take deep breaths and concentrate on what we'll do when we get there."

She swallowed hard, several times, looking pale. He checked in the back of the seat in front of him and was pleased to find a sick sack. *We might need this.*

Two hours later

Cybertech kept an apartment a block down from the plant, and they got there with no problems. Will knew the security codes and where the key was hidden. It was almost dark, but they still had a good view of the main gate.

Becky put her binoculars up to the window and scanned for the third time. "There's no one on the street. There are no lights on. I think someone just entered the guard shack. I didn't see anything visually, but I got a blip."

"Damn it, why doesn't the phone ring?" She'd said that every five minutes for the past half hour, with increasing frustration in her voice. This time, as if on cue, it buzzed. She picked it up, making sure Will's scrambler was activated.

"Yes?" Strain made Becky's voice harsh. "Of course I'm nervous. I'm scared, we've got no backup, the flight left me queasy, and it'll be dark soon." She paused and listened for a moment. "I can't see much, but we think there's one person in the guard shack. Talk to me. What's going on over there? Where's our help?"

She listened for several minutes, and her face fell.

We have a problem. Will recognized the expression. It was an, "Oh, shit."

"Are you sure?" she said. Becky listened some more.

"A woman?" she said. "That's terrible."

Will could only hear one side of the conversation, but the tone of her questions and the tone of her voice made it clear something was wrong.

"I'll call you back. Please hurry." She put the phone down and turned to Will.

"We're screwed. There's a squad of Peace Enforcers at your plant." She proceeded to describe the situation at Cybertech.

Will took several deep breaths. "The dead guard you described could only be Harry Conners. He was Dad's first sergeant and good friend. Harry all but raised me. He and Dad won medals together. Did you say the woman captive has gray hair?"

Becky nodded.

"That's my assistant, Kate Chambers. Harry must have resisted. He apparently put three of them down, and there are three left. Do you concur?"

"It's a good working assumption."

"The police won't intervene against Peace Enforcers. When will we have help?"

"They said 'soon.' I took it to mean no more than an hour."

"Not soon enough if Kate's being tortured."

"It's the storm." He could hear the frustration in her voice. "The roads are snarled. They're doing the best they can. What do you want to do?"

I want to run. I want to save Kate. Mostly, I want to make sure you don't get hurt.

Will didn't tell her any of those things. His mind was racing. "Let me think." Finally, he said, "I have a plan."

"Let's hear it."

"It's not complicated: I'll go in. It should be safe."

"Are you **crazy**?"

"Think it through. Those Peace Enforcers in the mountains could have killed me easily. Instead, they stalked me. They want to arrest me, not kill me out of hand. I can't compromise your friends, because I don't know who or where they are. I can't compromise you because you'll have your friends watching and will be long gone from this apartment before they can make me talk."

"Will, that's *insane*. What does that accomplish? Why give them two hostages?"

"I'll buy time. Maybe I can trade myself for Kate. She's of no real use to them, and they wouldn't kill her with me as a witness. When your help comes, you can rescue me."

He thought of his many-times-great grandpa, at the Battle of Trenton. A farmer standing alone and unarmed in the dark on that bleak, cold winter night, waiting to guide the small band of ragtag soldiers who'd come to fight their hopeless fight against the strongest army in the world. He'd always wondered how it felt. Now he knew. It was terrifying.

I guess in the end you do what you must. I can't abandon Kate.

"What about you?" Becky asked.

Will forced a smile, gave her his most confident look, and lied. "It's not a problem. There are only three of them left. Your security people can rescue me if anything goes wrong. Whatever happens, document it, and send it to the same place you sent the helicopter clips.

"My people will know what to do with what you send. There's a note in my pack proving you speak for me. If I'm arrested, tell my lawyers. Ask for Sam. He'll get me out."

She stood there looking up at him, feeling tears well up. He tilted her head and kissed her cheek. "Can you do that for me, Becky?"

"We're out of options. I'll do whatever you want."

"Don't take any chances. The access codes and disks you need are in my backpack. Get them back to your friends. That's important. Don't linger here if anything goes wrong. I'll go around and approach the plant from the opposite direction."

"Be careful. I came to save you. Not to...."

"There's no time." He kissed her again, this time on the lips, gently. "I have to do this. It'll be okay."

She stood back and looked deeply into his eyes. Finally she nodded. "I'll get you help."

"I know you will. Take care and stay safe yourself. Remember, if they get us both, we lose. It's game over if that happens."

"I understand." Becky watched him out of sight, as he slipped down the back stairs. Then she picked up the phone to call her friends back.

CHAPTER NINE

CYBERTECH PLANT

K ate regained consciousness slowly. She opened her eyelids slightly and then closed them, trying to avoid notice. Tanaka was sitting on the edge of Will's desk rummaging through a small toolbox. *If he thinks I'm still out, maybe he'll leave me alone.*

"I know you're awake, Katherine Chambers. Look at me, or I will hurt you more."

A stab of fear went through her. She opened her eyes. Tanaka was holding a small pair of pliers. He stood up and slowly approached her.

"Pain is part of life, you know." He smiled like a shark circling its prey. "Perhaps you can avoid some if you cooperate." Tanaka gestured at Will's computer. "How do I open the files?"

"I don't know." She tried to keep her voice calm. "I'm a friend of Harry's. I don't know much about computers."

"You're a bad liar. You're Dr. Giles' secretary. Before that you worked for his father."

"I don't have his passwords, and I'm not a computer expert." Kate's head was throbbing. She felt as if she had been screaming for days, but the clock on the wall said it was only mid-afternoon. She was losing her sense of time, and it increased her horror.

"So you say." Tanaka shrugged. "A workman needs proper tools, but sometimes one must improvise. These pliers will suffice. I am going to start removing your fingernails unless you tell me the passwords. There's no hurry. You'll tell me what I want to know eventually."

Peace Enforcer Barracks, Portland, OR

Lieutenant Matsu paced back and forth impatiently. He'd rushed from the landing pad to report to Captain Tanaka, only to find the barracks almost deserted.

"I'm here to replace Lt. Sasaki. My orders are to report to Captain Tanaka." He handed them to the duty officer, who was, in this case, a young and obviously inexperienced corporal.

"Captain Tanaka is at the Cybertech plant with a squad, Sir."

"Do you know why?"

"No, Sir. I wasn't told." He glanced down at his call log. "Sergeant Kami is with him. He called thirty-two minutes ago and requested reinforcements. He said to send everyone available and requested heavy weapons support. He reported they'd taken casualties.

"Heavy weapons. Is there a war going on, Corporal?"

"No, Sir." He hesitated. "I think they want to make a show of force."

They told me Portland was a peaceful area, Matsu thought. "Have you dispatched the relief force?"

"Not yet, Sir."

Matsu stared at the Corporal and shook his head. He did not expect to find such disorder and confusion. "I'm aware of Captain Tanaka's reputation. It would lead me to take it for granted his orders would be carried out efficiently."

The man lowered his eyes. "Sir, I'm doing what I can. We were told to stand down. There was a bad accident in the mountains. Many were injured or killed, and the rest were given leave to recover."

"I know that, Corporal. It's why I'm here," Matsu snapped. "What assets are available?"

The young man looked overwhelmed. "I can dispatch two vehicles and nine men with small arms and grenades now. Ten if you'd like to go along, Sir."

"That's *everyone available*?" The lieutenant was incredulous.

"The local communications are primitive, Sir. Other than our alert crews, the men don't carry communicators. They don't work reliably, and cell phones are not secure. I've been calling people at home and leaving voice messages."

Matsu shook his head. *Voice messages. Why not clay tablets?*

"I couldn't contact the helicopter pilots. Other than the duty crew who picked you up, they're on leave. We do have two Armored Personnel Carriers here. The APC crews were on standby. They're on their way, but haven't checked in yet." The Corporal looked embarrassed. "Portland's roads are noted for gridlock, Sir."

"Is there any good news?"

"Yes, Sir." The Corporal's face lit up with pride. "Our equipment is first rate. The helicopter that picked you up is a black swan with the intelligent weapons systems. Our APCs have the new hyper cannon and can kill heavy tanks. We're the first unit outside Japan to get these weapons."

"What force can you muster when everyone checks in?"

"In an hour, we could put together a combat team of over a hundred men, including two weapons squads with grenade launchers, anti-tank weapons, shoulder launched surface-to-air missiles, and heavy machine guns, plus the APCs and the helicopter gunship that brought you. Sufficient force to level half the city, Sir."

Matsu frowned, thinking furiously. *Why do these fools keep having accidents and taking casualties? Why is Captain Tanaka mobilizing a small army?*

The Peace Enforcers routinely suppressed riots, but unleashing an armored column on a peaceful city seemed excessive. He found himself wishing he'd not arrived in the middle of this. It was becoming painfully clear he was the ranking officer at the base and responsible if anything went wrong.

I need more information, he thought. This was his first field assignment and Captain Tanaka's reputation was fearsome. Nothing in Matsu's training had prepared him for this. "What else, Corporal?"

"Sir, we have no officers available to command such a large force. Lt. Noda is in the hospital. Our Senior enlisted men are with the Captain."

Matsu kept his face impassive. This would damage his career if he handled it wrong. One thing was certain: He did not need Captain Tanaka as an enemy.

"I'll take command of the relief force. Tell me precisely what the Captain's orders were. Should we send what's available now, or should we wait?"

"He said, 'Send everyone available.' I can't advise you beyond that, Sir."

"Did Sergeant Kami indicate the situation was under control?"

"Yes, Sir."

Matsu was remembering Tanaka's reputation for brutality. *He probably wants to make an example to cow the locals. Nothing else makes sense.*

It's best to bring an overwhelming force, even if I won't have to use it. Alternately, if Tanaka wants to start a war, he can. I'll be covered either way. I'm just following orders.

Thus it was that Lieutenant Matsu made his first and last combat decision.

"Break open the armory. I'm declaring a full alert. I want you to have a hundred-man force ready to roll in thirty minutes. Offload the tear gas and non-lethal weapons. I want the APCs and the helicopter armed with a mix of high explosive, armor piercing, and incendiary rounds. Tell the men this is not a drill."

"Yes, Sir!"

Cybertech Plant

Tanaka scowled at the knock on the door. He disliked being interrupted in the middle of an interrogation. It disturbed his focus. "Come in," he snapped.

The door opened, and Will stepped into the room followed by Sergeant Kami. He paused at the sight of Kate slumped in the chair with blood dripping from her hand. The sergeant prodded him with his gun barrel, and he took several more paces into the room.

Will recognized Tanaka from the newscasts of the riots in Bellevue. The small Asian was smiling beatifically.

It's true. He does enjoy hurting people. Will wondered what abnormal psychology would induce a person to enjoy inflicting human suffering.

The two men studied each other silently.

"I'm Dr. William Giles. This is my company. You're on private property and are not welcome here. Please leave and take your men with you."

Tanaka laughed and shook his head. "You misunderstand the situation. You're my prisoner. I have authorization from your government to occupy this facility."

"May I use the telephone? I'd like to call my attorneys."

Tanaka shook his head again. "I'm aware Americans still have the quaint notion of what you call 'Rights,' but you'll find my authority supersedes them. You have no rights, only privileges. I'll decide those after you've given me the passwords to your computer."

"We can discuss such things after you release my assistant. She's of no value to you. Let her go."

"I'm not done with her." Tanaka smiled coldly at Will, almost licking his lips in anticipation. "I'll enjoy it when you're begging to tell me the passwords, *gaijin*."

Surprisingly, the sergeant spoke up, concern in his voice. "Captain Tanaka, Sir. This is the man we followed in the mountains. He walked up to the gate, unarmed, and asked to be taken to my commander. The orders from Kobayashi-san and Ambassador Kumakura say he's not to be harmed, Sir."

Tanaka flicked an irritated glance at the sergeant. Will could almost feel the man cringe behind him.

"Your compassion is touching, but those orders are obsolete. For this mission, I was given no such constraints."

"Sir, our command did not know we'd be encountering this man. Shouldn't we ask for instructions?" The sergeant was almost pleading.

"I don't need any clarification of my orders. We're to do whatever is required to get this company's design information. Still, since you're so concerned, I'll let **you** interrogate him. Get a chair and place him in it. I want those passwords, Sergeant."

"Yes, Sir."

The sergeant set a chair next to Kate's. He gestured with his weapon for Will to sit down. Will glanced at the two warriors and complied, offering no resistance. The sergeant walked over and leaned his weapon against the wall. He came back to face Will and stood over him, between him and the Captain.

"Do you want me to tape him to the chair, Sir?"

"No, Sergeant, leave him free. If the *gaijin* leaves his chair or attempts to resist, you are to stop your interrogation and restrain him. Then he can watch me finish with the woman. As he noted, she is quite unnecessary, and, hence, expendable. One way or the other, I think he'll cooperate."

"Yes, Sir." The sergeant looked at Will with resignation. "Please give me the passwords."

Will shook his head and the sergeant hit him carefully, with measured force, an open-fisted chop on the shoulder. The blow still caused excruciating pain to shoot down Will's arm.

He screamed, involuntarily. His vision filled with bright flashes and then went black. A dark shade came down.

When he regained consciousness, the sergeant was standing patiently in front of him with the same dogged look on his face. Will glanced past him at the clock on the wall, surprised that over five minutes had passed. He needed to hold out as long as he could for help to arrive.

The sergeant hit him again.

Will struggled back to awareness through a thick black fog. Every part of his body hurt. He blinked, dazed, trying to clear his vision.

The sergeant was still standing over him, waiting. Will had been enduring the beating for almost an hour. He sensed his body had taken about all it could. He couldn't stall much longer. He'd given up hope help would arrive.

"What are the passwords?"

Will tried to speak, but only a croak came out. He tried again, but without success.

"Continue, Sergeant." Tanaka was in no hurry.

Will croaked again and shook his head. He'd bitten his tongue and his jaw wasn't working right. Finally, he managed to form words. "I'll talk." It came out AHH TAAAK.

"Sir, I can't understand him. May I give him some water?"

The sergeant held out a cup. Will tried to take it, but couldn't. He couldn't feel his feet, and his hands and arms were numb. He took several deep breaths and finally managed to reach out. He had to hold the cup in both hands to steady it. He finally managed to take a small sip, then another.

Will felt strength returning. He tentatively moved his arms, then his legs. He shifted the cup from hand to hand, flexing his fingers. Nothing seemed to be broken, despite the pain. *It's now or never. Much more and I won't be able to move at all.*

"Give us the passwords," the sergeant ordered.

"Don't hit me again. Help me over to the computer."

The sergeant looked relieved. Unlike Tanaka, he wasn't enjoying this. He reached down to help Will to his feet.

"No," ordered Tanaka.

"Sir?" asked the sergeant, in puzzlement.

"I'm not going to let him touch his computer. Have him dictate the passwords. I'll key them in myself."

"Yes, Sir." The sergeant looked at Will expectantly.

Will managed a raspy whisper. "Can't talk. Please, just one more sip." *This is the only chance I'll get.* He took several deep breaths and hoped his body would respond. He took a sip from the cup, then another.

The sergeant waited patiently.

Tanaka was smiling. "Perhaps you should give him some more encouragement."

Will cringed, letting his fear show. It wasn't difficult.

"Sir. He's trying to cooperate. Give me the passwords, Dr. Giles."

"Yes," gasped Will. "The password is my name, William Patton Giles followed by the numbers 666."

"Spell it out," Tanaka said.

Will did so.

"With no spaces?"

Will nodded. "Yes. Use all capitals. No spaces. Put 666 at the end."

Tanaka slowly walked around the desk and sat down at the computer. He keyed in the password and waited. It seemed to be taking a long time. Will kept breathing deeply, ordering his body to function, praying it would respond.

"It says 'command accepted,' Sergeant. Good work."

More time passed. The computer seemed very slow. Will kept taking deep breaths. He flexed his arms and legs in an attempt to get the circulation going.

"Now it's asking me 'please verify 666 command (Y/N)?' What should I do?"

The sergeant looked at Will. "What should he do?"

"Type 'Y' and then hit enter."

Tanaka smiled, tapping the keys. Then he gave a scream of rage as the screen flashed once and went blank.

The sergeant, startled, turned to see what caused this reaction.

Will dove for the sergeant's weapon.

He sprung from the chair and stumbled as his left leg collapsed. It didn't matter: *he had the carbine.* He remembered his father's training. One hand took the pistol grip, thumb flicking the safety off. The other slapped the grip under the barrel.

He was falling. It didn't matter. *Focus, get on target, and squeeze.* The sergeant was almost on him, charging into the gun. Tanaka was screaming in rage and just coming around the desk.

Will didn't squeeze -- he clamped the trigger down.

Brrraaaaap. The sound was deafening in the confined space. The weapon was on full automatic, bucking and almost tearing free although Will was holding it as tightly as he could. His hands weren't working right.

Will fired at least half a clip in one long burst. He cut the unfortunate sergeant almost in half, walking a line of fire diagonally up across his body at contact range.

The man was falling, but he was too close. His momentum carried him into Will, now down on his knees and desperately trying to clear the weapon for a shot at Tanaka. *I'm not going to make it.*

He was right. Tanaka kicked the carbine out of Will's hands with such violence it bounced off the wall. Almost casually, he flung the sergeant's body aside.

Will raised his hands in front of his face.

Tanaka laughed and broke Will's arms with two quick karate chops. He paused, smiled into Will's eyes, and kicked him.

Will groaned in agony. His vision went black. He couldn't breathe.

The Captain kicked him again and Will felt ribs snap. The next kick lifted him into the air and he collapsed on the floor.

Choking and gasping for breath, he still felt a surge of triumph. *They'll never use that computer again. They can examine it until hell freezes over. They'll get nothing. They won't even know I didn't leave anything on it to begin with.*

Tanaka kept kicking him, but the pain was becoming more distant. Eventually, it faded away entirely. Will's last thought was this was what dying must be like.

Outskirts of Portland

Keigo Ouchi peered through his goggles at the strange world of green and silver images formed by his thermal imager. He smiled to himself and wondered if it was because of choice or ineptitude that Americans always kept their roads torn up.

For once, it had proved convenient. The Peace Enforcer convoy was detoured off the freeway into an industrial district and forced to slow to a crawl.

It was the perfect place and the *yakuza* was ready.

Ouchi shielded his eyes and keyed his mike. "Kill the vulture."

Bars of glaring white light instantly rose skyward from three locations, and the helicopter hesitated in mid-flight and burst into flames. It fell like a wounded bird, trailing debris and burning fuel.

The Peace Enforcers were already returning fire. Turrets swiveled on both armored vehicles and contact-fused HE shells raked the face of a building with bright white flashes. He could hear engines racing over the crump of the explosions as the convoy tried to escape.

Excellent response time and precisely on target, Ouchi thought with approval. *That building was our only antiaircraft position in direct view of the column.*

"Contain them," he ordered. "Maximum indirect fire. Lay it on."

The two vehicles at the ends of the column died and with them the unfortunate Lieutenant Matsu, who never knew what hit him as his command car blew apart. The APC behind it tried to nudge the wreckage aside and was immediately hit by two rockets. It slewed sideways blocking the road. Its ready ammunition exploded in a bright flash that engulfed the truck behind it.

Men in black uniforms tried to scatter from the trucks, but were cut down by a rain of steel from the sky as a string of shells burst over the column. The remaining APC was still firing into the burning building, but it was trapped in the middle of the column and couldn't maneuver.

That's a major threat if it gets clear. "Kill the tank," Ouchi ordered.

It wasn't really a tank, but the weapons he directed were up to even that task, had it been necessary. The APC rocked on its tracks as it was hit hard, but its frontal armor held. It kept firing, the cyclic whiplash cracks of its hyper cannon clear over the other battle noise. The targeted building was disintegrating. Girders and large chunks of reinforced concrete rained down into the street.

The second hit was from a kinetic energy weapon that shredded the APC's armor like tinfoil and flipped it aside like a dog hit by a truck. Something internal exploded with a muffled *whump*. It was hit twice more, but the vehicle was already dead. It sat there with belches of yellow-orange flame gushing from its vision slits and hatches, but there were no secondary explosions.

Ouchi nodded to himself. "Antipersonnel weapons. Fire for effect."

The shell bursts were continuous. When the shooting stopped, nothing moved.

Ouchi glanced down at his clan emblem, the small snake tattooed on his wrist. He felt pride: His men had performed well against a superior force.

When they got home to Japan, they'd have a ceremony and drink the blood of the *Mamushi*. There'd be bonuses for this mission.

He gave his final order. "Disengage and disperse." The *yakuza* faded back into the night as if they were never there. Behind them, the flames were already starting to die down.

Cybertech Plant

Kate's eyes were blurry through the tears, but she was defiant. "I never had the passwords. Your only hope was lost when you killed Dr. Giles."

Tanaka stood in front of her juggling the pliers in his hand. He didn't bother to hit her again. She was already conditioned to where she'd cringe and start screaming when he approached. He'd removed three fingernails, but learned nothing useful.

Clearly, he was pondering whether to kill her and be done with it. Kate hoped he would. She was tired of the pain.

She saw motion behind the Captain. The door was slowly, silently opening. It was a large man with sandy hair and a face like an ax blade. He held a pistol with a thick barrel. She recognized it from the movies, a silencer.

"Don't move, little man. Drop the pliers."

Tanaka hesitated.

"Don't be stupid. I can blow your head off before you half turn around."

The pliers fell from the Captain's hand.

"That's better. Now raise your hands, slow and easy. Good." There was the drawl of Texas in the man's voice. He spoke in a slow cadence.

"I'm Captain Akai Tanaka of the United Nation's Peace Enforcers. This operation is ordered by our National Chief and authorized by your own President. My men are outside. They'll kill you if you don't surrender to me immediately."

The Texan laughed. "Your men are in hell, Captain. Including your relief column."

Tanaka stiffened. The smile froze on his face. "I don't believe you."

"I don't much give a shit what you believe. Step forward one pace. Good, now one pace to the right. Be very careful, Captain. Now two more paces to the right, real slow."

Tanaka obeyed.

He's putting me out of his line of fire, Kate thought.

The Texan slowly stepped into the room, glancing at the bodies on the floor but keeping his attention on Tanaka. "Do you enjoy torturing old women?"

His tone was one of mild curiosity. It was that of a man asking about the weather.

"I have my duty."

The Texan laughed again. "I thought you might say that. Turn around and back up slow, real slow."

Tanaka, no longer smiling, did as instructed. He moved slowly, facing the Texan, hands still raised.

"That's right, against the wall. Now lean back."

Tanaka complied.

"Good, put your weight on it. Now slide your feet forward. More. That's good."

Tanaka was in an awkward position, his shoulders against the wall, his body leaning back at an angle. "Why do you make me helpless, *gaijin*? Kill me if you dare."

The big man shook his head, relaxing slightly. "Don't need to, unless you force it. It's maybe better I leave you around to answer questions. Afterwards, they'll probably ship you home. You'll get to explain how you screwed up."

Tanaka's lips thinned.

The Texan lowered his gun and glanced left, looking at Kate. Suddenly, time seemed to stop. Tanaka's movement came without warning, so fast it was a blur.

His right arm snapped down, flinging a shiny silver object at the Texan's face. In the next instant, with a scream that froze Kate rigid, he was halfway across the room.

In that tiny, microscopic sliver of time, less than the blink of an eye, Tanaka's body was airborne, fully extended, both arms straight out. He was a living spear, a locus of energy launched to rip life from an enemy. Kate had never seen anyone move so quickly.

But the Texan wasn't there. He swayed aside, twisting, flicking his head so the shiny object just missed his ear. Somehow, incredibly, the Texan seemed to flow sideways, dropping to one knee, his gun coming up, his left hand slapping into position on the grip of the weapon to brace it.

Tanaka flew through the empty space, crashing to the floor with a dull thud. He tried to get up, pushing on the rug, but couldn't for some reason.

Time suddenly snapped back to its normal pace and Kate gasped as her muscles unlocked. She noticed bright objects bouncing on the rug. Shiny brass shell cases. Two were in mid-air, still falling. One hit the rosewood desk and rattled around with a tinkling noise.

Tanaka groaned and managed to roll over on his side. There was a tight pattern of holes in his shirt clustered over his heart. His black outfit was turning red.

The eyes of the two men met. The Texan's eyes were gray blue and held mild curiosity, a man studying a small but dangerous animal, waiting to see what it would do next. Tanaka's eyes were starting to glaze. He was having trouble breathing.

The Texan shook his head, holding his gun steady. "I went to the same school, Captain." It was the same tone, casual, this time with just a tinge of reproach.

Tanaka coughed and raised his head. Bright blood gushed from his mouth, running down his cheek and chin.

"You didn't give me a chance."

"You screwed up, Captain. Stupid move. You could have lived."

Tanaka lay there, wheezing, staring up into the big man's eyes.

"Lung shot's a bad way to die, isn't it?" There was no pity in the Texan's voice.

Tanaka coughed up more blood, but didn't try to speak. He continued to stare at the Texan.

Kate couldn't decide if the look was defiance, or if there might have been a silent plea in Tanaka's eyes. She could see air bubbling from his chest wounds and blood was starting to pool on the floor around him.

For a long moment, the room was silent, except for Tanaka's wheezing. He was fighting for each breath and clearly didn't have much longer.

Finally the big Texan nodded. Taking careful aim, he put one last bullet between Tanaka's eyes.

Without taking his eyes off his enemy, the Texan stood up and slipped a fresh magazine into his pistol. He took a deep breath, then let it out slowly, shaking his head.

He carefully unscrewed the suppressor and put it in his pocket. Finally, he holstered his weapon and glanced back at Kate. She would have collapsed except her arms were taped to the chair, holding her upright.

Kate tried to speak, but no sound came out. She swallowed, took a breath, and tried again. This time it worked. "He was going to kill me."

"Yes, ma'am. I'm a tad late." He looked at her hand and frowned. "I'm right sorry about that, ma'am. Got here quick as I could."

"I was sent to help. Dr. Giles told us to say 'purple flower.' To let you know I'm one of the good guys."

Kate looked up at the Texan, who was now removing the tape from her arms, trying not to hurt her. Her eyes flashed. "God. Men are so dumb."

"Purple flower." The big Texan frowned. "Isn't that the right password?"

"Yes, of course it's the correct password, but watching you handle the Captain was all I needed to know what side you're on." Kate sighed and pointed with her good hand. "*That's* Will Giles, next to Harry on the floor. I think they killed him.

"Why do men have to be heroes? Dr. Giles walked in here alone and unarmed to save me. He's a scientist, not a fighter. I thought he had better sense."

The Texan rushed over to Will, knelt down, and gently examined his injuries. "He's still alive, ma'am." He didn't sound optimistic. "I'd prefer not to move him unless we can get a stretcher and straps to keep him motionless. We need a medevac."

"I agree." Kate looked hesitantly at the bodies and blood on the floor. "This is going to be hard to explain."

The big man was studying the line of bullet holes stitched up the wall behind the desk with professional interest. "Did Dr. Giles do that?"

"He sure did. Sent the sergeant to hell and just missed Tanaka."

The Texan looked impressed. "Didn't do the paneling any good."

"I don't think we should call 911," Kate said. There was a question in her voice.

"No, ma'am," the Texan said. "There are four more bodies outside, but help is coming."

Fugitives can't call the police, Kate thought. "Does your help include a local doctor?"

"No, ma'am. But I've got transport and a damned good EMT."

"I know some people I can trust. We need to get Will to a doctor." *I could use one myself*, she thought.

The Texan frowned and shook his head. "I need to get you and him out of here, ma'am."

Her response was an irritated look. "Why are men so damned inflexible?"

The big man blinked.

"I assume you have orders to make sure nothing of value is left here for little bastards like him?" She glanced at Tanaka.

"Pretty much, ma'am."

"Well, to hell with your stupid orders. The situation has changed and so have your priorities. We'll get around to that, but right now saving Will's life is more urgent."

Her glare clearly indicted she would tolerate no argument. "Do you understand me, young man?" she snapped.

"Yes, ma'am. Like I said, I've already got help on the way with EMT transport. It's best we not try to move him until they arrive. We can have your doctor examine him if you wish, but we need to get him out of harm's way pronto. Oregon isn't safe. This is a kill zone."

"We agree about that, young man. Who are you? And who sent you?"

"Name's Reggie, ma'am, Reggie Metzger. Most folks just call me Rex. I work with some friends of Dr. Giles. They sent me to help." He looked down at the limp form with respect. "He seems to have a whole passel of friends."

Kate was rubbing her arms, trying to get the circulation back. She noticed the shiny object, a steel disk with points, was embedded in the wall behind where the Texan was standing.

He noted her glance. "Don't touch it, ma'am. It's a throwing star, a nasty weapon. They call 'em *shuriken*. Razor sharp edges. Sometimes they coat 'em with poison. The little Captain was real quick. He's bout quick as I've seen."

Kate was getting her strength back. She looked down at Tanaka's body. "Not any more, he's not. Now he's just real dead. And the sadistic little bastard deserved it."

"Do you think you can walk?"

"Damn right I can. If you'll help me up."

One huge hand took her arm and gently lifted her to her feet.

"I know a doctor we can trust."

"Yes, ma'am. What about the rest of it?"

"I made sure the paper records were shredded myself. I think the engineers already attended to the computers." Kate sighed. "They were gleefully deleting files and wiping disks when we closed down. They trashed mine so bad it doesn't work at all."

She looked at the big Texan. "But you're right. Your orders still apply. There are too many stories of security breaches even after experts have supposedly taken all the proper steps to prevent it. I'm going to personally make sure nothing is left here. *Nothing*."

"Yes, ma'am. I've got some C4."

"We can do better than that, Reggie." She paused and then spoke more softly. "Would you please get me some water? There's a drinking fountain in the hall."

The big Texan released her arm, grinned, and stepped back. "Yes, ma'am." He hesitated, watching her closely, a gentle look of concern clouding his rugged face.

Kate waved him toward the door. "You go ahead, now. I'm all right, thanks to you."

She knelt down next to Will and touched him gently with her good hand. His skin was cold. The pulse in his neck was very weak.

You were going to trade yourself for me, you silly, hopeless, lovable man, she thought. *Hang on. We'll get you to a Doctor. Just hang on.* She said it aloud, with firmness, "Hang on."

"I'll be right back, ma'am." The Texan was still watching her. "Are you sure you're okay?"

She smiled confidently and nodded, mostly to show him she wouldn't fall over. "On second thought, help me over to the desk. I need to use the phone."

The Texan did as requested, carefully avoiding the blood and bodies on the floor.

"The desk outside the door was mine. You'll find cans of gasoline in my cabinet. The key is in the center desk drawer. I'll show you how to disable the sprinklers and alarms.

"I have four boxes of dynamite stashed out in the shop. It's in the cabinet labeled 'cleaning supplies.' There's a gurney at the first aid station out there. Bring the med kit too. I'll need you to bandage my hand and give me some painkillers. It hurts like hell."

"Yes, ma'am."

The big Texan was shaking his head in wonder as he left to fetch the water. *Damn, she reminds me of Mom,* he thought.

BOOK THREE:
AFTERMATH

"In this snug over-safe corner of the world ... we may realize that our comfortable routine is no eternal necessity for things, but merely a little space of calm in the tempestuous untamed streaming of the world, and in order that we may be ready for danger. Out of heroism grows faith in the worth of heroism."

Oliver Wendell Holmes Jr.
Memorial Day 1895
(A veteran of Antietam and other Civil War battles)

CHAPTER TEN

RUSSELL SENATE OFFICE BUILDING, WASHINGTON DC

The office door burst open. "You have to see this. *Muy pronto.*"

Senator George Margolin looked up from his paperwork. Ernie's face was flushed, and he was out of breath.

Margolin raised an eyebrow. His chief of staff's accent was more pronounced when he was upset. *Yoo 'ave two cee theeese.*

"Relax or you'll bust a blood vessel, Ernie." The Senator smiled and spoke mildly to blunt any implied criticism. "This isn't a good time. I need to leave for a meeting."

"This is more important." Ernie was carrying a large envelope and waving a stack of videodisks. He set them on the desk, pulled out a handkerchief and mopped sweat from his swarthy face.

"My committee is meeting about military appropriations."

"Tell 'em you'll be late. Please. I need to brief you. There are big things happening."

The senator frowned and buzzed his secretary. "Grace, something's come up. Call Bill Simmons. Say I'll be late and ask him to please start the meeting without me. Apologize and say I'll explain later. Hold my calls and buzz me in fifteen minutes."

"Yes, Sir."

"I'm never late to those meetings. Please be quick."

The words spilled out rapid fire. "Japanese troops, Peace Enforcers. They just raided a technology plant in Oregon. Remember Cybertech? It was in the news a month or so back."

The Senator waved him into a chair and waited a moment for him to recover. He wrinkled his brow, pondering, and then spoke slowly. "I remember a flap in the media, but didn't pay it much attention. The CEO was a scientist, as I recall? A professor? Harney's State Department nailed him for something?

Ernie nodded. "Dr. William Giles. It was Commerce and the drug people that bitched. Their grievances were over the sale and export of unapproved security products. Cybertech makes encryption gear even the National Security Agency can't break."

"I'm familiar with their products. Has he broken any laws?"

"Unlikely, Senator. Giles is a bloody Boy Scout. Squeaky-clean. I have our legal staff checking, but Alex says this has come up before. There's never been proof Giles or his firm ever broke the law. Most of Cybertech's sales are here in the states, and the rest were approved.

Alex doubts the government has a case. Says no charges have been filed. He thinks it's just harassment."

"People have been arguing about freedom versus safety since before we were a nation. It's a damned fine line, Ernie."

"Yes, Sir."

"Edmund Burke said, 'The people are the masters.' He also said, 'Liberty too, must be limited in order to be possessed.' That was back in the 1700s, and it's gotten more confusing since then. What makes this worth being late to my meeting?"

Ernie took a deep breath, trying to regain his composure, frantic to explain. "Loss of sovereignty, murder of our citizens, and attempted theft. An act of war. Maybe treason." His words spilled out, rapid fire.

"Jesus, Ernie. Slow down. You have my attention. What happened now?"

"There was a small war out in Oregon, Senator. Peace Enforcers broke into Cybertech and killed the guard who was on duty. There are allegations of torture. Their goal, reportedly, was the theft of U.S. technology."

Margolin shook his head. "Serious charges if true, but difficult to prove. Peace Enforcers have been accused of assaults before. Harney's justice department won't do anything. It's probably a waste of time, Ernie."

"The Peace Enforcers are dead."

"What?"

"Six of their finest, led by Captain Tanaka himself. Deader than day-old mackerel."

"Good God, Tanaka will take revenge for that. You know his reputation. He likes to hurt people. It's just the excuse they've been looking for to expand their power."

"Tanaka won't do anything. He took four nine-millimeter slugs in the chest. Tightly grouped. Unusual ballistics, they said."

"That should have done the job."

Ernie's breathing was almost back to normal. "I think a sucking chest wound would discourage even a *muy macho hombre*, but someone apparently didn't think four bullets were enough. Finished him off with a head shot.

"There's more. Remember the recent news about those Peace Enforcer copters that went down in the mountains?"

"Advanced weapons, better than our troops have...."

Ernie nodded. "It was in Oregon, where Cybertech just happens to be located. I don't believe in coincidences. They're calling it a 'training accident.' We're still trying to get people in to investigate."

Margolin frowned. *Why would the Japanese deploy a heavily armed military force in a wilderness area?* It seemed needlessly aggressive. *Are these events related to Harney's new trade treaty?*

"There's more, Senator. The Japanese had *another* disaster. An armored column of Peace Enforcers was wiped out at about the time of the Cybertech incident. Details are unclear. Not a clue who did it."

"Where?"

"Also in Oregon. In Portland, their largest city. The state's population isn't large, but 80% live in the greater Portland area. Cybertech is in a small town near there."

"Were there any civilian casualties?"

"Some at the Cybertech plant. Those are the only ones reported."

"And we have no idea what the hell the Peace Enforcers were doing? Or what happened?"

"No, Sir. Not yet."

"I assume the explanation for the incident last week in the mountains is implausible."

Ernie nodded. "The PEs had no legitimate business there."

"I'll ask my sources to look into these 'training accidents.' Perhaps it's time the Senate asked Harney to explain why he allows unsupervised foreign military operations on our soil."

"Good idea," Ernie said.

"For now, let's stick to the events at Cybertech. What do you think happened?"

"A foreign assault on our citizens and private property, made by PEs acting under UN charter, sanctioned by President Harney, and led by Tanaka."

"Maybe." Margolin rubbed his nose absently. He did that when he was thinking. Broken when he was a POW and left untreated, it had never healed properly. "What exactly does 'unusual ballistics' mean?"

"You can cover the holes in Tanaka's chest with a playing card. The impact tracks of the two spaced the widest were at a slight upward angle. The other wounds had a very steep downward slant. Like he was shot from above."

"Is there an explanation?"

"Not so much an explanation as an argument. The Peace Enforcers say Tanaka was assassinated. They say that he and his men were ambushed and 'Gunned down in cold blood.' Oregon officials have a different story. They note Tanaka's violent history and say he was 'obviously' shot in self-defense."

"It there evidence to support Oregon's view?"

"Some. The ballistics proves that at least two of the four shots came from the same gun. They have crime scene photos and a statement from a witness. Local CSI experts did an autopsy and took measurements from the Oregon photos to reconstruct what happened.

"The photos show two bullet holes and blood spray on a wall about 15 or 20 feet from Tanaka's body, but about a foot lower than he would have stood."

"Blood spray," Margolin said. "Did they get a match?"

"I'll get to that. Stick with me about the photos. The holes are at about the right level if Tanaka was shot while crouching to spring. The CSIs think the first shots were rushed, snapped from hip level. If so, that's good shooting, but it's not the weird part."

The Senator gestured impatiently. "Ernie, I don't have a lot of time."

"The other two wounds, those with the downward slant, were within a centimeter of each other. The CSIs say those shots were fired at very close range.

"They timed Tanaka's moves from videos of his matches. I've viewed the clips. The man was *unbelievably* quick. I'm told he could spring the distance from the wall with the bullet holes to where his body was photographed in something under three-tenths of a second."

"So? What's your point?"

"If you buy the Oregon theory, Tanaka was attacking someone. His intended victim hit him twice in the chest as he leapt. The shooter was cool enough to stand fast, take aim, and nail him twice more in midair. That's four bull's-eyes in maybe a quarter of a second. Any one of the slugs would have killed Tanaka."

"Could a single shooter do that?"

"Barely. Oregon CSIs say yes. Peace Enforcers say no."

"What do *you* think?"

"I don't know, Senator. I talked with the FBI's top weapons instructor in handguns. He said he knows a few people who can shoot like that on a target range. But after we watched clips of Tanaka's matches, he shook his head and admitted it wasn't likely in combat." Ernie shrugged. "Maybe something slowed Tanaka down."

"Anything else?"

"The shooter was a scary thinker and very weapons savvy. Two slugs – the first two, if you buy the Oregon theory – made neat little round holes, front and back. One nicked a rib and it didn't deflect the bullet at all. The CSI people think these were armor piercing rounds. They know they were coated with Teflon, because traces were found on Tanaka's rib bone. Such ammo is used to penetrate bulletproof vests.

"The last two slugs were CORBON DPX. These are specialty bullets, made only in America, and extremely lethal. They are designed to penetrate, expand, stay inside what they hits, and tear it up. They ripped Tanka's heart and lungs apart. He would have bled out in seconds. Like I said, Senator, the shooter was scary."

"Tanaka deserves scary, Ernie. He was a cold-blooded killer." The Senator frowned. "You're absolutely sure it was Tanaka? You've gotten a positive ID?"

"Yes, Sir. I've got the photos." He waved the disk. "And I have testimony from witnesses who saw the body. They did fingerprint and DNA matches as well. We even have Tanaka's photo ID card. That part checks out."

"Well done, Ernie."

"I also have statements from two Oregon officials and from the woman the Peace Enforcers were allegedly torturing, a Katherine Chambers, sixty-two years old. She said Tanaka killed Cybertech's head of security and was going to kill her too. She said Tanaka was killed in self-defense."

"What else?"

"A lot. The Chambers woman said she's fearful for her life. She gave a statement. Apparently she rang up the Oregon State labor commissioner in the middle of the night. They are close friends. His name is Mike Fahey. He came right out to the plant along with an assistant DA from the State Attorney General's office to take her statement. I've got a film clip."

"Shot at the plant?" the Senator asked.

"Yes. She showed them the bodies of the Peace Enforcers, including Tanaka's. The DA took detailed photos to document the crime scene before it was disturbed. They're being used to reconstruct how Tanaka died."

"Is the woman available?" the Senator repeated. "We need to interview her."

"I'm getting to that. Things are a little confused out there."

Margolin glanced at his watch. "Go on."

"Something odd happened next. After Fahey and the DA took the woman's statement and evidence, they left the plant. They went off to have coffee and talk, and they didn't hurry. They conferred over what to do and discussed the jurisdictional issues."

Margolin sighed. "Did the DA make a statement?"

"Only that he claims jurisdiction for Oregon. By the time they got back to the plant, the police were already there, and the Chambers woman was gone."

"Someone else reported the dead Peace Enforcers?"

"No. The police were there because the plant was on fire. It's a total loss. The bodies, along with a small arsenal of weapons and other evidence, were neatly piled just inside the main gate. That's why no blood matches. Because of the fire, a normal crime scene investigation is impossible. Fahey and the DA have both given sworn statements testifying to the validity of their photos and videos."

"The fire was set?"

"Probably," Ernie said. "The Feds want to blame Chambers for it. They say they'll charge her with arson and murdering the Peace Enforcers. They tried to seize Fahey's evidence. He told them to go fuck themselves."

"He did what? He told Peace Enforcers to...."

"No, he said it to some guy from Treasury, ATF to be precise, who claimed to be in charge. The Peace Enforcers are a bit thin on the ground there right now. They've taken a number of casualties."

Margolin blinked. "What else?"

"Fahey got hostile when the ATF guy wanted to press charges against the Chambers woman. Weapons were cocked. One of the local TV stations taped it. I have a copy." Ernie smiled. "It was quite a scene."

"Has this been shown on the public news?"

"Not yet. There's a restraining order. Both the State and the Feds have asked for various court orders relating to jurisdiction and evidence. The media is screaming about freedom of the press. It promises to be a busy time for lawyers in Oregon."

"Summarize, please." Margolin looked at his Rolex. "Where do we stand now?"

"The news is on it. The Peace Enforcers and Feds want to blame the Chambers woman for everything. The locals want to blame the Peace Enforcers. There's been no explanation of what the Peace Enforcers were doing there."

"Has anyone been charged with a crime?" the Senator asked.

"Last I checked, no. It was a pretty confused situation. It got worse when a busload of women pulled up in the middle of the standoff, some fringe group of feminists called WOW. They had signs saying, 'Burn Cybertech,' with them."

"Why?"

"I'm damned if I know. They wanted to protest something, apparently. Whatever it was, they apparently changed their minds."

"Did they set the fire?"

"No one's accused them. There was a young kid on the bus who had ID as a Cybertech guard. He'd intercepted them before they got there. One of the WOW women claimed the kid harassed them. They got into a fight about that, on-camera no less."

"The women and the police?"

"No, the WOW women amongst themselves, pushing, shoving, and screaming. There are some good shots of a starlet named Tonya Wild hanging all over the kid.

"Ms. Wild said, and I quote, 'Billy's cute and was just doing his job.' I don't know what the kid's story is. He didn't say much. I wouldn't have either." Ernie grinned. "She's a looker."

"You've got to be making this up," Margolin said in a bemused tone. "This WOW group was arrested, I assume?"

"No. They promised to leave so no charges were filed. The kid said they were lost when he found them, and they hadn't done a thing to harm anyone.

"The starlet, Tonya, said it was all a misunderstanding. She started giving autographs." Ernie shrugged. "Whatever WOW's intentions, they'd apparently not done any harm."

"No harm, no foul?"

"My guess is there was too much else going on, and neither the police nor the DA want to spend time on a bunch of wacko broads. I think the WOW episode is just a sideshow. Probably unrelated. Oregon has a reputation for weird shit like that."

"Check it out anyway. I assume the Feds put this Fahey guy in jail? For obstructing justice, tampering with evidence, or something?"

"Actually, no." Ernie grinned. "Fahey and the DA must have done more than drink coffee. By the time he got back to the plant, he had backup – a dozen state cops and several squads of National Guard troops, none of whom came from Portland, incidentally. If the Feds want jurisdiction, they're going to have to fight it out in court."

Margolin shook his head in disbelief. "What's happening now?"

"They have road blocks up all over the state. The police are looking for the Chambers woman. Peace Enforcers are flying in to quote 'provide assistance' unquote."

"So Harney now has another bunch of alleged troublemakers, this time the government of Oregon, to crush in the name of national security and international harmony?"

"I don't know, Senator. Maybe, but if this is something Harney planned, it's gone wrong, and in a big way. There's something else odd about this. Tanaka and his men had letters of authorization for the operation with them."

"That's their normal procedure."

"Not exactly, Sir. Tanaka's orders were signed by Ito Kobayashi."

"The liaison to the White House?"

"The same. Technically he's Japan's Deputy Ambassador for Trade. He is not, however, anywhere in the Peace Enforcer chain of command. His employment history is ministry of trade. His background is technology policy. There's more. Tanaka also had letters of authorization signed by President Harney. I have a copy." Ernie tapped the envelope.

Margolin blinked. "You're sure? Signed copies?"

"It looks like Harney's signature to me. It's on White House letterhead. Fahey says it's Harney's signature. He has the original. He offered to let me see it, but won't let it out of his possession. That's why Oregon demands jurisdiction. 'To prevent the real or apparent possibility of foreign influence,' Fahey said."

"Get the best experts available and check it out. Select people you can trust. Be certain they keep their mouths shut. I need at least two credible independent opinions, and I want you to handle it personally."

"Yes, Sir."

The Senator ran a hand through his hair and looked thoughtful. "This is moving too fast. We need to get out ahead of it. Let's get back to the Oregon situation. Tell me more about the woman...."

"Katherine Chambers. She's Dr. Giles secretary at Cybertech."

"What's she charged with?"

"I don't think she's actually been charged with anything. The ATF guy wanted to charge her with murder and arson, but Oregon blocked it by claiming jurisdiction. There's an APB out to detain her, but for her own protection."

"What did Fahey say about that?"

"He says the Peace Enforcers are hunting her. He called them 'a bunch of Jack-booted jerk-offs.' I'll give you the **Readers Digest** version. Fahey says he went to high school and college with Kate—he calls her Kate—and that she's 'good people.' He says the notion of a woman her age taking out an armed squad of Tanaka's killers is nonsense."

"What's the official Oregon position?"

"I'm not sure. It turns out Fahey is pretty tight with the governor. She ordered National Guard troops out to protect him and made a public statement this morning."

"What did she say?" the Senator asked.

"She's demanding an explanation of what the Peace Enforcers were doing at the plant, which was closed and locked. She urges Mrs. Chambers to turn herself in to Oregon authorities and promises to guarantee her safety. She wants Chamber's torture accusations investigated. By the way, the governor is a well-respected member of Harney's own political party."

Margolin nodded. He knew that. "What's the White House say?"

"No comment," Ernie said. "That's the official position."

Senator Margolin glanced again at his watch. "I have to go, Ernie. This is now our top priority. Think about how we can help the Oregon Governor on this one. Put whatever you need and whomever you need on it. I'll be back by eighteen hundred hours.

"Oh, and get copies of everything made for our special team. Draft a cover note from me to inform them. I want a meeting in the morning to discuss this and brainstorm. Tell Grace I said to drop everything. She'll know what to do."

"Yes, Sir."

On cue, the Senator's buzzer sounded. He thanked Ernie and left, waving over his shoulder as he rushed out the door.

Siskiyou Mountains

The soft rain had resumed, and fog was starting to form. Becky eased the battered Ford van with Washington plates off the dirt road, being careful to get it out of sight under the trees without getting stuck. Until the last vehicle switch, a sequence of others had done the driving while she tended her patient, but now she was alone.

She closed her eyes and rested her head on the steering wheel, but dared not go to sleep. She straightened, took a few sips of water, splashed some on her face, and crawled into the back of the van. Will was unconscious and breathing shallowly, but the monitor showed no deterioration in his vital signs. Taking care to follow the procedures she'd been shown, she changed the bottle on his I-V drip.

The doctor said Will should be in a hospital, but that wasn't an option. Becky just hoped her amateur care and being bounced along the rutted back roads wouldn't do him more harm.

She checked her maps and navigation unit again, and looked around. This was the right place, but no one was here to meet her. *God, I hope there hasn't been a screw up*, she thought. *There's supposed to be a doctor here. He needs a real doctor, a good one.*

She leaned over, adjusted the oxygen cannula, and checked the flow. "Help is coming. Don't you *dare* die on me." She gently took his hand, careful not to bump the splints on his arms.

She was thinking about how he'd sent her to safety and went in alone and unarmed against Tanaka's killers. "You're a wonderful man," she said.

She impulsively kissed him and was astonished when his eyes flicked open. His gaze was unfocused for a moment, but then he saw her and smiled.

"Would you do that again?" His voice was weak.

She started sobbing, nodded, and did. "Don't try to talk. Help is coming."

He relaxed and his eyes closed. "Okay, whatever you say…"

"I'm getting you to a doctor. We're going to somewhere safe." She did her best to sound reassuring, but a small still voice in the back of her mind said, *I hope.*

He gave her hand a squeeze. She could feel the gentle pressure and responded. She carefully arranged some cushions and dragged a blanket over herself so she wouldn't have to move. She was afraid if she let go, he'd somehow lose his lifeline.

After a time the pressure relaxed and his breathing softened. He seemed to be sleeping normally.

At least she hoped so. She sat for a long time, holding his hand, careful not to disturb him. She dozed off wondering if he'd heard her first words. Outside, the rain continued. It seemed to be picking up.

When Becky woke up a black man was standing over Will, checking the monitors. She gasped, then blinked and beamed her recognition. He was one of their transportation specialists. She couldn't recall his name. Something ethnic.

"I've had med training. He seems stable. Are you okay?"

She nodded. "I'm sorry, but I can't remember your name. Is he going to be all right?"

He grinned. "Smith. Kunta Smith." The grin faded. "Why don't you clean up and have some coffee. I'll brief you then. We have a little time."

She noticed he'd not answered her question. *Either he doesn't know, or he's not hopeful.* "Just tell me what's next," she said, rubbing her eyes.

"I'll take you to an aircraft, a jet. You got out of Oregon just in time. They have roadblocks up and are stopping everything. That's why I'm late. The search hasn't moved this far south, though, so we should be fine.

"We need to get you out of the country tonight. They're going to lock down the borders tomorrow morning."

Becky frowned and shook her head. "We're already out of Oregon."

"Barely, and none too soon. Closed them just after I got through. Tomorrow, they seal off the adjacent states and national borders. You started a major shit storm, lady. Cybertech's all over the news. There's a manhunt on."

"A manhunt?"

"Not for you or Dr. Giles. They're looking for a woman named Chambers."

"Dr. Giles' administrative assistant. She's injured and should be in a hospital herself. Why are they after her?"

Kunta shrugged. "No idea."

She was glad she'd sent Kate with Rex. "They're not looking for Will and me?"

"Don't think so." Kunta shook his head. "You're not on their radar, so far as we know, but if they close the borders, you'll be stuck here. Need to keep moving."

"If there's a big hunt on, why are they waiting to close the borders?"

"Inertia." He grinned. "Flow. Got to go with the flow, lady."

Becky shook her head.

Kunta's grin got wider. "Drugs. We need to ride the tide."

"I don't understand."

"Everything legal gets inspected. Drugs don't. That's the quick way out."

"What are you talking about?"

"Safe transport. Go with the flow. Ride the tide. You best come in with the illegal immigrants and drugs, and go out on the deadhead runs. Drug transport is quicker 'cause the payload's worth big bucks, so I use those routes for my urgent shipments. Costs more, but worth every penny."

Becky recalled they'd once gotten her across the border in the back of a truck packed with farm laborers. It took forever. Probably that was what had delayed Rex.

She shook her head. "If they're hunting someone important, why don't they just cut the flow off and seal the borders? That should take about five minutes."

"Not how it works." Kunta shook his head. "Drug trade depends on moving a lot of product daily. Tons. Be total chaos if it got suddenly shut down. People lose their jobs. Economy goes down the toilet. Can't have that."

Becky felt like screaming. This man knew what he was doing, but she was more interested in getting Will to safety than discussing stupid social policies. The drug war's notion of defending people from themselves despite the cost and consequences never made sense to her.

"Safest way for hot cargo." Kunta chucked. "Trust me. Economics 101."

She recalled Kunta had an MBA. "What do you mean?"

"It's like prohibition back in the 1920s, only bigger, turbocharged, jet propelled, and on steroids. Illegal drugs be the biggest industry, and fighting drugs is the biggest piece of the budget. Politicians know they gotta be smart when they mess with the flow. We talking 'bout capitalism and global trade here. Lotta folks feed at that trough."

"That's crazy."

"Crazy world, but I don't make the rules. The tide's leaving. Your man here has gotta ride the tide or get stranded. Tomorrow's too late."

"We could kill Dr. Giles if we jostle him too much," Becky said. "The doctor was concerned about his injuries."

"I got him a good ride, fast and smooth. I got us an airplane with emergency medical facilities and a trauma doctor." He glanced at his watch. "It'll be landing in about two hours."

"Okay." She sighed. "Let me clean up. I'll take some coffee if you have any."

Japanese Embassy, Washington DC

The ambassador looked at his visitor. "You need not sit down, Mr. Kobayashi. I'll be brief."

Ito stiffened, trying to keep his face impassive. The American form of address was almost an insult. Skipping the pleasantries to start a meeting certainly was. In twenty years of government service, he'd never been snubbed this way. "Mr. Ambassador, what's the problem?"

"Do you recall my saying 'Don't make me ask you questions?' You neglected to tell me a few things."

"Sir?"

"You didn't mention anything about hiring American mercenaries to kill U.S. citizens."

"What? No, Sir, I...." The Ambassador silenced him with a gesture.

"My secretary will give you a videodisk when you leave. The photos and news clips may interest you. Captain Tanaka was using Americans to augment his force. Some were killed in the mountains."

"Yes, Sir. The accident. Some of our own men were killed...." Another gesture.

"There are angry relatives. One of the Americans had a brother whom he called just before they left on the mission. The brother gave an interview to an Oregon news station. He said four augmented squads were assigned to hunt down and kill an American businessman, William Giles. As you know, Dr. Giles owned Cybertech...."

Kobayashi was horrified. "Sir, I gave no orders to kill Giles...."

Another gesture.

"Don't interrupt me again. The Americans hated Captain Tanaka, and Dr. Giles has vanished. His neighbors haven't seen him for weeks. His car was found in the Peace Enforcer barracks' parking lot in Portland. Don't you think that's a rather odd place to find his vehicle?" Kumakura's tone was caustic.

"Yes, Sir." Kobayashi cringed as if struck.

"The highest-ranking survivor from Tanaka's foray into the mountains, a lieutenant, says Tanaka intended to kill the American. The rest say it's possible he did, but that they don't know what was in his mind. What do you say?"

"Captain Tanaka's mission in the mountains was a training exercise. He was only following the American, Sir."

"The governor of Oregon, a troublesome woman, had autopsies conducted. She says martial arts blows killed Cybertech's security chief. She notes Captain Tanaka and his men held black belts, and she highlights the coincidence."

"Yes, Sir."

"Do you think our PEs would have killed without direct orders from Tanaka?"

"I don't know, Sir."

"Was Captain Tanaka ordered to kill any Americans, Mr. Kobayashi?"

"Not specifically, Sir. But...."

A gesture. "But he probably did," Kumakura said with a sigh.

"I don't know, Sir. I don't think...." Kobayashi stopped for a long moment, and then bowed respectfully. "I'm sorry, Kumakura-san. Yes, Mr. Ambassador, it's possible."

"Can you explain the events in Portland itself? And at Cybertech? We've suffered many casualties."

"We don't know yet, Sir. There were no survivors from either of those incidents."

Kumakura gave a deep sigh and shut his eyes for a time. Finally he looked up at his subordinate.

"I've called off the search for Dr. Giles. The Peace Enforcers and Americans think he's dead. I'm inclined to agree, and I don't care about him in any case. My job is to de-escalate this crisis before it turns into a disaster."

Kobayashi bowed again, signaling his respect, but said nothing.

"You're responsible, Kobayashi-san." *He had said Kobayashi-san.* Ito's heart leapt with hope. The ambassador used the respectful form.

"You're responsible, but you are not *bushido*." The ambassador spoke the word distinctly and precisely, making distinct pauses between the three *kanji* characters that composed it. *Bu* (military), *shi* (man), *do* (way). There was a pause as both men reflected on the deep meaning of *bushido*, centuries old.

From Zen, came stoicism, indifference to suffering, and scorn for the weak and even for death itself. From Shinto, came deep, religious love for country. Shinto held that each lake, rock, and mountain was infused with the national spirit. From Confucianism, came the social ethic of relationships, the debt owed by subject to king, by salaryman to corporate president, by Kobayashi to his ambassador, Kumakura.

Japan's trade warriors practiced *bushido*, but both knew it was a weaker, paler form of the true art. Kobayashi should not lead true warriors. Kobayashi bowed deeply. "I understand."

"You are hereby relieved of all Peace Enforcer duties."

Kobayashi bowed again. "Yes, Sir."

"Much is at risk. You have a special relationship with President Harney. I want you to get a meeting and calm him down. I'm offering you a chance to redeem yourself, unless you prefer to be relieved and sent back to Japan?"

Both men knew the purgatory of becoming a "window watcher." Being disgraced and left in place as an example for others was so much crueler than being fired. Both knew Kobayashi wouldn't be given a second chance. *Not now. Not ever.*

"Thank you, Mr. Ambassador."

Badly shaken, Ito left the office.

CHAPTER ELEVEN

UNKNOWN LOCATION, CHIAPAS HIGHLANDS, YUCATAN

The *Viracocha* turned off his viewing device and bowed his head. Tears were streaming down his cheeks as he prayed for wisdom and guidance.

He hardly knew what was right anymore. He'd trained all his life for the vocation of *Viracocha*. His family on both sides had served the higher calling for generations. Right now, that training and tradition of service didn't help much. He was afraid.

Fear is the mind killer. He knew that, but this was his first assignment without a mentor. So much had gone wrong that pushing the fear away was hard.

He needed help from the council of elders, but it wasn't available. He was responsible for his decisions and actions, and mistakes were so horribly easy to make.

Fortunately, God had created people with free will instead of puppets, but the human tragedy was that some used their free will for evil. Watching Tanaka torture the helpless woman had shaken him, as had the violent aftermath.

He felt alone and inadequate. Powerful forces were gathering, and people were depending on him. *They never prepared me for this. I hope Rebecca hasn't overestimated Dr. Giles. We're running out of time.*

His feline companion sensed his discomfort. She was twitching her tail in alarm.

You're right, he thought. *I should concentrate on positive things, not dwell on the negative and fearful. Our attention shapes our intention.*

He stroked the animal until it calmed and started purring. Her luminous violet eyes studied him somberly, and he thought, not for the first time, how often cats had been linked to the Ancient cultures, to magicians, witchcraft, and telepathy.

Stay calm, little friend. Thank you for your comfort and help. We're safe for now.

There was so much anger, conflict, and distrust on the planet. It sometimes sucked him in and blurred his focus. His life's purpose was to be a civilizer, but during the bleak, dark moments, he wondered if he was making things worse.

His tiny band of followers was in mortal danger. Some were already running for their lives, killing to survive. His intention was peace and love, but he and his flock were being inexorably drawn into war and conflict. He was staring into the abyss, deep and dark.

Racial memories run deep. The same themes resurface in new contexts. People are dying. Is anything worth taking life?

"Yowl," the cat declared. Her eyes seemed to be looking through to his soul.

He met her gaze. "What are you trying to tell me?"

The words of his mentor came unbidden. *"Living well requires believing. To live fully, you must believe in something of such value it's worth giving your life.*

"Dare to believe. Dare to live. Dare to hope. That's how great things are done."

He thought for a time, watching the cat watch him, feeling faint stirrings of renewal and cleansing. Finally, he nodded. "Thank you, little friend."

The *Viracocha* stroked the cat gently. She made soft noises in her throat and squinted her eyes the way cats do when they're content. He took several deep breaths, closed his eyes, assumed the lotus position, and focused on his meditation. After a long time, he finally gathered his robes, stood, and went to join his followers.

The cat shadowed gracefully behind him, staying close.

Cathedral Hall, Unknown Location, Chiapas Highlands, Yucatan

The *Viracocha* waited serenely until he had their full attention, his hands together in prayer. When he spoke, he was glad his voice was calm. "One of us has killed. I'm deeply saddened."

His words echoed hollowly off the stone walls, falling into a long moment of silence. He looked around, meeting their eyes. A soft murmur spread through the crowd. Some blessed themselves, others looked fearful. Most just shook their heads in denial.

After some time, the bald American, the man who'd once been a Jesuit priest, spoke. "It was Rex Metzger, I presume?"

The *Viracocha* nodded slowly. *Of course he'd guess it was Rex.* The small band knew each other well. They'd been through much together.

"He's violent," the priest said.

"Reggie is a good man." An attractive young woman in a white dress jumped to her feet, demanding attention, her dark eyes fiery. "He wouldn't kill without a great need."

No one answered.

"He was acting to save lives."

The *Viracocha* smiled gently. "How do you know this, my child?"

"I'm no longer a child, *Viracocha*." She used the title as a term of respect, not obedience. She was learning. "I turned eighteen last month, and I *know* Reggie."

The priest scowled and started to say something, but halted at a gesture from the *Viracocha*.

"Did Reggie act to save lives?"

He nodded. "Yes."

"That's permitted. The priest has no right to condemn him."

The *Viracocha* spread his hands helplessly. She spoke truth.

"Reggie's done nothing wrong." She glared at the priest. "Some call him T-Rex as if he was a savage beast, but he's not an animal. He's a man, a good man, and he's needed for our troubled times.

"*Viracocha*, you have your own soldiers, your *huaminca*, to keep you safe, do you not? We need men like Reggie to protect us from those with evil intentions."

"What you say is true." The *Viracocha's* smile was tinged with deep sadness. "We may defend ourselves from human anger and violence just as we do from natural dangers. Still, how can you be sure what has happened far away?"

"I just *know*. I don't need your smoking mirror to see what happened, because I know Reggie's heart. He wouldn't kill without need."

"Rex has blood on his hands." The priest's voice was harsh. "He's killed many."

"To save lives," the girl said. "Reggie killed a whole squad of soldiers when the drug lords burned our village and raped me. He saved my life."

"Our doctors were worried for you, my child," the *Viracocha* said softly.

The girl had been badly beaten and was suffering dizzy spells when she'd first arrived. Her body recovered in a few days, but it took longer for her mind to heal.

The girl approached the *Viracocha* and took his hand, still glaring at the priest. She was starting to cry, but brushed the tears away, shaking her head with irritation.

"Their leader was a big man with bad breath and yellow teeth. A beast."

"He was the one who raped you in the village?"

"Yes. It caused his death. Reggie burst through the door and pulled him off me. He threw the man against the wall like a dead rat."

"You've never told me, child." *But I knew. It was obvious. I just never thought about it. I must be losing my spirituality. I need more time to meditate.*

The girl had a distant look. "When the big man drew a knife, Reggie dropped his gun and gestured him forward. He was smiling, taunting him, begging the man to attack."

"What happened?"

"It's like I told you. The man died."

"Rex removed the man's genitals with his own knife, *Viracocha*," the priest said. "It had to be terrifying to a young girl."

"You blame the wrong person, Priest." A woman's voice came from the middle of the crowd. "My daughter was sixteen at the time. She's alive and well because of Reggie.

"The doctors said watching justice done and knowing she was safe helped her. She knew that evil man could never threaten her again."

The crowd parted. A small woman in a brightly colored shawl made her way to her daughter and stood by her side, putting an arm around her, glaring up at the priest. "There are twelve of us here from my village. We all owe our lives to Reggie."

"It was a terrible thing for anyone to watch, much less a young girl," the priest said. "An unspeakably barbaric act."

"You weren't there," the woman said. "You don't know anything."

"Did Reggie frighten you?" asked the *Viracocha*.

"A little," the girl said. "I was afraid the man would kill him and then me. The man cut Reggie's arm. He still has a scar. I begged him to never take such chances again."

"He saved me too," a tall woman in the back said.

"And me, and many others," an old man with a bad arm said.

"Reggie just now put his own life at risk to save people, didn't he?" The girl's face was shining. "He used violence to stop violence, to prevent harm, to save someone. Isn't that what we're talking about?"

The *Viracocha* said, "He saved an old woman, a colleague of the man we seek, who was being tortured by the Peace Enforcers."

"Did he complete his mission?" the priest asked.

"He may have saved Dr. Giles as well, but he's badly wounded."

The *Viracocha* paused and studied the faces of his followers, trying to sense their thoughts. The girl was watching him intently, hands on her hips. Her eyes challenged him.

"Reggie killed to save lives," she said firmly. "That's permitted."

"It is," the *Viracocha* said. His gaze was infinitely sad as he turned to the priest. "Reggie's done no wrong. He's your brother. You must treat him with respect."

The priest lowered his eyes. "Yes, *Viracocha*."

"Is he safe?" the girl asked.

"Reggie and Rebecca are running for safety, but there is much confusion."

"Is he safe?"

"He's in no immediate danger," the *Viracocha* said, "but Reggie terminated the lives of some Peace Enforcers. One was the notorious Captain Tanaka."

There were gasps. The priest blessed himself.

"The Peace Enforcers now hunt the old woman Reggie saved. They blame her for Tanaka's death."

"They won't let that pass," the priest said. His tone was ominous.

A murmur ran through the crowd. He could smell the fear, but the *Viracocha* was watching the girl. She was smiling, unafraid, a serene look on her face.

"Reggie stayed to help the woman and keep her safe, didn't he?"

The *Viracocha* nodded. "How do you know?"

"I know his heart," she said softly. "We must bring the woman here."

"We can't..." The priest shook his head and started to raise a hand in protest, but the girl interrupted.

"We must bring them to safety." She pinned the *Viracocha* with her eyes. "This is a place of safety for those who seek us out. 'No matter who you are, no matter where you are on your journey of life, you are welcome here.' That's what you preach. You offer us sanctuary."

The *Viracocha* smiled, drawing strength from her words. "Our way is love, not fear. The woman is welcome here. So is Dr. Giles."

She turned on the priest. "Do you criticize your brother for saving an old woman from Tanaka's tortures? For defending his own life? For freeing a man who may save us? Would you turn away a woman who needs our help? If so, you should be ashamed."

He fell back before her words, holding up his hands in surrender. The group watched in silence.

Finally the priest shook his head. "Carmelita, Rex and I see different truths, but we both try to do God's will as best we can. Rex is strong. We need his strength to protect us from men with dark souls, from devils like Tanaka."

"What are you saying, Priest?"

"That I'm sorry. I abhor violence and I'm still afraid, but I apologize for what I said."

Slowly, the girl relaxed. She didn't speak, but nodded to accept the priest's apology.

The *Viracocha* sighed. *God's universe is beautiful and bountiful, but often it requires difficult choices.* "We'll offer the woman sanctuary if she can get here, but they're in great danger. The nets close swiftly."

The cat made a soft sound. She blinked, looked satisfied, and started grooming herself.

"Do we have a plan to get them back?" the priest asked.

More like a desperate hope, the *Viracocha* thought. "We will bring Dr. Giles to safety. We will need his help if we are to prevail, or even survive."

"What of my man?" demanded the girl.

"Our resources are fully committed to getting Rebecca and Dr. Giles to safety for now. We've sent an aircraft and medical assistance. Dr. Giles is badly wounded and near death.

"Reggie and the woman must rely on their own abilities." The *Viracocha* couldn't meet her eyes. "We'll send them help as soon as we can."

The priest said, "May God save us all."

Siskiyou Mountains

There was still a spark of life. Becky and Kunta had moved Will's stretcher and support equipment into Kunta's Jeep. He'd lapsed into unconsciousness again, but at least they'd managed the transfer without ripping loose the links to the medical devices that were keeping him alive.

Shifting the power connections from the van to the big jeep was tricky, but Kunta seemed to know what he was doing. Becky was exhausted by the time they were done. Between the cold rain and her own perspiration, she was soaked. Her waterproof jacket only seemed to make things worse and she was glad to let Kunta drive.

"We gonna be there soon. With this rig I be the baddest, blackest redneck in the whole mo fo forest."

Kunta was obviously trying to cheer her up, but she didn't answer. She didn't feel like chitchat. If they couldn't get Will to help soon, he was going to die.

The doctor at the hospital where she'd met Rex and Kate had run tests. Kate insisted he treat Will first. The doctor was able to stabilize Will, but afraid to do more. He said specialists were needed.

They'd decided Kate and Rex would lead any pursuit east into the mountains, while Becky took Will south, hopefully to safety. She smiled grimly at the memory.

Kate was in pain, but she was more worried about Will. She hugged me and insisted the doctor make sure the bandages on her hand allowed her to hold a weapon. She calls Rex "Reggie," and they're becoming friends. I hope I'm that feisty when I'm her age.

Kunta concentrated on his driving. Becky sat next to him, belted in tight, with Will's medical records in a packet on her lap. The jeep struggled up the steep and narrow trails, branches slapping at the fenders, its engine growling at the challenge.

The rain was intense again, coming down in sheets the wipers had no chance of clearing. Vision was limited. At times they were axle deep in mud, but Kunta somehow kept the vehicle moving.

Mostly they didn't speak. Her whole body ached. She was thinking furiously about what she should do.

"Son of a bitch," Kunta muttered as the jeep lurched over a log, slewing wildly. They teetered on two wheels. For a moment she was hanging from her seat belt expecting they'd roll, but he caught it somehow. They came crashing back down on their wheels with a jar that rattled her teeth.

Then they were sliding sideways with the engine roaring as Kunta fought the wheel and the big tires clawed for traction. Becky glimpsed a deep ravine through the globs of mud on her window and stifled a scream as they drifted towards the edge.

The tires grabbed and somehow Kunta regained control at the very edge of the rift. Then the gap was behind them. They had trees on both sides again, branches slapping the fenders.

She took a deep breath and waited for her heart to stop pounding, then looked back and checked that Will's stretcher was secure. Fortunately, they'd lashed everything down and the straps were holding. He seemed to be no worse. His medical monitors were still in the green.

"What kind of a road is this, anyway?" She pictured the jeep tumbling end over end down the mountain, but firmly forced those grim images from her mind. Antarctica prepared her for a lot, but this was scary. She didn't like feeling helpless.

Kunta grunted. "It's a son-of-a-bitching worthless mo fo bastard of a forest service road. They use it in the summers for fire watch." He was holding the wheel with both hands, his foot jammed hard on the accelerator as they lurched along.

They seemed to be gathering speed. That was frightening, but so was the alternative. She knew that if Kunta bogged down and got stuck, they'd miss their time window. If they missed the flight, Will would die.

All four tires were digging in and throwing streams of mud as the rig fishtailed back and forth across the trail. They'd slide to one side and start smashing through brush, but that ground was dryer. It was enough firmer that they gained traction and lurched back onto the trail. Then the cycle would repeat.

Becky was becoming mesmerized by the view out her mud-streaked window. *We're barely under control.*

She concentrated on keeping her mouth shut. *This is not a good time to distract him by screaming.* Once they did glance off a tree. She tasted blood and heard metal crumple, but somehow they kept moving.

"What time is it?"

At Kunta's words she unclenched her jaw and glanced down at her watch. "Almost two," she said, careful to speak calmly and distinctly.

"Gonna be okay. It's just over the top of this hill." They'd gained a little speed. The ground seemed to be getting firmer and the grade less steep.

They popped over the crest, and there it was, a dirt strip cut out of the trees. With firm ground under them, the jeep surged forward. Becky heaved a sigh of relief. There was a twin-engine airplane sitting at the far end of the strip, but it wasn't a jet. It had propellers. Two men were squatting under the wing, watching them approach.

Kunta carefully parked next to the hatch on the left rear of the aircraft. He opened his door as the men approached. "You made it," one said with relief in his voice.

I don't like jeeps. Becky was concentrating on regaining her composure before she had to say anything.

The first man, apparently the pilot, gave Kunta a high-five slap on the hand. "We got here early. Didn't dare try to get the Lear in here. Braking action sucks. The ground's slicker than whale shit." He jerked a thumb at the plane. "It's slower, but we have enough time and range to make the border."

"It's not a jet," Becky said dubiously.

"It's a turboprop, lady. Prop jet. It's better for this mission. It'll get the job done."

The man spoke confidently. She was glad someone was confident.

"I'm a doctor. How is he?" the second man asked. He sounded less confident.

"Bad," Kunta said flatly. "But still alive. She has his medical records. They took full scans. You can look at them while we're moving him into the plane."

Kunta and the pilot gently moved Will, still tightly strapped to a stretcher, to the airplane. They took great care not to jostle him or tear his tubes and sensors loose. The doctor climbed into Kunta's seat, and Becky handed him the packet of records.

"Should I be helping?"

He shook his head. "You'd just get in the way. Me too. Kunta and Tim know what they're doing, and we have life support equipment in the plane. How was the ride here?"

"Not good. The roads were terrible. I hope he's going to be okay."

The doctor frowned as he carefully studied the records and images, but didn't say anything. He turned on the dome light and held the scans up to see them better. His frown deepened. "Open your door, please. I need more light. I need to examine these."

She complied, and the doctor opened his door as well. The rain was letting up and the clouds were a lighter shade of gray. She didn't speak until the doctor was going through the records and images for the third time. "What do you think?"

"What do I *think*?" he asked, preoccupied, irritation showing in his voice.

"I want to know Dr. Giles's status. I need to make some decisions."

"You need to make some decisions? I don't know who you are, lady, but I'm responsible to my patient, not you."

"That *man* is Dr. William Giles, and he's probably the only one who can save us. That *man* is someone I care about a lot. Yes, he's your patient, but don't give me any crap, Doctor. Can you save him or not?"

The doctor blinked. "I'll do what I can." He reeled off some medical jargon that Becky didn't understand.

She felt like screaming, but forced herself to be calm. Finally she spoke, keeping the panic from her voice. "I don't understand what you're telling me. I've not had medical training and I need to know what his odds are. Can you tell me in plain English?"

The doctor took a deep breath and let it out slowly. "He's badly bruised, both arms are broken, and he has broken ribs and fluid in his lungs, but that's not what worries me. He also has internal injuries, he may have a concussion, and...."

"Plain English. What's his prognosis, Doctor?"

"He's dying."

"Oh," she said. It felt as if she'd been stabbed in the heart. *Don't ask the question if you can't stand the answer.*

"I'm sorry." The Doctor looked at her with compassion. "I do know who you are. I was briefed, but my attention was on the medical issues.

"It's not hopeful. There's been too much damage. I lack the skills and knowledge to save him."

"Surely there are procedures, transplants, and medications. There has to be a way."

The Doctor shrugged helplessly. "The *Viracocha* has access to a science beyond ours. I've seen some miracles, but I don't think this patient is up to the trip."

She looked at the doctor. "You need to do something."

"All I can do is make him comfortable and keep him on life support. I can't...."

"Don't tell me what you can't do, Doctor. Just tell me what you can do to help him," she asked softly. She tried to keep emotion or accusation from her voice and her tone gentle. She waited until the doctor met her eyes, and then added, *"Please."*

He averted his eyes and was quiet for a time. "I was an ER doctor, and a good one, at a major trauma center in LA. I did my residency at Johns Hopkins. We have intensive care equipment and a good nurse on that airplane, but....."

"Take him aboard," Becky ordered. "Stop talking, and take him aboard."

The doctor gave her a hard look.

"Now," she said softly. "If he dies, let it be on the way to safety, not out here."

"So be it." The doctor gave the signal to load his patient. "I've got him now."

The doctor put the medical records back in the envelope. He touched her compassionately on the shoulder and took his leave, taking the envelope with him.

Becky called after him, watching as they loaded him into the plane. "Thank you."

You'll do all you can. His care will be as good as if he were in a trauma center. Kunta came running back. "Get aboard. They are ready to go now."

"No."

He blinked and stared at her. "Say what?"

"There should have been a sealed pouch for me on the airplane," Becky said. "Did they give it to you?"

"Uh-huh." Kunta nodded, holding it out. "Said it's urgent."

"It is." She put the packet in her pocket unopened. "Send them off. I'm not going."

Kunta's eyes widened, the whites vivid against his dark skin. "You need to…."

"*No.* Damn it, get them the hell out of here," she snapped. "Every minute counts."

"Told me to get you to safety. To get your white ass on that airplane."

"Your instructions have just been changed. By me. I can't help Will medically, but I have a job to do."

Kunta stared at her for a long moment. "You 'da boss."

He rushed over to the airplane and stood at the hatch for a moment. He waved emphatically, and stood back as it slammed closed. Immediately, the right engine started and the propeller whined up to speed. Kunta walked slowly back to the jeep, got in, and backed it clear, to a position where the pilot could see them. By then, the left propeller was turning as well.

They got out and stood by the jeep in the rain, waiting, as the pilot went through his checklist, the engines now idling as the other systems came on line. She caught the glimpse of a wave from the cockpit. They waved back and the engines changed tone.

"He cycling the props now," Kunta said. "Cover you ears. Gonna get loud."

The engines gathered power. They roared as the plane leaned forward against its brakes. The pilot held it straining like that until the wheels started sliding. Then he released the brakes, letting the plane spring forward with its engines screaming at full power.

She could see branches on the trees behind the plane bending in the prop wash. A cloud of mud and spray trailed it down the runway. The instant it broke ground, the wheels started retracting. The plane turned steeply left to avoid the next hill. Climbing fast, it disappeared into the clouds.

They listened until the sound was gone and then Kunta turned to her. "They'll make it. Tim's good at that pilot shit."

"I hope so."

Kunta was looking at her, a question in his eyes.

"Thank you for getting us here safely."

He nodded.

"I need more of your help."

"Figured. Where we going?"

"Washington DC. Can you get me there?"

"Are you crazy, woman? Not looking for you yet, but they gonna be soon."

She looked at him.

"Bad idea. Belly of the beast. Hard to get you back out."

"That doesn't matter."

"It matters a lot if they catch your ass."

"I'm going. Are you with me or not?"

"You say so, I get you there." Kunta gave her a sharp look, then climbed into the jeep and started the engine. "But not out. Not gonna hang round that town. Not me."

"Fair enough. Just drop me off. I'll take full responsibility."

Becky was glad Kunta didn't ask any questions. She didn't feel like talking. She was wondering if she'd ever see Will again.

She'd been sent to rescue him, but he was dying and that was her fault. She'd let him go back to Cybertech and risk his life, when she knew her mission was to get him to safety.

CHAPTER TWELVE

SENATE FLOOR, CAPITOL BUILDING, WASHINGTON DC

Senator Margolin glanced up as his secretary crept into the chamber and sat down next to him, careful not to attract attention or interrupt his thoughts. They were debating his foreign military oversight bill. Despite dogged resistance and intense rhetoric from the White House, it had bipartisan support and seemed likely to pass.

He'd opened the session by saying, "Some say a Republic is a very bad form of government, but it's better than anything else that's been tried. I'm going to make sure ours keeps working if we have to sit here and debate until hell freezes over. Are you with me?"

The applause had been thunderous. He was confident he had the votes he needed.

"Good," he said. "Let's get at it. You all know about the recent events in Oregon. Our constituents want to know what foreign troops are doing on U.S. soil. They want to know why American lives and property have been lost. We're damned well going to find out, take appropriate action, and report to the public. The amendment to include that as a part of this bill passed 81 to 15, with one abstention, one absence, and two votes of present."

That had been two hours and nineteen minutes ago. Now he was waiting for the last subcommittee chair to finish speaking.

The junior Senator from Massachusetts, a member of Harney's own party, seemed about to wrap up, though it was difficult to tell for certain. "America didn't tolerate having her citizens assaulted at Lexington, Concord, and Bunker Hill, and she won't tolerate it in Oregon. We must get to the bottom of this matter…."

Margolin listened politely, poker-faced, as his colleague continued her oration. On the surface, the speech was typical politics. After all, the lady *was* up for reelection. The real news was what wasn't being said, what would never be mentioned. President Harney was starting to lose the support of his party. He was becoming a political liability.

Finally the speech ended, and Margolin stood up to help lead the applause. He stood until it was over, and Harney's Vice President banged his gavel to signal a short recess. The man had been unusually subdued. He'd made no comments whatsoever after the motion to table had been soundly defeated by a roll call vote.

Margolin sat down, glanced at his secretary and asked quietly. "Do we have a problem, Grace?"

She gave him an *I'm-not-sure, Boss* look, and passed him a handwritten note. He read, "A women insists on meeting with you. Says it's confidential and MOST urgent. Says she is your niece?"

The underlines were in red ink. Attached was a color shot from the office security camera. "Subject Unknown" was embossed across it in yellow. The AI system didn't recognize his visitor.

The Senator glanced at the photo and smiled. He'd had his family members and friends purged from the databases during one of the periods when the personal privacy extremists in Congress had gained superiority over the police state zealots. Since then the pendulum had swung back, but Rebecca had been out of the country. The watchers and cyber clerks had missed her in the tally.

Grace is very protective of my time. I wonder what Rebecca said to her. She not only got access, she even got Grace to come chase me down. It was really quite intriguing.

Even as a child, Rebecca had been formidable. He grinned and shook his head, recalling how she was so much like his sister, which was to say, domineering at times, though in an amiable way.

Rebecca would look at you with those big blue eyes and before you knew it, her inexorable logic had you agreeing to something unexpected. *She inherited her mother's eyes and powers for sure.*

He and Rebecca had been close. Hell, he was her Godfather. But he'd not seen her since her parents' funeral. He tried to recall how long ago it had been. Almost four years.

She had gotten her doctorate and left the country. He received an occasional card or photograph from strange places, but they'd not kept up with each other. She hated Washington. For him to get away was hard, except when he was campaigning and had no time to himself.

He looked at her photo more closely and frowned. She was thinner, looked tired, and the strain in her face was visible. *Yes, something is definitely bothering her.*

"Thank you." He spoke softly into Grace's ear. No one was close, but why take chances? "You acted correctly. Rebecca is my late sister's only child. Please get her anything she needs."

Grace's eyebrows went up slightly, but she didn't say anything.

The Senator glanced at his watch. "This should adjourn by six. Please reserve a secure room for Rebecca and myself and have dinner brought in. I think she'd like the soft-shell crab if it's fresh and perhaps a nice Chardonnay. It's PPC, Grace."

Grace nodded. PPC – Private, Personal, and Confidential – meant she was to have the office logs and camera photos sanitized and the staff alerted to deflect questions. The Senator was intense about protecting his private conversations. "Yes, Sir. Anything else?"

Margolin looked pensive as he folded the note and put it safely in his pocket. "Rebecca looks beat. Tell her she's free to use the cot and bathroom in my private office if she wants to sleep or clean up. Say she's welcome to stay at my place, or I'll have her dropped wherever she wants. I'll want a limo with one of my personal drivers waiting at 9:30 by the rear entrance."

"Yes, Sir." Grace joined the throng now rushing for the exits, and quietly slipped away.

The White House

President Harney had only seven months left in his term, but was wondering if he was going to survive that long. The protests were continuous, and both houses had assigned committees to investigate the events in Oregon.

A bill was expected from the Senate imminently to provide oversight of foreign involvements on U.S. soil. If it passed, they'd subpoena him to testify under oath about it.

What do I do now? Harney thought. *We're heading for a Constitutional crisis. I see it coming, but don't know how to avoid it. I can't stall the legislation much longer. Everyone knows it will pass, and my own party wants me to back off.*

The House already passed its version by an overwhelming majority. If the Senate bill passes, the law will be on my desk in hours. My people on the hill are warning me they'll have to support it. They'll override my veto.

"My god damned staff is worthless. There's no one I can talk to," he muttered aloud.

That damned woman Governor in Oregon is fighting me too. If she'd surrendered the documents from the Cybertech incident, it would have all blown over by now.

Oregon was in the news constantly, and Harney's dreaded yellow briefing packet got thicker every day. The Peace Enforcers had over a thousand troops there, its borders were sealed, and they'd **still** failed to locate one old woman.

I never should have put my instructions in writing. The woman's testimony, coupled with evidence, can topple my administration, Harney thought. The operation had seemed so simple. How had they failed so miserably?

The situation kept getting worse. His Attorney General not only refused to issue a warrant for the woman's arrest, he'd held a press conference and publicly offered his resignation. Oregon's governor was on the video feeds constantly, saying she could no longer guarantee the woman's safety, warning her to stay in hiding.

The bastards sold me out. They have to be working together, Harney thought. *They caused a firestorm, and now the hearings in the Senate are fanning the flames.*

From Oregon to the White House gates, demonstrators were chanting. "Leave Kate Alone. Harney Must Atone." Each day the crowds were getting larger. The missing woman had become a media event.

This all started because the Japanese wanted Giles over some arcane technology issues. I went along with it, and now they've lost interest in finding him. It was all for nothing.

That bastard in the Senate, Margolin, was relentless. Harney's supporters were either lining up behind him or ducking for cover. So far no one had threatened impeachment, but it was coming.

My best bet is the Peace Enforcers. They have as much to lose as I do. Hell, all they have to do is burn some documents and seize one old woman.

They didn't even have to kill her. If they just made her unavailable for a few months, it would all blow over. But the fools kept bumbling around, having accidents, shooting each other.

How could the Peace Enforcers be having such problems? Tanaka had subdued Seattle less than six months ago, and without any controversy.

The media supported suppressing the Seattle protests in the name of public safety. Now a secretary allegedly takes out Tanaka and an armed squad, and I have an insurrection on my hands.

Harney's thoughts were interrupted by the buzz of his intercom. He scowled and hit the button. "Damn it, Marta, not now. No fucking interruptions."

He screamed the words. He felt like smashing the unit with his fist.

There was a long pause. "Sir, it is Mr. Kobayashi. He insists on seeing you."

Harney took a deep breath. He reached into his desk drawer, poured a shot of whisky, and tossed it down in one gulp. The fiery liquid burned, but it helped push back the fear.

He took another deep breath, and spoke in a more measured tone. "Excuse me for snapping at you, Marta. Give me two minutes and then send him in." He needed time to compose himself.

Senator Margolin pulled open the door and beamed in delight. He rushed across the room, pulled Becky to her feet, gave her a massive hug, and kissed her on the cheek.

"It's been too long, girl."

Surprisingly, she started crying. She hugged him back, then pushed him away, wiped her eyes, and nodded. "It sure has, Uncle George. Too long, and too far. I've missed you."

"I'm going to go home now, Senator," Grace said. "Rebecca's not in the databases. She wouldn't let me fill out a card for her. It's up to you to get her past the checkpoints."

"Thank you, Grace. That'll be my pleasure."

He closed the door behind her, grinning broadly. "This room is swept for bugs. We can talk privately. How the hell did you show up here without being put back into the system? They're supposed to be checking passports these days."

"I got myself a French passport."

"You're kidding."

She grinned and showed him. It even had the appropriate stamp showing that she'd legally entered the U.S. The passport was valid. The stamp was a fabrication, though a very good one.

"You haven't given up your citizenship, have you?"

"No, of course not, Uncle George. I'd never do that. I spent a lot of time down in the Southern Hemisphere working with some French scientists. At times things were dangerous. They were worried about me."

"Why?"

"Americans get the best prices as hostages these days. My friends feared someone would discover you were my Uncle and that would make me a target. They said if I had a blue passport, I might get kidnapped. I know you could have gotten me a diplomatic passport, but they said that was worse. If I had a black passport and got kidnapped, they were afraid people might think I was with the CIA and kill me.

"So they got me a French passport instead, and it solved the problem." She smiled at his perplexed look. "I've learned to speak pretty good French."

George was shaking his head. Several questions rushed through his mind. He picked a safe one. "Where were you when you got this, ah, helpful document…?"

He tried to recall if there was any French territory in South America. He didn't think so.

"I was on Desolation. It's an island."

She's just like her mother, and I'll be damned if I let her shock me, Margolin thought. He stepped over to the bar, uncorked the wine, and poured them each a glass.

She took a sip, nodded in appreciation, and took a deeper drink. "That's good stuff, Uncle." She smiled. "You don't know where Desolation is, do you?"

"I think you made it up."

"No way," she said. "Desolation is where I started my dissertation. The actual name they put on the maps is Kerguelen Island. There are three smaller islands and a bunch of several hundred rocks that stick out of the ocean.

"Technically, it's an archipelago. A Frenchman named Yves de Kerguelen-Tremarec discovered the place in the 1700s but had the good sense to never step ashore. The French still keep scientists there."

"I've never heard of it. Not by either name." *And I'm on the foreign relations committee*, he thought wryly. "Where is it?"

Becky laughed. "Uncle George, it's not about where. 'Where' means you can say 'near this.' Desolation is *nowhere*, hence the name.

"The closest civilization, if you can call it that, is Cape Town and it's 4,000 miles away. Australia is slightly further. Antarctica is closer, but it's uninhabited. Desolation has no harbors and no airport. Other than moss and grass, there's no vegetation. It's just volcanic rocks.

"Its latitude is mid-way between what they call the Roaring Forties and the Furious Fifties. The subarctic wind blows clear around the planet with nothing to slow it. A full gale is a slow day, and it rains, sleets, or snows 300 days of the year."

He refilled their glasses. "Why would anyone want to stay there?"

"For practice. It's much more survivable a place than Antarctica. It's much warmer. The water keeps the temperature pretty constant, usually right around freezing. A warm summer day might hit 40 degrees.

"Seal hunters and whalers used to shelter on the East Side of Desolation. There are good anchorages there, and Mt. Ross, over 6,000 feet, breaks the wind. German surface raiders used it for the same reason during the last centuries' wars. Think of Desolation as the banana belt of that part of the world."

"It sounds awful."

She laughed. "You don't know what a hostile environment is until you've seen Antarctica. That's what we were practicing for. It's cold, it's cruel, and the air is thin.

"Do you know Antarctica is the world's highest continent? It's also the coldest, the windiest, and the driest. The average elevation is about 7,500 feet. The world's record cold temperature was measured there – minus 89.2 Centigrade."

Margolin said, "They quick-freeze foods at higher temperatures than that. A temperature that low would kill a person in a few minutes."

"Right," Becky said. "That's minus 129 Fahrenheit. It makes places like Alaska seem warm by comparison. You get dry ice by freezing carbon dioxide. A nippy day will do that, a mere minus 109 F."

Margolin blinked and shook his head.

"When the first winter storm hit, they waited till the wind dropped and gave me the rookie demo. One of the guys took a cup of hot coffee and tossed it up in the air. It hit the ground frozen solid," she said. "Antarctica's twice as cold as the North Pole and a hundred times more dangerous. If you touch anything your hands freeze fast. If you breathe air that cold, you get lung damage. Inhale too quickly thorough your mouth, and you crack your teeth.

"We had high tech masks that preheated the air, and we checked them before we went out," Becky said. "It was like living on Mars. Nothing works like you expect.

"Metal landing gears snap, plastics shatter, and batteries are useless unless you keep them warm. Exposed skin freezes in seconds. Glycol, antifreeze, is worthless – because it freezes solid. Without heaters, gasoline and heating oil quickly turn into thick, useless sludge. If you lose power in the winter for more than a few minutes, you'll die because you'll never be able to restart the heaters or generators."

"How did you get heat and power?"

"Vigilantly and with great determination." She grinned wryly. "Back in the 60s when the U.S. was wealthy, some of the military bases had nuclear power plants, but they've all been decommissioned.

"Sometimes I think Americans are crazy. We brought in a 413-ton nuclear reactor in 1961. Then we disassembled it and lugged out the radioactive pieces in 1972 when we got ecologically minded. It must have cost hundreds of millions of dollars."

The Senator nodded. That sounded exactly like something the government would do.

She took a sip of wine. "It amuses the scientists how Americans bounce from one extreme to the other. In the 60s, we stacked our waste on the frozen sea until the ice melted. Greenpeace – remember Greenpeace? – took photographs, and it embarrassed us.

"Ever since, we've hauled all our trash back to the states for disposal. We once had small radioactive thermal generators, RTGs, scattered around the continent to run automatic weather stations. All but one has been hunted down and removed. The lost one is legendary. It hasn't been seen for decades, but the old hands say people still come down to look for it."

George had to laugh. "Let me guess. To preserve the pristine Antarctic ecology, we then sent the *Exxon Valdez* down there with a load of petroleum?"

"You guessed it," she said. "They run tankers, small ones, down there once or twice a year. Our camp was small enough we could ship what we needed in steel drums.

"Oil heat, despite its problems, is politically correct again. We used diesel fuel to run heaters and generators, and for the snow cats. We had three independent sets of generators and kept two turning all the time when it was under twenty below. The generators powered the heaters on the fuel tanks."

"So the Antarctic now runs on fuel oil?"

"Pretty much. Gasoline is much too dangerous to keep near dwellings, though we had some in sheds for snowmobiles, ice saws, and other tools. We even had a spare building just in case there was a fire. If a fire starts, you can't put it out."

"Why not?"

"Think about it. Winds of 200 miles per hour have been recorded in Antarctica. Can you imagine the chill factors you get when you combine the world's extremes of wind and low temperature?

"You can't survive outside long enough to fight a fire. Even if you could, it wouldn't help. Everything is frozen solid except what's burning and the wind whips the flames into such an intense heat that steel melts like candle wax. Antarctica is tough to survive. A good fraction of the people who tried to stay through the winters have died there."

"I didn't have any idea it was so bad."

"It's a dangerous place, Uncle George. The explorers you read about in the history books typically dashed across Antarctica in the summer during good weather.

"The summer of 1911-12 was relatively warm. Admundsen's party reached the pole on December 14 and got back safe because they had dog sleds with fast teams. They got in and out quickly, and they lived.

"The second party to reach the pole, Scott's, focused more on science than speed. The time delay killed them all. They made it to the pole on January 18, but by then the weather was turning bad. A rescue expedition recovered their bodies and carefully kept scientific notes the next summer."

He nodded, thoughtfully. "I always forget summer in that part of the world is in our winter." *You grew up when I wasn't looking.*

"Could I please have some more wine?"

He filled her glass.

"The outposts in Antarctica hug the coasts where it's warmer and supplies can be delivered. By comparison, Desolation was easy."

"How many people are there on Desolation? Where do they live?"

"Most just passed through," Becky said. "There was constant turnover. A few times in the summer, we had 200 people. In the winters, we had maybe a hundred, tops. The hardy ones stayed in tents. You have to pile rocks on the tents to keep them from blowing away. There are a few sheds, but they had to bring the wood in and tie them down too.

"I lived on a converted oil platform in relative luxury. We had hot water, electricity, toilet paper, and everything. I stayed with a French biologist studying Patagonian toothfish, at least when she wasn't drunk or stoned, which was often."

Becky drained her glass, and held it out for a refill. "It was ugly."

"The biologist or the island?"

"The fish. Patti was cute. Very French and very sexy. Men liked her because she had a great body and a pleasant personality. Nice tits, as you'd say. She was funny. We laughed a lot. She'd get stoned, only grass, never hard drugs, and play her guitar.

"She had grow lights in the closet and sold pot to the fishing fleets that sheltered at Desolation to pay for her education. The island was just a rock, and the toothfish was repulsive. It was one of those geological throwback type things. We had one for dinner once, and it was a disaster. Mostly bone and teeth."

"Why was she studying toothfish?"

"To get her Ph.D., of course. It was sufficiently obscure as to be a good research topic. I got my Ph.D. in technical anthropology. I studied penguins. It changed my life."

It certainly did, George thought.

"Patti's teaching at the Sorbonne now. Her stupid fish wasn't any worse than my penguins. Patti was a good role model. I had a still in my closet and sold moonshine. I didn't need the money, but it was fun. It helped me make friends."

"It sounds like she's a friend." *I expect she was probably screwing someone in the French diplomatic corps*, he thought.

"Oh, yes. We were close. Patti got me my French passport," Rebecca said brightly.

Bingo. George smiled and poured himself another glass of wine. "Dinner will be here soon. Tell me more about, ah, Patti."

"She was great. One day we woke up and couldn't believe it. The sun was shining and there was a big cruise ship from Australia in the anchorage. It was December 24th, the peak of the summer, and they were visiting because Captain Cook spent Christmas day 1776 there. I thought it was a silly reason, but apparently it helped them sell tour tickets.

"There were 500 people on board. Patti organized a party, of course. They had a grand piano and she played quite well. She traded pot for Australian wine and French champagne."

"Tourists?" he asked incredulously.

"Yes, tourists." She laughed, remembering. "4,000 miles from nowhere, and we had tourists. Including a gaggle of secretaries, a collection of young divorcees, and even an all-girl rock band. Patti and I made the researchers bathe and put them on their best behavior.

"The ship stayed for four days. I think everyone had a good time."

"I imagine so." George sipped his wine, trying to imagine the dynamics of combining stranded French scientists with horny tourists, alcohol, and drugs in the middle of nowhere.

"The French helped me a lot. The other problem with Antarctica is the bureaucracy is as hostile as the environment. International treaties regulate everything. Mining is absolutely banned.

"The local scientific community bitterly resents outsiders, especially Americans, unless you are a card-carrying socialist. Research has to be approved by committees. If it's anything new, a dozen countries have to sign off on it first. I slipped through because my penguin research was pretty standard, the continuation of an approved program."

"So the French got you into Antarctica under a false flag to do your research?"

"Exactly." She nodded, and smiled at the memory. "Did I shock you, Uncle George?"

"Absolutely." In truth, he wasn't shocked at all even though he was pretty sure marijuana was illegal again. He wasn't positive – the laws kept switching back and forth – and he didn't really give a shit. Sex, wine, and drugs were a way of life to the French. *Vive la France.*

Rebecca was showing reaches of resourcefulness well past anything he'd seen lately inside the beltway. On her own she'd learned to build coalitions, manipulate the Globalists, befuddle the bureaucrats, outmaneuver the UN, and get what she wanted. She'd had fun, got adventure, and was awarded a PhD along the way. *Not bad. The girl had good genes.*

There was a knock at the door, and a waiter brought in their dinner. They didn't speak until he'd left. She looked at her uncle fondly and kissed him gently on the cheek. "You remembered I love soft-shell crab. It was always my favorite.

"I'm going to cut myself off on the wine though." She paused and a frown crossed her face. "I have something I need to discuss with you."

"Time enough after dinner, girl. Can you stay at my place? I've got plenty of room, and I promise no one will bother you."

"I'd like that. Thank you."

"It's my pleasure. It's damned good to see you again."

They savored their meal together, speaking softly and laughing quietly as the years fell away.

BOOK FOUR:
A VERY BAD SYSTEM

"A nation can survive its fools, and even the ambitious. But it cannot survive treason from within. An enemy at the gates is less formidable, for he is known and he carries his banners openly. But the traitor moves among those within the gate freely, his sly whispers rustling through all the alleys, heard in the very halls of government itself. For the traitor appears not traitor, he speaks in the accents familiar to his victims, and he wears their face and their garments, and he appeals to the baseness that lies deep in the hearts of all men. He rots the soul of a nation, he works secretly and unknown in the night to undermine the pillars of a city, he infects the body politic so that it can no longer resist. A murderer is less to be feared."

Cicero, 42 B.C.

CHAPTER THIRTEEN

THE WHITE HOUSE

President Harney scowled darkly at his visitor. "Things are not going well, Dr. Kobayashi. I sincerely hope you have some good news to report from Oregon."

Kobayashi studied the President carefully. He'd aged greatly in the last few weeks. There were dark smudges under his eyes and a slight tremor in his hands.

He doesn't show proper respect. He's discourteous. No pleasantries, not even an offer of tea, just a cold acknowledgment of my credentials. Still, this is not a good time to pressure him. He's weak and near his breaking point.

"The situation is evolving, Mr. President," he said calmly, seating himself.

The President stared at him, but didn't speak. He seemed to be having difficulty formulating what he wanted to say.

"There's not much to report. The storm broke. We finally got personnel into the mountains and recovered our crashed helicopters." Kobayashi felt no need to tell the President about the bodies and angry relatives. He'd learn soon enough.

The President continued to stare. A long moment passed before he spoke. "I don't give a damn about your helicopters. What about the Cybertech evidence?"

"We don't have it yet. That's what I came to discuss...."

"What about the Chambers woman? Do you have her yet?"

Kobayashi spoke carefully. "The Oregon borders are sealed. We have teams sweeping the state and AI links to all the Federal security cameras in the state set to automatically alert us if she appears. But that's just the airports, ports, border crossings, and federal buildings."

"What else do you need?"

"The Governor refused us access to the state and local public cameras. That's tied up in court. Perhaps you can assist us?"

"You've lost the woman, haven't you?"

"We'll have her soon with your help. She can't get out of the state."

"I dare not defy the courts." Harney shook his head emphatically. "My enemies are waiting for something like that. Surely you have the resources to locate one woman. What's your problem?"

"Not a problem, just a delay," Kobayashi said.

"Why?"

"The cameras are giving us an unacceptably high false positive rate, Mr. President. So far, we have detained one hundred and forty-three women with similar features to the fugitive. We've finished interrogating thirty-one. None of them knew anything about Katherine Chambers beyond what they could have learned from news reports."

"They all knew about her, though, didn't they?"

Kobayashi sighed. "She's become a local hero. We put up pictures of her everywhere, and now women are dressing to resemble her. It makes our job harder."

"I don't want to hear about your problems. You need to handle this."

"We are," Kobayashi said. "We've offered a substantial reward for information about the woman. We're following up on all leads."

What's the peculiar American expression about the futility of chasing wild birds? The local commander complains his men are being run all over the state. He dares not send them out except in squads.

The President was frowning, drumming his fingers on the desk. Kobayashi chose to ignore it. "We have roadblocks on the major highways, and patrols making house-to-house searches in the Portland area. Since Oregon authorities are refusing to cooperate, I came to request assistance."

President Harney spread his hands in supplication and then clenched them into fists, choking off a snarl. He shook his head. "Effectively you have Oregon under martial law. What more do you want?"

"You can declare an emergency and take over the National Guard, Mr. President."

The President groaned, put his head in his hands, and was silent for several minutes. Finally he took a deep breath, composed himself, and looked up.

"I needed your line of credit, so I did everything you wanted. I signed the letter agreements, but they require approval by Congress. The authorization for independent action by Peace Enforcers is a part of that legislation, **which has not yet been passed.**" Harney almost screamed the last words.

"We shouldn't let this get bogged down in minor protocols." Kobayashi put all the confidence he could muster into his voice. "We kept our bargain. We've advanced you the money as a show of good faith. You said you had the votes to get the enabling legislation passed, and the polls supported our agreements. Your popularity ratings went up significantly after your speech."

"You don't understand my country, Dr. Kobayashi. I'm bound by the Constitution. The President makes treaties with other countries, but they take effect only if two-thirds of the Senate approves."

"Our agreement is simply a loan, not a treaty, Mr. President."

"The Senate Foreign Relations committee ruled otherwise."

Kobayashi felt the conversation going adrift. He needed to take action. "Why are you so concerned over a minor procedural delay? Your country needs our money. Your legislation will pass. This is a time for boldness."

"I'll never be able to get two-thirds of the Senate to approve that treaty, you damned fool." Harney's face was flushed. His breath smelled of liquor.

Kobayashi kept his voice calm. "Mr. President, it's a loan, not a treaty. It's within your power to accept by executive decision." *You're falling apart, and it spells disaster for us all.*

"*No!*" Harney was breathing hard. He reached into his bottom drawer, poured himself a shot of whisky and drank half in one gulp.

Kobayashi frowned. "You've already accepted our loan."

"No, Dr. Kobayashi, to interfering with the Oregon National Guard. I will not nationalize them. And I don't find your opinions on Constitutional law helpful. You're placing my administration at risk."

He's close to a state of panic. "We're just having a discussion to explore alternatives. There's nothing to be concerned about. The situation is under control."

"I hope for both our sakes you are correct, but at present your Peace Enforcers are operating in a gray area of the law. I thought you had the woman located. What about that call from her, the one made from the Cybertech office? I authorized NSA and Homeland Security to give you full support."

Kobayashi sighed. "It didn't work out, Mr. President."

"What the hell does that mean?"

"The call traced back to AT&T. It was a dead end."

"That's impossible."

"No, Sir. That's your law. The call was made using something called IP Relay services, and it was placed by an AT&T operator. There's a law that allows the hearing-impaired to place telephone calls by typing messages over the Internet. FCC rules require that calls must be completed for customers who identify themselves as disabled. The service is widely used for things like the Nigerian scam, where goods are purchased with stolen credit cards and false bank accounts."

"How, exactly, does it work?"

"The typed messages are read aloud to the recipient by an AT&T call-center employee, and your Government pays for the call and for the service. About $1.30 per minute, I'm told. It's a lucrative business. The big advantage of the system is that it is anonymous. FCC rules say that the operators can't disclose the content of the conversation or validate who the caller was. The vast majority of the calls, about 90%, come in from overseas IP addresses."

"So how do you know it was this Katherine Chambers person?"

"We don't, but NSA thinks so. The times matched, but there was no useful voice communication in the first call. The IP relay call came through a minute or two later, to the same number. That one was from a call center operator at AT&T. We know what was said because NSA captured it. It matched Internet text sent from an IP address in Lagos, Nigeria. It's in some kind of cypher code. Both calls were placed to a disposable cell phone that was purchased in Portland, OR for cash. Like I said, it's a dead end."

Harney took a deep breath and let it out through his teeth. "You said the call was from her, from this Katherine Chambers."

"The first call might have been."

"Might have been?"

"NSA said it was, but I wonder. As I just explained, the system for keeping the call secure was improvised. It did not utilize Cybertech gear. That seems odd to me. May I summarize?"

Harney nodded.

"The first call was placed from Cybertech shortly after the incident on an open line, but only two words were said. 'Orange two.' The voice was muffled, but female. We don't know who placed the second call, but it did come in two minutes and seven seconds later. We know the content but can't break the cypher, so we have no idea what was communicated. Even if it's eventually decoded, it's likely of no help in finding the woman, because she's long gone by now. In any case it's a dead end, and not worth spending time on."

Harney put his head in his hands, and rubbed his eyes. Then he looked up. "You have just wasted valuable time for both of us."

"I answered your questions, Mr. President. You wanted to know these details."

"I suggest you find the woman and get control of the evidence so we can put this matter behind us."

"My options are limited, Mr. President. A delegation from your Senate is in the Oregon capital. This is not a good time or place to use force."

"What?" The flush on Harney's face had faded. He was pale. Beads of sweat were forming.

"We don't have control of the Salem airport. They flew in by private aircraft, bypassing our roadblocks and checkpoints."

"You didn't stop them?"

"We couldn't."

Harney finished his drink and set the glass carefully on his desk. His hands were shaking again. He looked at them, took a deep breath, and folded them carefully in his lap. "You didn't stop them?"

"Oregon Air National Guard fighters escorted them. Our local commander thought a confrontation would be unwise." *It's worse than I thought. The President can't help us. He can't even help himself. The man is falling apart.*

Kobayashi forced a smile. "Don't worry, Mr. President. Whatever the Governor showed the delegation could have been falsified. Modern technology makes proof difficult."

"Find the woman. I do not want her available to testify."

"We'll find her. This will pass. Soon the reporters will be off chasing the next news event and all will all forgotten."

President Harney didn't speak. The two men sat there for a long moment looking at each other, but there was clearly nothing more to say.

"We'll find the woman," Kobayashi repeated. When the President didn't respond, he excused himself and left, wondering what he could report to Ambassador Kumakura. He wasn't looking forward to that discussion.

Russell Senate Office Building

Senator Margolin opened the door and smiled at the guard. "Could you please ask one of the stewards to bring a fresh pot of coffee, Art? Tell him the meal was excellent and to offer the chef my compliments."

"Yes, Senator."

Almost immediately a waiter appeared. He left coffee and removed the food service cart. Becky noticed the door closed with a solid *thunk*.

The Senator poured her a cup of coffee. "You like it black, as I recall?"

She nodded and raised an eyebrow. "Is this room soundproof?"

"Very much so. It's screened as well. Art is instructed to keep folks away from the door. There are always too many lobbyists and staffers wandering around."

Becky pointed. "What about the food cart?"

"Checked by the Secret Service and my own security staff. It's safe. You can relax here."

"Thank you. It's been a bit crazy."

"So I gathered. You wanted to talk. Grace said you didn't want anyone to examine your bag, and you've managed to stay under our government's radar. I'm assuming you have something more than family matters to discuss."

Becky nodded.

"You're safe here. How can I help?"

"I was in Oregon recently, Uncle George."

The Senator blinked. "Jesus, girl. You were at Cybertech during the recent incident, weren't you? What the hell is going on out there? Are the police looking for you? Have you broken any laws?"

She shook her head. "I don't think so."

"But you were at Cybertech...."

"I wasn't in the plant, but I was close. I know what happened. Dr. William Giles was one of my professors. He's being harassed by our government and hunted by the Peace Enforcers."

"Do you know why?"

"To steal Will's technology. It's not just the UN and the Japanese. Our government is involved."

"What about the woman they're hunting? Did she murder Tanaka?"

"Absolutely not. It's a long story, Uncle...."

"Do you know who killed him?"

"I wasn't there." She shrugged, avoiding his question. "Does it matter? Tanaka was in the process of torturing Kate Chambers and Dr. Giles. He was killed in self-defense."

"A Peace Enforcer Captain is shot down, and you brush it off as unimportant?"

"Tanaka and his men broke into the plant, killed the guard, and were torturing American citizens. He was shot as a consequence of his assault on Cybertech, his invasion of private property, and his brutalizing of innocent civilians."

"They say it was a legal operation," the Senator said.

"You know better. The thing you should be asking me is who's behind this."

"Do you know?"

She nodded. "President Harney."

"Can you prove it?"

A stricken look crossed her face, and she dissolved into tears. He slid his chair over to her, reached out, and put her head gently on his shoulder. She relaxed against him and they sat like that for several minutes. He started patting her back. Slowly her sobs became less frequent. She took deep breaths, trying to regain control.

Finally she pulled back. Her eyes were red, and her makeup was streaked down her face.

The Senator dampened a napkin and held it out to her. She nodded gratitude and wiped her face. Finally she produced a mirror from somewhere. *It tears me apart remembering how Will looked. Please, God, let him be all right.*

She looked into the mirror disapprovingly and then back at the Senator, shaking her head. "I've had a rough few days, Uncle George."

He smiled reassurance.

"I've not had much sleep and I'm worried about Dr. Giles and his people. I've been living on energy bars, vitamin pills, and coffee. I don't want to embarrass you, burden you, or put you at risk."

"Just relax. You're safe here."

"I wanted to look nice for you. I wanted to impress you with my Doctorate and all the things I've learned. Instead I break down and blubber like a little girl." She smiled ruefully. "Is there someplace where I can clean up?"

He pointed at a door across the room and helped her up.

She was more composed when she returned. "How do you feel about what's happening out there."

"In Oregon?"

She nodded.

"I don't like it. You may have just witnessed an act of war. I'm troubled that President Harney is involved."

He gets it, Becky thought. "Thank you. Remember how we'd talk when I was in college and you were a junior Senator? Remember what you said about the beliefs that make America unique?"

"Of course," he said. "It's been a part my speeches for years. Liberty and Exceptionalism. Doing the right thing. The freedom for each person to be all they can be. The American Dream."

"I believed you, especially the part about our being free to create new things and to own the creations of our mind. What if I told you about technologies that let people see their friends across time and distance, and that let them share their thoughts in private? How would you feel about that?"

"I'd feel great." He smiled. "You'll notice we're talking in a secure room. I feel pretty strongly about freedom and privacy."

"Will Giles is persecuted because his products allow privacy. By our own government. What do you say about that?"

"Some people are afraid, Becky." The Senator shrugged. "Powerful technology can be used for good or for evil. In the wrong hands, technologies like you describe could be very dangerous. We still argue over mature technologies, like firearms, but we allow them. Many nations don't. Some still ban printing presses, fax machines, and free newspapers."

"What happens if President Harney and people like him steal Will's technology for their own totalitarian interests? What happens to our freedoms when Big Brother has all that power?"

"Paul Harney is a weak and fearful man, a small man." A dark look came over the Senator's face. "He's desperate. Desperate people do desperate things."

"How can our government go along with that?" She was looking intently into his eyes. "Others have to know what he's doing."

He shifted uncomfortably. "It's not uncommon for bureaucrats to think if they could just control everything, people would be safe. Harney prefers safety above freedom. I strongly disagree. Trading freedom for safety is naïve."

Becky nodded. "Ben Franklin said, 'They that give up essential liberty to obtain a little temporary safety deserve neither liberty nor safety.' "

The Senator nodded. "That's often quoted. What's missed is that he said it long before the American Revolution, in 1759. He said it when living under the rule of a tyrant."

"You used to say, 'It's often safer to be in chains than to be free.' "

"I got that quote from Kafka, actually."

It's time to tell him, she thought.

"Uncle George, I'm working with a group of scientists who have rediscovered powerful ancient technologies. They allow us a control of time, space, energy, and matter well beyond our present science."

"Really?"

"Really."

"It sounds like science fiction," the Senator said.

"Most of the marvels we take for granted in our daily lives were once science fiction. The past golden age is persistent legend, Uncle George, and from many religions besides the Christian bible."

"Does this ancient science actually work?"

"Yes."

"How do you know?"

"I've seen demonstrations. We don't understand much yet, but we're learning. We need a secure place to work. I'm convinced we need to keep it secret."

"I'm aware of Cybertech's security products. We use them ourselves. Why are you so worried about privacy?"

"New technology can be highly disruptive."

He frowned. "I'm not sure what you're saying."

"The printing press and the longbow ended Feudalism. Airpower and missiles replaced battleships. Internet access eventually replaced the network news and telephone monopolies. What if airplanes became obsolete? What if we had cleaner, better power sources than petroleum? What if electric power grids were obsolete?"

He was watching her closely. "Can you say 'rolling economic collapse'?"

"I can say much worse, Uncle George. What's a small power source that efficiently converts matter into energy? Coupled with a way of transmitting matter across space?"

His gaze darkened. "Nuclear weapons and unstoppable delivery systems?"

"It's a possibility. Some of our scientists think something happened over ten thousand years ago that almost knocked the Earth off its axis. That's speculative and so are our technologies, but the coincidence of their both coming from the same era is intriguing to our deep thinkers."

"Why were you at Cybertech?"

"We have secrets to keep. We needed their technology."

"What else? I know you, girl. You're personally involved. Don't deny it."

"I volunteered to go because I could see what was happening to Will Giles and wanted to save him. He's a good person who's trying to ensure personal freedom and make the world a little better. People are trying to destroy him for that."

"How close are you and Dr. Giles?"

"We were becoming very close," she said softly. "He's been running for his life and I've been helping him. His technologists scattered for their own safety. Will trusted me with the information of where to find them and code words to instruct them to help me."

"Do you have proof President Harney set him up to be murdered?"

"Proof....." She sighed. "I'm not sure what the word means anymore. I have truth. That's all I can offer. I've come here to offer it to you."

She held her case out. He took it without opening it.

"What's in it?"

"Truth," she said. "Copies of a document initiating the Cybertech harassment that President Harney received in a briefing packet and annotated with 'stonewall it' in his own handwriting. Videos of meetings between Harney and Japanese officials planning the theft of Will's technology by the Peace Enforcers. Videos of PE troops breaking into Cybertech, killing the guard, and torturing Will's secretary."

"Let me see what you have."

She reached into her bag and handed him a folder. "This is a good start."

He spent several minutes looking through it. Finally he turned to her with an odd expression on his face.

"How'd you get this? Some of us in Congress have been moving toward Harney's impeachment. This would cinch our case."

"No, it won't."

"Why not?"

"It wouldn't stand up in court. When you see the images and videos, you'll realize no known science on the planet could produce these clips. Except perhaps for the cinematographic science of Hollywood special effects."

"Oh," he said.

"I can only bring you truth, Uncle George. You'll have to rely on other means to get legal proof."

The Senator was quiet for a long time, thinking. "There must be a way we can use this. Can you testify?"

"No." She shook her head and stifled a sob. "I wasn't there myself for any of these meetings or events, so the lawyers would dismiss anything I said as hearsay. I hate lawyers."

"So did William Shakespeare." The Senator smiled. "The feeling's been around for centuries. What about Dr. Giles? Can he testify?"

"No." She shook her head again. "I suggest you show my packet only to people whom you can trust to keep a secret."

The Senator nodded. He waited for her to continue.

"Will doesn't know about these videos or this technology. I never got the chance to show him. Another reason he can't testify will become obvious when you view the packet. It contains video clips of his being brutally beaten by Captain Tanaka."

"Is Dr. Giles all right?"

"No." The word seemed to hang in the air, sucking all joy and lightness from the room. "When I last saw him he was dying. I came here to bring you the information I showed you about President Harney. It's all I have. I hope it's enough so you can do some good with it."

"It's valuable," the Senator said firmly. "My friends in the intelligence community can keep secrets. They value knowledge more than proof. We'll think of some ways to use this. You have done your country a great service."

"I hope so."

She took time to gather her thoughts. He waited patiently. "I need your help. My friends are trying to get Will to a safe place outside the country. He's not safe here."

"Perhaps not."

"I couldn't protect him, and I'm not certain you can either. I want to be with him. I need to get to any large airport in Mexico, but the borders are sealed."

"When do you want to leave?"

"*Now*, Uncle. Now would be really good."

"Are you sure you don't want to get a good night's sleep first?"

"I dozed in your office and can sleep while I'm traveling. Can you help me?"

"I can." He handed her a dollar bill.

She looked at him questioningly.

"As of now you're on my staff. I hereby order you to go down to Mexico and help the United States protect its technology. Report back to me when you can. I'll give you a phone number to call if you need help."

"The government isn't trusted. You must promise not to have me followed."

He looked her directly in the eyes. "You have my word."

"That's more than I dared hope. Thank you, Uncle."

"What else can I do?"

"Help me. I need to go to him now."

"Okay, let me see if I can get you some fast transport." The Senator walked over and threw the door open. "Art, have someone get me Easy Ed out at Andrews on a secure line. Patch it in here and bring me a scrambler phone."

"Yes, Senator." In a few minutes, the door opened and a secure phone was passed in. "We have Major Shay on the line. I'll just plug it in over there and hook it up to the speaker."

The guard left discreetly, closing the door behind him. The phone rang immediately. The scrambler's green light flashed, then came on solid.

"Ed, is that you?" Margolin queried gruffly.

A chuckle came over the line. It sounded hollow with the multi-level pseudo random encryption, as if the man was laughing into a rain barrel. "Who the hell else would be out here in the middle of the night?"

"Good point. Are we secure?"

"Yes, Sir. That's what they tell me. I've got solid green at this end."

"I need to get one of my staffers down to Mexico pronto. How soon can you get her there?"

"Depends. How soon can you get her here?"

"Thirty minutes. Minor problem: she won't have an ID. I'll bring her myself. Can you clear it with the guards?"

"No problem. I'll meet you at the gate and have an F-32 preflighted and waiting with a hot pilot and long range tanks. Where in Mexico do you need her delivered?"

"Any airport with a customs service we can trust to lose the paperwork. South is good. The Yucatan is best."

"Stand by one, Sir." He was back on the line in under a minute. "If you can settle for somewhere near the Gulf of Mexico, we can make a supersonic run down over the water and get her there in a little over an hour. How about Mérida?"

The Senator looked at Becky. "It's in the Yucatan. You can be there in less than two hours."

She nodded. "That's perfect."

"That'll work, Ed. She's five foot eight and about 130. Can you find a flight suit that size?"

"Not a problem, Senator. We'll be waiting."

Margolin thanked him, punched the disconnect, and unplugged the phone.

And I thought I was getting too old for miracles. "Thank you, thank you, thank you, Uncle George. I really appreciate this."

"That's what uncles are for." The Senator grinned. "Let's go, girl. We can talk more in the car."

CHAPTER FOURTEEN

TWO WEEKS LATER, CAPITOL BUILDING, WASHINGTON, DC

The room was crowded, and the arrangements were awkward. Normally the long table held the twenty-four members of the Senate Armed Services Committee, plus a few guests and the staffers, by custom only one for each member, sitting along the wall behind their Senators. Today the room seated eighty-two people, and there was an overflow crowd leaning against the walls or kneeling on the floor in front of the large screen that was set up at the long end.

To the right of the screen was a speaker's podium. The Chair and Vice Chair sat next to each other along the table to the left of the screen, with the rest of the committee members arranged around the table behind nameplates.

The periodic filing in and out of speakers burdened with materials added to the general inconvenience and claustrophobia. When a briefer finished, they were required to leave with their materials before the next one came in to set up. It was disruptive, but unavoidable, given the sensitivity of the information presented. There hadn't been much discussion, yet.

The questions asked had mostly been for clarification or to request more detail. There was a growing sense of discomfort in the room, but so far no one had voiced specific concerns or expressed an advocacy. The committee members were free to take handwritten personal notes, each taking responsibility for leaks. There were, of course, no recording devices or cellphones permitted in the room.

The last specialist finally finished, and Senator Margolin tapped the mike for attention. "Thank you, Bill. That concludes our briefings."

The speaker squeezed down the gauntlet on the table's edge – amid the flurry of mutters and chair shuffling that had become the norm – and took his exit. Margolin waited until the commotion died down, and then ordered those who lacked both all-sources clearances and a committee sponsor to leave. The room was swept again, and the door was closed before he continued.

Fifty-two people remained. Margolin passed a signup sheet around and said, "Thank you for your patience. You've heard evidence and testimony from our nation's leading intelligence and forensic experts. You've been briefed as to possible ramifications and consequences in the areas of foreign relations, economics, technology, and trade policy. In a moment, I'm going to order a short break."

He looked around the room, making sure he had everyone's full attention. Recess announcements usually prompted a rush for the door, and he had other issues he wanted to address first.

"I remind you the materials you have just seen are all classified Top Secret, Special Intelligence, and NOFORN. This is 'eyes only' intended for the use of members of this committee alone. I need not remind you of the oaths you and your staff members have signed to preserve the privacy of these discussions. After the break, we'll discuss action plans."

George looked around the room, meeting each set of eyes. "We've agreed the materials you've seen will not be discussed outside this committee until we are prepared to make recommendations to the full Senate."

No one spoke.

"Are there any questions or comments before we break?"

One hand went up.

"The Chair recognizes the Senator from Oregon."

"Mr. Chairman, as you know my State is at ground zero for the recent events. I'd like to request five minutes to speak. I ask we clear the room of all but the committee members. I'd like the staffers to leave as well."

"Is there any objection?" George looked around the room and saw none. "So ordered."

The room was cleared. George waited until the door was again sealed. They were now down to twenty-four. *Good.*

"I'd like us to go off the record now and suspend the agenda to allow open discussion. Can I have a show of hands in favor?"

Many hands went up, and George nodded.

"So ordered. We are now off the record."

"Bart, come on up here and tell us what you want to say. You have the floor."

Bartholomew Roberts was the most junior member of the committee. He was thirty-two, but looked younger in his wire rimmed glasses and short-cut curly hair. He usually kept a low profile at these meetings and said little.

Bart got up and walked to the podium. He looked over at his colleague, the Vice Chair and minority leader, and then back at Senator Margolin, somewhat uncomfortably. "The recent troubles we've been discussing are centered in my home state. You've all seen the news. Most of us who represent Oregon are members of President Harney's party. Nonetheless, I think we need a proactive, bipartisan approach to these distressing and most serious events."

He looked briefly around the room.

"My home state suffers from what is, in effect, a foreign military occupation. Citizens have been killed. Some have had their property stolen or destroyed. There have reportedly been at least two military engagements, with casualties. Our state capital is under siege. The Oregon National Guard has been called in to protect it.

"Our nation's legal system is based on the concept of 'due process' and being 'innocent until proven guilty,' but a woman who is not charged with any crime is at present being hunted by foreign troops. It's alleged the White House may be complicit in this.

"Oregon's Governor has warned she cannot guarantee this woman's safety. We've apparently lost the basic ability to protect our citizens.

"Such actions have not been seen on American soil since the Revolutionary War. They were, not coincidentally, one of the major causes of that war."

He paused, scanning the faces in the room. No one spoke. "My sister is in Graduate School at the University of Oregon. She's 23 years old and is a victim of this conflict.

"She was detained by Peace Enforcer troops and held without being charged or allowed the benefit of legal counsel. She was interrogated for three days and then released without explanation. She is now recovering from exhaustion, dehydration, and trauma.

"This is not an isolated occurrence. Some two hundred women in my state have been similarly detained and interrogated, and the number mounts daily. There have been clashes between foreign troops and locals. In at least seven instances shots were fired.

"These actions are clearly acts of war. We've now seen compelling evidence that the President of the United States, a member of my own party, has, directly or indirectly, sanctioned this foreign aggression. That perfidy adds to my concern."

"Harrumph...." The young man paused, frowning, as a heavyset older Senator rudely cleared his throat into his microphone.

"Does the Senator from Mississippi wish to say something?" Bart asked.

"Boy, you need to get control of yourself, before you wet your pants. You're way out of line here making insinuations of misconduct. I work with my colleagues across the aisle. I'm a good dog with which to hunt, but I have not seen any damn evidence.

"It's all been most entertaining, but you have no proof of anything. Nothing we've seen amounts to a hill of horse pucky, including those fantasy film clips our Chair pulled out of.... Well, now, we just don't know where he obtained them, do we?"

Margolin banged his gavel and started to rise. He stopped at a private word from the gaunt Senator next to him, took a moment to compose himself, and slowly relaxed back into his chair. He flashed a sardonic smile at the Senator who'd interrupted the younger man.

"Marvin, you're out of order," he said dryly. "And this is bad time for partisanship. With the Senator from Oregon's permission, I'll turn the floor over to our Vice Chair, the gentleman from Ohio, Mr. Brock."

"I yield to Senator Brock," said the younger man after a moment's hesitation. He looked unsure as to whether to be angry or relieved.

Senator Brock was tall, thin, highly respected, and finishing his fourth term in the Senate. He walked with a limp and favored his right arm, courtesy of a terrorist assassination attempt during one of his early political rallies. Everyone remembered the video clips of the shots, the screams, and the images of bodies and a shattered podium covered with blood.

They also remembered how the young candidate had grabbed a pistol from the fallen security guard who'd shielded him. Left handed, Walter Brock had carefully put two rounds into the head of the terrorist before he collapsed. He was still in the hospital when he learned he'd won by a landslide.

What happened next changed history and the dynamic of self-defense in America. Senator Brock instituted a policy of encouraging Concealed Carry Permits for his staff. His motto was, *"No more Gabby Giffords!"*

Brock's security people embraced the policy, which turned into periodic classes and weapons training exercises. It was popular in Brock's state, but protested in California and New York. After media controversy, it turned into a "Don't Ask, Don't Tell" program.

An attack on a vocal anti-gun Member of Congress was thwarted by this policy within the year. The assailant died, and the liberal Congresswoman was reelected. She became an advocate for responsible gun rights.

Walter stood and slowly limped across to the podium. He paused and looked around the room, meeting each set of eyes. "These are difficult times. Our nation has been through a lot, dear colleagues. We've depleted our resources and our treasure, mostly for just and good causes, but also by pursuing some very ill-advised programs. We've been tainted by corruption and embarrassed by bungling and scandals.

"We're recovering, but does anyone think we'd be serving America well if we impeached our President for high crimes? Do we want to put our country through such divisiveness?"

There was silence.

"I don't think so, either." He looked around the room. "Have any of you conferred with President Harney recently?"

There was a soft murmur and some shuffling, but no one spoke.

"He's not a well man. It would be a tragedy if we allowed our nation to blunder into an unnecessary war because one man became unstable, wouldn't it?"

No one said anything.

"Americans will not tolerate a foreign occupation, but the impeachment of a President opens deep wounds."

He paused. There was total silence. This was a raw subject.

"My friend, Senator Margolin, is a reasonable man. Neither of us wants this matter to escalate further. We've agreed to work together to come up with solutions that avoid impeachment, prevent war, and get the UN out of Oregon. Does anyone here oppose that?"

No one spoke.

"Good." Brock pinned the Senator from Mississippi with a disapproving look. "During the break, Marvin and I are going to go out behind the barn and have a serious talk. Anyone from our party who'd like to join us is welcome."

The room was silent as he limped back to his seat. After a moment of silence, Margolin ordered the recess.

Unknown Location

Will gradually became aware of sensation. His first thought was astonishment his body wasn't hurting. He could sense light and warmth, and for some reason he felt peaceful and safe.

How odd. Each time I awoke all I could feel was pain, but it's stopped.

He slowly opened his eyes. The ceiling was lit by a soft white radiance that seemed to come from everywhere. He tried taking a deep breath. *It doesn't hurt,* he thought. He wiggled his fingers and moved his arms. Everything seemed to work. When he touched his ribs, there was no pain. Nothing was grating as he breathed.

He heard a sound, slowly looked to his right, and recognition came. Becky was sitting quietly in a chair next to his bed, looking at him. Their eyes met and she smiled. *God, she looks beautiful when she smiles.*

"You have beautiful eyes, Becky. Azure, like the sky." His voice sounded weak, even to him.

Her smile broadened, and she took his hand. "How do you feel?"

"Peaceful, like I'm drifting. At least nothing hurts."

"Our doctors put you into a deep sleep. They didn't want you to wake until the pain was under control."

"How long have I been out?"

"Five days. It was my fault."

"No." He shook his head. "You didn't want me to go back to the plant, but I insisted. I wanted to help my people."

"You did help. You bought us time. We got Kate out. The company records are safe."

"How's Kate?"

"She'll be fine."

"Tanaka's an evil man. I tried to stop him, but he was too much for me."

"Tanaka's dead. That's over. He won't bother anyone again."

"I remember waking up in the back of a truck with tubes stuck in me and my arms in casts. You were standing over me looking worried."

"You were in bad shape. We got you to medical care just in time."

"Where are we?"

"That's a long story, but the main thing is you're safe. Things are getting better. Because of what you did, because of what you brought us, we're all safer. Please don't worry about it now. You need to rest and heal."

"I don't hurt, but my mind seems clear. Do they have me on drugs?"

She shook her head. "Our doctors needed your conscious and unconscious minds functional. They took you off the narcotics shortly after you arrived.

"Western medical science doesn't know how to rebuild vital organs, but we do. Our methods are helping your body to rebuild itself."

"They beat me for a long time. At first there was pain, but near the end everything was numb. I couldn't move. It was like I was watching from far away. I think I was dying."

"You almost did." A dark cloud crossed her face. "It was a near thing, but you're going to be fine. You had broken bones, several injured vital organs, and nerve damage, but we got you here in time. Our healers have been channeling life energy to help your body regenerate itself, and they tell me it is working. Your biological systems are responding."

"Are you sure? I have so many things I want to say to you."

"I'm sure. Our doctors say you'll recover fully. Part of good health is belief, and it's especially important now. Your mental energy is part of the cure, and it's important you know the damage to your body is being repaired."

He nodded. It didn't hurt.

"Your lungs, kidneys, and liver are almost back to normal. Your blood counts and vital signs are within limits and getting better by the hour. You'll come out of this in better health than before. You're weak and tired, but rest, food, and exercise will fix that."

"We need to talk...."

She put a finger on his lips. "Shush. Your doctor said we should give your body a chance to rejuvenate. Concentrate on getting your strength back. Get some rest and I'll make sure they get you a nice dinner. We can talk then."

"Okay." He closed his eyes. He drifted off to sleep with her still holding his hand.

Cascade Mountains

Rex peered through the telescopic scope intently, his finger gently caressing the trigger. But he didn't fire. Instead he sighed and, keeping low, cautiously eased himself back off the ridge. When he was safely out of sight, he jogged back to the cave where Kate was waiting.

Without waiting for his eyes to adapt to the dimness, he entered and approached her sleeping bag. "We got trouble, ma'am."

"You're getting careless, Reggie."

The voice came from behind him, and he jumped, startled. He turned carefully.

Kate chuckled, lowered her pistol, and flicked on a flashlight, careful to keep it aimed at the ground. "I had to be sure it was you. What's wrong?"

"A squad of Peace Enforcers is heading our way. On foot. I think our friends took out their transport. Remember, we saw those helicopters go down a few days back?"

They'd heard the powerful engines and saw the distant cluster of black dots in the sky. The copters had dropped out of sight before Reggie could get a good count. They'd heard distant explosions.

"Four days ago."

"Yes, ma'am. I don't think they know we're here, but they're right determined little shits. They're coming over the big ridge to the west. I counted twelve."

Kate felt a chill of fear. "They must know we're here."

"I don't think so, but they're on the trail. They seem to be sweeping the hills, taking their time. They act confident, like no one is around.

"I had a good bead on their leader and could have gotten three or four more, but it won't help. It'd give us away and they'd just call in reinforcements."

"So what do we do?"

"Good question, ma'am. They'll find us if they search this area. Running is a bad idea too. We'd stand out."

"You think I can't move fast enough for us to stay ahead of them?"

"No, ma'am. We've about run out of places to go anyway." The big Texan frowned. "Our friends said they'd be back, but they're days overdue. That's a bad sign.

"My guess is roads are blocked and PE troops are covering the ports, airports, bus depots, and rail lines. We're stuck. We've more gear here in the cave than we can carry."

"Yes."

"We could leave it and try to get to a town." *I've never wanted hot water and electricity so badly,* Kate thought. *I dream about having a soft bed with warm blankets, hot tea in the morning, and not having to use my injured hand.*

She looked at Reggie, and that brought her back to harsh reality. He was shaking his head. "Wouldn't that work?"

"No, ma'am. They'll be searching the towns house by house. They've got pictures of you up everywhere by now.

"They want to flush us out, Ms. Kate. If we run, they'll head us off and hunt us down. We're better off to make a stand here. It's our best hope."

"We can't beat a squad of Peace Enforcers. We can run. I won't slow you down."

He shook his head.

"You could easily get away if you left me. Why do we have to fight?"

"It's simple, ma'am. If they're dead, they'll stop hunting us."

"There are too many of them." She could hear the fear in her voice.

"Don't give up yet, ma'am. Firepower and surprise can beat numbers." He put his hand on her arm reassuringly. "Sometimes."

Kate took several deep breaths, forcing herself to relax, trying to draw strength from his touch. That seemed to help. Calmness came slowly.

"Here's the thing. We have to get them all. If even one gets away or gets off a message, we're done for. We have to take them all down quickly. It's our only chance."

"They're not going to give us a chance. They're professionals."

"They'll have to bunch up when they approach the cave, and we might get lucky. If only one or two get away, I can handle 'em."

"You don't need to die. Leave me."

"Can't, ma'am. Couldn't live with myself. Decide what you want to do, but I'm not letting them take me, and I'm not leaving you."

Kate sighed. "I'll do whatever you say."

"We're only going to get one chance at this. The first few seconds of an ambush are crucial. We need to lay down effective fire. Can you shoot to kill?"

"I can try. Just tell me what to do." Her voice sounded more normal. She was thankful for that.

"Our first targets are the squad leader and the radioman," Reggie said. "The leader has a yellow armband and his SATCOM radio guy has a backpack and wears glasses. We need to drop both targets with our first volley."

"I understand," Kate said. *Targets, not people.* "I know how to shoot. My dad used to take me duck hunting."

"Good. I'm counting on you." Reggie grinned. "They'll approach up the trail. We'll set up the cave so it looks obvious, but not too obvious. They'll want to check it out. We'll hide off to the sides, but close enough so we have good fields of fire.

"You find the leader and focus on him. He's your target. I'll take down the radioman first. The instant he falls, kill the leader."

She thought for a moment, visualizing the ambush. "In the back?"

"Good place to start. Shoot him in the back, blow his head off, or shoot him in the legs and shoot him more when he falls. Main thing is put him down quick.

"It don't much matter which way he's facing or where the holes are, Ms. Kate, but it matters a whole bunch if we don't get hard kills." His eyes searched hers intently.

"I know this ain't fair, but there's no chance to practice. We need to get it right the first time. Can you do it?" His tone was apologetic.

Kate sighed deeply. "The alternative is singularly unappealing."

"First firefight is always the worst, ma'am. Our only chance is surprise, and it's important you don't hesitate. Most newbies get killed because they freeze up and don't use their weapons. You need to shoot and keep on shooting. Even if you can't hit a bull in the ass with a bass fiddle, they don't know that."

"I'll do my best," she said. "I used to be a good shot, Reggie."

"Stay in place long as you can, and if you have to pull out move straight back up over the ridge. I'm going to plant claymores in the forest between you and the cave. It'll slow 'em down, and we might get a few if they get careless."

"Claymores?"

"Antipersonnel mines," he said. "I'm going to set up a kill zone where we have good fields of fire. Use your rifle first. Two or three aimed shots per target are best, but the leader is worth more. You need to take him down hard."

"I understand."

"Go full auto if they bunch up or try to rush you."

He put her thumb on the fire selector. It had three positions, *single*, *double*, and *auto*. It was on the top one, *single*. She practiced running it up and down with her finger on the trigger, feeling the click of the detents.

The safety was on the trigger guard. She touched it gently, moved it to *fire*, and then clicked it back to the safe position.

"Good." Reggie nodded approvingly. "Keep your extra clips out where you can reach them and save your pistol in case they get real close."

"Okay," she said. She played the scene in her mind, imagining the leader falling and her shifting fire to the others on her left.

"It's not much different than ducks. Just stay real still until they pass. They may have body armor, but don't worry 'bout that. Your rifle's got a lot of punch and every second round is armor piercing."

She nodded.

He was looking at her with a question in his eyes. "Remember, center of mass is the best aim point. Two rounds are best for effect: a 'double tap.' That's the middle click on your fire selector. Main thing is when you shoot, stay on the leader till he drops."

"I understand." *He's worried about me*, she thought. *He's repeating himself.* "Whatever happens, I'm going down shooting."

"Good plan. If they rush you, be happy."

"*What?*"

His grin was a flash of white in the dim cave. "If they come at you, they won't be bothering me. Just hunker-down, stay in position, and keep shooting. I'll cover you."

"Even if I miss, maybe I can create a diversion and give you more of a chance."

"Try to hit something, but the main thing is to lay down fire and keep them off balance. And if you see anyone with a large weapon, maybe a rocket launcher or light machine gun, it's rock and roll time."

"Rock and roll?"

"Yes, ma'am. Full auto. Hose him good, because one rocket grenade can ruin your whole day. Short bursts are best, but the important thing is to take 'em down."

She nodded.

"War ain't sporting or glamorous. It's about killing, and this time we need to get them all. If they break and run, you shoot 'em in the back. Remember, if any get away, they'll come back with more force."

"I understand," she said. "I'll practice it in my mind while I'm waiting."

"Not just your mind. Don't think too much. Put your hands through the motions a few times. You want to train muscle reflex so they'll know what to do when the time comes."

She nodded.

"If you're on auto, aim low. Your weapon will want to ride up."

"I won't let you down." She spoke emphatically, forcing a calm voice. And she hoped it was true. *Kate's last stand. I'm not going to let myself be caught and tortured again, and you refuse to leave me. So I'll get as many of them as I can.*

"The main thing is to keep your nerve, ma'am."

"Sure." Kate tried to sound confident. She hadn't fired a gun in thirty years.

CHAPTER FIFTEEN

CASCADE MOUNTAINS

Reggie and Kate put on thermal underwear and camouflage suits. Reggie found a good spot and carefully put an insulating blanket down on the ground for her. He took a tube of ointment from his pack and blackened their faces, checking his in a steel mirror he produced from somewhere. Then he draped a camouflage net over the bushes, gave her a cover, made sure she was comfortable, and stood up.

"You'll be safe here."

She looked at him dubiously.

"Well, safe as anywhere." He grinned, looked down at her, and pointed in the direction of the cave. "You have a good field of fire."

She raised her head. The forest was mostly tall fir and dense underbrush, but she had a good view. The glade was in direct sun. She could see a faint trail of trampled grass leading to the cave entrance. It was a dark shadow amid the gray granite boulders on that side of the clearing. She could see small animals, probably chipmunks, scurrying amongst the rocks.

"I'll set my sights for a hundred yards," she said.

"Close enough. It's an easy range but remember to hold low, cause you're shooting down hill," he said cheerfully, standing up and flashing a grin.

"Thank you." Kate tried to smile back. It wasn't very successful.

"It's about time," he said. "Stay put 'till I come for you. Remember, you're most vulnerable when you're moving."

"And when I'm reloading."

"Yes, ma'am."

"I'll be okay."

He straightened and looked around carefully, sniffing the wind, sensing the environment, peering down at the kill zone. Finally he nodded. "Best we can do."

Heigh-ho. Twelve to one odds and he almost makes me hopeful. She was surprised Reggie didn't clank when he walked.

He was holding a scoped sniper rifle casually in one huge hand. He had a short-barreled grenade launcher clipped diagonally across his vest in front where he could reach it easily. A nasty looking assault carbine with a suppressor slung muzzle-down over his right shoulder in back. A pistol hung at his belt and a combat knife in a scabbard was strapped to his left leg.

She tried to hand him his pack, but couldn't budge it.

"I brought extra ammo, ma'am. Just in case."

Reggie grinned. He handed her two energy bars, a canteen, and a pile of twenty-round clips for her rifle. He wrapped a hand around the straps, easily lofted the pack, and faded off into the woods.

He's counting on me. I need to be ready.

After he left, Kate practiced ejecting and inserting clips with her injured hand. It hurt like hell. At first she couldn't do it. She kept dropping the clips.

The slightest touch on her fingertips was agony, but she finally developed a system. If she braced the gun on her arm, turned it sideways, and used her palm to shove the clips into place she could reload. She practiced until she could do it automatically, without thinking.

The cocking lever made a *tch-clack* sound as she eased it back, released it, and clicked the safety off. She did the same with her pistol and laid it beside her.

Kate waited as time passed and the shadows slowly lengthened. Waited for Tanaka's avengers to arrive.

Heavily armed.

Grimly determined.

Thoroughly pissed.

Looking for her.

Senator Margolin's Office, Washington DC

"May I offer you some more tea, Kumakura-san?" The Senator looked at his guest politely.

I wonder what the hell brought him to my office. I've met him a few times through my duties on the Foreign Relations Committee, but it's rare for an ambassador to visit. Why did he insist on meeting with me in private?

"Thank you, Senator. You're most gracious." The ambassador's dark eyes met the Senator's. "You have an interesting history, Sir. We Japanese appreciate history more than most."

Margolin raised his eyebrows. "Indeed?"

"You're a patient man. That's unusual for Americans, especially those who hold high office."

"Some would disagree with you, Mr. Ambassador."

"Your former President was one." Kumakura waved a hand in dismissal. "No matter. He was mistaken.

"You were in the Navy. You retired and ran for the Senate because of disabilities suffered when you were shot down and interrogated."

Margolin nodded.

"I think you were held prisoner for two years?"

"Two years, three months, one week, and five days. I received better treatment than most because of my rank. It was stupid of me to be there. I was in intelligence. I wanted to get a closer look at their new antiaircraft defenses." Margolin shrugged and gave a wry smile. "They gave me one."

"That government didn't survive," Kumakura said flatly.

"Not for long. Abdul Nassid was toppled a few years later."

"A most fortuitous event. My country is pleased they're now a modern democracy and a good trading partner." He paused. "You were on the Senate Intelligence Committee at the time, weren't you?"

What an interesting question, thought Margolin. He nodded.

Ambassador Kumakura gave the Senator an appraising look. "We were surprised when President Harney resigned so suddenly. His Vice President says he's going to retire. Your name is being mentioned as a candidate."

"I think it's premature for me to discuss that." Margolin paused and looked at his guest carefully. "As you know, I've been somewhat... curious... about some of the arrangements between President Harney and your government...."

The Ambassador sipped his tea and was quiet for a long moment. Margolin tried to place the expression on his face. Regret was there, but mixed with something else. He tentatively categorized it as sorrow.

"We Japanese are said to be patient, Senator. It's not always true. Sometimes, some of us are impulsive. Sometimes we do foolish things too."

Margolin nodded. It was the human condition.

"Did you know my youngest son was a sergeant in the Peace Enforcers?"

"No."

"Teruyuki was my namesake. He was very bright, but more interested in the martial arts than in philosophy or political history.

"We finally agreed he'd do one term – hitch, I think you Americans call it? – before he went on to graduate school. He'd been admitted to your Stanford University, but they agreed to wait for him."

"Yes, we call it a hitch. You must be proud of him. I'd always wanted a son, but we have two daughters."

"My son is dead. He was under Captain Tanaka's command. He died at the Cybertech plant. I grieve for him."

Margolin stared at his guest. "I'm sorry for your loss."

"I've seen the Oregon evidence. Captain Tanaka committed murder and other atrocities. He is responsible for many such acts."

"And for the death of your son."

"Exactly." Kumakura's face was like stone.

"Tanaka died at the plant."

"It's not yet over yet. Others made mistakes. They are being rectified.

"I want you to know Mrs. Chambers will be left alone. Our Peace Enforcers will be removed from Oregon. Those orders are being carried out as we speak."

Margolin looked at his guest and waited, politely.

"Did you know that at the time of the Cybertech incident, Captain Tanaka reported to a person assigned to me, Dr. Ito Kobayashi?"

"I was briefed on that." Margolin nodded. "I'm also aware of Dr. Kobayashi's agreements with President Harney."

"Kobayashi was one of the impatient ones. He was tragically misguided. Did you know he jumped to his death from his tenth-floor apartment?

"There's a small notice in today's *Washington Post*. Your networks seem preoccupied with the Harney resignation, so it's not gotten much attention."

"I missed that myself," Margolin said.

"Kobayashi left a suicide note apologizing and asking for forgiveness. I brought you a copy." He handed the Senator an envelope. "My nation shares in the disgrace of Tanaka's actions. I came to apologize."

"Thank you, Mr. Ambassador. But why are you apologizing to me?"

"Your future is bright, Senator." Kumakura took a sip of tea. "Not long ago, my country was in worse economic shape than yours is now. Now our positions are reversed. Do you know how we recovered?"

Thank you, Helen Branson. I can actually answer the question. "Wise economic policy. Quashing and punishing corruption and cronyism. Allowing free markets and entrepreneurship. Intertwining your economic future with that of your neighbors."

"You are very kind, Sir. Our policies helped, but there is more."

Margolin nodded, waiting for him to continue.

"We learned it was permissible to fail, Senator. That was the hard lesson."

"I see," said Margolin, not seeing at all. *What's your point?*

"The answer is simple: Admit failure and stop. We learned from the Koreans. They allowed their weak companies to fail. They abandoned their flawed policies and social programs. In very little time they were leading the economic recovery in Asia. The Chinese did much the same when they finally abandoned Communism in all its forms."

"What are you trying to tell me, Mr. Ambassador?"

"Your country has pursued some foolish policies. When they failed, you built bigger bureaucracies and threw more money into them, even though you knew they weren't working. That's folly. You've done yourselves much damage."

"We say, 'it didn't work' and we stop? Is that what you are suggesting?" asked Margolin.

Kumakura nodded gravely. "It sounds trivial, doesn't it? I can assure you it's not. It's simple, but not easy. We almost allowed our country to be destroyed before we acted. After we'd made the tough decisions, our recovery was rapid."

"Thank you, Mr. Ambassador." The two men searched each other's eyes for a long moment. Margolin took a deep breath and waited.

"One of my countrymen, a famous writer, said watching the United States was like a 'test run for the decline of the human race.' His prediction proved correct. You fell from greatness, but you can recover. I personally hope you do."

"Why?" Margolin asked bluntly.

"I'm not sure," Kumakura said. "Perhaps because you've helped us in the past. Perhaps because we've had foolish policies of our own. Maybe I'm just an old man mourning his son. In any case, I wanted you to know we're not your enemy."

"Thank you, Mr. Ambassador. Some of us are trying to get back to our roots. A smaller and less intrusive government. The Constitution. Liberty. Freedom. Individual Responsibility. None of this is a threat to your nation."

"It will be interesting to watch." Kumakura finished his tea and gently set the cup down. "I brought one more document for you." He handed over a larger envelope. "Your Senate was right to abrogate President Harney's treaty."

Margolin raised his eyebrows.

"This letter, which I leave for you to convey to the proper authority, offers a formal apology for Captain Tanaka's deplorable conduct. My government also would like your country to keep the monies that we advanced to President Harney as a gift."

Holy shit. Can he be serious? "A gift?"

"An indefinite, interest-free loan, to be precise. You can pay us back when you've recovered."

"Why are you doing this, Mr. Ambassador?"

"You helped us rebuild after the wars of the last century. You provided a shield for us during the Cold War. This is the least we can do."

"That's a lot of money," Margolin said carefully. "What do you expect in return?"

"As I said, it's a gift. Though I would appreciate another cup of your excellent tea, sometime."

"You may have one now, Mr. Ambassador, if you wish."

"Thank you, but no. I'll look forward to that pleasure sometime in the future."

The two men shook hands and Kumakura bowed respectfully and took his leave. After he left, Margolin sat for a long time thinking about their conversation and its ramifications.

That was a signal of a major Japanese policy change. I think the smooth son-of-a-bitch is nudging me to run for President.

He buzzed his secretary. "I need you to find Ernie. I need to see him *muy pronto.*"

Cascade Mountains

I can't let Reggie down. Kate tried to remember what her father taught her. *Keep the stock tight against your shoulder and squeeze.*

Of course, ducks didn't wear body armor and shoot at you with automatic weapons. She occasionally looked at her watch. At first, time seemed to be passing quickly, but then it started to drag.

More time passed. Kate concentrated on staying motionless. She had a clear view of the cave and the trailhead, but saw nothing. *I mustn't make a sound,* she thought. The forest was very quiet.

She saw something, a flicker of motion. She reached carefully for her weapon. Peering through the trees, she saw a man in black flow out of the forest and approach the cave. He was carrying a rifle. Another man appeared, then two more. All carried weapons, but none had a backpack or a red armband.

Then she saw the leader with his red armband. He stood up and strolled casually into the clearing, accompanied by his radioman. She couldn't hear what they said, but they were talking, peering into the cave. The radioman was on the right, just as Reggie predicted.

The leader gave a hand signal and two more of his men stepped into the clearing. He said something. They spread out, weapons pointed at the cave.

Kate lifted her rifle, lining the sights on the man with the red armband. Nothing happened. She waited. Every leaf and blade of grass seemed vivid. She could hear a slight breeze ruffling the trees. The men in the clearing were fully alert, turning slowly with their weapons, scanning the area.

One had a thermal imager. She crouched, sliding the cover over her head for concealment.

They finished a full circle and focused back on the cave entrance. Kate let her breath out slowly in a silent sigh of relief, putting her sights back on target.

The leader gestured and three of his men approached the cave slowly. One had a white armband. Perhaps a sergeant. He slung his rifle, drew a pistol from his right hip, cocked it, and aimed into the cave.

"Come out with your hands in sight."

Kate could hear the words clearly.

She waited.

"Last chance," the man called.

Kate started counting in her head. Before she got to three the man started firing into the cave. She saw the gun jerk in his hand and the shell casings fly out. He took his time, aimed carefully, and squeezed off six shots. She heard a bullet whine as it ricocheted off rock.

Then there was silence again.

The sergeant gestured and his two men charged into the cave. The explosion came instantly, a bright flash, followed by the blast and screams. The sergeant dropped his pistol and gripped his stomach with both hands, trying to push back intestines and bright blood. Then he was falling.

So was the radioman, smashed to the ground by an invisible hand.

Kate squeezed her trigger and the rifle kicked savagely, a double tap. The leader staggered. He started to turn, and she fired again. One of the rounds caught him in the cheek, spinning him half around as he fell.

He dropped his gun and was screaming in agony. The two men on his right dropped like stones. She heard the heavy rolling booms of Reggie's sniper rifle echoing off the hills.

Kate swung her gun left and flicked the selector to full auto. She fired short bursts, the gun pounding into her shoulder, bucking, trying to ride up. Her hand was hurting again, but she saw the last man fall just as her weapon clicked empty.

Eight down, she thought, trying to reload.

She dropped the clip. *Damn.* Her hand wasn't working right. She saw blood on the bandage.

She bit her lips suppressing a moan and, ignoring the pain, picked up another clip. She slipped it into the gun, slapped it into place with her palm, and chambered a round.

Kate heard distant screams. She saw movement in the clearing. The leader was crawling crab-like toward the bushes. A man ran out and grabbed his arm to help.

Chook, Chook, Chook, Chook, Chook. The muffled thumps of Reggie's grenade launcher were followed by a walking string of explosions across the clearing, lashing the men and bushes with shrapnel. When she looked again, there was silence. Nothing moved in the clearing.

Nine down. There's still three more out there.

She waited, motionless, terrified, straining her ears. Did she hear something? She wasn't sure. Then she was.

A man stood up not fifty feet in front of her. His shoulder was bloody. One arm was dangling limp, but he was swinging a weapon toward her. Everything seemed to be happening in slow motion.

Kate felt her rifle kick and saw the man's body jerk. His gun drooped and he fired into the ground. He looked at her for a long moment with sad eyes, trying to raise his weapon.

She fired again, his knees folded, and he collapsed.

Kate put two more shots into the body. When nothing happened, she shifted to a better position, aimed carefully and put two more rounds into his head.

Her hands were shaking. She took deep breaths until they stopped. Then she picked up another clip and reloaded.

Time passed, and Kate waited as the shadows lengthened. The breeze had died down and the forest was very still. Her left hand was throbbing, the bandage red with blood. She took a pill for the pain, chasing it with a swallow of water, and draping the cover carefully over her head.

This night was going to be a long one.

BOOK FIVE:
RENEWAL

"There is a well-known saying that power corrupts, and absolute power corrupts absolutely. I disagree. It is not that power corrupts so much as immunity. That is, corruption results not from being able to wield power per se, but from being able to wield it without consequences."

John W. Campbell

"The name of American, which belongs to you...must always exalt the just pride of Patriotism.... It should be the highest ambition of every American to extend his views beyond himself, and to bear in mind that his conduct will not only affect himself, his country, and his immediate posterity; but that its influence may be co-extensive with the world, and stamp political happiness or misery on ages yet unborn."

George Washington

CHAPTER SIXTEEN

UNKNOWN LOCATION

Three days ago, Will was first able to stumble to the bathroom without assistance. He smiled to himself grimly. *A major milestone.*

He was still weak and sleeping most of the day, but the physiologist said he was doing fine. They'd brought an exercise bike into the room and insisted that he work up to thirty minutes a day.

Today he'd managed that, though at the lowest setting. Becky had rushed off to fetch the doctor and give her the news. They were chatting excitedly when they entered.

Dr. Salazar was a young Mexican who'd gotten her MD in the U.S. She was proud of how well Will's tissues and organs had regenerated. "I rebuild you from scratch, *señor* Will. When you got here, only the machines were keeping you alive. Now everything works."

"It's starting to."

"You are my best patient. My mentor is very happy. After this, I will have my own clinic for sure." Her English was strained, her accent delightful – *veer-hee app-hee* – and she was so exuberant about his recovery he could barely understand what she was saying.

Is she glad I was an extreme case, a total wreck? Or glad because I recovered and saved her from professional embarrassment? He didn't like feeling like a guinea pig, but, in any case, his strength was returning, and he had no pain. *How do I respond to that?*

"Thank you," he finally said.

She favored him with a radiant smile. "This is…." she struggled for the correct word. "Today, you graduate. You are released.

"You are 'good to go,' like you Americans say, *señor*. Now we move you to an apartment of your own. We get you to into rehabilitation. You are good now and soon you will be better than new."

Becky was beaming encouragement.

"Better than new," Will said. "What exactly does that mean, Doctor?"

"We're going to train you to get more power from your mind and body. With proper training you can help your body recover faster and stay healthy.

"I am done with you, Mister Will, except you must come back for checkups. I work with sick people, but you are well. Now you just need to not let bad people hit you with things."

"I'll try to avoid it," he said dryly. "What's next?"

"I have an extra room in my apartment," Becky said. "I can help you acclimate. Or you can have your own, but right now I need to take you to another doctor."

He nodded, not wanting to commit until they had some time to talk in private.

"You get dressed. I'll be right back. You'll find clean clothes and shoes in the closet."

The shoes turned out to be sandals. The clothes were his size, but fit loosely, especially the pants. He'd lost weight. He put them on and cinched the heavy brown leather belt as tight as he could. Even on the last hole, it was still loose. He had to hold them up when he walked.

Becky was back in a few minutes. She looked him over approvingly. "Not bad, but don't go outside in those sandals."

He looked at her.

"Snakes."

"What kind of snakes? Where are we?"

Becky grinned. "The kind you don't want to bite you. Two thousand years ago, they called it the northern Maya lowlands."

He blinked. "Where?"

"I'll show you tomorrow. I've got a new pair of hiking boots coming for when we get out for exercise. We left yours in Oregon, but I found a pair in the same brand and size that will be here tomorrow. I'll get you some pants that fit and a smaller belt too." Her grin broadened. "Don't suck your stomach in or those are coming down."

"Yeah, I know," he said. "Can you find me something to put another hole in the belt?"

"Maybe. Take it off, give it to me, and I'll be right back."

She returned in a few minutes, handed him the belt, and watched him put it on. "I think that's better."

"It will work," he said. "Thanks."

She led him down the corridor to his next appointment. The corridor, like his room, was lit by a warm glow from the ceiling.

Will stopped and put his hand on the wall, then touched the floor. They were very smooth, as if they'd been carved precisely and polished.

"It's made from blocks of granite." Becky showed him the seams between the blocks. They were very fine lines, so thin that he didn't think he could slide a paper between them.

How unusual. He started to ask about that, but she shushed him. "Later. We have to get you to your appointment."

The doctor was a tall man with auburn hair, a neatly trimmed beard, and striking pale blue eyes. He wore a white robe, tied around the waist, and sandals. The room was cool with soft white lighting, and the decor was a mix of rustic and modern.

The walls were stone, like the corridor, but rougher and less finished. The furniture was rather crudely made from wood. Strangely, there was a big white cat perched in a chair by the door. It studied him – totally relaxed, paws tucked in – with intense golden eyes.

That's a most serious cat, Will thought. He ruffled its ears and was rewarded by a beatific look and a purr.

You're welcome. Will smiled. He placed himself in the chair indicated.

There were normal things you would expect in a doctor's office – a stethoscope and blood pressure monitor, a notebook computer, and a sink – but Will had never seen anything like the pair of devices the doctor was holding. "What kind of doctor are you?"

The doctor grinned. "Damned good, but you do test us."

That broke the ice. Will and Becky chuckled.

"Mine is an unusual specialty by your standards. The closest you come in your society is something along the line of empathic psychiatry and holistic medicine. I'm going to ask you a few questions and test your neural responses. We're going to wear these small headbands." The doctor held them up. "The devices help me link better to your thoughts and feelings.

"The purpose of this session is to help gauge your core convictions and to see if certain training methods we have would be appropriate for your psycho-physiology. I'll also check your physical health, though Dr. Salazar is most pleased with your progress. Is it your wish that Rebecca be in attendance?"

"Shouldn't she be?"

"It's entirely your choice. At the end, if you wish, I can share some personal information with you about what I've learned.

"Your society is not healthy, and that often makes its people unhealthy. Your lives are grounded in fear, not love, and in scarcity and competition, not abundance. Most of you are closed and distrustful. You tend to guard your thoughts and live in isolation."

Will thought about that. Finally he nodded.

"You think distrust is safer because you don't know whom you can trust, but you pay a high price for that safety. I'm impressed that you're sufficiently open as to want another person here. Are you two close?"

Will thought about the past few weeks with Becky. *Good question. I think so.* "Yes."

"No," she said.

They both looked at Becky.

Will blinked. *Women are so confusing. I wish they came with instruction manuals.* "I admit we've not had much of a personal relationship. I've been a little stressed. Now that we're not running for our lives would it help if I gave you some flowers?"

"It wouldn't hurt. Some wine would be nice too. A girl appreciates things like that…"

The doctor was watching them with a bemused smile.

Becky looked at Will. "We're becoming close. I'd like to stay if he'll allow it."

The doctor glanced at Will, who nodded. "I want her to stay."

"You've been through this process, Rebecca. You know that all we discuss is private and not to be shared without Will's permission?"

"I agree."

"Is there anything you want to tell him before we start?"

"This doctor can be trusted. We call those in his specialty the 'Shining Ones,' a term of honor. They can help as spiritual advisors and psychologists. Use him to help you learn about yourself. I did, and it helped me to grow."

The doctor proceeded with his tests. He asked a series of questions about Will's formative years, about valued things, about fears and hopes.

He sat next to his patient, with the tips of his fingers touching Will's forehead gently. Will answered as honestly and completely as he could.

Becky mostly listened, occasionally adding her insights. She knew more about him than he'd realized.

They talked for a long time. The doctor took no notes, but instead gazed into space with a look of concentration. Finally, he nodded and took his hand away. He removed the headbands and placed them on the small table next to him.

The doctor produced a small device which he passed slowly over Will's body. He paid particular attention to the vital organs and frowned once when the device beeped. He made some adjustments and pushed a button. The device hummed for a time, then beeped twice.

"That's it. All done."

"That's all?"

"Unless you have questions."

"Of course I have questions. Did I pass?"

"There is no pass or fail. We are what we are. All life is valuable."

Will frowned. "Perhaps I phrased that incorrectly. Did you find anything abnormal?"

"You've suffered major trauma to your body, but it's rebuilding properly. You need food and exercise, but you'll be fine. Beyond that, you need to change your habits so your life force can become more harmonious."

"I don't understand."

"You've been living under considerable stress. You haven't treated your body as well as you should. You need to think better of yourself."

"How so?"

"Fear and despair are toxic. Even before you were injured, you had deterioration in both kidneys. Untreated, it would have killed you eventually. The regeneration is nearly complete. I will prescribe dietary supplements and exercises that will help you maintain full functionality.

"Beyond that you need to choose your path." The doctor smiled. "We'll help you develop your talents, but only you can decide how best to use them."

Certainly their medical technology is very advanced. "Can I stay here?"

"That's between you and our *Viracocha*, but I see no reason why you couldn't. You're not a damaged personality. You're not addicted to substances or destructive habits."

Will looked at Becky.

"The *Viracocha* is our leader. You'll meet him soon."

Will nodded.

"My recommendation to him will be positive. Your mind is healthy, and there is no evil or hate in your heart. You strive to do good, to better the human condition. I personally hope you'll choose to stay.

"If you do, you're welcome to learn any knowledge that we can share with you. Still, knowledge is dangerous. If you accept education in our methods, you also accept training to suppress selected higher knowledge when placed under conditioning, pain, or in a situation where you lose control of rational processes."

"You mean if I'm tortured or interrogated under drugs?"

"Exactly. It's dangerous for evil people to acquire advanced scientific knowledge. They might do harm to themselves and to others. Advanced science without spirituality and ethical behavior is dangerous. There must be absolutes about right and wrong."

"Like the Ten Commandments?"

"An excellent example: Simple, clear, and absolute, setting a bright line between right and wrong. With nuclear and biological weapons a few barbarians can cause much destruction. As science gets more powerful, the risk of misuse increases exponentially.

The doctor was staring into his eyes, as if trying to examine his soul. "Our conditioning methods are for your own safety. Will you accept them?"

"Have you and Becky had that conditioning?"

They both nodded. "We have," Becky said.

"Then I agree."

Becky was beaming, thanking him with her eyes. "Do you remember when I was telling you about ancient maps and long ago events?"

He nodded.

"There's so much more. I didn't tell you about pyramids or the portals."

"About the *what?*"

She waved him down. "We can talk about all that later. Right now please use this time to your best advantage. This doctor is from an advanced society. There are only two Shining Ones on Earth and they are cherished. Use your time well. You can ask him whatever you want to know about yourself."

Will looked at the man. "Why has my life been so bleak and unrewarding?"

The doctor started talking....

Cascade Mountains

"Don't shoot, ma'am. It's me." The voice was soft.

"Come ahead."

Reggie materialized out of the dark forest like a ghost.

"Where are they?" Kate whispered.

"We got lucky." He was smiling. She could see the glint of his teeth in the moonlight.

"What do you mean?"

"They were sloppy. Totally lost their weapons discipline when you took their leader down. Instead of laying down suppressing fire, they stood around in the kill zone looking for targets. Too bad for them."

"You got the last two?"

"Yes, ma'am. Did a body count too. Eleven plus the one out there in front of you, and he ain't moving."

"He's not breathing either. I put my last two shots into his head."

"Twelve kills then. We got 'em all. My friends are coming to get us out of here."

Praise God, Kate thought. *We live.*

Unknown Location, two days later

Becky took Will to the small cafeteria for coffee, the first he'd had since they were in the mountains together. It seemed like a lifetime ago. So much had happened. He took a sip and nodded in appreciation.

"That's excellent."

"Guatemalan." She smiled. "It's the good stuff."

They sat close together, holding hands without saying much. Will found himself just sitting, watching people, savoring being alive and with someone he cared for. This felt good, but then he remembered his responsibilities. He remembered Kate and frowned.

"What's wrong?"

"My people are scattered and hiding. I was just thinking about them, about Kate."

"She's going to be fine, Will. She's here. They're giving her your old room."

Thank God. "Can I see her?"

"Of course. She got here last night and she's been asking about you."

Will felt as if a weight had come off his shoulders as they strode down the corridor. Becky rapped on the door and they heard a gruff, "Come in." It wasn't a woman's voice.

But Kate was there, propped up on pillows sipping a glass of fruit juice. She saw him and smiled as he rushed to her bedside.

"You look a hell of a lot better than the last time I saw you." Kate started crying, but she was still smiling.

Will hugged her and then sat down in the chair by the bed, the same chair where Becky kept her vigil all those weeks. Kate wiped her tears away, still smiling, and looked at him.

"You look a lot better too. Are you all right?"

"I'm fine, thanks to you. And to him." She glanced over his shoulder.

Will glanced back. There was a big man nonchalantly leaning against a wall, watching him. He was about 250 pounds and six four or five. His shoulders and arms were massive, bulging with cords and sinews. These were not "gym muscles," they looked like those of a professional athlete in top form.

Then Will noticed the weapons, the first he'd seen in this place. The man had a pistol slung on his belt, and a big knife strapped to his leg. They both looked like they'd seen a lot of use. So did he.

I wouldn't want to meet him in a dark alley, Will thought, noticing the scars and feeling a tinge of apprehension. "Do we know each other?"

"Yep, sorta," the man said in a soft Texas drawl. "You look a heap better than the last time I saw you."

There was an air of restrained violence about him, as if he was wary of accidentally breaking things. Will noticed a deep scar on his right arm and wondered idly what had happened to the person who inflicted it.

Tanaka's men were like attack dogs, but this one is a timber wolf. Independent, undomesticated, and lethal, an element of nature. Dad's old sergeant, Harry Conners, had that look. A wolf only loses one fight, and it's his last.

Will remembered Harry, dead on the floor. The image was burned into his mind like a picture. Harry went down fighting, doing his best to protect his friends. *Greater love hath no man....*

He thought of Kate strapped to the chair in his office with blood running from her ruined hand. A wave of dizziness swept over Will, and he swayed for a moment.

"Are you all right?" Becky looked concerned. She put her hand on his arm.

"Give me a minute. I was just having a flashback to the last time I saw Kate."

"It wasn't my best day," Kate said. "Permit me to introduce Reginald Metzger. I call him Reggie, but most people call him Rex."

She was looking at them both fondly. "Reggie and I got you out of Cybertech, but you probably don't remember. You were unconscious at the time."

"I'm very glad to meet you." Will stuck out his hand and watched it vanish into the big man's grip. Rex shook it gently. He gave it back intact and stood there grinning.

He's careful not to hurt people. Kate trusts him. More than that, she likes him, and she's a good judge of people.

Becky looked up at Rex. "Thank you." She stepped over to him, hugged him, and kissed him on the cheek.

It looks like a small kitten hugging a ferocious tiger, but the kitten is totally unafraid, and the tiger looks embarrassed. Will started to relax.

Rex glanced at Will. "Miss Kate told me about you. You got a lot of balls. I don't know many civilians who'd stand up to Peace Enforcers. You weren't even armed."

"You were in my office at Cybertech during Tanaka's raid?"

"Right at the end."

"I didn't do much good. Tanaka was beating me to death."

"You were just creating a tactical diversion." Rex smiled encouragingly. "If you were in the Army, they'd probably give you a Gawd damned medal."

They'd give me a medal for hitting Tanaka in the boots with my kidneys? How odd. "You got me out of there?"

"Kate and I did."

Will shuddered. "Tanaka liked to hurt people."

"Not anymore," Kate said. "Rex shot him five times."

Will looked at the big man, "No kidding?"

The Texan shrugged. "Five's what it took."

"Tanaka won't be bothering anyone again," Kate said. "Not ever."

"For sure," the Texan said. His eyes were friendly.

"That's a fact," Becky agreed, "and one for which many people are grateful."

"Ahem." Kate cleared her throat. "I should remind the *men,*" somehow she made the word sound accusing, "before we go into a serious testosterone overload here, that it is I who was officially credited for thwarting Captain Tanaka and his nefarious minions. And with one hand tied behind my back."

She held up her injured hand to prove it.

Will looked at Rex and blinked in astonishment. "Really?"

Rex was laughing so hard that tears were running down his cheeks. Finally he caught his breath and nodded.

"It's Gospel truth, so help me. The Peace Enforcers have her down as a major Badass, with a capital 'B.' They had a small army chasing all over Oregon trying to catch her. I think we're going to maybe see Kate in the history books."

"The victors get to write the history," Becky said softly.

"She thwarted the hell out of Tanaka." Rex nodded solemnly. "It's official."

He dissolved into laughter again.

Kate's face was a study in one-upmanship. "You're definitely looking at history here."

"Actually, the charges against Kate have been dropped." Becky gave a dramatic sigh, rolled her eyes, and fluttered her eyelids pathetically. "But they always try to blame the woman...."

Will couldn't restrain himself – he broke out laughing. Apparently that was okay, because Becky, Kate and Reggie were laughing too.

They finally agreed they'd all saved each other, and were still laughing when Dr. Salazar returned and chased the visitors out of Kate's room.

CHAPTER SEVENTEEN

UNKNOWN LOCATION, CHIAPAS HIGHLANDS, YUCATAN

After a good night's sleep, they were both ravenous. The breakfast was delicious: huevos rancheros with black beans, rice, and the excellent hot black coffee.

"I'm glad you like Mexican food," Becky said. "That, plus seafood, pretty much defines the local cuisine. There's a nature area nearby where we can talk and relax."

As they emerged from a long stone tunnel into bright sunshine, Will stopped, turned, and looked back. His jaw dropped. "It really *is* a pyramid."

"Told you."

"I thought you were kidding. Is it like the ones in Egypt?"

"Same basic construction. Pyramids have been found all over the world, though most people associate them with Egypt. Ours here is bigger than most. The ones in this hemisphere typically don't have the same shapes as those in Egypt on the Giza plateau, the ones you see in the tourist brochures. Those at Giza have the classic pyramidal shape. Some argue that's because the big one there was a geodetic marker and the architects wanted to make it distinctive."

"A marker?"

"As societies advance into sea travel and beyond, they need precise navigation. One key problem is the need for a prime median, a longitudinal starting point. In 1884 to develop common maps, the major nations of the world met in Washington to standardize on a zero point."

"Greenwich Mean Time," Will said. "The zero meridian runs through Greenwich, England. That's how we set time zones all over the world."

Becky nodded. "The British ruled the seas at the time, so they prevailed. But the ancient maps, the few that were accurate, and the portolans, used a meridian that was thirty-one degrees eight minutes east as their zero line."

"What's a portolan?"

"The word means 'port to port.' In medieval times land maps and nautical charts were different things. Portolans, ancient nautical charts, were considered state secrets."

"Does it matter?"

"It did back then. Possession by anyone unauthorized was punishable by death in many countries. Portolans were incredibly accurate, and no one knows why. There were arguments at that same meeting in 1884 to use their zero line for the prime meridian, but the proposal lost."

"So?"

"That meridian line runs exactly through the Giza Pyramid. Its positioning is just as precise for latitude. We measure it at 30 degrees 6 minutes North, but due to atmospheric refraction it appears at exactly 30 North when viewed from space. It's in the center of the earth's habitable landmasses and would have stood out from orbit because it was faced in highly polished mirror-like stones."

"There aren't any polished facings," Will said. "Even in old photos, it was just rough rock."

"Not always. There was a major earthquake in AD 1301 that shook the casing blocks loose. Most were later removed to build Cairo, but enough were left that scientists measured them in the nineteenth century. Today's technology can't grind big blocks to those tolerances.

"The facing stones weighed ten tons each. The pyramid's core structure consists of much larger blocks of granite. Didn't you ever wonder why sane beings would build structures from 200 ton blocks?"

"Instead of easier-to-handle sizes?"

"Yes."

"There's nothing sane about it. It was hubris, pure and simple. Pyramids are works of ego, monuments to dead kings."

She smiled. "Have you considered alternative explanations?"

"Why bother? It's ancient history."

"Because the explanations don't fit the facts. Think about it as an engineer. Those huge blocks were carved to high precision. We couldn't build anything like that today. Even if we could, we wouldn't. It'd be too expensive."

"What are you suggesting?"

"What if the ancient pyramids were machines? What if they had a purpose, a function?"

"They did. They were tombs."

She shook her head. "That doesn't fit the facts. They've *never* found an ancient mummy in a pyramid."

"Sure they did. What about King Tut's tomb? I saw the exhibit once."

"No." She was smiling and shaking her head. "That common belief isn't supported by fact. Tut's tomb was in the side of a hill in the Valley of the Kings, hundreds of miles from the pyramids. Egyptology has become rigid, if not strident, but its dogma doesn't hold up to scrutiny."

"For example...?"

"The astronomical alignments of the ancient pyramids are so precise they're almost uncanny. Why would anyone need such precision for tombs?"

"I have no idea."

"Pyramids are found in groups, often in triads. Usually one is significantly larger than its two satellites, and always they are formed from huge blocks of the hardest rock available. The granite in the Giza pyramids came from hundreds of miles away. Why?"

"Beats me...."

"Pyramids have been found in Mexico, Central America, and all the way down to high mountain lakes in the Peruvian Andes. There are over 100 pyramids in China's Shenshi province, more than in Egypt. It's a forbidden zone for foreigners so you don't hear much about them."

"I didn't know that," he said. "Big ones?"

"The 1,000-foot 'white pyramid of Xian' is the largest one known. Even isolated places like Tenerife had pyramids. These places couldn't have had any contact with ancient Egypt unless there was an advanced society at the time."

"Where the hell is Tenerife?"

"On an island, way out in the Atlantic Ocean, down near Morocco. Nowhere near Egypt. The Mesopotamians and the ancient Kush, in Sudan, built pyramids before Egypt even existed. Does it make any sense that all over the world, dozens or hundreds of kings in disparate primitive societies all developed compulsions to be buried in pyramids?"

"Perhaps not, but it's possible...."

"Is it possible all these primitive societies concurrently got the same capability in advanced astronomical science and the same ability to precisely machine and transport multi-hundred ton blocks of stone? All without machine tools or power sources, not even animal power?"

"They had animal power, didn't they?"

"No. Even those who support traditional dogma admit Egypt didn't get horses until later. The Western Hemisphere didn't get them until the 1500s. The myth that slaves using hand tools built such massively precise structures is simply not possible."

I give up, he thought. "Maybe not. So what?"

"When you eliminate the impossible, what's left, however improbable it may seem, must be considered."

"Aristotle?"

She grinned. "Sherlock Holmes."

"What does this have to do with you and me?"

"A lot. It brought us together. I figured, 'What the hell? What if conventional history is wrong?' I got interested in trying to link history to advanced technology. That journey led me to rescuing you from the Peace Enforcers. Now it's led us here. What do you think of that?"

"I'm not laughing, if that's what you're worried about...."

"Good. Penguins were interesting. I'm glad to have my Ph.D. Here's the thing: That's not why I was freezing my ass off in Antarctica. There were other reasons."

He glanced at her questioningly, but she looked pensive and didn't say more. The day was warm and humid. Will was getting his strength back and enjoyed the walking. She led him to a clear lake, and they took off their shoes and stuck their feet in the water. It felt good.

"There are scientists who think there may have been technological civilizations on Earth long before modern times. We don't talk about it publicly because they'd dismiss us as nuts."

Will smiled. "It's a career limiting topic?"

"More like career suicide. I'd never have been allowed to do research in Antarctica if I'd told them the truth. I'd be ridiculed."

He remembered her tirade when he'd mentioned Atlantis. "This has to do with the old maps, doesn't it?"

"Exactly right. The maps demonstrated an advanced technology, both by their accuracy and the mathematics upon which they were based. The center of their focus was around what we now call Antarctica. The real reason I went to the Antarctic was to find relics, to find proof."

"What proof?"

"Pyramids. The ancient construct that most withstands the ravages of time. We found a grouping of pyramids buried in Antarctica. And it was still functional."

"Under the ice?"

"Deep: over three-quarters of a mile down. We had a cover story about trying to reclaim a lost B-24 aircraft from World War II named 'Wedding Belle.' We brought a lot of special equipment to do subsurface scans and melt through the ice."

She smiled. "Several rare aircraft have been collected from under the ice in Greenland and other less hostile places. This was the first attempt in Antarctica. We wrote the expedition up in *National Geographic* as a failure. Technically, it wasn't even a lie. We found no airplanes."

"You said, 'Still functional.' How can a pyramid be functional? It's just a pile of rocks that sits there."

She shook her head. "Ours was a power source, an ionospheric tap. Apparently, the ancients tapped terawatts of electrical power from the ionosphere. It's like using the whole planet as an electric generator. It's a superior technology."

"Why?"

"There's no pollution, no waste products, and you're not using up a resource that can't be replaced."

"There must be some disadvantages. Everything's a trade off. That's engineering 101."

"Sure. That much energy release is dangerous. For one thing, it puts tremendous stress on the structures. That's why huge masses of rock were needed. The great pyramid in Egypt weighs six million tons and is seated on bedrock."

"Terawatts." He computed briefly in his head. "Our modern civilization doesn't consume that much energy. As an engineer I'd worry about side effects."

"You should. We think the triad we found caused the holes in the ozone layer at the South Pole. We know they've diminished since it shut down."

"Keep talking."

"Ionosphere taps depend on the relative motion of the earth's spin. They work by cutting lines of magnetic force with a beam. Their efficiency is low in Polar Regions, and exactly at the poles they don't work at all.

"At the equator they'd work too well, like short-circuiting a generator. It is possible that misuse of ionosphere taps for power could have caused an ancient disaster that wiped out advanced civilizations. Many suspect ancient disasters. There are other theories that range from Mega Volcanos to earth crustal displacement, to, of course, the Biblical flood."

"Let's stick with the ionosphere taps. Assuming they exist and work, for the sake of argument, whatever did the Ancients need so much power for, Becky?"

She didn't reply for some reason.

"Well?"

After a long pause, she finally said. "This is where it gets crazy. Let's walk while I think about how to say what I want to tell you."

They hiked for about an hour. The air was warm, but not too hot. The Doctor prescribed vigorous walking, and they carried water to keep themselves hydrated.

She insisted he stop and drink periodically, reminding him of the doctor's orders. She'd even brought sun block lotion in several forms, which they carefully applied.

They eventually came to a pleasant glade. Becky sat down in a patch of sunshine and leaned against a tree. Will sat on the grass, facing her.

"Do you believe in teleportation?" she asked abruptly.

"Like in Star Trek? I've seen the old videos. *Beam me up, Scotty.*"

"I'm not talking about Hollywood. In the real world."

"Actually, I do. Quantum teleportation is a well-known phenomenon," Will said. "First demonstrated back in 1997. Caused quite a squabble at the time. The Americans proposed it theoretically, and the Austrians, Italians, and Japanese all demonstrated it at about the same time. It's the basis of modern quantum cryptography. I'm quite familiar with it."

"I didn't know that." She had an odd look on her face. "Are you're saying we can beam matter around without problems?"

"I doubt it," he said. "It's quantum craziness. The theory works, but not like in the movies. We can teleport particles, not people. I doubt we'll ever be able to send people."

"Why not?"

"Because we don't know how. And even if we did, there are many problems. The amounts of energy involved are enormous." Will took a stick and drew Einstein's famous equation in the dirt.

$$E = mc^2$$

Becky looked at him.

"Energy equals mass times a very large number, the speed of light squared. Converting a few grams of matter to energy releases the energy equivalent of megatons of TNT. It works the same way in reverse. Our entire civilization doesn't produce enough energy to teleport my wristwatch, much less a person."

"Maybe there's something we don't yet understand. Maybe we'd have enough power if our civilization was more advanced."

He was staring at her. "This isn't about movies or science fiction, is it? You know something."

"Pyramids. We didn't tap much power in our Antarctic digging. We only managed to get our triad to just barely work and only for a few minutes, but it was enough to activate an automatic transport device."

"What?"

"The doctor who examined you is one of five people who were transported here. They came from an outpost on a planet of the double star Sirius."

Will thought about it. *In my grandfather's day, rockets, computers, and atomic energy were science fiction. Today, they're common tools. Any sufficiently advanced technology is indistinguishable from magic.*

"Five healers? Like the doctor that saw me?"

She shook her head. "The leader is the *Viracocha*, a civilizer. His job, his vocation, is to carry civilization to isolated parts of the universe. His team includes two Shining Ones, doctors, and two technician soldiers."

"*Viracocha's* a job?"

"It's a profession, a vocation, perhaps a calling. Apparently disasters that cause civilizations to regress are not uncommon. They keep emergency teams on duty, just in case a lost portal opens. The *Viracocha* said there hasn't been one open to Earth for over four millennia."

No little green men, just people with human frailty trying to cope. Man is a tool-using animal. Without tools, he is nothing. With tools he is everything. It seemed to fit, somehow. "I'd like to meet him," Will said.

"He wants to meet you too. He sent me to get you."

"In the mountains?"

She nodded.

"Why?"

"I asked to go. I said we needed your technology, and he agreed. You're honest, competent, and I trust you."

"Do you trust this *Viracocha*?"

"Absolutely. It goes far beyond normal trust. I've lived with this team for over a year, and I know they're here to serve. Remember what the doctor said about how our civilization teaches fear and distrust, and that being unhealthy?"

"Our poets and priests say the same. Distrust is our only defense."

"What if that is wrong? The human mind is intrinsically empathic. We all have latent telepathic abilities as children, but we don't train them. What if we could truly sense what was in our brothers' hearts? What if we knew a higher purpose?"

She asks difficult questions. "I'd expect life would be better or much worse."

"Why?"

"Better, because evil, treachery, and ignorance would be obvious, and we could cull it out. We'd know better who to trust, who to dare love."

"All the great spiritual leaders of mankind have preached that message. Most major religions in the world are based on love."

"You are assuming we'd also know who to hate. People like Tanaka."

"Yes."

"What if we didn't? What if we were sucked into the dark side instead?"

"Why would you say that?"

"Hatred, greed, and fear are far more common than love," Will said sardonically. "The dark side has enormous appeal."

"Think about it. The most evil leaders in history started off as very popular. It gets even worse when religions turn to evil. People kill each other over religion. Religion has caused most of the wars in history."

"Religion and politics." She sighed. "God gave us free will, so we use it to kill each other. We'll never become a higher civilization if we can't get past that."

"That's why I said things could get worse. Things aren't going well now, are they?"

"No, and the *Viracocha* is tortured. It's his first mission as leader. The hate and fear on our planet makes it an overwhelming challenge."

"Why can't he cope if he's trained for that role?"

"His civilization isn't warlike. They lack nuclear bombs, poison gas, and biological weapons. They'd never conceive of building such horrible things."

"Our science is ahead of theirs?"

"Some of it. Apparently, we're savages who possess advanced weapons technology. They're far ahead of us in many things, especially physics. They're able to generate energy and build large structures without environmental damage."

"Like shaping and moving multi-hundred ton blocks of granite?"

"Exactly. I think our civilization is soul-sick. This visitation is a miracle, one that might well save us."

It would be nice to hold more hope for mankind than I do now, Will thought. "Let's go meet your *Viracocha*."

"You'll help us?"

"Probably. I've been following your lead ever since you first found me in the woods back in Oregon. It seems like a lifetime ago."

Inside the Pyramid

"Thank you for coming, Dr. Giles" The *Viracocha* was stroking a large white cat. The cat was watching Will with luminous violet eyes.

Why do they have these cats? This one resembled the one the doctor had, except for the eyes and its size. This cat was even larger, and its eyes almost glowed. Will felt them searching inside his head, peering into his soul. He forced himself not to look away.

Will was nervous. He reminded himself this person wasn't an alien creature, just a man. He looked much like the doctor except for the sad eyes. Again the eyes were different.

The *Viracocha's* eyes were those of a saint: honest, sincere, and troubled. There were flecks of gray in the auburn hair.

"Will said, "I'm grateful to you for saving my life and offering me sanctuary, but I don't want to bring danger to your group."

The *Viracocha* studied him for a long moment. "I sense that. You bring us no more danger than we already have. The Peace Enforcers are no longer seeking you."

"Are you sure?"

"Yes." The *Viracocha* smiled and nodded. "Some good things have happened, partially because of you. My doctor – we call his profession *hayhuaypanti* – was impressed with you as is Rebecca. You're welcome here."

"Because you need my products?"

"We do, but more. You have great potential. You possess an advanced sense of ethics and responsibility for one from your society. You've spent your life doing what you could to help serve freedom and better mankind."

"Don't overrate me. I've failed at the things most important to me."

"Why do you say that?"

"My company is gone. I've failed at business. I've no personal life. Some hate or fear me because of the things I've tried to do. Some seek to steal what I've created. I've let down people who depended upon me. People who trusted me got hurt."

"I could say the same." The *Viracocha's* voice was soft. "I'd have to add that all governments on your planet would hate and fear me if they knew of my presence. If our group was discovered we'd all die, and because of me."

"Why? Everything I've learned about you testifies you advocate peace and love."

"That's why. Your early United States focused on freedom and did its best to center its power in the people. That's a rare exception to what normally happens on your planet. You distrust those who want to set you free, and you kill your peacemakers. That is your nature and your Earth's history, is it not?"

"I don't understand what you are saying, *Viracocha.*"

"Surely, you must. A famous writer, Dostoevsky, gave you a clear warning about human frailty shortly after your nation was founded. It was almost directed to America as a nation, with the notions of God-given unalienable rights being so explicit in your founding documents. Why did you not heed the warning? Why did mankind not heed it?"

"Who? What warning? I have no idea who or what you are talking about."

"Fyodor Dostoevsky. A Russian novelist. Don't you know him?"

"The name is vaguely familiar...."

"**The Brothers Karamazov.** That was his book."

Not a clue, Will thought. "How old is this book?"

"He started it while in prison few hundred years ago...."

"A few hundred **years**...?"

"The book is still in print. It's still taught."

"I'm sorry. I studied science, not classic literature."

"The notion was The Grand Inquisitor. Have you heard of that?"

Will shook his head. "No, *Viracocha.*"

"Wait." The *Viracocha* closed his eyes and put a hand on his temple, trying to recall. When he spoke, his words were almost mechanical:

"The fundamental tension in 'The Grand Inquisitor' is between God, in the form of Jesus, and worldly power, in the form of the Roman Catholic Church or the State. According to the Grand Inquisitor, the two cannot coexist in the modern world; one must give way because they require different things from their followers."

He blinked, gave a slight headshake, looked at Will, and spoke normally. "Do you understand me now?"

"No, Sir. I do not. I'm sorry."

"Jesus **refused** to make things easy for his followers. He could have given them bread when they were hungry in the desert and satisfied in one gesture their need for material comfort and their need to see miracles. But he refused, demanding instead that his followers believe on the strength of their faith alone, without any proof. God will not force people to believe in him, or to follow him. Each person must be free to choose his own path."

"I agree with that, *Viracocha*. Freedom. Free will. Rights and responsibilities. Yes, my country, America, was founded on that notion. That's our Constitution."

"Ah, but many do not agree. God's road to salvation, says the Grand Inquisitor, is appropriate only for the very strong. Ordinary people are too weak to find this satisfying, as he explains: "Thou didst promise them the bread of Heaven, but. . . can it compare with earthly bread in the eyes of the weak, ever-sinful and ignoble race of men?""

"Handouts. Something for nothing. That's the call of socialism, communism, despots, fanatics, and tyrants," Will said. "Is it not?"

"Exactly so. And it's what directly causes religious wars, jihad, and holocaust. The Grand Inquisitor says it's God's fault, not the fault of the wicked or weak."

Will was frowning. This was heavy stuff. "How so?"

"The Inquisitor says, 'People seek to worship what is established beyond dispute, so that all men would agree at once to worship it.' This is the reason for religious wars: people demand that everyone believe as they do, and for the sake of common worship they've slain each other with the sword. In placing the freedom to choose above all else, God has permitted this misery. And yet, 'man is tormented by no greater anxiety than to find someone quickly to whom he can hand over the gift of freedom.' In short, says the Inquisitor, God does not understand the true nature of human beings. Now do you understand?"

"American tradition, and Christianity, says it differently," Will said. "All the deals with the Devil in our folklore are based on trading instant gratification for eternal damnation."

"Yes." The *Viracocha* smiled softly. "That's it. I'm glad you know the concept."

"It's hard to know who to trust," Will said. "People lie. The wrong ones come to power."

Yowl, the cat said. It sounded like agreement.

The Viracocha glanced at the animal. They exchanged a look and then returned their gazes to Will.

"Your history is tragic and bloody. Through the ages, leaders who preached peace and nonviolence were hated. Often they were assassinated or tortured and put to death, mostly by their own governments, friends, or those they tried to help."

"That's our history," Will agreed. "It's not pretty. Becky says you come as a professional civilizer. You offer us hope. Is that true?"

"It's my life's purpose. My parents on both sides have been *Viracochas* for seven generations. Still, your planet is difficult almost beyond imagining. Others before me have failed here, and now our group is at risk."

"*Viracochas* have helped us before?"

"Several times. Two at least, but I think perhaps more."

"Why don't we know these things?"

"When you regress, you erase your history. There were records in ancient Rome predating the famous Greek library in Alexandria, but in the winter of AD 406 the Rhine froze solid. Hundreds of thousands of savage barbarians crossed and the Roman Empire fell. They pillaged Europe and Asia, destroying all the writings and libraries they found. The golden age survives only in legend."

"Is there any proof of previous visits?"

The *Viracocha* smiled gently. "Proof is in the eye of the beholder. There are faint signals that suggest it to one of my training. I think there was a team here in 10,450 BC."

"Why?"

"In that year, and in that year only, the patterns of the pyramids on the ground in Egypt are an exact reflection of the stars in the sky, with the Nile as the Milky Way galaxy. The Great pyramid at Giza maps into the star Alnitak in Orion's belt, which is where our major transport hub for this sector is sited. There's similar evidence, based on Stonehenge's alignments, of a visit around 2,500 BC."

"Were there other visits?"

The *Viracocha* nodded. "Almost certainly. Perhaps the Nazca lines in Peru or the pyramid that houses us now are testimonials to such past efforts.

"The destruction of records in this hemisphere was systematic, ruthless, and most thorough. The conquistadors destroyed Aztec, Inca, and earlier records because they deemed them to be religious heresy. Spanish bishops built bonfires from astronomical documents, manuscripts, and codices. Records on tablets of gold were looted and melted down. It's all lost."

"Surely your civilization has its own records?"

"Our records go back over sixty thousand of your years. What of it?"

Will's furrowed his brow. "What do you mean, 'What of it'? What happened to higher civilization on earth?"

"I don't understand what you're asking. A disaster ended your planet's golden age. There were probably several attempts to rebuild that civilization. Each time, the civilizers failed. I think they died here, isolated and alone."

"You *think*? What do your records say?"

"I'm not sure. I vaguely recall something from one of my classes, but it was long ago and the details are fuzzy. It was one of several baffling cases they use to curtail the pride of young postgraduate students. At the time I assumed the case was an artificial construct, because it was so intractable. Now I suspect it may have been based on this planet."

"You don't have access to your own records?"

The *Viracocha* shook his head. "My team consisted of twelve plus myself, but only a few were quick enough to make it through before the portal collapsed. Our librarian, engineers, and heavy equipment did not."

"Portal collapsed…?" Will frowned. "I don't understand."

"Forgive me. I've not communicated sufficiently well. My society's core technology is the portals, just as yours is based on oil. I'm told your general relativity theorists might call our portals 'macroscopic wormholes.' They serve as our roads to the stars."

"Quantum teleportation."

"Our engineers use different words." The *Viracocha* shrugged. "I'm sorry. It's a specialized field and I'm not a scientist."

"What can you tell me about your portals? What are their limitations?"

"They consume much energy, so we normally transmit information, not physical objects. A power equivalent beyond that of your entire planet was needed to transport my team here."

"Our theoretical scientists advocate developing quantum computers to bypass the light speed limitation on data transfers," Will said. "Unfortunately, while such machines hold promise, they've not yet been invented."

"We've used portals for millennia. They're proven, trusted, and safe. I've never heard of a portal collapsing, but this one did." The *Viracocha* shuddered. "It was awful.

"We'd never experienced an environment like your Antarctica. We'd have died there without Rebecca's help. None of our engineers would ever site a portal in a polar region. The portal *collapsed*. That just doesn't happen.

"My advance team was equipped for emergency response only. A full team consists of hundreds of trained people. We're few, we have only our personal gear, and we're stranded here."

"Stranded?"

"That's right. We'll die here."

"Why?"

"The few portable devices we have with us can only transmit information and tiny bits of inert matter. Eventually, your civilization may learn to transmit large objects, but I'm afraid it won't be in my lifetime."

"Can you teach us?"

"Be careful what you ask. A civilization that possesses so much power without deep wisdom and maturity invariably destroys itself."

"Our legends contain cautionary tales about the danger of knowledge."

"Rightly so," the *Viracocha* said. "It's dangerous to take a bite from the apple. Would you dare trust your people with such power? It could destroy you."

"All advanced science has that potential. After almost a century, we've used atomic energy only for building bombs and boiling water. Many distrust the ability of government or business to manage it."

"What do you think yourself?"

"I think you should try," Will said.

"Why?"

"The current situation is unstable. Our civilization is regressing."

"Yes," the *Viracocha* said. "Is that a reason?"

"I think so. There's so much to gain. Dependence on petroleum and coal is fouling our nest, and the only useful alternative we've found, nuclear fission, is too hazardous. Offer us a better alternative and we might just make it."

Yowl, the cat said, looking at Will.

The *Viracocha* stroked it and nodded. "You can't manage what you have, so you ask for more. Is that sane?"

"Seeking knowledge is always sane," Will said. "We haven't destroyed ourselves yet."

Yowl, the cat said. It sounded dubious.

Becky reached out and stroked it gently. "We're damned if we do and damned if we don't. Ignorance is the universal enemy."

The *Viracocha* was silent for a time. "I need your help, Dr. Giles."

"What do you require?"

"Scientists and engineers we can train. People of goodwill who can keep a secret. It's our only hope of rebuilding an advanced civilization here."

Thank God, Will thought, relieved. *It's just an engineering problem.* When he looked up, his relief vanished. The *Viracocha* was shaking his head.

"There's a greater challenge. Most governments on this planet have evolved into despotic technocracies that view individual freedom as dangerous. Your preferred organizational form, the bureaucracy, fears and resists new things."

"It does indeed," Will said. "I've fought that most of my life."

"Your weapons are advanced. If we're discovered, we'll perish. Even a small force could easily overwhelm us."

"They won't use violence. Not if you're helping to save us."

Yowl. The cat sounded doubtful.

Becky was shaking her head. "You know better."

"Most people wouldn't use violence," Will said.

"Most doesn't matter. It only takes one person in power," she said. "Just one."

Will sighed. She was right.

The *Viracocha* stroked the cat for a time. His smile was sad. "They nailed your Christian God to a cross for preaching love, compassion, and forgiveness."

"That's what we're taught," Will said.

"I've seen your movies," the *Viracocha* said. Would Hollywood cast me as an alien invader or as a visitor who came to help and was accidentally stranded here?"

"This isn't a movie."

"What happened to the alien who came in peace bringing a warning in *The Day the Earth Stood Still*? What happened to ET, the gentle creature who befriended a child?"

"They died. Well, ET almost died. He escaped and went home."

"People tried to kill them. That's the general theme, isn't it?"

"Don't take it personally," Will said.

"How can I not? The norms of behavior here make me afraid. I fight my fear every minute of every day. If I were able, I'd take my team and run."

"But you can't."

"No." The *Viracocha* watched the cat watch Will.

"It's your decision," Becky said. "But time's running out."

The *Viracocha* nodded but didn't speak. The cat's eyes were almost glowing. It stared at Will appraisingly as the silence lengthened.

Will touched the *Viracocha's* fingers to get his attention. He looked into the sad eyes. "If you've studied our Christian religion, you know it teaches us, *Be not afraid.*"

The *Viracocha* smiled. "Even though I walk through the valley of death…"

"Don't give up. And whatever you do, don't stop. Keep walking, or we may all die."

The *Viracocha* sighed. "You're right, of course. I know we must proceed. That's why I sent your friend Rebecca to get you. Didn't she tell you?"

"Well, yes…" Will took a deep breath. *I just wasn't listening closely enough.*

"What you offer us is more valuable than I'd dared hope. Civilization everywhere tends to backslide as governments and other groups centralize and seize power. Societal decline and oppression is a universal problem."

"Why are my encryption devices so important?"

"The ability to speak honestly and openly in private with one's friends is the most basic freedom of all. You Americans cherish your Constitutional right to public free speech, but isn't the right to speak one's mind privately to your brothers an even more fundamental freedom?"

"We don't think that way."

"It's important you learn. The more advanced the society, the more essential one's right to personal privacy becomes."

"How can my technology be that important?"

"If we succeed here, your devices can help people on many worlds."

Will looked at the *Viracocha* searchingly, seeing honesty in the man's eyes.

"We need your help."

Will nodded slowly. "I'll do what I can."

"Thank you." The *Viracocha* gave his soft smile again. "Don't underestimate how much you can contribute. You gave me the right answer: *Be not afraid*. But it's difficult."

"It sure is."

"We'll try," the Viracocha said. "When good people work together for a higher purpose, great things can be accomplished."

"I hope you're right, but I'm with you in any case." Will took a deep breath, feeling free and alive, feeling the faint stirrings of hope. He felt better than he had for years. Despite the risks, he'd found friends and renewed purpose. He smiled at Becky and took her hand.

BOOK SIX:
SIMPLE, BUT NOT EASY

"We the people are the rightful masters of both Congress and the courts, not to overthrow the Constitution but to overthrow the men who pervert the Constitution."

Abraham Lincoln
"The solution to 1984 is 1776."
Iron John Giles

CHAPTER EIGHTEEN

UNKNOWN LOCATION, CHIAPAS HIGHLANDS, YUCATAN

Twelve days ago, the Doctor had released Will. He was feeling good. Physically, he had more strength and stamina than before his ordeal. He still had bad dreams, but didn't wake up screaming anymore.

The doctor said his posttraumatic stress would take longer to heal than the physical abuse. He'd prescribed exercise and relaxation.

Becky had him on her own therapy program. She was demanding courtship and not being especially demure about it. She said he was getting stronger every day and she should know.

The days had fallen into a pattern. They'd get up at six. He'd exercise in the gym for an hour and take a long shower. He and Becky would breakfast at eight. Then they'd hike somewhere, packing a lunch and not returning until dinnertime.

Will was surprised at the diversity of the environment. There were lakes, mountains, and an abundance of wildlife. There were birds everywhere, some quite large, including peacocks and a species of turkey he'd never heard of. Their heads and necks were blue and covered with red, wart-like growths. Their tail feathers had green-blue eyespots and an iridescent purple cast.

They'd been cautioned about snakes, but he laughed about it. "It's like dolphins and sharks. If you see peacocks, there's not going to be any snakes around."

Peacocks loved to feed on young snakes, and he was told the turkeys did too. He made a point to ensure the birds were around before they spread their blanket on the ground. He even packed food to attract them. Despite his scoffing, he was careful not to sit on rock piles.

Becky was more cautious. She'd put an emergency radio, a snakebite kit, and a .45 with alternating birdshot and hollow point loads in her backpack. Will had spotted some peacocks eating a small, brightly colored snake two days ago. After as close a look as had seemed advisable – the snake was still struggling – she'd declared it harmless.

"That one's supposed to be safe. Just remember, 'Red on yellow - kill a fellow.' They're the bad ones."

"After Tanaka, I'm not going to worry about snakes."

"Shush," she said. "That's over with."

This was a special day, and they were going to celebrate being alive. Becky had talked the Doctor into allowing him alcohol. They'd packed two bottles of the local wine.

The valley floor was lush jungle, but the mountains were sparser and drier. Will preferred the high ground, the open areas.

Today they'd trekked up into the mountains and were sitting next to one of the many streams that fed the lakes. They found a flat rock in the middle of the stream, spread their blanket, chilled the wine in the water, peeled their clothes off, and basked in the warm sun.

She smiled at him. "I love the flowers."

The *Viracocha* had offered gifts in exchange for promises not to worry about Cybertech or do any work for two weeks. Will's request was for wine and to ensure bright flowers were on Becky's plate for their meals. She'd put some in her hair.

He grinned, filled her glass, and kissed her gently.

She kissed him back, less gently. Quite some time passed before they disengaged.

Will was quiet for a long time, watching the stream as it rippled over the rocks. *We need to talk. We need to plan.*

"I've been thinking, Becky," he finally said.

"Don't you *dare* start thinking about business. You promised, and, besides, I'm not done with you yet."

"We can't stay here forever."

"When was the last time you took a vacation?"

Will sighed. "A long time...."

"Months?"

"Longer. Before Dad died. Three years, maybe...."

"That's what I thought." She sipped her wine. "Me too. This is my prenuptial honeymoon, big guy, and I'm enjoying it far too much to stop now."

She chuckled at his look.

"Big guy?"

"Sure. I'll show you." She giggled, reached out, and started stroking him. "A hard man is good to find...."

That was the end of any thoughts he'd had about getting back to work. Will carefully set the wine aside and rolled over to reciprocate. She moaned softly.

Several hours later, they woke up, bodies still entwined. "How about a dip in the water before it gets too cold?" he asked.

Becky smiled dreamily and nodded. After their swim, they climbed up on the bank, dried off, and put their clothes back on. "What was it you were trying to say earlier? I think you got distracted...."

"I'll be good."

"You were," she said. "But that won't help us talk about work."

"It's a great kindness that our friends insisted that we get some time away."

Becky sighed and glanced at the sun. "We have an hour or so before we have to start back. What did you want to talk about?"

Will felt the joy of the moment slip away. A crushing sadness replaced it. A darkness of the soul. It was as if someone had turned the sun down just a notch.

She was looking at him with sudden concern. "What?"

He took a deep breath. "Cybertech is gone, Becky."

"The building burned, but we have what's important. You're safe and so are your people, even Kate."

"Not all of them. What about Harry?"

"It wasn't your fault."

"It was my responsibility. I'm broke, and my company is bankrupt. Cybertech's assets have been confiscated by now. It's gone."

"Why do you say that?"

"We had those 30-day letters. There is no way my lawyers could fight them with all our witnesses gone and the firm's records destroyed. Before I met you in the mountains, I'd decided I needed to go back."

"Oh. You've not seen the news, have you?"

"How could I see the news? I woke up in a hospital inside a freaking stone pyramid. Do they even have a video feed here?"

"That and more. We have many ways of monitoring the outside world."

He looked at her.

"Damn," she said. "I'm so sorry. I wasn't here when you arrived. I thought you knew. I thought certainly you'd been told."

"Told what…?"

"No wonder you want to talk about work…."

"You're going to make me crazy, woman. What are you talking about?"

She took his hands, looked into his eyes, and smiled radiantly. "You silly man."

"What?"

"When you told the *Viracocha* to 'be not afraid,' I was sure you knew. But you didn't, did you? You were just acting from faith."

"Why don't you just assume I don't know anything? I don't know shit. Specifically, I don't know what the hell you're talking about."

She put her arms around him and kissed him. "It's all turned out fine, Will. A lot happened while you were unconscious.

"Those 30-day letters were withdrawn. The Japanese apologized to the U.S. government which has, in turn, apologized to Cybertech and promised reparations."

He blinked in disbelief.

"Some of your employees are national heroes. Your large black woman is a hot item on the talk show circuit."

"Sarah?"

"Kate too, when she gets back," Becky said. "The political winds have shifted. The Peace Enforcers were pulled out of Oregon. President

Harney resigned, and there's a bill in Congress to assure Cybertech gets compensation and damages. Several groups are holding forums on electronic privacy. It promises to be a major issue in the next election.

"Mentioning the election, my uncle's party is supporting his candidacy for President. He wants you to loan him Sam Goldstein for his Justice Department."

Will's mouth was hanging open. He closed it slowly. "Your uncle...?"

Becky smiled, uncorked the second bottle of wine, and poured him a glass. "Here," she said, holding it out. "You look like you need a drink..."

"What uncle...?"

"I guess I never mentioned Uncle George to you. George Margolin. He's a U.S. Senator. He was one of the leading critics of the Harney administration. He's my Godfather."

"I know who Senator Margolin is, but I..." He let the words trail off and shook his head, feeling dazed. "He chairs the Senate Armed Services Committee. I heard him speak once."

"He's on Foreign Relations as well."

"I feel like Rip Van Winkle. What else did I miss while I was asleep?"

She started talking....

CHAPTER NINETEEN

TWO DAYS LATER – MÉRIDA, IN THE YUCATAN

The jeep came around the curve too fast trailing a cloud of dust. Will jammed on the brakes, and let it slide to a stop on the rough gravel road. He turned off the engine and put both hands on the wheel, in plain sight.

Rex, next to him, shifted slightly, but didn't raise his weapon. There were two men blocking the road in military camouflage uniforms.

Becky spoke up from the back seat. "Take it easy and slow. Please. Those are U.S. Marines. They're on our side."

"Yes, ma'am," Rex said. "Just let's check out their ID, okay?"

The officer, a young lieutenant, walked up to the jeep. He had one hand on his sidearm, but kept it in its holster.

His man, a corporal, had an assault rifle and a serious look. The weapon had a long magazine, maybe thirty rounds, and a flash suppressor on the barrel. It wasn't quite pointing at them. He was watching them closely.

The lieutenant approached on Rex's side, eyeing the big man cautiously. He was careful not to come between them and his man.

Rex said, "Stand easy, Lieutenant, we're expected. The lady in the back seat is Dr. Rebecca Rider. Can we check your ID?"

The lieutenant nodded, handing his to Rex.

Rex studied the card carefully. He checked both sides and passed it back. "You don't look as good as your photo, Lieutenant Como."

"Some days are like that."

"Roger that." The officer stepped back, never once blocking his corporal's line of fire. "The lady's expected, and so is Dr. Giles. But you're not."

"They can vouch for me."

"We can't let anyone onto the airfield with weapons." The lieutenant was eying Rex's short-barreled shotgun.

He's lucky Rex's traveling light, Becky thought.

Rex looked down at his weapon as if seeing it for the first time, then back at the Marine. "My job is to protect these people. I'm just a civilian, but if you're doing your job right someone is looking at me through a scoped up rifle right now."

The lieutenant looked at him appraisingly. "You think?"

"If you're not, I'll be damned if I'm going to entrust the safety of my people to you just because you've got a uniform, some shave-tail bars, and a plastic card."

The lieutenant gave an arm signal. Two more men stood up behind the jeep.

Both held assault rifles at the ready. At a signal from the lieutenant they lowered them.

Rex looked back and nodded. He turned to the lieutenant. "Where's the sniper?"

The lieutenant signaled again and pointed. A man stood up on a hill overlooking the trail.

"Nice."

"We try."

"We're not in the United States. Is this one of those Halls of Montezuma things?"

"Senator Margolin will be arriving shortly. We're here to make sure he's safe. I'll need to take your weapons."

"Can't do that, son…."

"Lieutenant," Becky interrupted. "We're all on the same side here. Do your orders extend to keeping me and Dr. Giles safe?"

"Yes, ma'am."

Becky cleared her throat and tapped Rex gently on the shoulder. "Please put your hands up in plain sight. You're making this young man and his soldiers nervous."

"Yes, ma'am." Rex opened both hands and slowly held them up.

"Put them up and grip the top of the windshield."

He glanced at her, then at the Marine, as he complied. His expression was one of total innocence.

The officer relaxed and gave another hand signal. His men vanished silently into the bushes at the side of the trail.

"Would it be acceptable if my bodyguard waited in the jeep at the edge of the field until the Senator arrives and I can get him properly cleared? You may stay with him, if you wish."

The lieutenant frowned.

"Rex has a job to do, and I feel safer with him around. I'll vouch for him and ask Uncle George to get him proper clearances. We don't want to cause you any problems."

"Let me check, ma'am." The lieutenant pulled out a small radio and spoke into it for a few minutes.

Finally he nodded. "Yes, ma'am, that's fine. If you don't mind, I'll ride in the jeep with you. Some of my people tend to be a little excitable."

I'll bet they do, Becky thought. She nodded, and the lieutenant climbed into the back with her, sitting behind Rex.

The Senator's jet landed a few minutes later. They watched it roll to the end of the runway, braking hard, spoilers deployed, engines screaming in full reverse thrust. It stopped, turned, and taxied back. The door popped open, and George Margolin hopped out.

Becky started to greet him. "Just a minute," he said, peering into the sky.

A moment later a pair of fighters appeared, moving fast. Margolin held his hand up, waving, as they roared over the field.

The leader rocked his wings and they tapped their afterburners, climbing steeply and breaking away to the east in a wave of rolling thunder. They swiftly became specks and vanished into the clear blue sky.

"The runway here's too short for them to land. They're going off to refuel. They'll come back in time to escort me home. Have we got a place where we can talk?"

"We do. But first you need to rescue my bodyguard from your Marines."

"Not a problem." The Senator grinned. "We'll be right back."

He and Becky strode off briskly to attend to details, conferring in low voices, leaving Will standing on the ramp shaking his head.

"So that's it," Senator Margolin said. They were sitting around the small table sipping chilled drinks. The Senator's plane had ice cubes, a welcome treat.

"Harney resigned, his VP agreed not to run, the Peace Enforcers stood down, and it's all fading into history."

"And the Japanese gave us a trillion dollars as a gift?"

"In a pig's eye, Dr. Giles." Margolin chuckled. "Nobody *gives* anyone that much money. They were in a tough spot. This is an accommodation.

"We'd already spent most of their money. Harney was going down for treason. The Japanese had committed at least one atrocity and several acts of war. They knew I was the main guy leading the chorus against them, so they had me announce the so-called gift and say they were pulling their troops out."

"If it's not a gift, then what is it?" Becky asked.

"Beats me." George shrugged. "My own staff doesn't agree about the true intent of Japan's transfer of funds. Hell, the National Security Council doesn't either.

"We'll find out someday. What's for sure is they gave me a gold-plated invitation to run for President. They also replaced the people responsible for attacking Cybertech."

Will looked at the Senator. "Replaced them terminally?"

The Senator gave a noncommittal shrug. "There were some accidents."

"The Japanese are both more polite and more brutal than we are," Becky said. "What about us?"

"All charges are dropped. Dr. Giles can come back and startup Cybertech anytime he wants."

"You mean the regulators and agencies aren't going to give me grief about selling security products?"

"No reason to. We've checked you out in detail. Your firm was squeaky clean. The United States has always maintained a careful balance between freedom and security."

Becky was watching her uncle closely. "What about our safety?"

"You're safe now. Like I said, the charges have been dropped."

"We need more than physical safety," Will said. "Citizens need to be able to communicate in private. Our prosperity comes from innovation, from ideas, from freedom. How can people do business if they can't keep their ideas private? They can't."

"I agree. We need help watching the watchers and making them accountable."

"What kind of help?"

"Help at the margins to provide strategic intelligence and targeting for legislative action. Congress can get us back to the Constitution. Think about it: The states can ratify an Amendment to ensure Congress can no longer exclude itself from the laws it passes. What's missing?"

"You tell me."

"We need ways to choke chain the tyranny of our own unaccountable bureaucracies."

Will shook his head. "How? America has come to look like the old Eastern Europe under the Soviets. My plant was invaded, my assistant was tortured, and I was almost killed."

Senator Margolin nodded.

"Forget the margins. The *core* is the problem. The President of the United States **personally** sanctioned shutting us down. He was helping people steal our technology."

"Yes. Politics sucks, doesn't it?"

Will frowned.

"We don't deserve this abuse," Becky said. "He doesn't. I don't. Our Country doesn't."

"True." The Senator nodded. "There's a proven solution, you know."

They both looked at him.

"I'd like to hear it," Will said.

"Me too."

"It's simple, but not easy." The Senator smiled thinly. "*The solution to 1984 is 1776.*"

Oh. Will blinked. "My father said that, a long time ago. Few listened."

"I was there when he testified, but I'd forgotten about it until the recent events. Congress wanted him to give us an easy technical solution, but instead he gave us a political problem."

"You brought it on yourselves." Becky was frowning. "Will's father is missing or dead, and he is lucky to be alive. It's getting damned hard to tell the good guys from the bad guys."

"Not that hard." The Senator met their eyes. "Not really. The solution isn't found inside the beltway, it's here. Out here with the people: *By and for the people.* I think it's time. All we have to do is restore the Constitution, to restore our honor, our culture, and our values."

Becky's eyes narrowed. "You're serious?"

"A bipartisan group of us have been waiting for the right moment."

"Exactly when is this moment, Uncle?"

"We'll move right after the election. Early in the next President's term."

"Why now?" Will said.

"Because the mood of the country is right for it and because we have no choice. Without advanced cyber technology, our enemies will crush us. But this very technology will crush freedom unless we get control away from the bureaucrats and back to the people, as our founders intended. People sense this."

"How do you propose to make Washington give up power?"

"We are still a nation of laws, and both parties are guilty of crimes and misdemeanors. You're going to see selective impeachments and legal action."

Will shook his head dubiously. "Is this a campaign speech?"

"Absolutely not. This is a private discussion. I expect you both to keep it in confidence."

Becky was nodding slowly. She touched Will's arm. "I believe him."

"Why do you think I'm down here Dr. Giles?"

"Because of Becky?"

"In part, but I came to speak with you. Do you study history?"

"Some...."

"What if I could give you the history of the world in two sentences? Where did it all start?"

Say what? "I don't know. The primordial soup, I guess."

The Senator smiled. "That's the secular view, abiogenesis, an unproven theory. What if you looked at it from a spiritual or philosophical view? A political, humanist view, versus an evolutionary science view."

"No idea. You tell me, Senator."

"Warm Fuzzies."

"Huh?"

"In the beginning, especially for America and Western Civilization, there were Warm Fuzzies. Absolutes for right and wrong. Hopeful thoughts. Myths of heroes and patriots. That was embedded in America, designed into our Constitution, written on stone tablets. It's the Judeo-Christian ethic. It's why we put 'In God we Trust' on our money and monuments."

Warm Fuzzies? Why does this conversation remind me of the Viracocha? "I'm afraid you've lost me, Sir."

Will glanced at Becky. It didn't help. She was staring at her uncle. Waiting for something. She smiled, but didn't speak.

"Millions and millions of Warm Fuzzies," Margolin said. "Good thoughts. Then people started worrying that we were going to run out of Warm Fuzzies. Do you know what replaced them?"

Will shook his head. "No idea."

"Cold Pricklies. That's where we are now, politically. Institutionalized fear."

"Evil is ever-present and unpredictable, and only compliance and powerful government can save us? Like when we were conditioning passengers not to resist hijackings before 9-11?"

The Senator shook his head. "No, more intense, more totalitarian. Like when Bush started TSA to accommodate Political Correctness. Like Gore and Global Warming, like ObamaCare."

"State of Fear," Becky said.

"Exactly right." The senator's smile broadened. "That is why I'm down here, personally. Dr. Giles is a poster child for Warm Fuzzies."

"Huh?" Will said.

"State of Fear is a novel by an American scientist, Dr. Michael Crichton. His premise was that politicians and special interests were systematically using fear to corrupt science and scare people into giving them power. Did you ever read it?"

"A long time ago. They called him a nut, and the book got bad reviews."

"Crichton was blacklisted and threatened," Margolin said. "He was personally attacked, demeaned, and ridiculed. He suffered thuggery and Saul Alinsky tactics. Evil seeks to destroy Warm Fuzzies."

"They didn't try to kill him."

"He got death threats. For writing a novel."

"Oh...."

"That's why I need *you*, not just your technology. The totalitarians and socialists want Cold Pricklies. They seek stories to spread fear and divisiveness. I need uplifting stories to unify and energize."

"Why me?"

"Technology uplifts. It drives prosperity and progress, but I need more. You inspire. You exemplify exceptionalism, and the American Dream. I need examples of success.

"You and your dad built a prosperous company, and you did it by helping with freedom. We in Government need to protect you. We need to protect your property rights and freedom, in order to protect our other citizens' rights to privacy and to own property themselves."

"All this is good, but you came here for something specific."

Margolin nodded slowly. "I did."

"What exactly do you want from me?"

"What Congress needs to get started are trustworthy legal experts from honest entrepreneurs who've been abused, so we can defund the right things, kick the appropriate asses, and end the sinecures. Can I count on your support?"

Will met his eyes. "I'll speak with Samuel when I get back."

"Thank you. There's more: Thanks to the research you and Becky are doing, we'll soon have better ways of identifying foreign agents and enemies. My view is that actions by outside groups to destabilize our government and undermine our Constitution should be considered as acts of war. We in Congress take sacred oaths to defend the Constitution."

Will blinked. *What's he talking about now?* He stared at Becky, not having a clue. He was trying hard not to let his bafflement show. He felt like his brain was sizzling. *These are heavy concepts. How'd we get from Warm Fuzzies to treason and acts of war?*

Becky kicked him under the table. "That's why I had to leave and trust other people to get you to safety. I needed to see my uncle. I used your devices to help him."

Will kept his face turned away from the Senator. He was pressing his lips together so hard his jaw was starting to hurt. Becky's look said, *Let me handle this!*

"We need to slow down," Becky said. "Will was badly beaten by Captain Tanaka. He was disoriented and has been a bit out of touch, but he's going to recover fully."

"We'll give it time, as long as he needs."

Becky was staring at him, her eyes like lasers. "We can discuss the details later."

Will nodded slowly. "Sure...."

The Senator gave a reassuring look. "It's over. Cybertech is safe, Dr. Giles."

"She's been bringing me up to date...."

"There's just one more thing."

They both looked at the Senator. Becky's expression was one of polite interest. Will kept his lips pressed together.

"The consensus on fighting global terrorism allows me, ah..., certain discretion in sources and methods. You have no idea how much trouble you have saved our government. I'm going to be offering you retainers to serve as covert resources."

"Um...."

Margolin said, "You'll be working *with* us, not *for* us. I'll be your only contact. From time to time, I'll ask you for information."

"But...." Will started to speak, but closed his mouth at a sharp look from Becky.

"I just need to know if you are interested. We can work out the details when you're fully recovered."

Will took a deep breath, let it out slowly, and then nodded. "Okay. Sure...."

"Good." Margolin looked relieved. "Thank you, Dr. Giles."

"There is something we need from you, Uncle George," Becky interrupted in her sweetest voice. "I know you're busy, but...."

"Speak up, Girl. I'm not *that* busy."

"We're going to get married and then take a long honeymoon without anyone bothering us. Would you be willing to give me away?"

Margolin started to say something but was drowned out by a silky roar from outside. Two fast moving shapes flashed by the windows, so low they kicked up dust on the ground. The Senator's escorts were back. Smiling, he waited for the noise to subside.

"Bet your ass, Girl. I wouldn't miss your wedding for anything. I'm sorry, but I'd better get going now. I have to get back to Washington."

Becky hugged him, and he and Will shook hands.

"I'm looking forward to having you in the family, Dr. Giles," the Senator said. "May I ask you a favor?"

"Of course."

"You should start calling me George, now that you're in the family."

"Yes, Sir."

"I have two daughters. You know how women are..."

Will nodded. He didn't, of course, but men were expected to fake it.

"They want autographed pictures of your assistant, Katherine Chambers. My colleagues on the Armed Services Committee would like copies as well. So does my secretary. I need twenty-seven copies. I can get you a list of names."

"Certainly, Senator, but...."

"Captain Tanaka was widely disliked, even hated."

"He almost killed me...."

"But Kate Chambers thwarted him. Four nine-millimeter slugs in the chest, tightly grouped. We've not had a national hero like her for years. My girls *insist* on meeting her...."

"Oh," Will said. "I'm not...."

Becky had a hand over her mouth and was making choking sounds.

"Are you all right?" Fortunately, the Senator was focused on Becky.

Will closed his gaping mouth. He pressed his lips together and brushed one hand across his face.

Becky blinked, coughed several times, and finally got control. "I'm fine."

The Senator said, "You two have been through a lot. Much has been happening...."

"It sure has," Becky said. "You'll like Kate. She's a heroic woman and the doctors say she'll be fine. I'll bring her to Washington and get you all the pictures you want."

"Perhaps at a campaign event?"

"Sure." She grinned. "Why not?"

They walked the Senator to his plane. Becky hugged him again and gave him a kiss on the cheek. Will shook his hand.

The Senator climbed aboard, the door closed, and the engines started. They stood there waving, as his plane took off and climbed northbound, with the fighters loitering protectively overhead. They watched until it was out of sight.

CHAPTER TWENTY

THE MÉRIDA AIRPORT, IN THE YUCATAN, HALF AN HOUR LATER

Will turned to Becky, looking to confirm there was no one within earshot. The Marines were forming up to board helicopters and seemed fully occupied with the task. "Well?"

"Well, what?"

"What exactly did you and the Senator agree to?"

"Uncle came down here to get your agreement, to get your help. That was his agenda. The rest was social, and about us. That was my agenda."

"Help for what? What's this research we're allegedly doing? Why is he giving us a retainer?"

"I told Uncle we had an experimental quantum camera technology."

"Do we?"

"We do." She looked around, faced him, and mouthed the word silently. "Portals."

"I thought that technology was lost."

"We have some personal devices. They can't transport any significant mass, but, like you said, particles are easier."

"Say more."

"Light is made of photons, which are particles. Light lets one make photographs and digital images."

"Yes, of course." He was watching her carefully. "So?"

"I gave Uncle George the pictures that helped him nail President Harney and his Japanese conspirators. He and our government are very grateful."

"I'm beginning to understand...."

"There's more: Uncle has agreed we're going to help you find your dad as a test case for our new technology. It will be our first project: Finding a missing Congressional Medal of Honor winner, an American hero. He liked that."

Will stood there looking at her, feeling a heavy weight lift off his shoulders. He closed his eyes and took several deep breaths. He wiped them, brushing tears away. A long time seemed to pass. *Thank God. No matter how it turns out, at least I'll know....*

When he opened his eyes, Becky looked concerned. She put her hands on his shoulders, steadying him. "Are you all right?"

"It was just a shock. I think about Dad a lot."

"I know."

"Thank you." He bent down and kissed her gently.

"You don't need to thank me. I did it for myself too. It's the right thing. We can help my uncle root out traitors in Washington. Every elected official swore a sacred oath when they took office."

"I will support and defend the Constitution of the United States against all enemies, foreign and domestic...."

Becky nodded. "That's the one."

"Which they have not been doing."

"Not for decades and it's been getting worse with each Administration. We've forgotten our own heritage and our foundational laws."

Will was watching her skeptically. "So now he reminds them?"

"Not alone, and with deeds, not words. Congress and the courts will start enforcing the oath, one case at a time. My uncle thinks Harney can be prosecuted without tearing the country apart."

"That will be the test case?"

"Possibly." Becky shrugged. "If not, there are others...."

"Do you honestly think this can work?"

"It has to. We've stared into that abyss, and we're out of time."

Will took a deep breath. *This is one hell of a woman. You're a lucky man.* "I love you."

"Good," she said. "Me too: You. You know that, don't you?"

"Yes, but I think I'm about ten steps behind you. Should I propose now?"

"Not here, silly. I hate airports. Let's go home...."

The End

FACTOIDS OR FANTASIES?

I hope you enjoyed my novel and thank you for sharing the journey with me. My non-fiction book *Engines of Prosperity* included a quote from Dr. Alvin Toffler, the futurist. He said, "The sophistication for deception is increasing at a greater rate than the technology for verification. This means the end of truth." My novel is fiction, but in today's world there can be a lot of truth in fiction, and a lot of fiction in truth.

Ancient Science and Civilizations: There are hundreds of myths and legends of ancient advanced civilizations, which appear in virtually all languages and cultures. One book that inspired my back-story was Graham Hancock's *Fingerprints of the Gods* and his more-or-less sequel, with Robert Bauvel, *The Message of the Sphinx*. These discuss ancient but incredibly accurate maps, the Viracocha and other ingredients of my novel. For those with a practical engineering bent, Christopher Dunn's *The Giza Power Plant* is more technically precise. I was privileged with being able to visit pyramids in Egypt and the Western Hemisphere, and, while visiting on business, my Arab hosts arranged a private tour of the backrooms of the (very old and once Royal) Museum in Cairo which contain thousands of never-displayed ancient artifacts, some of which are very different from the later-era mummies and relics that interest tourists.

Disasters That Wipe the Slate Clean of Human Knowledge: Why were the ancients so consumed and preoccupied with a need to precisely measure the stars? Bauvel's *The Orion Mystery* and a fascinating little book, *When the Sky Fell: In Search of Atlantis*, by Rand and Rose Flem-ath, make interesting reads. It is here we learn of Charles Hapgood's incredible theory of crustal displacement, and his book *Earth's Shifting Crust*. Albert Einstein found Hapgood's theory compelling and wrote the foreword. Professor Hapgood was also fascinated with ancient maps. His book *Maps of the Ancient Sea Kings* is better known. Gavin Menzies has an excellent best-selling book *The Lost Empire of Atlantis* that makes persuasive claims that a forgotten civilization, the Minoans, discovered America thousands of years before Christ and sparked the Atlantis legend. Also, not all such lapses are ancient, which is the topic of *How the Irish Saved Civilization* by Thomas Cahill.

Antarctica: This least-known continent has long fascinated us. Sir Ernest Shackleton's *South: The Endurance Expedition* relates one of the most incredible stories in history. I have personally viewed the *James Caird*, Shackleton's open longboat that crossed 800 miles of the worst ocean weather in the world. My late uncle, George O. Noville, was Admiral Byrd's second-in-command at both poles, and I inherited some of his papers. Also, Sara Wheeler's *Terra Incognito: Travels in Antarctica*, is enjoyable and informative.

The Yakuza: It's real, violent, powerful, and politically connected. One good book is *Yakuza: The Explosive Account of Japan's Criminal Underworld*, by David E. Kaplan and Alex Dubro.

Edgy Science: Quantum Teleportation has been demonstrated. See *Scientific American*; Beam Me Up, December 22, 1997. Cold fusion is real too, but controversial as experiments are not repeatable with any consistency. It was first demonstrated in America, but when the U.S. Patent Office called it "junk science" and refused patents, Fleischmann and Pons moved abroad to work in secret for commercial interests. (This is mentioned in the "Factoids or Fantasies?" section of my own novel *God's House*.) A Google search is useful, and http://www.infinite-energy.com/ is a good start. For a lay treatment of hyperspace, see Michio Kaku's *Hyperspace: a scientific odyssey through parallel universes, time warps, and the 10th dimension*.

The Loss of Privacy: This is obvious and disturbing in our post 9-11 world. What's less known is that digital intrusion has been embedded in U.S. law and communication systems since the early 1990s. The government has repeatedly been embarrassed when its own information was compromised. WikiLeaks was a debacle, a major breach, one from which America's enemies benefited. Already we have killer drones. Can the "hunter seekers" of *Dune* be far behind?

The Stellar Wind Project: It's real, it's huge, it's beyond Top Secret, and it's in Utah. It's been confirmed publicly that NSA has warrantless access to AT&T and Verizon billing records, databases containing trillions of records. There are persistent rumors that Google and social network firms also participate, but, at this writing, that's not been confirmed. Wired Magazine and The Blaze occasionally report on this.

There is a lot of information out there about privacy issues if you look. Websites are being hacked with regularity, loss of privacy is escalating, the situation is fluid, most things electronic are compromised, and some seek government (or UN) control of the Internet. Google searches are useful (though neither private nor secure themselves). Some good places to start might be:

EFF: https://www.eff.org/

CALEA: http://www.eff.org/issues/calea

CARNIVORE: http://www.epic.org/privacy/carnivore/

The pyramids are real too. I was personally assured of this by a Sphinx.

ABOUT THE AUTHOR

John Trudel has authored two nonfiction books and two Thriller novels, *God's House* and *Privacy Wars*. He graduated from Georgia Tech and Kansas State, had a long career in high-technology, wrote columns for several national magazines, and lives in Oregon and Arizona. Visit http://www.johntrudel.com/.

14310339R00159

Made in the USA
Charleston, SC
04 September 2012